ATTILA: THE SCOURGE OF GOD

ATTILA

THE SCOURGE OF GOD

*The story of Flavius Aetius,
the last great Roman general, and of his
friend who became an enemy:
Attila, King of the Huns*

Ross Laidlaw

First published in Great Britain in 2004
This edition published in 2007 by
Polygon, an imprint of Birlinn Ltd
West Newington House
10 Newington Road
Edinburgh
EH9 1QS

www.birlinn.co.uk

9 8 7 6 5 4 3

ISBN 13: 978-1-84697-012-2
ISBN 10: 1-84697-012-1

British Library Cataloguing-in-Publication Data
A catalogue record for this book is available on
request from the British Library

Typeset by Palimpsest Book Production Limited,
Grangemouth, Stirlingshire
Printed and bound by Creative Print and Design, Wales

To Margaret my wife, Kenneth my son,
Ruth my daughter, Bill her husband, and their
little son William MacKinlay

ACKNOWLEDGEMENTS

My warmest appreciation to the following for their generous help in supplying me with information from the Internet etc.: Bill Paget, Dr Alberto Massimo, Roy Ellis, and Barbara Halley; also to Helen Simpson for her superb editing. A special word of thanks to my publishers Hugh Andrew (who sowed the seed and made it grow) and Neville Moir, for their steadfast support and encouragement.

Contents

MAPS AND PLANS

GLOSSARY OF LATIN TERMS AND
PLACE NAMES

Note: the short form of compound place names such as Augusta Treverorum or Tigernum Castrum is Augusta or Tigernum.

adscriptus glebae	(lit: tied to the land) serf, villein
adventus Saxonum	the coming of the Saxons
Aemilian Plain	Lombardy
agens (pl: *agentes*) *in rebus*	courier-cum-spy
ala	military 'wing'
Aluatica	Tongres
Anderida	Pevensey
angon	barbed javelin
Appenini	the Appenines
Aquincum	Budapest
Aquitania	Aquitaine
Arar river	the Saône
Arduenna Silva	the Ardennes
Arelate	Arles
Aremorica	Brittany
Argentaria	Horburg, Alsace
Argentorate Stratisburgum	Strasbourg
Ariminum	Rimini
Arvernum	the Auvergne
Augusta Taurinorum	Turin
Augusta Treverorum	Trier
Aureliani	Orléans
Autissiodorum	Auxerre
auxilium	auxiliary infantry unit
ballista	giant crossbow-like catapult
Bantisus river	the Ob
barbaricum	barbarian territory
barbaricarii	officers' armour-makers

barritus	battle-cry
Basilia	Basle
biarchus	junior officer, equivalent to NCO
Boiaria, Boii	Bavaria, Bavarians
bora	regional north wind
Boreal	far north, Arctic
Borysthenes river	the Dnieper
Branodunum	Brancaster
bucellarii	landowner's private retainers
bucellatum	military rations biscuit
bucina	military trumpet
bucinator	army trumpeter
byrrus	hooded cloak
Caesarodunum	Tours
Caledonia	Scotland
calidarium	hot room of bath-house
Cambracum	Cambrai
Cambria	Wales
campidoctores	army drill-sergeants
canonicarius	financial overseer
Cantium	Kent
capsarius	army medical orderly
carae epistolarum	officials in charge of financial correspondence
carbonarii	charcoal-burners
cardo	main street
Carpathus Mountains	the Carpathians
Carthago Nova	Cartagena
catafractarius	heavily armoured cavalryman
Cebenna mountains	the Cévennes
centenarius	(i) junior army officer; (ii) horse which has won 100 or more races
Chersonesus of Thracia	the Gallipoli peninsula
Choson	Korea
circitor	foreman/NCO of *bucellarii* or regular troops
clibanarius	armoured cavalryman
Colchis	trans-Caucasia
colonus	tenant farmer
comes	count
comes rei privatae	Count of the Privy Purse
comes sacrarum largitionum	Count of the Public Purse
comitatus	retinue, group of followers

compulsores	collectors of tax arrears
conductor	foreman
cuculli	hooded cloaks
cuneus	attack formation
cuniculi	drainage channels
curialis	leading citizen
cursor	messenger
cursus velox	imperial post/courier service
Danubius river	the Danube
decemprimi	inner committee of city council
decurion	(i) army rank; (ii) town councillor
defensor, defensor civitatis	magistrate
Deva river	the Dee
Divonum	Cahors
Dor river	the Doré
ducenarius	army officer
Durocatalaunum	Châlons-sur-Marne
Durocortorum	Reims
femenalia	underpants
Elaver river	the Allier
Entia river	the Enza
erectores	chariot-race officials
Etruria	Tuscany
Florentia	Florence
foederatus	ally
foedus	i) alliance; (ii) oath of allegiance
follis	money-bag
francisca	throwing-axe
Fretum Gallicum	Straits of Dover
Gallia Narbonensis	Narbonne province
Garannonum	Burgh Castle
gladius	short sword
Grinnicum	Cannes
Hadrianopolis	Adrianople
Haemus Mons	Balkan Mountains, Bulgaria
harpastum	ball game
Hellespontus	Dardanelles
Hibernia	Ireland
Hispania	Spain
Imaus Mons	the Urals
insulae	'high-rise' buildings

Italia	Italy
iugatio	land tax
iugerum	unit of land measurement
kontos	heavy spear
Lacus Benacus	Lake Garda
Lacus Brigantinus	Lake Constance
laetus	P.O.W.-turned-soldier
lanista	gladiatorial instructor
lares et penates	household gods
latrocinium	robbery
Lauriacum	Lorch
Lerina	Lérins
Lexovium	Lisieux
Liger river	the Loire
limitanei	frontier troops
Limonum	Poitiers
lituus	*cavalry trumpet*
Locus Mauriacus	the Catalaunian Plains
ludus latrunculorum	board game
Lugdunum	Lyon
Magister militum	Master of Soldiers
mappa	white cloth used to signal start of chariot races at the Circus
Mare Caspium	Caspian Sea
Mare Suevicum	Baltic Sea
Massilia	Marseille
Matrona river	the Marne
Mediolanum	Milan
Metaris Aestuarium	the Wash
Metis	Metz
Mons Matronae Pass	Genèvre Pass
Mosa river	the Meuse
Mosella river	the Moselle
murcus	'Draft-dodger', self-mutilated to avoid conscription
Naissus	Niš
Narbo Martius	Narbonne town
Narbonensis	Narbonne province
naufragium	(lit: shipwreck) crash in chariot race
Nemetacum	Arras
Nicer river	the Neckar

Glossary of Latin Terms and Place Names

Nemausus	Nîmes
Novae	Sistova, Bulgaria
Noviomagus	Chichester
numerarius	financial official
numerus	infantry unit
nummi	coins
Oceanus Germanicus	North Sea
Oechardis river	the Irtish
Old Dacia	Transylvania; Romania
onager	(lit: 'kicking ass') catapult
palatini	central groups of the Roman field army
papilio	army tent
Paralia	Malabar
pedites	foot-soldiers
perditi	criminals, outlaws
Phrudis river	the Somme
pilleus pannonicus	soldier's cap
Placentia	Piacenza
Pontus Euxinus	Black Sea
Portus Adurni	Portchester
Portus Dubris	Dover
praenomen	forename
praepositus	regimental commander
pridie	the day before
primicerius	most senior NCO in Roman army
princeps	highest rank in courier service
principales	inner committee
procuratores	overseers, managers
Propontis	Sea of Marmara
protector	senior army officer
Provincia	Provence
quaestor	magistrate
Rauraris river	the Hérault
Regulbium	Reculver
res privata	Emperor's private income
Revessium	Saint-Paulien
Rha river	the Volga
Rhenus river	the Rhine
Rhodanus river	the Rhône
Rutupiae	Richborough
Saba	Yemen

Sacrae largitiones	imperial finance ministry
Samarobriva	Amiens
Sapaudia	Savoy
Scaldis river	the Scheldt
scholae	Emperor's personal bodyguard
scriptorium	book-room
scutarii	light cavalry
Secies river	the Seccia
Sequana river	the Seine
Serdica	Sofia
Singidunum	Belgrade
Sirmium	Mitrovica, Kosovo
solea ferrea	cavalry horseshoe
solidus	gold coin of high denomination
sparsor	chariot-cleaner
spatha	sword
spina	barrier down centre of the Circus
sponsio	bribe
status belli	state of war
Sufes	Sbiba, Tunisia
Sufetula	Sbeitla, Tunisia
suffragium	the going rate for purchase of office
susceptores	tax-collectors
taberna	inn
tablinum	study, library, office
Tamesa river	the Thames
Tanais river	the Don
Taprobana	Sri Lanka/Ceylon
Tarus river	the Taro
tessera	token; small cube of stone, glass, etc.
Thusuros	Tozeur, Tunisia
Ticinum	Pavia
Tigernum Castrum	Thiers
Tolosa	Toulouse
tractator	intermediary
tremissis	gold coin worth one third of a solidus
triclinium	dining-room
Turnacum	Tournai
Utus river	the Vid
Vectis	Isle of Wight
venatores	hunting-gangs

Glossary of Latin Terms and Place Names

Vesontio	Besançon
vexillatio	cavalry unit, detachment
Viadua river	the Oder
vicomagistri	nightwatchmen
vigiles	police
Visurgis river	the Weser
Vosegus Mons	the Vosges

HISTORICAL NOTE

In AD 376, exactly a hundred years before the end of the Western Roman Empire, an extraordinary thing happened. An entire German nation, the Visigoths, assembled on the banks of the River Danube pleading for permission to cross the river into the Roman Empire. The reason: a terrible race of mounted nomad-warriors, the Huns, had suddenly fallen on them from the east with such ferocity and in such overwhelming numbers that the Goths were forced to seek safety across the Roman frontier. Entry was granted, and all might have been well; the Goths would probably have settled peacefully as workers on the land and recruits for the legions. But exploitation by corrupt Roman* officials (for example, when reduced to starvation the Goths were given dogmeat in exchange for their sons sold into slavery) provoked the Goths into rebellion. In 378, at Adrianople in Thrace, they destroyed a huge Roman army, killing the Eastern emperor, Valens. (The empire had recently been split into two halves, with capitals at Milan and Constantinople.) This was Rome's worst disaster since Cannae, where in 216 BC her forces had been massacred by Hannibal.

The danger passed, thanks to firm but diplomatic handling of the Goths by Theodosius I, Rome's last great soldier-emperor. The empire, apparently strong and secure once more, was briefly re-united at the end of his reign, but when he died in 395 it was divided – this time permanently – between his feeble sons, Honorius (West) and Arcadius (East).

With the strong hand of Theodosius removed, inherent weaknesses showed up, and the West plunged into crisis. The Goths, under their leader Alaric, broke out and proceeded to ravage the Balkans and invade Italy. Stilicho, the West's brilliant Vandal general, defeated Alaric time and again but always let him escape, perhaps out of reluctance to finish off a fellow German. Then, on

---

* From AD 212 all free inhabitants of the empire were accounted Romans.

the last day of 406, disaster struck. A vast host of German tribesmen – Vandals, Suevi, Burgundians, etc. – crossed the frozen Rhine, then poured across Gaul and into Spain. Distracted by grandiose plans to wrest the Balkans from the Eastern Empire, Stilicho failed to intervene; as a result, he fell from power and was executed. Alaric then re-invaded Italy, and in 410 captured Rome itself, only to die within the year. (The Goths soon withdrew from Italy, taking with them Honorius' sister Galla Placidia, who was captured when Rome fell; she was eventually sold back to the Romans for half a million measures of wheat.) Denuded of troops by a usurper, Britain was instructed by Honorius to fend for itself against the depredations of Saxons, Picts, and Scots (from Ireland).

At this critical juncture for the West, the situation was stabilized and to some extent reversed by a remarkable Roman general, Constantius. His policy of persuading the German tribes to settle peacefully as federates in the provinces they had invaded had considerable success; so much so that in 421 Honorius appointed him co-emperor as Constantius III, and sanctioned his marriage to Placidia, by whom he had a son, the future Emperor Valentinian III, and a daughter, Honoria, whose scandalous involvement with the Hun king, Attila, very nearly brought the Western Empire to a premature end. (Plans for recovering Britain were indefinitely shelved.)

Unfortunately, Constantius died within months of receiving the purple. But his great work, to try to preserve the empire by forging a state of harmonious co-existence between the Romans and their German 'guests' (as the federates were euphemistically termed), was to be carried on by another Roman general with vision, Flavius Aetius. Their task was complicated by a religious problem. Catholic Christianity was now the official religion of the Roman state. The Germans settled within the Empire were also Christians, but of a different brand – Arian. Arianism held that Christ the Son was inferior to God the Father, a doctrine in tune with the Germans' paternalistic society. In the eyes of Romans this made them heretics, and therefore beyond the pale.

In AD 423 (when this story begins) Honorius died without issue, and this immediately created a power vacuum. The Eastern emperor, Theodosius II, the son of Arcadius, renounced his claim to the Western throne, backing instead the next legitimate heir, Valentinian, the infant son of Constantius III and Galla Placidia.

(The empress and her little son were then the guests of Theodosius in Constantinople.) Meanwhile, a usurper, Iohannes, had proclaimed himself emperor at Ravenna, which had become the Western capital. Accompanied by Placidia and Valentinian, an expedition was despatched from Constantinople to depose Iohannes, who appealed for help to Aetius. Anxious to prevent Placidia coming to power as regent for Valentinian – something he saw as potentially disastrous for the West – Aetius agreed to back Iohannes. With a large force raised from among his friends and allies across the Danube, the Huns (among whom he had lived as a hostage when a boy), Aetius set out for Italy. As spring wore towards summer in the fateful year of 425, the two armies converged in a collision course upon Ravenna.

PART I

RAVENNA
AD 423–33

PROLOGUE

Cursing, Titus Valerius Rufinus slapped at a mosquito which had bitten the back of his neck. Even here, a hundred feet up on the roof of Ravenna's Basilica Ursiana, Bishop Ursus' new cathedral, the pests were active. Eastwards, the angry red disc rising above the Mare Adriaticum threatened another day of scorching heat. The towers of the imperial palace suddenly glowed in the early rays, followed by the crenellations of the city walls, the topmost arches of the aqueduct that Emperor Trajan had built three centuries before, and the cupolas of the churches that were everywhere replacing the pagan temples. The banks of mist that always seemed to shroud the place partially shredded away, revealing the great causeway that connected the city to its port of Classis three miles to the south-east and to the sprawling suburb of Caesarea in between. All around stretched a dreary landscape of marshes and lagoons, its monotony broken only by clumps of bog-willow, isolated vineyards, and the glittering line of the Fossa Augusta, the mighty canal joining the city to the River Po.

Soon, twinkling flashes from armour and weapons, threads of smoke from cooking-fires, and the faint blare of trumptes told Titus that the enemy encampment – dispersed throughout the buildings, squares, and smallholdings of Caesarea – was astir. An hour crawled past. Then the enemy force, cavalry from the Eastern Empire, commanded by Aspar, son of the veteran general Ardaburius, began to form up on the causeway. Extending an arm with fist bunched, Titus began to make a rough estimate of numbers: fifty horsemen between two knuckles; ten, twenty, thirty ranks . . . The more distant formations merged into a gleaming blur, making an accurate count impossible, but he thought the total could not be less than five thousand, perhaps nearer ten.

Muted by distance to a tinny bray, trumpets sounded. Like a monstrous caterpillar, the vast column began to creep along the

3

causeway towards the city. When they were five or six hundred paces from the walls Titus was able to pick out the various types of cavalry in the van: *catafracti* armoured head to toe, looking strangely unhuman; *clibanarii* in hooded chain-mail coats; light cavalry armed with javelins, unprotected save for small round shields and helmets; horse archers, and various intermediate types. All these impressions Titus stored away in his head, using the old Ciceronian trick of 'memory palaces': an imagined suite of rooms, each containing a segment of information which a walk through the suite would instantly recall.

Time to move. Filing into the city through the Aurean Gate would slow the column, as would its exit via the Ariminum Gate. But every second Titus could shave from his journey back to base to deliver his report would gain his commander, General Aetius, precious time to prepare for the battle that now seemed inevitable.

Titus clambered back down through the trapdoor giving access to the roof, and down a ladder to a platform supported by scaffolding, where artisans were finishing a wall mosaic. It showed Christ enthroned on a globe of the world, separating the sheep from the goats at the Day of Judgement. The face was wonderfully depicted, its expression combining tenderness with strength, compassion with power. Momentarily overcome with emotion, Titus knelt before the image and made the sign of the cross. (A pagan for almost all of his young life, Titus had recently converted to the new faith.) Feeling strangely comforted and strengthened, he descended more ladders to the floor. A subdeacon, who had smuggled Titus into the cathedral, was waiting at the foot of the scaffolding. The pair hurried through the vast building with its five naves, fifty-six marble columns, and glorious mosaics glowing blue and gold in the dim light. The cleric unlocked the great double doors.

'Farewell, my son.' He pressed into Titus' hand a Chi–Rho amulet, the crossed Greek letters symbolizing the Christians' faith. 'Let Christ and His holy angels have you in their keeping, and may Fortune favour your enterprise.'

From the slight eminence where Aetius had set up his headquarters in front of the Hun encampment, Titus watched the enemy deploy half a mile to his fore. Tinged with fear, excitement churned in his stomach. Aspar had chosen his position well, extending his forces in a triple line on a stretch of comparatively firm ground between swamps so that he could not easily be encircled. Protecting his flanks were the heavy cavalry – *catafractarii* and *clibanarii* – with the light cavalry and horse archers forming the centre. Well to the rear were parked the supply wagons. Titus looked behind him to where the Hun riders waited, an impatient, milling horde.

This was going to be exclusively a cavalry battle, he reflected, something virtually unprecedented in Rome's long history, where until comparatively recently victories had been won by heavily armed legionaries. The transport ships carrying the Eastern infantry from Constantinople had been dispersed by a storm and their commander, Ardaburius, captured. On the Western side, barring a small Roman entourage, Aetius' force was drawn from his allies beyond the Danube, the Huns. They were mounted archers, probably the most formidable light horsemen the world had ever seen.

Supremely skilled equestrians, whose marksmanship was unrivalled, Aetius' Huns vastly outnumbered the Eastern cavalry. But, unlike Aspar's tightly disciplined troops, they hardly constituted an army in the strict sense. None of the tribes making up the force owned allegiance to any of the others. And each warrior fought very much as an individual, totally lacking in loyalty to his fellow tribesmen and motivated solely by plunder and reward. Nevertheless, the Huns made terrible opponents. Nearly fifty years before, they had fallen on the Goths, one of the most warlike of the German tribes, forcing them to seek refuge within the Roman Empire.

After receiving Titus' report on the strength and movement of the Eastern army, Aetius, then camped a few miles from Ravenna, decided to offer battle to Aspar. Realizing the futility of trying to fight a pitched battle in the swamps surrounding the city, he had moved north-west to less waterlogged terrain.

Accompanied by a knot of officers and tribunes, and, as always, wearing his dented cuirass and carelessly tied scarf, Aetius emerged from the command tent and joined Titus' group of dispatch riders, scouts, and junior officers. A young man of middle height, the general radiated energy and confidence. He squinted at the sun, which was a quarter of the way through its arc, and shook his head wryly.

'I'd like to hold things off until the ninth hour at least,' he declared.* 'We'd have the sun behind us and those lobsters over there would be frying in their armour. But I'd never hold the Huns back that long.' Smiling, he looked round the circle of faces. 'So, gentlemen, unless anyone's got a better plan I suggest we open the games. Bucinator, sound the advance.'

The trumpeter put his lips to the mouthpiece of his circular instrument and blew a series of sonorous blasts. The Hun horsemen trotted forwards: squat, powerfully built men with flat Asiatic faces, dressed in filthy skins and mounted on ugly but tough-looking brutes; each man carried a short recurved bow and densely packed quiver. Titus watched in awe as they flowed round the hillock on which the Romans stood, and rolled across the ground between the armies in an accelerating tide which seemed to extend to the horizon on either hand.

Despite their lack of formal organization, the Huns behaved as though animated by a collective will. In a precise cavalry manoeuvre which equalled anything a crack Roman *ala* could perform, the riders in the van broke right and left when a hundred paces from the East Roman front, then galloped parallel to the enemy, discharging dense clouds of arrows. Their place was immediately taken by the next wave of archers, so that the scene resolved itself into two vast whirlpools of horsemen revolving in front of the static ranks of Aspar's cavalry. The expression 'the sky darkened with arrows' Titus had previously dismissed as exaggeration. Now he saw that it was true.

After about an hour, the Huns withdrew out of bowshot to breathe their horses, and the results of the encounter could be observed. They were unimpressive. Judging from the windrows of shafts scattered to their fore, the Hun arrows had bounced harmlessly off the armour of the Eastern heavy cavalry. Elsewhere, the barrage seemed to have been mainly absorbed by the centre's bucklers, which now resembled giant hedgehogs. On Aspar's side, casualties were light: here and there a fallen horse or rider, with a trickle of wounded filtering back to the field hospital. Lacking armour or shields, the Huns had come

---

* The ninth hour was mid-afternoon. The Roman day – from sunrise to sunset – was divided into twelve hours, which varied in length according to the season. Midday corresponded to the sixth hour.

off worse, the row of corpses marking the line of their attacking van testimony to the efficacy of the Eastern horse archers. Now, at the start of May, it was still too early in the year for the Huns' grass-fed horses to be in peak condition, especially as the wetlands of the Po basin yielded scant pasture for fodder. The East Romans, on the other hand, had enough grain in their supply wagons to keep their horses fit and in the field for a long period.

'This is no good,' said Aetius, sounding remarkably unperturbed. 'As long as Aspar holds that formation, we could keep on charging him all day and get nowhere.' He raised his hands in mock supplication. 'Ideas, gentlemen. Give me ideas. Well, come on – I'm waiting.'

'Surely sir,' volunteered a grizzled duke, 'if we kept on attacking, we'd wear them down eventually, even if it meant heavy losses on our side. The Huns being so many, you'd scarcely feel the difference.'

'Brilliant, Marcus, quite brilliant,' responded Aetius with affectionate sarcasm. He clapped the veteran on the shoulder. 'Huns aren't Romans, you old dunderhead. You can't tell them what to do. They want immediate results, and if they don't get them they pretty soon lose interest. And then handling them becomes a major problem. We Romans may think of them as *ballista*-fodder, but I suspect your average Hun takes a rather different view. Their horses are in poor condition, remember. I don't know how many charges they've got left in them; not a lot, I should guess.' He looked round the group expectantly. 'Any other suggestions?'

There was a silence, which began to stretch out uncomfortably, when Titus suddenly found himself speaking. 'If there were only some way to take them in the rear, sir. I know those marshes on their flanks *look* impenetrable, but if we could find a way through . . .?' He broke off self-consciously, realizing that, as possibly the most junior person present, he might be speaking out of turn. 'My father pulled off something on those lines at Pollentia,' he pressed on gamely, 'against Alaric's Goths.'

'And saved the day for Flavius Stilicho, as I recall,' added Aetius approvingly. 'Full marks, young Titus. I was about to make the same suggestion. The Huns are at their deadliest when they can outflank an enemy, so it's definitely worth a try. Right, we'll make a reconnaissance. Groom, saddle Bucephalus. Titus, Victorinus, mount up. Marcus, keep the Huns in leash till I get back.'

'Right, let's head for home,' Aetius said to his two companions. He dashed sweat from his face. 'At least we tried.'

Making a wide circuit to the enemy's right flank, they had managed, with considerable difficulty, to pick a passage through the mosquito-ridden hell of the swamp, eventually emerging on firmer ground several miles to the rear of Aspar's lines. What had been just feasible for a tiny party was clearly impossible for a large body of horsemen.

'Sir, look!' exclaimed Victor, a normally phlegmatic Batavian youth. He pointed to four horsemen in the distance, probably an Eastern scouting-party. Three, judging by their javelins and small round shields, were light horse, while the fourth had no shield and so was probably a heavy cavalrymen to stiffen the patrol. Spotting the West Romans, the four immediately spurred to intercept them.

'Run for it, lads,' ordered Aetius.

As the three urged their mounts to a gallop, they were presented with a dilemma. They could only hope to outdistance their pursuers by keeping to the firm ground away from the marsh. But this course must eventually bring them dangerously close to Aspar's lines. The problem was resolved unexpectedly.

The chase had continued for some time, with the West Romans beginning to draw away, when a cry from Victor in the rear made the other two pull up. Encountering a swampy patch, he had become mired. He had dismounted and was tugging desperately at the bridle, but the horse had sunk almost to the hocks and was stuck fast.

'Leave it!' shouted Aetius, racing back accompanied by Titus. Reining in close to the edge of the bright green surface of the bog, he leapt to the ground and extended a hand towards Victor, now himself in some difficulty.

'Ride on, sir,' urged Victor. 'Don't put yourself at risk. I'll give myself up.'

'Don't be a fool,' snapped the general. 'They'll kill you; cavalry never take prisoners.'

Victor struggled to the edge of the morass, grasped the general's hand and was hauled clear.

'Get up behind me,' ordered Aetius, grabbing his horse's mane and swinging himself into the saddle. But as the young Batavian reached for a rear saddle-horn, a javelin came arcing through the air and struck him in the back. He gave a choked cry, blood gushed from his mouth, and he crumpled to the ground.

The delay had allowed the pursuit to close. The leading three were only yards away, the fourth, the heavy cavalryman, some distance behind.

'Take the one on the right!' Aetius shouted to Titus, wheeling Bucephalus and charging the other two leaders.

Suddenly, time seemed to slow for Titus. As in a dream, inconsequent details registered on his mind: his opponent's arm still upraised from hurling the missile that had killed Victor; the helmet with its tall crest, nose-guard and huge cheek-pieces giving the man an ancient, almost Homeric appearance; the pair of rampant wolves painted on his shield; his horse's hoofs lifting and falling no faster than a galley's oars.

Then time came back to normal. The two horsemen hurtled towards each other, Titus drawing his sword, a long, cutting *spatha*, while the other plucked another javelin from the leather bucket at his saddle-bow. They passed in a blur of confused movement; Titus hacked, his blade biting air, while the other's javelin flew wide. They wheeled to face each other again, paused briefly to take stock and ready themselves.

Titus, an experienced horseman, noticed signs of restiveness in the enemy's mount: it was shying and fighting the bit. At some stage, horse or rider had lost his nerve, he decided. Probably the rider, whose lack of confidence transferred itself to the animal. The Eastern cavalry had recently seen hard action on the Persian front; some units, if exposed to constant attack by the superb Persian horsemen, would have become demoralized. Trusting that the horse would flinch and spoil its rider's aim, Titus bent low over his own horse's neck and rode straight at his opponent.

Things transpired as he had hoped. Daunted by Titus' direct charge, the enemy's horse reared as its rider flung his weapon – Titus felt the wind of its passage past his cheek as he drove his sword-point into the exposed armpit. A jarring shock travelled up his arm as steel struck bone; then the blade slid deep into yielding flesh. Wrenching his *spatha* free, Titus wheeled, preparing for another clash. No need. Blood spurting from a severed artery, his adversary swayed in the saddle and slid to the ground. His legs kicked spasmodically, then he lay still.

Turning towards Aetius, Titus saw with dismay that the general was hard pressed. He had dispatched one of his opponents, and was engaged in a sword duel with the other, the closeness of the combat precluding a javelin-throw. The pressing danger came from the fourth cavalryman the armoured *catafractarius*, who was galloping to his comrade's assistance.

With no time to think, scarcely enough to react, Titus spurred towards the monstrous figure bearing down on his commander. The *catafractarius* presented an appalling sight. Every part of his body was covered in metal: limbs encased in laminated bands; hands, feet, and body protected by articulated plates reinforced with chain mail; the spherical helmet completely concealed the face and head, giving the wearer an inhuman appearance. The horse, too, was armoured, its head and chest covered by moulded plates, its body by a housing of metal scales. Couched in the attack position the *catafractarius* held a heavy *kontos*, the deadly twelve-foot spear which could transfix a man like a rabbit on a spit.

Converging on this apparently unstoppable killing-machine, Titus saw that the *catafractarius* was vulnerable in only one place: the narrow gap between helmet and body armour. Knowing that he would have only one chance, he slashed at the gap with all his might. The other's impetus prevented him from swerving to avoid the blow, which landed true. The *spatha* was nearly torn from Titus' grip as the *catafractarius* thundered past, blood jetting from his neck in a crimson spray.

Abandoning valour in favour of discretion, the surviving trooper broke off his fight with Aetius and fled. Meanwhile, the *catafractarius*' horse charged on, then slowed and finally came to a halt, its lifeless rider still upright in the saddle.

'I owe you my life.' The general grasped Titus by the arm. 'This I will not forget.'

Titus's mind flashed back eighteen months to when it had all begun . . .

ONE

Ill-smelling seven-foot giants with tow hair
Sidonius Apollinaris, *Letters*, c. 460

Although it was only October, the wind from the Alpine passes that ruffled the leaden surface of Lacus Brigantinus* and roared around the barrack blocks of Spolicinum was bitterly cold and held a hint of snow. The Roman sentries pacing the walkway of the fort's crumbling walls shivered beneath their cloaks and blew on reddened hands gripping spear-shafts. Unlike the tough German mercenaries whose cantonment lay a few hundred yards off beside the lake, not all these men would survive the coming winter. For the Roman element in the increasingly Germanized army tended these days to be drawn from the sweepings of the great estates: *coloni* too puny or infirm to work their farms profitably, and so handed over by their landlords for arrears of rent.

In his tiny office, Titus Valerius Rufinus, the fort's senior clerk, made a swift calculation on his abacus and entered the latest consignment, a cartload of iron pigs and mouflon horn for bow laths, in the codex tagged '*Supply*'. Before replacing the bulky record, he removed from its hiding-place at the back of the shelf a scroll bearing the label '*Liber Rufinorum*'. He unrolled a foot or two of blank papyrus, weighting it down on his desk with a bronze inkwell and an oil lamp. Then, after checking through the window that the duty tribune wasn't on the prowl, he dipped a reed pen and began to write:

Spolicinum Fort, Province of 2nd Raetia, Diocese of Italia. The year of the consuls Asclepiodotus and Marinianus, IV Ides Oct.**
Following a terrible quarrel with my father, Gaius Valerius

* Lake Constance
** 12 October

11

Rufinus, retired general and veteran of Hadrianopolis and the Gothic Wars, I've decided to take up the task that he began, namely the keeping of the *Book of the Rufini*. Aware that these are critical times for Rome, my father wanted to record for posterity the key events he had lived through and in some of which he had taken part; he also expressed a wish that his successors carry on the task after his death. Having broken the old man's heart, I feel I must pick up the baton – if only as an act of reparation. For I doubt if Gaius Valerius now has the will to continue the compilation of the *Liber*.

The cause of our quarrel was twofold: my decision a) to become a Christian, and b) to marry a German. Now, to Gaius, a diehard pagan and a Roman of the old school, two things, Germans and Christianity, are anathema: Germans because to him they are unruly savages who threaten the very fabric of the empire; Christianity because, by turning men's minds away from earthly affairs to the afterlife, it is sapping Rome's will to survive. (To me, faith in a single loving God, incarnated for a short time on earth in the form of Jesus, seems infinitely more valid than belief in a pantheon of beings who, if they exist at all, behave like so many petty criminals or malicious children. Also – let me be honest – being a Christian has practical advantages: pagans are debarred from promotion in the army and civilian administration.)

Foolishly (as I now realize), I convinced myself that I could talk Gaius round to accepting my position. When I paid a visit to the Villa Fortunata, our family home near Mediolanum,* to introduce him to Clothilde, my beautiful betrothed, a dreadful scene erupted.

'They don't *look* very dangerous,' laughed Clothilde as they waited beside the atrium's central pool, pointing at an array of little bronze figurines on a low table. They represented the household gods, the *lares et penates*, which until lately would have been found in practically every Roman home. By openly displaying them, as Titus had explained to Clothilde, Gaius Valerius risked incurring savage penalties.

* Milan.

'Don't be fooled. These little fellows could land us in a lot of trouble. The government's determined to stamp out all pagan practices, even something as trivial as this.'

'Wouldn't it be sensible just to keep them somewhere private?'

'You'd think so, wouldn't you? But that's Father for you. Principle. He should have been a Christian back in Diocletian's time; he'd have made a splendid martyr. Ah, here he is.'

Accompanied by the slave sent to summon him, Gaius Valerius shuffled into the atrium, supporting himself on a stick. At sixty-five, he was hardly ancient, but with his bald head, wrinkled skin, and stooped posture, he could have passed for eighty. A lifetime of hard campaigning and the cares of running an estate in straitened times had taken their toll.

The old man's face lit up. 'Titus! It's good to see you, my son,' he cried in a reedy quaver. 'You should have let us know you were coming.' He propped his stick against a wall and they embraced warmly. Releasing the young man, Gaius regarded him fondly. 'That uniform suits you. Pity that as a civilian you can't wear armour. In a muscled cuirass and crested helmet you'd look splendid.' He paused and added wistfully, 'As I did myself once. You should have seen me at the victory parade after the Battle of the Frigidus . . .' He trailed off as a faraway look came into his eyes.

Titus was afraid that his father was about to embark on one of his rambling reminiscences, but Gaius collected himself and announced briskly, 'But you've heard all that before. Now, some wine. There's still an amphora or two of Falernian in store.' He paused and seemed to notice Clothilde for the first time, then shot Titus a quizzical glance which held a hint of disapproval. 'Your companion . . . ?' He left the question hanging in the air, his breeding preventing him from putting into words what he obviously wondered: was she his son's personal slave, or perhaps a concubine? (To Gaius she had to be one or the other; no alternative relationship was conceivable between a Roman and a German. And Clothilde, from her dress and colouring, was clearly of Teutonic origin.)

Titus took Clothilde's hand. 'Father, this is Clothilde, from a noble Burgundian family. We hope that you will give us your consent and blessing for our marriage.'

Gaius' face paled and he stared at his son in shocked disbelief.

13

'But . . . you can't,' he faltered. 'She's German. It's against the law.'

'Strictly speaking, that's true,' Titus conceded. 'But you know as well as I do there are ways round it if you can pull the right strings. After all, Honorius himself was married to the daughter of Stilicho, who was a Vandal. If you were to put in a good word for us with the bishop, I'm sure the provincial governor would—'

'Never!' interrupted Gaius, a red spot burning on each cheek. 'A son of mine marry a German? Unthinkable. It would bring eternal shame on the house of the Rufini.'

This was all going horribly wrong – beyond Titus' worst imaginings. 'I'm sorry,' he mumbled wretchedly to Clothilde, signing urgently to the hovering slave to show her out, until the storm should have passed.

'That was uncalled for, Father,' Titus said accusingly, once they were alone. 'Clothilde's a fine girl. You couldn't ask for a better daughter-in-law. Just because she's German . . .' He stumbled to a halt, anger making him incoherent.

'Germans are the enemy of Rome,' declared Gaius, a steely edge creeping into his voice. 'They are the cancer that is eating at the empire. We must drive them out or they will destroy us.' He paused, and when he spoke again his voice had softened, held a note of appeal. 'You can see that, Titus, surely? Look, we can't talk here; the slaves will start eavesdropping. Let's continue this discussion in the *tablinum*.'

Limping, the young man followed his father down a short corridor to his study-cum-library. (A childhood riding accident had left Titus lame in one leg, debarring him from military service which, as the son of a soldier, he would otherwise have been compelled to take up. However, his post as a clerk attached to the army conferred quasi-military status and entitled him to wear uniform.) The room overlooked the peristyle with its fountains, statues, and pillared arcades. A pleasant blend of sounds drifted through the open shutters; plash of falling water, distant lowing of cattle, the soft cluck of chickens. The walls were lined with all the old classics, Virgil, Horace, Ovid, Caesar, Suetonius and others. There were even a few moderns, such as Claudian and Ammianus Marcellinus. The two men sat on folding chairs facing each other.

'We can never mix with those people, my son,' said Gaius with earnest urgency. 'They're illiterate barbarians. They have disgusting manners, they stink, let their hair grow long, dress in furs and trousers instead of decent clothing, despise culture . . . Need I go on?'

'They may be everything you say, Father,' Titus replied. 'But I've found them also to be brave and honourable – unlike many of today's Romans. And once you've made friends with him a German's loyal to a fault. Anyway, whether we like them or not is academic. They're here to stay. We can't beat them, we need them in the army; the best thing we can do is try to get along with them. You know, they actually admire most things Roman, and *want* to integrate with us as stakeholders in the empire. We'd be insane not to take full advantage of that. Constantius made a good start, forging friendships with the tribes before he died. And this new general, Aetius, seems to have the same idea.'

'Defeatist talk,' retorted Gaius, his voice hardening again. 'Aetius is a traitor to his people. We destroyed the Cimbri and the Teutones under Marius. We can do the same again.'

'That was five hundred years ago,' Titus exclaimed in exasperation. 'Things have changed just a little since then, don't you think. What about Hadrianopolis? You were there, remember? Rome's worst disaster since Cannae, they say.'

'Rome recovered after Cannae,' Gaius retorted, 'and went on to defeat Hannibal.'

'I can't believe I'm hearing this,' Titus sighed. He plucked the first scroll of the *Liber Rufinorum* from its pigeon-hole, unrolled a section and began to read: '"Having inflicted severe losses on the Goths, as we ourselves had sustained many casualties we decided on a tactical withdrawal to the city in order to regroup."' He furled the scroll and replaced it. 'You've convinced yourself Hadrianopolis really *was* like that, haven't you? You know what your trouble is, Father – you can't face the truth about what's happening to Rome. You blame the Germans, when you should be blaming Rome herself.'

'Explain yourself,' snapped Gaius, nettled by his son's blunt criticism.

'If Rome really wants to get rid of the Germans, she needs one thing above all else: patriotism. Well, that's being very efficiently destroyed by the Roman government's corrupt tax policy. The "barbarians", as you call them, are being welcomed as deliverers by the poor, who are being taxed out of existence. People are ceasing to care whether Rome survives or goes under. Is any of this registering with you? No, I can see it isn't. I take it, then, you're not having second thoughts about my marrying Clothilde?'

'Once he has made his mind up, a true Roman does not change it.'

'That's the most pompous, stupid thing I've ever heard!' Titus shouted, aware that he was widening the gulf that yawned between them, but past caring. 'There's something else you should know. I'd meant to break it gently, but we seem to have gone beyond such niceties. I've decided to become a Christian.'

A terrible silence grew. At length Gaius rose. 'Go,' he said, in a flat, expressionless voice. 'And take your German slut with you. You are no longer my son.'

With his ties to home and family irrevocably sundered, Titus felt a huge loss and sadness. But in a curious way he also felt free. He knew that, like Julius Caesar five hundred years before, he had reached a crossroads in his life, a Rubicon. In a flash of insight, he saw what he must do. First, he would send Clothilde back to her own people, pending arrangements for his baptism and their marriage. (There might be tribal barriers to overcome, but no religious ones; unlike most of her fellow Germans, who were Arians, Clothilde had been raised a Catholic.) Then he would try, somehow, to join Aetius, whose policy of integrating the German tribes into the structure of the empire seemed to offer the best, perhaps the only, way forward for Rome. Having come to a decision, Titus felt relief tinged with excitement sweep over him. The die was cast.

TWO

Hail Valentinian, Augustus of the West
The Patrician Helion, presenting the child Valentinian
to the Roman Senate, 425

Flavius Placidius Valentinianus, Emperor of the West Romans –
the third of his name to wear the purple – son of the Empress
Mother Galla Placidia, Most Noble One, Consul, Defender of
the Nicene Doctrine, et cetera, et cetera, was bored. Earlier, he'd
given his tutor the slip (anything to avoid another history lesson
about the Carthaginian Wars) and hidden in the palace gardens
where, at the edge of the miniature lake, he'd caught six fine
bullfrogs. It had been tremendous fun blowing them up with a
straw until they burst. They swelled up like bladders and just
before they popped, their eyes, staring into his, had blinked.
That gave him a wonderful feeling of power. He looked forward
to the day when he was old enough to take over ruling the empire
from his mother. Then he would have power over Romans, not
just frogs. He could kill anyone he wanted to, just for fun if he
chose. Would his victims blink before they died? The thought
gave him a delicious thrill.

He could hear in the distance, his tutor, a Greek freedman,
calling him. Valentinian chuckled. The man sounded not just
anxious but terrified. As well he might: if his royal charge was
found to be missing, he could expect a severe whipping plus
loss of manumission. The frog episode had left Valentinian
feeling both excited and restless. No good looking for cats to
bait; the strays that prowled the palace grounds had long since
learnt to hide on sighting him. Then a delighted smile broke over
the boy's face as a faraway sound came to his ears, the clucking
of chickens from the imperial hen-coop. Uncle Honorius, the
late Emperor, had doted on the fowls; hand-feeding them had
been his favourite occupation. Though they were now surplus
to requirements, no one had found a pretext to remove them.

17

Eyes shining with anticipation, the Emperor headed for the chicken-run.

'I want you to take a message to Galla Placidia,' Aetius told Titus. They were in the villa outside Ravenna that the general had commandeered for his headquarters. (Since the incident with the *catafractarius*, Aetius had taken Titus more and more into his confidence.) 'Tell her my terms are these: that my Huns be paid off in gold; that I dismiss them on condition that they be ceded Pannonia; and' – Aetius grinned wolfishly – 'that I be made Count.'

'You can't mean it, sir!' exclaimed Titus, shocked by the cool effrontery of the general's demands. 'We're hardly in a position to bargain, surely? The battle with Aspar was a stalemate. And with Ioannes betrayed and executed three days before we arrived, it seems to have been, well, a bit of a futile gesture, if you ask me. Pannonia – you're actually proposing to give it away? To use a Roman province as a bargaining chip?'

'My dear Titus,' sighed Aetius, in the tones of a patient school-master explaining a point to a slow-witted pupil, 'you're failing to grasp the bigger picture. In fact, we're in an excellent position to put pressure on our beloved Empress. Aspar can't wait around indefinitely; he's needed back in the East. And with the Franks and Burgundians flexing their muscles in Gaul, Placidia daren't withdraw troops to counter any moves I might make. Also, she's desperate to see the last of my Huns. As to Pannonia, it's finished anyway; devastated during the Gothic Wars and never really recovered since. If we let the Huns have it, at least it becomes a useful barrier against further German encroachment. And Ioannes? He was never destined to be more than a puppet, with me pulling the strings. With him gone, at least I can play an open game.'

'Sir, may I ask you a question?'

'You may, young Titus, you may.'

'There's something that's been bothering me for some time, sir.' Titus paused uncomfortably, then pressed on. 'Why is it, sir, that you're so against Placidia taking power in the name of her son? After all, Valentinian is the legitimate heir. To some, your stance might seem like treason.'

'Careful, Titus,' rapped Aetius. '"Treason" is a dangerous word to use around generals. I'll let it pass, as you obviously speak from ignorance. The position is this. Placidia in full control would be a disaster for the West. She's achieved a status vastly exceeding her actual ability, through a series of colourful adventures: prisoner of the Goths after the sack of Rome; married to Athaulf, Alaric's brother-in-law; dragged in chains by Athaulf's assassin; sold back to the Romans; married General Constantius, who went on to become co-emperor . . . She's vain, stubborn, stupid, and ambitious. Unfortunately, she's also beautiful and alluring, which enables her to attract and use powerful men. As for her ensuring that Valentinian gets the proper training to fit him for the purple—' Breaking off, Aetius smiled wryly and shook his head. 'She's hopelessly indulgent, gives in to his every whim and tantrum. Result: a spoilt brat eventually ruling the West. We might end up with another Nero or Commodus. That's why, for the sake of Rome, their power must be curbed. Satisfied?'

'Of course, sir,' said Titus contritely. 'I should have realized . . .'

'Yes, you should, shouldn't you?' replied Aetius tartly. 'Anything else troubling you?'

'Naturally, sir, I'm honoured you've asked me to approach the Empress on your behalf. But why send me? Surely a visit from yourself in person would carry much more weight.'

'You should study the politics of animals, Titus. Ever watched how street cats behave? The lower-ranking ones approach the head tom, never the other way round. By sending you, I'm not conceding dominant status to Placidia.' Aetius shrugged, then his face broke into a disarming grin. 'I know – it all sounds utterly childish. Small boys scoring points. Important, though.'

They rehearsed the items Titus was to present to Placidia, then the general waved in dismissal. 'Right, off you go. I'll want a full report when you get back.'

Wearing the better of his two uniforms (red long-sleeved tunic, short cloak, broad military belt, and *pilleus pannonicus*, the round undress pillbox cap worn by soldiers of all ranks and by clerks attached to the army), Titus approached the imperial palace. The huge rectangular building with its guard-turrets and massive outer walls, each pierced by an arched gateway, was more like a fortress than a royal residence. At the west gate, he was challenged by two guards of the household troops. With their long spears, enormous round shields, and ridge helmets whose central crests had been extended into huge, flaring cockscombs, they seemed like throwbacks to the time of Horatius Cocles and his defence of the Tiber Bridge. Titus produced a scroll made out by Aetius' secretary in the general's name, requesting that the bearer be granted audience with the Empress.

'You'll need to see the Master of Petitions,' said one of the soldiers, after scrutinizing the document. 'Straight through the gardens, then you'll come to a passage between the four main blocks. You want the second block on your left. Ask at the chamberlain's office. Can't miss it.'

But miss it Titus did. Seduced by the beauty of the gardens, with their fountains, pergolas, flower-beds, and statuary, he decided to treat himself to a brief tour of exploration before attending to his mission. Some time later, after several futile casts to find his bearings amidst a mane of hedge-lined walkways, he was about to seek out a gardener to ask directions, when there was an outburst of squawking nearby. Curious, he turned a corner – and witnessed a bizarrely repulsive sight.

In a low-walled enclosure caged off at one end, a boy of about six was engaged in plucking the feathers from a struggling chicken. Cackling in distress, terrified birds, some of them naked of plumage, rushed distractedly about the feather-strewn yard, or flapped against the walls in a vain attempt to scale them. Such was the child's concentration that he failed to notice the stranger vaulting into the enclosure.

'You vicious little brute!' shouted Titus. In two long strides he reached the boy. Tearing the tortured fowl from his grip, Titus upended the infant and delivered a ringing slap to his bottom.

The boy wriggled free and whirled to face his chastiser. His face, white with astonished fury, worked silently for a few seconds. Then he screamed in outrage, 'How-dare-you-how-dare-you-how-*dare*-you!' He gulped for breath then added, 'You'll be sorry you did that.' This last was uttered with such venom that, although coming from a child, it was disturbingly chilling. Then, in a swift movement, the boy reached for a whistle hung round his neck and blew a shrill blast.

After that, things happened very quickly.

Like actors responding to cues in a Terence farce, palace guards appeared from behind hedges and pavilions, and raced towards the chicken-yard.

'Kill him! Kill him!' shrieked the child as two of the guards leapt into the enclosure. 'He attacked me.'

A spear whirred past Titus' head and clanged against the cage. The near miss had a steadying effect on the young man; his mind clicked into focus and began to function fast and clearly. Unlike the frontier units or the mobile field armies, palace guards were recruited more for their fanatical loyalty than for their fighting abilities. Titus was sure that, man for man, he was more than a match for any of them.

After Titus' riding accident, his father had purchased an ex-gladiator to instruct the lad in self-defence. (The closing of the gladiatorial schools a few years previously had flooded the market with slave fighters, so Gaius was able to pick from the best.) Titus proved an apt pupil; hours of daily practice with a wooden sword against a post, or fighting with staves, or using only hands and feet as weapons, had honed his skills to a level which more than compensated for his disability. 'You're a dead man walking,' his instructor used to intone during these sessions, repeating a catch-phrase of his own *lanista*. On the day when Titus was able to catch a fly in flight, the old gladiator stopped saying it.

As the guard drew his sword and rushed forward, Titus grabbed the fallen spear with his right hand and feinted. The guard parried; flicking the spear to his left hand, Titus swept it in a scything blow across the other's shins. The man collapsed, his shield and helmet flying. Titus reversed the spear and whacked the butt against his opponent's skull, stunning him. Then, whirling the weapon round his head, he charged two guards closing on him and drove them back against the enclosure wall. A savage kick between the legs sent one man rolling on the ground in agony; a split second later the spear-shaft slammed into the other's sword-arm, snapping it with a brittle crack. With a howl of pain, the guard clutched the injured limb, his weapon thudding to the ground.

Three down. Titus looked around – and knew despair. From every direction guards were racing towards him. He was indeed a dead man walking. Retrieving his first opponent's shield, Titus backed against the cage, determined to sell his life as dearly as possible.

'Stop!'

The command came from a tall and beautiful woman in her early thirties. Everyone froze, except for the child, who with a yell of 'Mother!' rushed through a gate in the wall to be scooped up by her.

'Valentinian, tell us what this is about.' Concern showed through the regal tones.

Valentinian? Titus went hot then cold, as the enormity of his predicament dawned on him. He had assaulted the Emperor.

'I was convinced my last hour had come, sir,' said Titus, when he was safely back at Aetius' headquarters. 'When they bound my hands I thought I was about to be marched off for summary execution. Then, when I told Galla Placidia you'd sent me, she ordered me to be released, although it was obvious she was longing to have me put to a horrible death for daring to smack her son. I was escorted down this long peristyle and through a portico to the imperial apartments, where I was given an audience in the reception chamber.' He looked at Aetius with admiration. 'You must have huge influence where she's concerned, sir. When I told her your demands I could see she hated them and felt deeply humiliated, yet she agreed to everything – in writing.' Titus handed the general a scroll. 'I witnessed this myself. The whole thing was bizarre. There was Valentinian, all decked out in a purple robe and diadem, with me having to put your points through him to his mother. I actually had to place my finger against the little monster's forehead – to make the procedure binding, I suppose.

'Well, sir, I seem to have failed spectacularly as your emissary,' Titus went on bitterly. 'I've embarrassed you, and made a fool of myself. You can have my resignation now, sir, if you like.'

For a few seconds Aetius regarded him inscrutably. Then, to Titus' astonishment, he burst out laughing. 'My dear Titus,' he chuckled when his mirth had subsided, 'you're so refreshingly unsophisticated. Far from wanting your resignation, I wouldn't part with you for all the corn in Africa. You've done me the best service you could possibly imagine. Remember what I told you about animal politics? Well, by smacking the royal arse *in loco meo*, you've reinforced – in a uniquely powerful way – my dominant status in relation to Placidia and Valentinian. Unfortunately, as far as you're concerned the Empress won't rest until she's evened the score.' The general spread his hands apologetically and gave a wry smile. 'As from today, you're a marked man.'

In other words, a dead man walking, thought Titus grimly.

THREE

*A large head, small deep-seated eyes, a flat nose, a few hairs in
place of a beard, broad shoulders, and a short square body –
powerful but ill-proportioned*
Description of Attila: Jordanes, *Gothic History*, 551

The first the bear knew of something being wrong, was when a
chamois – a creature not normally found this far down the mountain – trotted across the glade he was resting in. The wind changed;
snuffing the air, he caught a whiff of the hated man-scent. Instinct
prompted him to retreat downhill, but intelligence combined with
experience told him that that way lay death. To survive, he must
take cover and let the hunters pass him, or break through them
to the safety of the higher slopes.

He was a huge animal; at twenty, past his prime, but still
extremely powerful and with his cunning unimpaired. These traits
he owed to his inheritance. He was perhaps the great-great-
grandson of a pair whose strength and intelligence alone had
ensured survival from the Roman *venatores*, gangs who, until a
few years previously, had been employed in large numbers by
contractors to capture wild beasts for the games. Their depredations over centuries had wiped out most large animals from the
Baltic to the Sahara.

Moving with surprising agility, the bear began to climb, looking
for a suitable spot where his great bulk could be concealed.

'Get back, Roman dog.'

'All right, I can hear you, Hun savage.' Using the most insulting
gesture he knew, Carpilio extended the index and little fingers of
his left hand at Barsich, the beater immediately to his right.
Nevertheless, he obediently backed his horse until the other's
signal told him he was once more in line with the other beaters.

He and Barsich, a Hun lad of his own age, had become firm
friends during the hunt, now in its final day. Sitting among the

adult hunters round the evening camp fires, the two boys had shared their food, chunks of mutton roasted on sticks over the embers, and swapped lies about boyhood exploits. During the day, when unobserved by their seniors they had shown off to each other, making their horses caracole and dance near cliff-edges, or swinging under their bellies then remounting at full gallop.

Carpilio couldn't remember being happier. He had accompanied his father, Aetius, on a diplomatic trip beyond the Danubius river to visit the general's friends, the Huns. He thought with quiet glee of his schoolfellows back in Ravenna, scratching away at their waxed tablets under the ever-present threat of the master's birch. Even that snivelling little beast Valentinian would be hard at it. Everyone had heard and laughed about the Emperor's misadventure with the chickens, and that his Greek tutor had been replaced by a stern disciplinarian imported from Rome. Meanwhile, his formal Roman dalmatic exchanged for baggy trousers and loose tunic, Carpilio was enjoying a glorious freedom, with nothing to do all day but ride, swim, wrestle, and shoot, with other boys. His greatest joy had been riding the Arab–Libyan stallion that was a gift from Attila, his father's closest friend among the Huns, nephew of Rua, an important chieftain. The Arab showed as much endurance as the hardy though ill-conformed Hun horses, but unlike them displayed spirit and intelligence – invaluable assets in an animal with whom a rider could establish rapport.

The hunt was the climax of the visit. Five days previously, the Huns and their Roman guests had ridden out from their encampment to form a huge circle, extending for many miles, among the wooded foothills of the Carpathus mountains. The circle then began to contract, with the result that the animals within it were driven into a smaller and smaller area which eventually became the scene of mass slaughter. The secret of a successful hunt lay in ensuring that the containing cordon remained intact, with no gaps where animals could slip through. Carpilio marvelled at the skill and discipline with which the beaters – young men and boys with a stiffening of veterans – maintained the line over difficult terrain: ravines, rivers, dense scrub, and clumps of woodland.

The line was moving again. Using only the lightest knee-pressure, Carpilio guided his mount down a scree-covered incline. Away in the distance, flashing sunbursts marked the course of the Tisa. Beyond the river stretched the steppe, a sea of grass rolling to the far horizon, its wind-rippled surface creating an uncanny illusion of waves. A thousand feet below, Carpilio could see the natural amphitheatre that would form the killing-ground. Ahead, the thickets boiled with game, with here and there a deer or goat-antelope breaking cover to race across a clearing. Excitement surged through Carpilio. Like the other boys, he would not be allowed to touch large or dangerous animals such as bison, lynx, or wolf; those were reserved for adults. But there would be plenty of pickings for the young-sters: marmots, blue hares, and the smaller hoofed creatures.

'Carpilio!'

The young Roman looked back. Above him, just beginning to descend the scree, was Aetius, mounted on Bucephalus, his favourite steed. Beside him rode Attila, a short but powerful figure, with a huge head and immensely broad shoulders.

'Good hunting, Father,' Carpilio called eagerly, returning the general's wave.

'The same to you, son.'

At the bottom of the slope, the line of beaters paused to straighten out, the delay allowing Aetius and Attila to close the gap, then it pressed on into a tract of dense-packed bush.

Suddenly, from a copse directly to Carpilio's fore, burst an enormous brown bear, the biggest animal the boy had ever seen. With its powerful muscles bunching and sliding beneath the shaggy pelt, its little red eyes blazing with fury, its open jaws revealing its vicious fangs, the creature was terrifying. Carpilio was gripped with paralysing fright and his bowels seemed to turn to water. He felt the horse beneath him start to tremble. On either side of him, he was aware of the young beaters' mounts beginning to rear and plunge. Knowing that a horse's instinct is to flee when faced with danger, but aware too that attempted flight, with the bear directly in his path, was probably his worst option, he placed a reassuring hand on the stallion's neck. Such was the empathy he had already established with the animal that it quietened immediately.

'Hold still!' roared a mighty voice in Hunnish – Carpilio had picked up enough of it to understand the words. Attila kneed his horse into the line of panicking beaters. 'Present your lances; he won't face the points.'

But the advice went unheeded. The line wavered, then broke, as first one youth then another dug his heels into his horse's flanks and bolted. In a few moments, all the beaters in sight of the bear, except Carpilio, were galloping pell-mell for safety. Last to flee was Barsich who, turning in the saddle, presented to his friend a face contorted by terror and anguished guilt. Left to confront the enraged bear were Carpilio, his father, Attila, and an elderly foot-retainer with three hunting-dogs in leash.

The old man loosed the dogs, huge, wolf-like brutes with spiked collars. They flew at the bear, which reared up on its hind legs, displaying to the full its awesome size and menace. A forepaw armed with sickle-like claws flicked out; the foremost dog cart-wheeled in the air, its back broken like a dry stick. Undeterred, the remaining pair leapt at their quarry, sinking their teeth into its flank and haunch. With an ear-shattering roar of pain and rage, the bear struck its tormentors with those terrible claws. One spun to earth, howling, the pink coils of its intestines spilling from a gashed belly; the other dropped lifeless, its skull stove in like a crushed eggshell.

'Keep still, boy,' Carpilio heard his father whisper as the bear turned its attention to its human adversaries.

Attila charged, his lance aimed at the bear's chest. As the point struck home, in a blur of movement too fast for the eye to follow a paw connected with the horse's head, hurling rider and mount to the ground. Towering above them, the lance embedded in its body, the dying monster raised its arms to smash the life from the man pinned helplessly beneath the screaming, blinded horse. But before it could deliver the death-blow, Aetius, vaulting from the saddle, ran forward to confront it. Head swinging to face this new opponent, the bear roared, blood gushing from its gaping jaws. Simultaneously, Aetius thrust upwards with his spear. Impelled with all the power of a strong and desperate man, the blade drove through the creature's palate deep into its brain. For a moment, the stricken animal stood still. Then it swayed, and toppled with a crash that shook the earth.

Like ripples from a stone dropped in a pool, a hush spread through the assembled tribesmen. All, on horseback as tradition dictated, were from the same clan as the disgraced beaters. Headed by Rua, the venerable leader of the chief division of the Hun

Confederacy, those who would decide the fate of the offenders filed in cavalcade into the central space cleared for them: Attila and his brother Bleda, Aetius, and five senior elders. The culprits, ten in number, cowered bound and terrified on the ground. Carpilio, as the one beater involved in the incident who had stayed at his post, and was therefore an important witness, was also present.

'We're not here to discover the guilt or innocence of these boys,' announced Rua, speaking in a surprisingly loud, clear voice for one so old. 'Everyone knows they ran away, thus putting at risk the lives of our Roman guests, as well as that of my nephew Attila. It was a shameful thing to do, bringing dishonour not only on themselves but on their families, their clan, and indeed their whole tribe. All that remains is to decide their punishment.' He turned to face Aetius. 'General, as our guest, whose hosts betrayed your trust, it is for you to recommend an appropriate penalty.'

'Friends and fellow Huns,' said Aetius, speaking in their language. 'I feel that I may address you thus, having lived among you as a hostage when a boy. What are we to do with these young men? We could, I suppose, be merciful; many among you may think that their lapse was not so very terrible. Faced suddenly with appalling danger, is it not understandable that untried boys should flee? And should we not on that account forgive them? I say we should do both. Not to understand, not to forgive – that would call for hearts of stone indeed. But' – Aetius' gaze moved round his audience, holding it – 'I say we should also punish. I say this not from any petty personal desire for revenge because their cowardice put my son's life in danger, but because not to punish them would weaken your clan, and in the end destroy the guilty ones themselves. If out of misguided pity we were to spare them, think of the consequences. Next time a wolverine attacked the goats in his charge, the herd-boy, fearing to face such a terrible animal, might also flee, knowing that he could expect to be excused. The rot would spread like a grass-land fire. Courage and hardihood – these are the twin thongs that bind your clan together. Loosen them, and the clan falls apart. Understand that mercy can have cruel consequences.'

'And what punishment would you suggest as fitting?' asked Rua.

'To remove the cancer that, left untreated, would grow and spread throughout the clan, there can be only one penalty.'

Mingled with whickers and neighing from horses, a stir and murmur swept round the assembly, then gradually subsided. Rua looked round enquiringly at the members of the tribunal. 'If any other would speak, let him do so now.'

'Flavius, old friend,' said Attila in a deep rumble, addressing Aetius rather than the audience, 'you and I go back a while. We have both seen and done things which at the time seemed past mending, but which in the end came right. Surely, in this special case, mercy could be shown. These lads have learnt their lesson. I would be willing to swear, by my honour and the Sacred Scimitar, that they will never re-offend.' His broad Mongol features puckered in a frown. 'When all's said and done,' he went on, a hint of appeal creeping into his voice, 'they're only boys.'

Aetius, sitting upright in the saddle, shrugged impassively and remained silent.

'Must *all* be put to death?' remonstrated Attila, leaning forward over his horse's neck. 'Would it not suffice if lots were drawn?' The note of entreaty was now unmistakeable. 'Yesterday, Flavius, you saved my life. Do not make that debt harder to bear by forcing me to plead.'

Aetius conceded, and so it was decided that lots be drawn. The prisoners' hands were unbound and a jar containing pebbles – seven black, three white – was passed around them. White meant death. When Barsich's turn came, his eyes sought Carpilio's. The boy withdrew his clenched fist from the jar. For a long, agonizing moment the friends' eyes locked.

Barsich opened his hand. The stone was white.

The tribesmen assembled near the top of the cliff to witness the sentence, watched in silence as the three condemned were led towards the five-hundred-foot drop. Two began struggling and crying for their mothers as they were dragged to the edge before being hurled over. Bodies twisting and flailing, they screamed all the way down. Pleading with his guards, Barsich prevailed on them to release him, so that he could die with honour. Freed from their grip, he walked calmly to the lip of the precipice and stepped into the abyss . . .

'Did he really have to die, Father?' Carpilio fought to keep his voice from breaking.

The general placed a hand on his son's shoulder, which was shaking with the boy's suppressed sobs. 'Some day you'll understand,' he said gently. 'As long as it stays strong and brave, a people will survive. Just so long – no longer. We Romans should remember that.'

The love and admiration Carpilio felt for his father were joined by a disturbing intruder. Fear.

FOUR

Athaulf himself was badly wounded in the assault [on Marseille,
in 413], by the valorous Boniface
Olympiodorus of Thebes, *Memoirs, c.* 427

General Flavius Aetius, Master of the Horse in Gaul, second-in-command in Italy, and now (thanks to the hold his Huns had given him over Placidia) Count, was in a sanguine mood as he rode home from the imperial palace. His campaign against Boniface was going better than he'd dared to hope. So well in fact that, less than an hour ago, Placidia had promised him that the imperial summons recalling Boniface from Africa would be on its way by fast courier that very afternoon.

Boniface: virtual ruler of Africa, and commander of all its forces; terror of the barbarians; friend of the clergy, especially Augustine, the saintly Bishop of Hippo; loyal champion of Placidia, sticking by her during her exile in Constantinople and the usurper Ioannes episode. The Count of Africa was now the only obstacle between Aetius and supreme power in the West. It had ever been thus in the Roman world (or in either of the two Roman worlds that now existed), the general reflected. There had never been room for two rivals to co-exist: Scipio *v.* Cato, Octavian *v.* Marcus Antonius, Constantine *v.* Maxentius, Placidia and Valentinian *v.* Ioannes. And now Aetius *v.* Boniface. For the victor, either the purple or command of the army. For the loser, death. (A vanquished rival, always a potential focus for disaffection, was too dangerous to be permitted to live.)

Yet what was at stake was immeasurably more significant than a personal vendetta, Aetius thought, the pounding rhythm of his horse's hoofbeats somehow conducive to the free flowing of ideas. It involved nothing less than the proper governance, and perhaps even the survival, of the Western Empire. For all his good points (and he had many, Aetius conceded, courage and magnanimity being the most outstanding), Boniface lacked the ruthless will and clarity of vision demanded of whoever ruled the West. His unshakeable loyalty to Placidia would ensure that, should he gain power at the expense of Aetius, he would share it with the Augusta, like some latter-day Mark Antony to Placidia's Cleopatra. And that would be disastrous for Rome. Placidia's priorities were narrowly dynastic, and her indulgent treatment of Valentinian, who already showed signs of a weak yet vicious nature, would mean power eventually transferring to an unstable degenerate.

'When did it all go wrong for Rome, old friend?' he murmured to Bucephalus, feeling the muscles bunch and flow beneath him as the great horse ate up the miles in an effortless canter. 'You were not born when it started, and I was but a boy.' His mind flashed back twenty years to that fatal crossing of the Rhenus* by a Germanic confederation, which had brought about a fundamental change in Rome's stance regarding the barbarians: accommodation rather than exclusion.

The consequences today of that mass invasion had been cataclysmic. With its field forces withdrawn to Gaul, Britain was under attack from Saxons, Picts, and Scots from Ireland; Hispania was overrun by Suevi and Vandals and, for the time being at least, virtually lost to the empire. But Africa and Italy were still secure, and so, if precariously, was most of Gaul. It was of vital importance that whoever ruled the West should shape his strategy according to the new realities. Constantius, Honorius' co-emperor, had coped superbly, pacifying the powerful Visigoths by granting them, after their many years of wandering, a homeland in Aquitania,** and halting the Burgundian encroachment into imperial territory, just west of the Rhenus. But Constantius was dead these six years, and Rome's federate 'guests' grown restive once again. The former north–south axis of power, Mediolanum to Augusta Treverorum,† had gone for good, thanks to the increase of Frankish raids into the Belgic provinces. The new axis was east–west, Ravenna to Arelate in Provincia,‡ a situation which he, Aetius, was well placed to exploit re his ability to influence the government.

* The Rhine.
** Aquitaine.
† Trier.
‡ Arles, Provence.

'Who would you choose to rule the West, my beauty,' he chuckled to Bucephalus, 'myself or Boniface?' The horse's ears pricked up as if in empathy. 'You might be wise to pick the Count of Africa. For if your master wins, one thing is sure – cavalry will be hard-used as never before.'

Boniface was the last person who should hold the reins of power. His approach to dealing with barbarians was head-on confrontation, an outdated strategy almost bound to fail. The tribes settled within the empire were too entrenched and numerous to be removed by force – unless the West received massive military backing from the East. Which wasn't going to happen; those days had ended with the death of Theodosius. He, Aetius, on the other hand *knew* barbarians, having in his boyhood been a hostage first of Alaric, then of the Huns. He could sense when it was politic to make concessions to them and when to apply pressure, the right moment to be diplomatic, or to take an uncompromising stand. And he fully grasped one all-important fact: the power of barbarians could often be neutralized by pitting them against each other; Huns against Visigoths, Visigoths against Suevi, et cetera. This called for skill and cunning based on understanding of the barbarian mind – something he, Aetius, possessed in abundance, his rival not at all. Boniface was good at killing barbarians; of handling them, he knew little and cared less.

As in a game of *ludus latrunculorum* or 'soldiers', Aetius reviewed the relative strengths and weaknesses of himself and his rival as regards the coming struggle. On the surface, Boniface appeared to have one supreme advantage, the confidence of Placidia. But Boniface was in Africa, whereas Aetius was here in Ravenna, able to exert all his considerable charm and powers of persuasion to poison the Augusta's mind against her favourite. By posing as her devoted friend and ally (even to the extent of being pleasant to the royal bratling), he had, over the past few weeks, gradually melted her hostility and won her trust. This had enabled him to undermine Boniface by means of hints and innuendo, reporting 'rumours' that he was secretly plotting against her and stirring up sedition among courtiers and army officers. And his efforts had now been crowned with success, it would seem.

Boniface was too honourable and trusting for his own good, Aetius thought with a twinge of conscience. Totally loyal and incorruptible himself, the Count of Africa was naive enough to ascribe those qualities to those in whom he put his trust. What he failed to understand – and herein lay his great weakness – was that most men (and women) were weak and could be manipulated, given enough pressure or inducement. Yes, politics was a dirty game; there were times when Aetius found it hard to avoid feeling self-disgust at his involvement in its machinations. But the end, so long as it merited achievement, could usually be made to justify the means, even when that involved deceit and betrayal. And, if he were honest, Aetius loved it all: the excitement of pitting his cunning and resources against a worthy adversary; the thrill of combat; the heady joy of victory.

Arriving at his villa, Aetius flung Bucephalus' reins to a groom, and strode through the suite of halls to the *tablinum* – more office than library, in his case. As usual, the place was in chaos, with books, papers, and accoutrements, scattered everywhere in disorder. Not that he could blame the house-slaves; he had given strict orders that, basic cleaning apart, the room should remain undisturbed in order to preserve the integrity of his 'system'. The books were mainly on military matters: Vegetius (an idiot who conflated tactics from the time of Trajan and Hadrian with those of the present); *On Matters of Warfare*, an interesting treatise by an anonymous author on army reform, advocating greater use of machines to save manpower; a precious copy (updated) of the *Notitia dignitatum*, a government list of all key offices of state for both empires, including military posts and the units under their command.

Now for the second part of his campaign against Boniface. Dropping his sword-belt over a bust of the Count (Aetius believed in the principle 'Know your enemy'), he made to call for his secretary, then changed his mind. What he intended committing to papyrus was so perilous that it was best not seen by any eyes but his own and the recipient's. Rummaging among the clutter, he finally located pen, ink, and scroll, then began to write.

The task completed, Aetius cast about in his mind for a suitable person to deliver the letter. Someone utterly reliable, discreet, and a good rider. It was essential, of course, that his message reach Boniface before Placidia's. He had it: Titus, the perfect choice. The lad was an excellent horseman, of proven loyalty, and of an unquestioning nature. He dispatched a slave to summon the lad.

'Ah, Titus Valerius, I've an important job for you. Ever been to Africa?'

'No, sir.'

'You'll like it. Nice people, good climate, no barbarians. You'll deliver a letter to Boniface. In person – that's absolutely vital. You should find him in Bulla Regia or Sufetula.'*

'Boniface?'

'The Count of Africa. One of the finest generals Rome's ever produced – I say nothing of myself, of course. Working together, the two of us could revive Rome's fortune's in the West. Now, details. Here's a travel warrant from the Master of Offices, valid for Africa as well as Italy. It'll let you change saddle horses at the imperial post's relay stations. Ariminum–Rome–Capua–Rhegium–Messana–Lilybaeum–Carthage, that's your route. Take passage on the fastest vessels you can find for the crossings. Time is of the essence, you understand. Cash: this purse of *solidi* should more than cover your expenses. Any questions?'

Surveying the latest batch of recruits standing by their mounts for morning inspection, the senior *ducenarius* of Vexillatio 'Equites Africani' groaned to himself. A poor, scratch lot, thought Proximo, who had been a centurion of the old Twentieth when it was recalled from Britain for the defence of Italy. In Proximo's view, these new units – *vexillationes* (cavalry) and *auxilia* (infantry) – couldn't hold a candle to the old legions, half of whose men had been wiped out during the Gothic Wars and which were now in process of being phased out. His present unit had been raised from the notoriously inferior frontier troops, and upgraded to field status in the Army of Africa. At least the horses were good quality – better than the men – though of the chunky Parthian type the Roman stablemasters would insist on sending. More sensible to use the local African breeds, which were small and wiry, but better adapted to the heat. He sighed; some things the army never seemed to learn.

Rising above the east curtain-wall of Castellum Nigrum – one of the chain of forts established by Diocletian to check raiding Moors and Berbers – the sun flooded the parade-ground with harshly brilliant light, instantly raising sweat on men and mounts. The valves of the south gate creaked open to admit the day's first supply-cart, disclosing a vista of irrigated vineyards and olive

* Sbeitla, in central Tunisia.

groves stretching away towards the distant snow-capped peak of Jurjura, thrusting above the blue rampart of the Lesser Atlas. An arresting, vivid scene, Proximo conceded, but not to be compared with the softer beauty of the British landscape. Oh, for just one glimpse of the silver Deva* winding through green meadows, with the mist-veiled Cambrian hills lifting to the west!

Proximo walked slowly down the line of young men – many of them clearly nervous or unhappy – his practised eye looking for the slightest sign of sloppiness in the cleaning of tack or weapons.

'Rust,' he declared with grim satisfaction, pointing to a cluster of brownish speckles on the otherwise bright blade of one recruit's *spatha*. He leant forward till his face was nearly touching the other's. 'There are three sins in the army, lad: asleep on sentry-go, drunk on duty, and a rusty *spatha*. And wipe those grins off your faces,' he snapped at the youths on either side who, in their short stay at the fort, had already heard this litany several times. Proximo grabbed the lead identity-disc hung round the culprit's neck. 'I want that sword clean by Stables,' he went on, tugging the disc sharply, while simultaneously giving a deliberate wink. 'Understand?'

'Y-yes, Ducenarius,' stammered the other in mystified tones.

Inspection over, Proximo dismissed the recruits to the care of the *campidoctores* for a session of drill. He felt a stab of sympathy for the frightened boy he had reprimanded; with luck, the lad would pick up his veiled hint. (Lead rubbed over intractable rust-spots on steel, magically caused them to 'disappear'.) The cash-strapped army was forced to keep on issuing ancient, worn-out gear, Proximo reflected sourly: That rust-pitted *spatha* could have seen service at the Milvian Bridge. Unlike his predecessor (nick-named '*Cedo Alteram*' – 'Give me Another' – from his habit of demanding a fresh vine-staff to replace the one broken over an offending soldier's back), Proximo believed that you got more out of men (and horses) by treating them with patience tempered by firmness, than by using brutality.

'Well done, lad,' grinned Proximo at late parade, inspecting the sword-blade, now a uniform silvery-grey. 'We'll make a soldier of you yet.'

* River Dee.

Later, on his rounds, he dropped into the new recruits' barrack-room. An informal, off-duty chat with the men was time well spent. That way you got to know who were the weak and strong links in the chain, who the barrack-room know-alls, who the likely trouble-makers, or informers. Also, by listening to soldiers' grievances (often incurred by something trivial, such as the reduction last week of the daily bread ration from three to two pounds, the loss being made up with biscuit), you could often take steps in time to defuse a potential crisis.

'All right, lads?' enquired Proximo, looking round the long room. Of the twenty recruits, most were seated on their bunks cleaning kit; the rest were crouched on the floor, engaged in a noisy game of *duodecim scriptorum*, a kind of backgammon.

'Can't complain,' volunteered one, 'now that we're back on full bread rations – thanks to you Ducenarius.'

'Good,' said Proximo. 'So, nothing bothering anyone?'

Collective head-shaking and muttered denials.

'Liars,' said Proximo cheerfully. 'Touch your toes, soldier,' he commanded the one who had spoken up. Looking puzzled, the man complied, whereupon Proximo delivered a smart tap on the buttocks with his vine-branch staff. The youth emitted a muffled yelp of pain.

'Thought so: saddle sores,' pronounced Proximo. Most recruits in the early stages of learning to ride acquired raw coin-shaped patches from chafing of the skin. He looked round the room. 'Come on, admit it, you've all got 'em.' No one disagreeing, he went on, 'Axle-grease, that's the thing. You'll also need *femenalia* – drawers – to keep the stuff in place. Any of the Berber women who hang around the fort'll run you up a pair. You won't be needing them for long, just till your bums harden up.'

'But . . . wearing drawers,' one anxious recruit objected, 'isn't that against regulations?'

'It is lad, it is,' purred Proximo, adding with simulated fierceness, 'And if I find any of you wearing them you'll be on a charge so fast Mercury couldn't catch you. But then,' he continued in his normal voice, 'unlike "Cedo Alteram", whom you've no doubt heard of, I don't carry a mirror on the end of a stick when I take parade, so I'm hardly going to know, am I?'

In the ambience of relaxed banter that followed, the *ducenarius* found himself fielding questions about conditions of service, donatives, the prospect of action, and their legendary supreme commander, the Count of Africa, famed as much for his strict impartial justice as for his feats of arms.

'Is it true he killed Athaulf, Galla Placidia's first husband?'

'Half-killed, I'd say. He severely wounded Athaulf when the Goths attacked Massilia.* But Athaulf recovered, much to Placidia's relief – devoted to her man, was the Augusta.'

'But he did kill a soldier accused of adultery with a civilian's wife?' pressed one trooper hopefully.'**

'Now that one *is* true,' Proximo confirmed. 'But you don't want to hear about it. Oh, you do, do you?'

It was noon before they sighted camp, a neat grid of the leather tents known as *papiliones*, 'butterflies', each holding eight soldiers. All around rolled a bleak landscape of undulating plains, sparsely clothed with esparto grass, thistles, and asphodel. To the north rose the wall of the bare, gullied Capsa Mountains. Southwards, shimmering mirages floated above the sparkling salt crust of the Shott el-Gharsa, one of the chain of salt lakes demarcating the limit of Roman rule. The lakes fringed the Great Sand Sea, which was traversed only by caravans bringing gold, slaves, and ivory across five hundred leagues of desert from the lands of the black men.

The camp was a temporary mobile settlement, erected at one of the stopping-points on Boniface's annual tour of what had become almost a personal fiefdom, rather than the Roman provinces of Africa Proconsularis and Byzacena. He had come to the decision that these peregrinations were a useful reminder to the local populace that Rome still had a mailed fist and was prepared to use it to maintain order and justice – Roman justice, not the primitive 'eye for an eye' code that prevailed beyond the frontier. Though officially 'Roman' for the past two hundred years, the natives were still tribesmen at heart. They were apt to become slack and unruly unless kept in check, witness the present unrest caused by the Donatists, a militant anti-Catholic sect guilty

---

* Marseille.
** The incident is recounted in Chapter 33 of Gibbon's *Decline and Fall of the Roman Empire.*

of whipping up tribal sentiment among the peasants (many of whom had Punic blood) against their Roman masters.

Boniface thought longingly of the bath and clean clothes that awaited him, followed by a cooked meal washed down with Mornag, the excellent local red wine, in contrast to the hard biscuit, sour wine, and salt pork on which he and his men had fared these past three days. A Berber war-party had been raiding villages in the vicinity of Shott el-Jerid, a huge salt lake on the Roman frontier. A punitive expedition was entirely successful, the insurgents being chased back across the border with heavy losses. Nevertheless, the affair had proved a costly diversion for the Romans; while in pursuit, several troopers had inadvertently strayed from the safe path, plunged through the salt crust and been instantly engulfed.

Arriving at the camp, Boniface thanked the soldiers, detachments from the Vexillationes 'Equites Mauri Alites' and 'Equites Feroces', and dismissed them. Then, dismounting, he flung the reins to a groom and walked swiftly to the command tent, which was fronted with the unit's standards. Crouching by the entrance flap was a young native in a worn jellabah. He rose as Boniface approached. He was a Blemmye, judging by his tribal markings, and looked vaguely familiar.

'Lord Boniface,' the man addressed the Count in tones of quiet desperation, 'my petition – you remember?'

A tribune emerged from the tent carrying a goblet of wine, which he handed to the general. 'Sir, I'm sorry about this,' he said apologetically, indicating the native. 'He insists that you promised to see him. I sent him packing, of course, but he kept coming back and repeating his story. He seems harmless enough, so eventually I let him wait here. But I'll get rid of him if you like.'

'No, let him stay,' said Boniface, his memory suddenly clearing. He had been about to hear the man's case at his customary morning tribunal when the news of the insurgency had arrived. He had immediately cancelled proceedings and prepared to depart for the south. That was three days ago; the poor fellow had been waiting for him all that time! His plea must be an urgent one indeed.

'Have you eaten while you've been here?' he asked the Blemmye.

The man shook his head.

'And you never thought to feed him?' Boniface barked at the tribune.

The tribune paled before his commander's anger. 'He – he was given water, sir.'

'How considerate,' sneered Boniface. 'Perhaps a spell of duty supervising the digging of new latrines will remind you of our common humanity. Bring this man some food at once.'

The Blemmye's story, recounted while he devoured a bowl of couscous spiked with lamb, was a pathetic one. He was a date farmer near Thusuros,* whose living had been destroyed when his palms, inherited from his father, had been submerged in the worst sandstorm in living memory. (Boniface could well believe it. Everyone knew the story of the legion caught in a sandstorm which had blown for four days. The men had kept alive by stamping up and down in the raging sand. When the wind stopped, they found themselves standing level with the crowns of palms a hundred feet high.) To pay for food for their baby, the farmer's wife had consented to sleep with a soldier billeted on them. When he was posted to another base, she had accompanied him as his concubine, he having refused to pay the rent he owed unless she agreed.

'She only did it for the baby,' the young Blemmye pleaded, his face an anguished mask. 'She is a good woman, but– ' He broke off, then continued in a trembling whisper, 'She loves the child, my lord. We both do. I could not stop her.'

Boniface felt a surge of compassion for the young man. Unlocking a strong-box, he withdrew a bag of coin and handed it to the other. 'This will help you restart your business, and feed your family meanwhile. If what you say is true, my friend, you have been gravely wronged. But I'll see that you have justice, never fear. Be here at my tribunal in the morning.' Dismissing the Blemmye's stammered thanks, Boniface sent for the *primicerius* to make enquiries about the offending soldier's posting.

So much for rash promises, thought Boniface wryly, as he rode north towards the Capsa Mountains. Having told the Blemmye to attend tomorrow's tribunal, it was imperative that, he Boniface complete his mission before then, both to keep his word to the plaintiff, and to maintain his reputation as a larger-than-life heroic

---

* Present-day Tozeur in Tunisia; then a Roman outpost marking the south-west extremity of the empire.

figure, guaranteed to mete out swift and terrible justice. Boniface chuckled to himself; living up to this carefully nurtured reputation was hard work. It was, however, important that he do so, not from vanity, but because it promoted high morale and loyalty among his troops.

He had learnt that the soldier was now billeted in a village just to the north of the Capsas. It was a mere ten miles away as the falcon flew, but several times that distance by the standard route, which detoured round the western end of the mountain chain – a choice barred to Boniface. The Seldja Gorge, he had learnt, did lead directly through the mountains, though it was used only by the foolhardy or the desperate. To have any hope of keeping his promise, that was the route he must take.

Obeying instructions given to him at camp by a Berber scout, Boniface skirted the foot of the range till he encountered the Seldja river. He followed it as it suddenly angled into the mountainside, and found himself entering a rocky portal hitherto invisible. This natural gateway debouched into a wilderness of shattered rock, choked with debris from the heights above, and impossible to traverse save by keeping to the river-bed itself, which was fringed by spiky reeds and tamarisk. His mount, slipping and starting over the chaos of boulders, disturbed sandpipers and wagtails that skimmed the surface of the brook. Boniface emerged eventually into a fantastic canyon whose winding vertical walls maintained a distance apart of some thirty yards. High above, cliff-swallows and rock-doves swooped and fluttered.

Here, the track left the stream and ascended the gorge's right-hand side. Never before had Boniface's nerve and control of his horse been so severely tested, as he pressed on and up along a track barely eighteen inches wide, with a sheer precipice to his left. The danger was compounded by the presence of snakes. Several times, the general heard an angry hiss issuing from the rocks that strewed the path, and once a cobra rose up before him on its massive coils. Retreat being impossible, Boniface halted his trembling mount and tried to calm it, while the huge snake's hissing rose to a furious crescendo and its throat swelled ominously. But after a few nerve-shredding seconds it glided off, apparently deciding that the creatures confronting it posed no threat.

After a few miles, to Boniface's immense relief the canyon opened out, its sheer walls giving place to easy slopes up to a

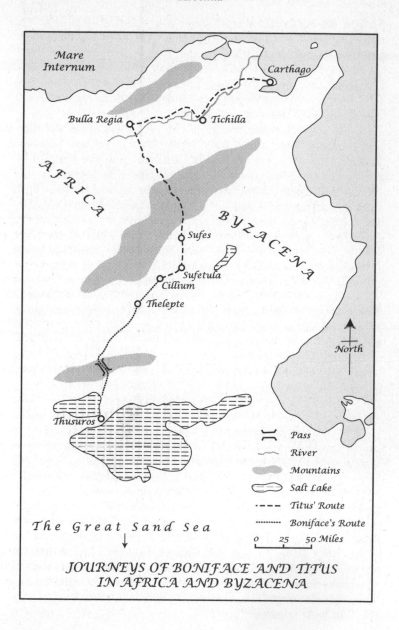

JOURNEYS OF BONIFACE AND TITUS
IN AFRICA AND BYZACENA

plateau. Soon, Boniface was descending the north flank of the range, and by early evening had come in sight of the village – a scatter of one-storeyed mud-brick buildings, with here and there the black goat-skin tent of a nomad family. Militarily, the place was an outpost of Thelepte, a largish town some distance to the north, where two *numeri*, or infantry units, the Fortenses and the Cimbriani, were temporarily billeted.

A few questions to a couple of villagers elicited the information required. Boniface knocked on the door – painted the ubiquitous blue – of one of the larger buildings, and was directed by the landlord to an annexe at the rear. He ripped aside the goatskin curtain that screened the entrance and stepped inside. Dim light from a small unglazed window revealed, besides domestic clutter, and soldier's kit hanging from pegs, a cot with a sleeping infant, and a bed containing two figures, one a native woman, the other a huge, fair-haired man. Both sat up and blinked at the intruder.

Boniface rapped, 'Soldier, she came with you under duress did she not?' The man shrugged but made no attempt to deny it. To the woman, the general said gently, 'Tomorrow, you will return with your child to your village, and rejoin your husband. I will arrange an escort.' To the soldier he said, 'Get dressed and say farewell. I'll wait for you outside.'

In silence, Boniface and the soldier marched to a cypress grove a little way beyond the village. Admiring the man's stoic courage in the calm acceptance of his fate, Boniface drew his sword . . .

Attempting to return through the Seldja Gorge in darkness would have been tantamount to suicide, so Boniface took the safe but much longer route round the mountains. Dawn was breaking as he approached camp, and a ghostly radiance shimmered over the pale expanse of the Shott. As the sun's disc lifted above the horizon, he gazed in wonder as an extraordinary phenomenon developed: an apparent second sun beginning to detach itself from the other. The two orbs separated; the upper rose aloft, the lower wobbled, sank, and deliquesced into the Shott.

An hour later, bathed and shaved, imposing in his parade armour (a splendid though antique suit dating from the time of Alexander Severus, and handed down from father to son through seven generations), Boniface was seated in his command tent, ready to hold tribunal.

First in line was the cuckolded Blemmye.

'Today, your wife and child return to you,' the general informed the peasant.

'And . . . the other, lord?'

'Fear not, my friend, he'll trouble you no more.' And with a grim smile, Boniface emptied at the man's feet the contents of a sack – a severed human head.

Titus' ship docked in Carthage's commercial harbour (warships had their own), overlooked by the capitol on Byrsa Hill. Regretting that time did not permit him to explore the great city, Titus showed his travel warrant at the central post station, and pressed on at a gallop straightway for Bulla Regia as instructed. His route took him south-west along the beautiful valley of the Majerda river wide and flat with extensive vineyards for the first twenty-five miles, after which the terrain became gradually more hilly, terraced vines giving way to olive groves, with broom and terebinth covering slopes too steep for cultivation.

Titus had been born and raised near the border with Gaul, in what had once been the non-Roman territory of Cisalpine Gaul, where his family had been settled for over four hundred years. To Titus Italia proper had always seemed in some ways like a foreign country. Apart from changing horses at a post-station outside the city on his journey to Africa, he had never even been to Rome!

After the flat, misty reclaimed land and small provincial towns of the Po basin, Africa came as a revelation. The brilliant light in which even distant objects stood out sharp and clear; the teeming, cosmopolitan city of Carthage, full of impressive monuments and huge public buildings which seemed almost to be the work of superhuman beings; the staggering fertility – the wheatfields, vineyards and olive groves: all this made a great and lasting impression on the young man. Such evidence (much of it admittedly at least two centuries old) of Rome's power and far-flung influence almost convinced Titus that the Western Empire was not in serious jeopardy. The barbarians could surely never overthrow a race capable of producing such mighty works. Could they?

After an overnight stop at Tichilla,* a small town with a postal

* Present-day Testour.

mansio catering for travellers, Titus pushed on at first light, pleased at having covered eighty miles the previous day – almost half the distance to Bulla Regia. Woods of cork oak, red kites flashing in the air above their glades, stippled the valley's sides; they were joined by stands of holm oak, pine, and laurel as he neared his destination. The *cursus velox*, the express post, enabled him to change horses every ten miles, and he made excellent progress, reaching Bulla Regia in the afternoon.

When he entered the city, Titus passed a theatre (clearly of recent construction) on his left, then turned right into the main *cardo*. Leaving his mount at the post station, he proceeded on foot past a busy market to the forum, which was flanked on opposing sides by an ancient temple (boarded up) and a huge basilica. He enquired in the latter where he would find the president of the *decemprimi*, the inner committee of the city council, and was directed to a villa at the north end of the town. His route took him past a disused temple fronted by statues of city fathers, and a monumental fountain enclosing the Springs of Bulla around which the city was founded. Titus was enchanted by the beauty of the place – the gleaming marble of its splendid public buildings made a striking contrast with the dark foliage of pines and cypress, which everywhere gave grateful shade. Could this really be the place that Augustine, the Church's moral mouthpiece, when haranguing the citizens in the very theatre Titus had just passed, had denounced as a sink of sin and a den of iniquity?

At the villa, Titus was conducted by a slave through a peristyle, then, to his astonishment, down a flight of steps to a vaulted hallway. This led to a large *triclinium*, or dining-room, flanked by pillars and with a splendid floor mosaic depicting Venus riding a seahorse; several corridors led off the room. The soft glow of oil lamps made a welcome change from the glaring sunlight. In all respects the house resembled a well-appointed Roman villa, except that it was all built underground.

'Cool, even on the hottest days,' said a languid voice. 'African summers can be *so* trying.' The speaker, an elderly man in a loose white robe which Titus guessed owed more than a little to native dress, rose from a couch. 'Our subterranean dwellings are quite a feature of Bulla, you know. Romans of Rome affect to despise us, calling us cave-dwellers. Little we care; at noon they sweat while we stay comfortable. Well, young man, now that you've disturbed my midday sleep, you'd better tell me what it is you want.'

Titus obeyed.

'Count Boniface is away on his annual inspection of the central provinces,' said the president, 'which suits us decurions – means we can relax a bit and work six instead of twelve hours a day.' He smiled wryly. 'Don't misunderstand me; we all love the Count. It's just that trying to keep pace with him can be exhausting, to put it mildly. No one takes any liberties when Boniface is around, I assure you. Why, on tour last year, he tracked down one of his own soldiers who'd seduced a native's wife, and cut the fellow's head off. What a man!

'Where is he now? Let me see. He's due back in Carthage soon, so he'll probably have finished his sweep of the desert frontier and be heading north. My best advice would be to take the main road south to Sufetula. That way you'll probably meet him.'

The president's offer of a bath and a meal was gratefully accepted, and Titus was on his way later that afternoon. He crossed a vast plain where a large river joined the Majerda, after which the terrain rose steadily. By sundown, when he stopped for the night at a lonely mansio, he had reached the foothills of the Dorsale Mountains whose crest delineated the boundary between the provinces of Africa and Byzacena. The following day he pushed on into the mountains (the road looping in most un-Roman fashion to accommodate the gradients), past dense stands of holm oak and Aleppo pines. Crossing the summit ridge in the late afternoon, he found himself in a changed world. Southwards, in the rain-shadow of the mountains, an endless expanse of dusty grassland, sere and yellow as a withered leaf, rolled away to the horizon. A gust of wind like the breath from an oven, fanned his cheek. This, Titus felt, was where the real Africa (the continent as opposed to the province) began. The swift tropical darkness was spreading when he reached his stopover for the night, the little town of Sufes,* a rustic backwater whose only claim to distinction lay in being another place to have incurred the censure of Augustine. Here, for the first time, he gleaned news of Boniface; the Count was reported to be three days' march away, at Thelepte, and heading north.

* Now Sbiba.

45

Much encouraged, Titus set off next day at dawn, and after an easy journey of some twenty miles, reached Sufetula, a han some town, completely Roman despite its Punic name. Built on a grid pattern in a striking ochre-coloured stone, it boasted a theatre and amphitheatre, aqueduct, public baths, a cathedral, and no fewer than three triumphal arches. Boniface's advance guard was already in the streets, requisitioning billets and ordering grass to be cut for fodder. Titus could travel much faster than cavalry on the march, so he pressed on, hoping to catch up with Boniface's advancing force at the fortress settlement of Cillium, some thirty-five miles further on. He arrived there to find the general's troops pitching camp outside the place, which was not large enough to provide adequate billeting. A tribune conducted Titus to where the Count was pacing up and down in a grove of figs.

'A courier from Ravenna with a message for you, sir,' announced the officer. 'Says it's urgent.'

'Ah, they all say that,' murmured Boniface, breaking off his perambulations to face them. 'A message that was not urgent – now that would be breaking the mould. Well, we'd better have a look at it.' And he held out his hand to Titus.

Titus found himself staring at an extraordinary figure who might almost have stepped down from the Arch of Constantine. It was not so much that the man was huge (he must have stood at least six and a half feet), as that his appearance commanded attention. He was wearing parade armour which looked as though it dated from the time of Gallienus or Aurelian: a muscle cuirass complete with Gorgon's-head pectoral, and an old-style Attic helmet which had gone out in the West with Diocletian. And – a real period piece – instead of the modern *spatha*, a short *gladius* sword depended from the general's baldric. Even the cut of his hair – a brutal stubble extending to both face and scalp – seemed to echo the fashion of that distant era. But there was nothing brutal about Boniface's manner.

'You like my uniform?' the general enquired affably, as he took Aetius' letter from Titus. 'Yes, it is indeed a bit outdated, but as it's been handed down in my family for seven generations I feel a certain obligation to wear it. However, you must be tired after your journey. The tribune here will see that you can bathe and change and have a meal. Later, we shall share a flask of wine and you will give me all the news from Ravenna.'

When Titus had departed with the officer, the Count unrolled the letter and began to read.

Written at Ravenna, Province of Flaminia and Picenum, Diocese of Italy, in the consulships of Hierus and Ardaburius, VII Kalends Jul.* Flav. Aetius, Master of the Horse of All the Gauls, Count; to my lord Boniface, Count of Africa and commander of all forces there, greetings.

Most noble and excellent Count, I write this in haste and secrecy as a true friend, out of concern for your welfare and for that of Rome. I have it from the most impeccable of sources that you will shortly receive, in the name of the Emperor, a formal summons from the Empress Mother Aelia Galla Placidia, ordering you to return forthwith from Africa to Ravenna. What has transpired to make her take this step I cannot say, but the palace is a hotbed of intrigue, swarming with scheming eunuchs and courtiers whose only concern is to advance their own careers. I know only that there exists a faction, jealous of your success and power, which drips poison into the Augusta's ear, turning her against you. You, who of all her subjects have served her the most loyally. Such injustice! My friend, I urge you in the strongest terms I know: do not obey the summons when it comes. For if you do these creatures will encompass your destruction. Remember Stilicho, who, after his fall from favour presented himself at Ravenna without armed supporters and was summarily executed. Rome can ill afford the loss of the foremost of her servants. Meanwhile, I shall plead your cause with the Augusta; be sure these lies will be exposed in time. Farewell.

Sent by the hand of my trusted agent T. Valerius Rufinus.

Boniface reread the letter in growing incredulity. How could the Empress believe such perfidy? Placidia of all people, whom he had stood up for through thick and thin. Well, at least he was forewarned, thanks to Aetius. There were still, it would seem, some honest Romans left. What to do? If he returned to Ravenna, assuming the summons came, that would be equivalent to signing

* 25 June 427.

47

his own death-warrant, as Aetius' warning had made clear. But if he refused, that would be construed as revolt, in which case an armed force would almost certainly be sent to arrest him.

However, if his enemies imagined he would give in meekly, they were in for a surprise. He would put his troops in a state of readiness, and prepare to resist. Of their loyalty he had no doubt, but of their ability to repel an expedition in force he was less certain. His Roman troops supplemented by Berber auxiliaries were adequate for occasional campaigns against insurgents. But faced with the might of an Imperial army . . . ? Well, the Gods (sorry, God, he amended to himself with a touch of gallows humour) would decide.

As soon as he spotted the distant but rapidly approaching dust-cloud, Boniface sensed that it spelled trouble. The cluster of dots at the cloud's centre swiftly resolved itself into a knot of hard-riding soldiers. They pulled up at the camp's perimeter; two decurions in full armour dismounted and marched purposefully towards him.

They saluted, then one handed Boniface a scroll. He did not need to unroll it to know what it contained: a summons, written in purple ink, to return to Ravenna.

'You are to come with us, sir,' said the officer respectfully but firmly.

For a moment Boniface hesitated, weighing up the enormous repercussions of ignoring an imperial summons.

'That won't be possible,' he said, gravely courteous. 'I regret, gentlemen, that your journey has been wasted.'

FIVE

And absolutely, with a master's right, Christ claims
our hearts, our lips, our time
Paulinus, Bishop of Nola, *Letter to Ausonius, c.* 395

Pacing nervously in the palace of his friend the Bishop of Carthage, Aurelius Augustinus – Bishop of Hippo in the diocese of Africa, famed author of *Confessions* and *City of God*, universally revered for his piety and spiritual example – was apprehensive. For today was the first of January, the day of the naming of the consuls, and of the most popular and eagerly anticipated festival of the year, which from time immemorial had been celebrated throughout the Roman world, the Feast of the Kalends. And he, Augustine, was about to go into the forum of Carthage and denounce it.

It had not been an easy or a quick decision. It came to him that, in a sense, it was a decision for the making of which his whole life had been a preparation.

The world into which he had been born, the golden afterglow of the reign of the great Constantine, was, Augustine reflected, very different from the one he now inhabited. Then Christians, their faith established by Constantine as the official religion of the Roman state after years of savage persecution, had been willing partners in a compact with the empire, and Christianity had become a unifying force in a realm once riven by divisions and disharmony.

But the empire, apparently so strong and stable, had within a generation descended into crisis. Disaster had succeeded disaster: Adrianopolis, the Gothic invasions, the crossing of the Rhenus by German hordes, the sack of Rome. In place of stability and confidence – chaos and insecurity. Yet, even as the empire weakened, its child the Church grew in power and authority. Had not Ambrose, Bishop of Mediolanum, forced the mighty Theodosius to kneel before him and do penance for his sins? The recent

49

consensus between Church and state broke down as Christian leaders increasingly stressed the irrelevance of earthly matters, and began to contemplate what had previously been unthinkable: a Church surviving in a world without the Roman Empire.

All this, happening within Augustine's lifetime, had strangely mirrored the events of his own career. His hedonistic student days when, not yet a Christian, he had lived for the sweet embrace of women and the addictive thrill of the arena, had been matched in the world by an easy-going co-existence between Christianity and other faiths. Then had come that blinding moment of epiphany, when he had seemed to hear a child's voice exhorting him to seek inspiration in the Christians' Bible: '*Tolle, lege* – Take up and read.' From that moment, even while storm-clouds gathered round the empire, and the Church – abandoning its relaxed attitude to pagan gods – declared virtual war on heresy, he had tried to give himself completely to the service of Christ, eschewing worldly affairs and pleasures. It had not been easy. 'Give me chastity and continence – but not yet' had epitomized the sharpness of his struggle, as he had recorded in *Confessions*. Others too, like his friend Paulinus, Bishop of Nola, in rejecting the world for God, had had to make agonizing personal choices. In Paulinus' case, this had meant ending relations with his dearest friend, the cultured and worldly poet Ausonius.

It was the terrible trauma engendered by the sack of Rome that had crystallized these aspirations, and prompted Augustine to begin writing his *magnum opus*, the *City of God*. No more should men concern themselves with the Earthly City, he had argued; instead they should strive towards the New Jerusalem, the Heavenly City, with its promise of union with God. With this vision had grown a conviction that men could not gain entrance to the City of God by their own striving. Sin barred the way. All men were sinners, but could not of their own free will purge themselves of sin. For this they needed Grace, a dispensation God alone could grant. But those who were vouchsafed this gift – the Elect – were already predestined to receive it. In the matter of salvation, God's will was everything, man's nothing. The bishop intoned to himself the rubric that formed the bedrock of his theology: 'Grace, predestination, divine will.'

The moment of truth was now at hand. If the beliefs expressed with such passionate conviction in his sermons and writings were not to appear so much hypocrisy, he could not allow the Feast of the Kalends – given over to drunkenness, gluttony, debauchery, exchange of gifts, and competitive displays of wealth – to pass while he remained silent. The feast was a flagrant celebration of everything the old pagan Rome had represented. To stand by and say nothing would be shamefully to condone it. With thumping heart but with mind resolved, Augustine left the palace and set out for the forum.

Of the great Phoenician city of Carthage that Hannibal had known, barring the harbours nothing remained. Its conquerors had, with truly Roman single-mindedness, destroyed it then rebuilt it according to their own models. The second city of the West, through whose streets Augustine now walked, was, with its forum, basilicas, theatre, and university, barely distinguishable from other great urban centres of the Imperium Romanum.

Halfway up Byrsa Hill leading to the capitol and forum, Augustine had to pause for breath. Age was catching up with him, he thought ruefully; soon he would be seventy-five. Drawing in grateful lungfuls of cool winter air, he surveyed the scene. To the north, beyond the city limits, loomed the headland of Cape Carthage, while below him to the east extended the vast double harbour – the elliptical one for merchant vessels, the circular for warships. Westwards, beyond the (deconsecrated) Temple of Neptune, stretched the suburbs of Megara, dominated by the circus and the vast oval of the amphitheatre, with the arches of Hadrian's mighty aqueduct striding away into the far distance towards the spring of Zaghouan, sixty miles inland.

Augustine entered the forum. It all looked innocent and joyful he thought, looking at the gently swirling crowds, the happy, excited faces, the cheerful colours of best garments looked out for this most special of occasions. But this smiling persona hid an ugly reality. Augustine's sacred duty must now be to tear away that mask and expose the lust and depravity that lurked beneath. Suddenly, he felt calm and confident, as though God's grace had touched him; the pounding of his heart stilled. He held up his hands, and – such was the greatness of his prestige – the murmurous jubilation in the forum died away as people recognized the tall, spare figure and began to spread the word: 'It's the Bishop of Hippo . . . It's Augustine himself . . . He's come to bless us.'

'People of Carthage, friends and fellow Christians,' Augustine began, 'I rejoice to see you gathered here today, as a loving father rejoices to see his children playing. But what if the youngsters' games should cause them to stray into a wadi, where deadly snakes and scorpions lurk concealed? Would he not warn them? And would he not be wanting in a father's duty if he failed to do so?' A ripple of agreement passed through the throng. Not one among them but could recall a parent's anxious warning not to play in scrubland or deserted buildings.

A good start, Augustine thought. The trick when addressing an audience was always to speak with them, not at them; the *Homilies* of Chrysostom, the 'Golden-mouthed' Archbishop of Constantinople, had taught him that. His confidence growing, he pressed home his argument.

'God your Heavenly Father loves you, and would warn you through me, His unworthy servant, of the perils you incur by partaking of this holiday. Because you are blinded by its pomp and glitter, deafened by the noise of its seductive music, you cannot see the cockatrice beneath the stone, nor hear the serpent's angry hiss. With all my heart I urge you to turn aside from the temptations of this profane festival. Think instead of God's love, and ask yourselves: "Will I deny that love, and place my soul at risk?" For, by celebrating this sinful feast, that is what you do.'

Augustine paused, suddenly aware that, carried away by the power of his own eloquence, he had forgotten his audience, the time and place, everything except the urgent need to impart his warning. He glanced at the sun: it was past its meridian. He had begun speaking at the fourth hour, so he must have been speaking for . . . over two hours! He looked at his listeners. Constrained by respect for his authority, they had not drifted away, but they had become restless and inattentive. Many seemed puzzled or anxious; more looked bored and sullen, resentful of this intrusion into their merrymaking. Realist enough to recognize that he had failed to win them over, that if he continued he would merely antagonize them further, Augustine prepared to wind down his address. 'And so, friends, I would conclude by saying—'

'Oh, spare us, please – you've said enough already.' The interruption came from a stocky, plump young man whom Augustine vaguely recognized. Macrobius was the author, he seemed to remember, of a treatise on the Saturnalia, and a *rhetor* at the university, the very institution where Augustine himself had won the prize for rhetoric. Appalled, the bishop heard a titter greet the young scholar's sally. The crowd, sensing conflict, perked up. Augustine fought to retrieve the situation.

'If, among these poor words of mine you remember but one thing, let – let it be this . . .' Augustine floundered to a halt, aware that he sounded weak, apologetic. It would never do to end thus. He began again. 'Bear only this in mind, my friends. Without God's Grace we are helpless. By ourselves, we can—'

'Do nothing?' Macrobius turned Augustine's statement into a query. 'Most Reverend' – the formally correct mode of address was tinged with subtle irony – 'you keep stressing the Grace of God. But what about the will of man? Are you suggesting that we cannot help ourselves?'

'Are *you* implying that man, by his own unaided free will, can achieve goodness without help from God?' countered the bishop hotly. Self-control, he urged himself, self-control; give way to anger in an argument, and you were lost.

'Not at all,' replied the other easily. 'Since it appears you're unwilling to answer my question, I shall answer it for you. God's Grace may well exist; I don't deny it. But only as a form of divine assistance. Heaven helps those who help themselves.'

Augustine was horrified. To deny the supremacy of God's will was tantamount to heresy. The man was dangerous, clearly a disciple of that misguided Scottish monk Pelagius, who insisted that salvation could be attained through individual endeavour.

'In fact, your theory of Grace and Predestination leads to some very bleak conclusions,' Macrobius went on. 'According to your philosophy whatever happens is predetermined anyway, so we should let the barbarians overrun the Roman Empire – your Earthly City – without lifting a finger to stop them.'

A muted growl of approval swept through the audience. Though nominally Christian, most still retained a pagan, worldly cast of mind; as a guarantee of personal security, the survival of the empire was to them a matter of no small concern.

'The Roman Empire and the Earthly City are *not* the same,' protested Augustine, unhappily aware that he was being forced on to the defensive, even being made to appear unpatriotic. He felt a stab of something very like panic as his grip on the situation seemed to slip. Desperately, he glanced around. Where were the *defensores*, the Church's guards, who had the power to arrest religious agitators? Nowhere to be seen, of course, he thought bitterly; on this day of public rejoicing, any attempted arrest might easily stir up mob violence.

'The Earthly City is the realm of the unrighteous – fallen angels, the souls of the wicked, sinners alive in the world,' he heard himself shout, knowing as he did so that his words were falling on deaf ears. With a shock, he realized that, for the first time in his life, he had lost his audience.

The forum darkened as sudden storm-clouds raced across the sky: a typical north-west winter squall. Hailstones bounced on paving-stones and tiled roofs, scattering the crowd. Macrobius waved an ironic farewell to Augustine and called out cheerily, 'A timely intervention, Bishop – by the Grace of God?'

Shaken and humiliated, Augustine returned to the bishop's palace, thankful that the streets had emptied. He had failed. But that, he vowed, would not stop him continuing the fight. God's enemies were powerful and ever-present. They must always be engaged and, God willing, defeated.

SIX

Acts are judged by their ends
St Augustine, *Letters, c.* 400

To the growing file labelled *'Boniface'*, Aetius added the latest report from Africa, just brought in by one of his *agentes in rebus*, couriers-cum-spies who kept him apprised of the rapidly developing political situation in that diocese. In his private journal, the general wrote: 'The net begins to close round Boniface. By acting on the advice contained in my letter, he was guilty only of disobeying an imperial summons – a serious enough offence, but not, in his case, a capital one. Though I have caused him to believe otherwise, Placidia would never have had her erstwhile hero put to death for that alone. Now, however, by repelling with arms the force sent to arrest him, he has crossed the Rubicon and declared himself an enemy of the state.'

A pity that a fine man must be destroyed to serve the greater good, Aetius thought with genuine regret, as he retied the thongs securing the codex, a set of thin waxed boards between exquisitely carved ivory covers: a gift from Placidia 'to a faithful friend'. His choice of medium for recording these private thoughts was deliberate. 'Always write on wax' had been the advice of his father – like himself a Master of Horse, and an adroit political survivor; 'ink is the executioner's ally.' Aetius had been assiduous in following that advice. True, there were his contradictory letters to Boniface and Placidia, but they fell almost into the category of state secrets, and as such were virtually proof against investigation. His file on Boniface consisted of dry and factual reports, hardly evidence of malicious intent. As for anything recorded on those waxed tablets, it could instantly be erased by the blunt end of the stylus. As long as he continued to be careful, his hands would remain clean – at least in the eyes of the world. And that was all that mattered; wasn't it? After all, had not Augustine himself adopted a teleological position

55

regarding the morality of how one acted? 'Acts are judged by their ends,' the bishop had reassured his friend Consentius, when the latter confessed to lying in order to save an otherwise blameless official guilty of a single act of peculation.

His plans were maturing well, rather like Falernian wine laid down for a year in a cool cellar, Aetius reflected wryly, thanks largely to the fact that Boniface, being a good and uncomplicated man, had put his trust in Aetius, thereby becoming the agent of his own destruction. By his most recent action, Boniface had made himself guilty of treason. As any forces he could muster were quite inadequate to repel a full-scale imperial invasion, it was only a matter of time before he was brought back to Ravenna in chains. There would follow a brief trial, then the Count of Africa would be marched outside the city walls, to bend his neck to the executioner's sword. Time now to clinch matters by sending another message to the beleaguered general, applauding his defiance and urging him to stand firm. Even as he felt exhilaration at the thought of his rival rising to the bait, Aetius experienced a prick of shame at engineering his downfall.

In a state of mind approaching desperation, Boniface paced the garden of his headquarters back in Carthage. It had increasingly become a refuge, a sanctuary where he could marshal his distracted thoughts and try to form a plan to cope with the burgeoning crisis that threatened to overwhelm him.

A gerbil scampered from its burrow and, darting in front of the general, sat up expectantly. Smiling, Boniface tossed the creature its usual dole, a handful of wheat grains. 'You at least, my little friend, are on my side,' he murmured.

He was grateful to Aetius for the approval and moral support shown in his last letter. But Aetius was a thousand miles away, and unable to offer material help. The grim truth was, that, unless Boniface could secure the backing of a powerful ally, he was doomed. But there *were* no potential allies.

Or were there? The Count stopped pacing as, unbidden, a siren thought slid into his mind. Immediately, all his instincts and training rose up against the idea, urging him to reject it. It was crazy; it was disloyal . . . It was his only hope. In a mood of sombre fatalism, he returned to his tent and called for his secretary.

SEVEN

*Of medium height, lame from a fall off his horse, he had a deep
mind and was sparing of speech; luxury he despised, but his anger was
uncontrollable and he was covetous*

Description of Gaiseric: Jordanes, *Gothic History*, 551

The encirclement of the village was almost complete. Ringed
about with steep rocky eminences, along whose crest the Vandal
cordon was moving into position, its only remaining exit was the
harbour mouth – and that would shortly be stopped up by Roman
galleys captured at Carthago Nova,* and now waiting in the next
cove.

A greyness shimmered briefly in the east, then vanished; the
false dawn. But already the sun was rising above the Baleares;
soon the ridges surrounding the village flamed in its early rays.
Light swept down the slopes, disclosing the raiders' objective: a
scatter of stone houses surrounding a square, one side of which
was bounded by a church. As the cocks began to crow, the prow
of the first galley emerged round the nearest headland. Gaiseric
raised a rams-horn trumpet to his lips.

Gaiseric, half-brother of Gunderic, King of the Vandals, was
angry, bitter, and frustrated. Not that there was anything extraordinary in that; he was angry, bitter, and frustrated almost all
the time. But this morning, he felt those emotions even more
keenly than usual. The immediate reasons for his ill-humour were
that the village, which his scouts had hinted was wealthy and
populous, looked as if it could scarcely keep a cat; that he had
been seasick on the short voyage along the southern coast of
Hispania; and that his fine Roman vessel had been damaged on
rocks just before dropping anchor. (The steersman had paid for
his clumsiness by having his right hand stricken off, which had
alleviated Gaiseric's anger a little.)

* Cartagena

57

The underlying causes of his choleric temperament were more deep-seated and complex. He was short and lame, whereas his brother was tall and sound of limb. He was illegitimate, while his brother had been born in wedlock, his royal blood fully recognized. Above all, despite his superior intelligence and gift of leadership he was nothing, whereas his nonentity of a brother was king. All this rankled deeply with Gaiseric, permanently souring him.

He had been a child when, twenty-one years ago, his people, along with the Suevi, Alans, and Burgundians, had crossed the frozen Rhenus and swept into Gaul.* Together with the Suevi, the Vandals had pushed on into Hispania, and, after defeating a Roman army sent to suppress them, had settled in the south of the peninsula, subsisting largely on plunder and piracy. Surrounded by a hostile population, and living with the constant threat of renewed punitive expeditions, the tribe's position was, to say the least, precarious.

As the horn-blast echoed round the crags, the waiting Vandals emerged from hiding and surged down the slopes to converge on the doomed village. Barring a trio of women at the well, and a boy driving some cows to pasture, no one was astir. As ordered to, the warriors fanned out into the houses, forcing outside the sleepy and terrified inhabitants; some, not having had time to fling on any clothes, tried to cover their nakedness with their hands. Totalling some three hundred, they were herded into the square, where their olive colouring contrasted with the fair skins and blue eyes of their captors. Apart from the crying of some babes-in-arms, there was silence; the silence of fear and foreboding.

The silence stretched out as the shadow of the church began to ebb back across the square, while a detail proceeded to ransack the buildings. The looters re-entered the square and cast their findings on to a blanket spread before Gaiseric: a pitiful hoard consisting of a few rings, coins, cloak-pins, brooches, and kitchen utensils. Most articles were of bronze or iron; only a few jewellery items were of gold or silver. A Vandal emerged from the church carrying a missorium and chalice, which flashed in the morning rays. 'Silver,' he announced proudly, adding them to the pile.

'Poor man's silver,' growled Gaiseric, his eyes glinting with

* On 31 December 406.

58

fury and disappointment. 'It's pewter, you fool.'

He glared balefully at the assembled Hispano-Romans. 'Which of you is the priest?' he asked in broken Latin, speaking in a slow, measured voice which, although husky and low-pitched, carried to every corner of the square.

Silence, punctuated by muffled sobs and wailing of children.

Gaiseric nodded to two of his henchmen, who plucked a man at random from the crowd. In an almost casual movement, one of the Vandals drew a dagger across the man's throat. He gave a choking gurgle then fell, blood sheeting from his severed gorge. A gasp of horror arose from the villagers.

'Which of you is the priest?' repeated Gaiseric in the same slow monotone. This time, a tall, middle-aged man stepped forward from the crowd. Though visibly shaking, he made an effort to comport himself with dignity as he addressed the Vandal leader. 'I am the priest, barbarian. I protest against your treatment of my flock, and the murder of this innocent man. I demand that—' He was abruptly silenced as a spear-butt smashed against his mouth, pulping his lips.

Gaiseric issued a few curt orders; a party of his men proceeded to drive the villagers into the church, encouraging the tardy with shouts, and blows from spear-staves. Ominously, before locking the doors they conveyed combustible materials – furniture, firewood, handcarts, oil, hangings – into the building.

Gaiseric turned to the priest. 'Where are your church's treasures, jewelled reliquaries, silver ewers and the like? I know you Romans would rather beggar yourselves than see your altars go unadorned.'

'We cannot afford expensive plate,' mumbled the priest, spitting bloodied teeth from his ruined mouth. 'We are only poor fishermen and peasants. That is all of value that our church possesses.' And he indicated the pewter vessels.

'Then we shall be generous and return them to you. Tell me, priest, do you believe that Christ the Son is equal to God the Father?'

'He is very God of very God, of the same substance as the Father, and equal to the Father.'

'Deluded heretic,' snarled Gaiseric. 'How can a son be equal to his father? He is younger, therefore inferior.' A fanatical Arian, he despised Nicene Catholicism almost as much as he hated

Romans. 'Drink your Saviour's blood, them. Not in wine, but in the cup itself.'

A cauldron was produced, a fire kindled, and the missorium and chalice soon reduced to a bubbling pool of liquid. The priest's arms were gripped, a funnel rammed between his jaws, and a stream of molten metal poured into the opening. He convulsed in silent agony; released, he writhed and flailed on the ground, then shuddered and lay still.

'The king comes!' called a Vandal warrior, pointing to the sea. A large galley, its sail embroidered with Gunderic's personal symbol, a charging boar, was moving into the harbour; the vessels blocking the entrance rowed back hastily, to give clear passage.

Ignoring this, Gaiseric called for torches to be lit and thrown inside the church. The men were about to comply when Gunderic, a commanding figure with yellow hair swinging about his shoulders, strode into the square followed by his retinue.

'Hold!' he roared. 'Have I not said, brother, we must befriend the Romans, not give them cause to hate us? If we intend to live among them, we should remember that.'

'Better they should fear us – brother,' replied Gaiseric with studied insolence. Taking a flaming brand from one of his men, he tossed it through an unshuttered window high up in the wall. Within seconds, smoke began to gush out; mingled with screams, loud crackling issued from the building. The screaming rose in intensity as flames leapt from the roof and shot from the windows.

Gunderic's face whitened with anger. 'I came to tell you, brother,' he said, raising his voice above the roar of the flames, 'that the Romans have appealed to us for help. The Count of Africa has sent an envoy. He asks that we join forces with him to resist the Emperor.'

In Gaiseric's cunning mind, a train of thought began to run. Africa. Here might lie the fulfilment of his own and his people's destiny.

In the Vandal camp that night, he approached an ancient crone, skilled in the preparation of salves. And poisons.

EIGHT

Could any other name but that of barbarian, which signifies savagery,
cruelty and terror, fit them [the Vandals] so well?

Victor of Vita, *History of African Persecution*, after 484

'It grows dark, old friend, yet surely at latest it can only be the eighth hour.' Augustine, Bishop of Hippo, scourge of heretics, the foremost intellect and most influential churchman of the West, raised his wasted head from the pillow of his sick-bed, and gazed at the Count of Africa with a puzzled smile.

Looking through the window of the upper room, Boniface pretended to scan the sky: it was a brilliant blue without a speck of cloud. Beyond the walls of Hippo Regius (so named because it had once been the capital of Numidian kinglets), he could see the Vandals sweltering in the August heat to build yet another of their versions of a siege tower. Like all its predecessors, it was a hopeless construction, destined to fall apart under a few well-aimed shots from one of the *ballistae* mounted on the ramparts.

'It's the sand-wind, Aurelius,' replied Boniface; the hot south wind could at times obscure the sun with whirling veils of sand. Dread clutched at his heart. It had come, then. Death was stalking the room, about to take from him his dearest friend and only source of comfort in this dreadful time. He thought, with guilt and horror, of the consequences of his appeal for help to Gunderic, King of the Vandals.

In the midst of preparations to mobilize assistance, Gunderic had died suddenly, of a mysterious sickness. His half-brother Gaiseric had assumed the kingship and, with a fleet of captured Roman vessels and ships eagerly donated by their 'hosts' in Hispania, had transported the entire tribe across the narrow strip of water between the Pillars of Hercules.* Once in Africa, however, instead of coming to Boniface's aid the Vandals under their terrible

---

* The Straits of Gibraltar.

61

leader had rampaged eastwards, wreaking havoc and destruction, their numbers swelled by Moorish rebels, slaves, and Donatists – these last a numerous and savagely persecuted sect spearheaded by gangs of Rome-hating ruffians.

Paralysed by remorse, bereft of the decisive brilliance that had once enabled him to crush the Moors, the Count of Africa had mounted but a faltering resistance – and had seen his troops scattered by the triumphant invaders. Boniface groaned to himself; by one stupendous act of folly, he had lost the West its richest diocese and the source of half its grain.

It would have been a blessed relief to end his life. In similar circumstances, the ancestor who had first put on the armour he now wore would undoubtedly have fallen on his sword – the same sword that now hung at Boniface's side. But that once honourable option was no longer open. For Christians, suicide was a mortal sin, as Augustine, perhaps fearing his friend's intention, had gently reminded him: his life was not his to take, but was God's.

It was cold comfort to reflect that his clash with the imperial government was now resolved. Partly through the good offices of Augustine, an influential court official named Darius had been persuaded to mount a full enquiry into the reasons behind Placidia's recall of Boniface, and his refusal to obey. With Aetius temporarily absent in Gaul, the investigating commission was able to insist that Placidia surrender Aetius' letters to her, maligning Boniface, which were compared with his letters to the Count, advising resistance. Aetius' perfidy was exposed, and Placidia and Boniface were fully reconciled.

Boniface was hurt and baffled by Aetius' betrayal. He had come to trust the general as a friend, and cherished a vision of their working together to rebuild Rome's power in the West. Operating out of strong bases in Italy and Africa, between them they could surely have tamed or crushed the barbarians in Gaul and Hispania, then gone on to restore the Rhenus and Danubius frontiers. It had been done before: a hundred and fifty years earlier, Aurelian had achieved no less in circumstances just as desperate. He sighed. That bright vision lay in ruins, and Rome's future looked dark and uncertain indeed.

A call from the sick-bed jerked Boniface from his gloomy reverie. 'The light fades – it's gone darker, much darker. I can hardly see you.'

Hurrying to the bedside, Boniface knelt and grasped Augustine's hand.

'No need to shield me from the truth, old friend,' the bishop murmured. 'It's the end, isn't it?'

'Not the end Aurelius,' replied Boniface, mastering a sob, 'but a glorious beginning. Soon you will be with Christ and His company of angels.'

So they stayed, hand in hand, the tough soldier and the saintly scholar, until, a little later, the bishop gently breathed his last.

A pity his friend could not have lived a little longer, thought the Count, brushing away tears. The siege, now in its third month, would soon be raised; reinforcements were coming from Italy, to be joined by Aspar and an Eastern army – the same Aspar who had foiled Aetius' attempted coup to install Ioannes as Western emperor. Gaiseric and his savages would be wiped out, or at the least defeated and driven from the soil of Africa. Perhaps, after all, the West's future was not so dark.

The Roman army was drawn up on rising ground to the east of Hippo. Composed of powerful contingents from both empires, and supplemented by the remnants of Boniface's Army of Africa, it made a brave showing. In the centre was the infantry: a few of the old legions still proudly displaying their eagles and standards, their ranks swelled by German mercenaries; the bulk of the force was formed of the new, smaller units, *auxilia* and *cunei*, the latter being attack columns intended to pierce the enemy's front. To right and left (that is, to north and south) of the centre was the cavalry: Aspar with his seasoned Eastern troopers to the right, Italian horse to the left. (Conspicuous by their absence were the units of Aetius' Gallic Horse.)

Opposite the Roman positions and about two miles distant, the Vandal forces were assembling on a hill to the south of the city. The churning mob of trousered warriors were armed mostly with spears and javelins, their only defensive equipment being a round shield with an iron boss. A few men, wealthy or important tribal leaders, carried swords; even fewer, from the same class, were mounted.

The setting in the fertile *tell* was idyllic. Vineyards and wheat-fields, interspersed with groves of oak and cedar, surrounded the neat little city, whose extensive harbour sheltered the two imperial fleets. Blue with distance, the Lesser Atlas rolled along the southern horizon, their foothills stippled with woods. Between the two armies, but closer to the Roman side, flowed the little River Sebus, its banks lined with trees.

Surrounded by senior officers, prefects of legions, and *praepositi*, or commanders of smaller units, Boniface surveyed the scene. As supreme commander of the joint enterprise, on him fell the responsibility of devising a plan to defeat the Vandals. For the first time in many months, he felt cheerful and positive. Like all barbarians, the Vandals lacked the skill and patience to invest walled cities and had given up the siege, at least for the time being. They might be individually brave but they lacked discipline, and their only tactic consisted of a wild charge. Break that, Boniface told himself, and victory was virtually assured for, in the event of a charge stalling, the Vandals, lacking helmets and body armour, were very vulnerable. The one factor that gave them cohesion and direction was their king. War-leader as well as monarch – functions not normally combined in German kings – Gaiseric inspired in his warriors an awed respect which commanded total obedience. This did not stem from fear, an emotion to which the Vandals, like all Germans, seemed impervious. A war-leader was accepted only for as long as he brought success; should he fail, he was quickly replaced.

Looking at their army on its hill, Boniface felt encouraged. The Romans outnumbered them greatly. Really, all he had to do was wait. His disciplined troops would keep formation indefinitely. But that was not in the Germans' nature; they would soon grow restive and impatient, until not even Gaiseric's iron will could hold them. Then they would rush down from their vantage-point – to break in red ruin on the Roman line.

He turned to the Commander of the Eastern army and smiled. Well, Aspar,' he said, 'this time I think we have them.'

'Perhaps. But I wouldn't rely on it. Gaiseric's a cunning fox. Something tells me he may have a nasty surprise in store for us.'

Aspar's suspicions were confirmed a few minutes later, when a scout came galloping up. 'Vandals in the wood, sir,' he gasped to Boniface, pointing to a stand of pines on the far side of the river. 'They're well concealed. I dismounted and crawled as close as I dared; I'm not sure of their numbers, sir, but I'd say they're there in force. I got away without being spotted; I'm certain of that.'

The elation that had begun to lift the Count's spirits suddenly evaporated. Should the scout be right, the situation was completely changed. If he stuck to his plan to await the German attack, he would be caught between two fires – the Vandals on the hill would engage his front, while those in the wood would strike him on the flank. But if he took the initiative and advanced to the attack, the ones in the wood would join their comrades on the hill before he could intercept them. Together, they would launch a charge which their combined impetus would render irresistible.

Suddenly, Boniface felt exhausted; tired to his very bones. He knew he must make a decision – and rapidly – but his mind refused to function. The terrible guilt resulting from his causing the Vandals to invade Africa came surging back, coupled with lingering depression over the death of his friend Augustine, eroding his confidence, petrifying his will. Dimly, he became aware of Aspar trying to communicate, and forced himself to pay attention.

'Sir,' Aspar said urgently, 'don't you see? We can turn this to our advantage. Gaiseric's made the mistake of splitting his force. Assuming the scout wasn't seen, Gaiseric doesn't know that we've discovered his dispositions. If we send our best infantry round behind the wood, we can flush the Vandals out. If our men advance along the river, they'll be screened by the trees, and can take them by surprise. Once the Vandals are in the open, our cavalry can hit them hard. With the slope in our favour, they'll be cut to pieces before the ones on the hill have time to intervene. Those we can then deal with separately. With half their force destroyed, they won't stand a chance.' Aspar paused, waiting for the Count's reaction. When none came, he almost shouted, 'It will work, sir, but only if we don't delay – surely you can see that? Give the orders now, sir.' And he proffered his own set of diptychs, hinged pairs of waxed tablets, used by commanders in the field to transmit messages.

Aspar's plan was bold, simple, and would probably succeed, Boniface acknowledged to himself. But the thought of detaching the cream of the infantry and leaving his centre exposed, if only temporarily, was worrying. He opened his mouth to summon gallopers who would convey the appropriate orders. But no sound came. Frozen by fear and irresolution, he hesitated while the precious moments bled away.

Mistaking the Count's silence for contempt, Aspar exclaimed

furiously, 'I see. You think because I'm an Alan – to you a barbarian – my opinion can be overlooked!' His fine-boned, delicate features, the result of the strong admixture of Persian blood possessed by members of his race, darkened with anger. 'Then fight Gaiseric your own way, Roman. You deserve each other.' Wheeling his horse, he cantered off to join the Eastern cavalry.

With numb horror, like that experienced in a nightmare when safety depends on speed but the limbs refuse to move, Boniface watched the Vandals descend the hill, and swarm across the intervening ground towards the Roman front. With a deafening clash, the two sides came together. The sheer ferocity of the German attack sent the Romans reeling, forcing them to give ground. Their line bent, but held, then slowly straightened again. Protected by armour, welded by discipline and training into an efficient fighting-machine, the Romans began to push the Vandals back. The Germans in the Roman ranks fought particularly well. Unlike the untrustworthy federates – whole tribes allowed to settle in the empire in return for a promise to fight for Rome under their own chiefs if called on – the Germans were individually recruited volunteers, and provided Rome with the best and bravest of her soldiers. Once sworn in, they always stayed loyal, even when required to fight against their fellow Germans.

Suddenly, just when it seemed that the tide was turning in its favour, the Roman line began to crumple from the right, as the Vandals in the wood launched their flank attack. The onslaught compressed the ranks on the Roman right, sending a destabilizing shock wave along the entire line. Cohesion crumbled and the Roman advance wavered to a halt, the men jammed together, unable to wield their weapons properly. With no orders issuing from their commander, demoralization then panic swept through the Roman army. Yelling in the sheer exultation of battle, which seemed to lend them near-superhuman strength, the Vandals inflicted terrible damage with their spears, which sometimes punched clean through scale armour or chain mail to deliver a mortal wound. Like a wax figure placed too near a fire, the Roman formations lost definition and began to dissolve. Then, with horrifying speed, the army disintegrated, transformed in a twinkling into a fleeing rabble inspired by a single thought: escape.

The cavalry fared best. A man on a horse is always intimidating to a man on foot; by sheer weight and speed, most troopers and their officers were able to cut their way through the disorderly press of Vandals. The footsoldiers were less fortunate. Vast numbers were killed or taken prisoner, and only a sorry remnant reached safety behind the walls of Hippo; so few, in fact, that it was decided to embark the civil population along with the surviving soldiers. A broken man, Boniface watched from the deck of his transport ship, as the African coast slowly vanished in the distance. In the space of a few months, he had lost two battles, the flower of Rome's armies, and the richest part of the Western Empire.

NINE

If God the Father and Son accept this holy plaint, my prayer may once again restore you to me
Ausonius, *Letter to Paulinus, c.* 390

Villa Basiliana, Ravenna, Province of Flaminia and Picenum, Diocese of Italia [Titus wrote in the *Liber Rufinorum*]. The year of the consuls Bassus and Antiochus, *pridie* Kalendas Sept.*

The capital buzzes with rumours about Aetius, who is in Gaul, considering his next move as regards Placidia. The situation is this: Boniface has returned from Africa, not, as one might expect, in disgrace for bringing in the Vandals and losing the diocese, but in something like triumph: given a hero's welcome by Placidia, raised to the rank of Patrician, made master-general of the Roman armies, and showered with medals! How can one believe it? Aetius, on the other hand, has been vilified at court – blamed for the African disaster, and now *persona non grata* as far as the Empress is concerned. People are saying he drove Boniface into appealing to the Vandals for help, by misrepresenting him to Placidia. Which puts me in a quandary: I hate the idea of showing disloyalty to Aetius (who has always been good to me) by even listening to the rumours. On the other hand, it would be irresponsible to ignore them – at least until I'm satisfied that they're unfounded. But if they *should* turn out to be true, what then? Could I, in conscience, go on serving a master whose scheming has so damaged Rome? Perhaps prayer to my new God will help me to see the way ahead clearly.

Meanwhile, on Aetius' orders I stay here at his head-quarters near Ravenna, gathering what information I can

---

* 31 August 431.

68

about political developments. He wants a full report on his return from Gaul. It's far from easy; as one can imagine, I'm not exactly in Placidia's good graces since that wretched business with the chickens. With Aetius out of favour, the palace is barred to me, so I'm reduced to snooping around the markets and wine-shops for scraps of gossip, which I then have to sift and evaluate.

Now, on a personal matter, some good news. I am a father! Recently Clothilde gave birth to a boy. We've christened him Marcus; he's a sturdy little chap with a fine pair of lungs. For the moment he and his mother are living with Clothilde's people, the Burgundians, in that part of eastern Gaul ceded to them first by the usurper Ioannes, then confirmed by Honorius. So for the time being, until I can afford a little farm in Italy, he's being brought up as a German. And I'm glad of that. He'll grow up strong and hardy, and learn to value loyalty and courage – qualities in short supply among today's Romans. Time enough for him to acquire some Roman polish later. I visit them from time to time when I get leave, which is fairly frequently – or rather was, prior to Aetius' departure for Gaul. He may be a hard taskmaster, but stinginess isn't one of his faults.

I worry about my father. The rift between us seems as wide as ever; he doesn't answer my letters, but family friends keep me informed. Poor, stubborn old Gaius! It appears he's much reduced in health and circumstances. It's his own fault, of course. If he'd moderate his pagan stance a little, or just pay lip-service to Christian rites, the authorities would probably turn a blind eye. With him, though, where principles are concerned it's a matter of honour not to give an inch. He's been fined, stripped of his civil decurion status and of his army pension. He survives through the generosity of friends and the kindness of the *coloni* on his estate. If only there were a way to resolve this senseless breach between us.

It was cool and dark inside Ravenna's great cathedral, a suitable place for Titus to focus his thoughts. He stared at the great, recently finished mosaic of the Enthroned Christ separating the damned from the saved on the Day of Judgement. The Saviour seemed to gaze back at him, calm, strong, filled with loving compassion, but also with the stern authority of a terrible judge. Titus opened his heart in prayer, pouring out in silent words his dilemma concerning Aetius. But it didn't help; he had no sense of a caring, listening Presence. Perhaps that image on the wall, formed of tiny cubes of coloured stone and glass, was all there was. Perhaps, after all, Christ was not Risen, was just a heap of mouldering bones in a forgotten sepulchre in Palestine. He continued to pray, increasingly unable to prevent the feeling that it was futile.

He failed to notice a cloaked and hooded figure, which had been watching him from behind a pillar, glide silently from the building.

Feeling empty and depressed, Titus left the cathedral. He was surprised to notice how much the shadows had lengthened; his attempts at prayer had taken longer than he'd realized. Better hurry before the city gates were closed; he'd left his horse at a livery stable outside the walls. As he was about to move off, he noticed a one-legged beggar sitting near the great double doors. Propped beside him was a crutch, and on the ground before him were a begging-bowl and a placard stating: '*Proximo, disabled soldier, African campaign*'.

Titus was always sympathetic to the plight of such ex-soldiers, whose pension instalments were often late, or subject to fleecing by corrupt officials. 'Which *unit*?' he asked.

'African Horse,' replied the other proudly, 'and before that the Twentieth Legion – the old "Valeria Victrix", stationed at Castra Deva* in Britain for nigh on four hundred years in all.' He indicated his leg, which had been severed above the knee. 'Doctors took it off after the recent battle with the Vandals. A right shambles that was, I can tell you.'

Interest displacing his concern for the lateness of the hour, Titus pressed the man for details. Perhaps he might learn something.

'We were doing well against the Vandals, until they launched a surprise attack on our flank. Then our commander, Count Boniface, seemed to freeze up. With no orders telling anyone what to do, there was chaos. In the end we broke, and what began as a rout became a massacre. Myself, I wasn't that surprised. Boniface, poor devil, lost his grip the moment the Vandals invaded – blamed himself for asking them to come over from Spain to help him. Ah, but you should have seen him in the old days, sir.

* Chester.

What a soldier! Suevi, Goths, Moors – take your pick; he'd thrash the living daylights out of any of them.'

'You say he asked for Vandal help. Against whom?'

The veteran shook his head in disbelief. 'What empire have you been living in, sir? Against the imperial Roman army, of course – thought everyone knew that. But it wasn't Boniface's fault, not really. It was that General Aetius who turned the Empress against him. Sent a summons, she did, recalling him from Africa, but he wouldn't go. Can't say I blame him, either.'

Titus' head whirled. Court gossip he had largely learnt to discount; usually about nine-tenths of it was mischievous froth. But among soldiers it was different. Perhaps because it bore on basic realities like pay, provisions, hardship, and death, it usually contained a nub of truth. Proximo's account, crude and simplistic as it was, he was inclined to believe.

Titus felt in his purse for a donation. He still had a third of the funds Aetius had given him to cover expenses for his African mission. When he had tried to return the surplus, Aetius had responded, with careless generosity, 'For God's sake keep it. You're too honest, Titus. Know the first rule of being in the army or the civil service: "Always double your claims, and never give back anything you're not entitled to."' But Titus, uneasy about spending money he hadn't earned, had kept by the remainder unused. Now he felt justified in giving a little of it away.

'God bless you sir. A few *nummi* would have done,' said an astonished Proximo, when Titus handed him a *solidus* – two months' income for a small artisan.

'You're welcome, Proximo,' replied Titus. 'You've helped me more than you know.' He bade him farewell, and plunged into a narrow alley, a shortcut to the Aurean Gate.

Passing a doorway, he suddenly felt something whip round his neck from behind, jerking him back into the darkness. The ligature tightened, choking off his breath; a roaring filled his head and his vision darkened. He struggled helplessly, hands clawing at the cord throttling him, all his skill in self-defence of no avail. 'I'm a dead man,' he thought, in panic and despair, 'a dead man walking.'

All at once, he became aware of a swirl of violent movement beside him, then the pressure on his throat relaxed. Drawing in great whooping gasps of air, Titus looked around, saw Proximo leaning on the wall beside him, and between them on the ground a crumpled figure in a dark cloak. A thread of blood trickled from a crater in the man's temple.

'Dead, sir.' Proximo waved his crutch, which he held by its base. 'Swung properly, it's like a sledgehammer. Lucky I watched you come down here. When you vanished suddenly, I got suspicious and decided to check.'

'Thank God you did,' said Titus shakily, massaging his throat. He'd live.

'Sneak-thief after your purse, probably. Can't be too careful these days.'

But Titus knew it was no thief. Placidia, burning to avenge her son's humiliation, had set one of her creatures on his trail, with orders to dispatch him. Without Aetius to protect him, vigilance would have to be his watchword.

They weighted the corpse with prised-up cobblestones, then, making sure they were unobserved, slipped it into one of Ravenna's many canals. Titus solved the problem of what to do with the balance of his African funds by giving it to his rescuer. The old soldier need beg no more; there was enough for him to set himself up in a small business. 'A small enough return for saving my life,' he said, cutting short Proximo's stammered thanks.

He reached the gate just before it shut. As he cantered back towards Aetius' villa, two things struck him with the force of revelation. Was it chance or destiny that had brought about his meeting with Proximo, a meeting which had confirmed his suspicions regarding Aetius, and resulted in his deliverance from assassination? And the man's old legion was 'Valeria Victrix'. Valeria – Valerius: the name of his father's *gens*.* Could it be that he was meant to seek his father's advice as to what he should now do? The weight of centuries of his family's pagan tradition – in reality a polite scepticism underpinned by Stoic principles – seemed to press down on him, urging rejection of such irrational thoughts. But part of him, the new Christian part, insisted that his meeting with Proximo might have been more than blind chance.

Perhaps, after all, his prayers in the cathedral had not gone unanswered, and he had been vouchsafed a sign?

* Clan.

TEN

Your [Rome's] power is felt even to the farthest edge of the world
Rutilius Namatianus, *On His Return*, 416

Written at the Villa Fortunata, Province of Aemilia, Diocese of Italia, in the year of the consuls Bassus and Antiochus, Kalendas Sept.* C. Valerius Rufinus, formerly commander of the Primani Legion, ex-decurion of Tremeratae; to his friend Magnus Anicius Felix, former tribune in the Primani Legion, senator, greetings.

Magnus, my dear old friend, having lost touch with you many years ago, I rejoice to hear (from a mutual acquaintance) that you are in good health and living in your ancestral homeland of Aquitania – now, alas, allotted to the Visigoths. My commiserations on your plight: having to share your province with stinking, skin-clad brutes can't be pleasant. You must come and visit me, although I fear you will find my hospitality a touch threadbare, my circumstances being somewhat straitened at this present. I will not bore you with the details; suffice to say that the authorities do not quite see eye to eye with myself over certain matters, as a result of which I am now *persona non grata* in their eyes. However, my cellar is not entirely empty yet; it would be good to re-fight old campaigns together, with a cup or two of Falernum to stimulate the memory.

Do you remember that August evening thirty-seven years ago when we waited, in the valley of the Frigidus, to hear if Theodosius had decided to withdraw?'

Moving among his legionaries, giving a word of encouragement here, a gesture of sympathy to a wounded soldier there,

* 1 September 431.

73

Gaius Valerius Rufinus, commander of the Primani Legion, watched, as, further down the valley, Arbogast's troops pitched camp for the night. Along the northern horizon rolled a range of low hills, outriders of the Julian Alpes, pierced by the white ribbon of the road from Aquincum.* From either host, details were digging long trenches to receive the dead, stacked in piles like so much cordwood. On Theodosius' side, the slain were mainly Alaric's Visigoths – bearing out the Goths' complaint that, when it came to fighting, the Romans preferred to spend the blood of their barbarian federate allies, rather than their own.

Arbogast, the Frankish Master of Soldiers, had treacherously murdered the young Western Emperor Valentinian II, and set up his own puppet, Eugenius, on the vacant throne. Just the latest in the seemingly endless series of attempted usurpations that at times had shaken the empire to its foundations. But the German's bid for power (via Eugenius, for no one of Teutonic blood could assume the purple) had been challenged by the Eastern Emperor Theodosius. The rival armies had clashed in the valley of the River Frigidus, where the road from Pannonia emerged from the hills to approach the great city of Aquileia at the head of the Adriatic.

The first day's fighting had been bloody and inconclusive, the advantage if anything lying with Arbogast, despite one of his generals having deserted to Theodosius.

'A messy business, sir,' remarked one of Gaius' officers, a young tribune from the great Anician family of Rome. 'If I were Theodosius, I'd be inclined to withdraw under cover of darkness, and regroup to fight another day.'

'That would be the sensible choice,' agreed Gaius reluctantly. 'But a pity to be forced to do it, all the same. The longer that serpent Arbogast remains unscotched—' He broke off, suddenly alert. 'You felt that, Magnus – a breath of wind?'

'I think so, sir. A cold breeze – seems to be coming from the hills.'

'It's the *bora*!' exclaimed Gaius. 'I've just remembered.'

'The *bora*, sir?'

'It's a seasonal north wind which blows with ferocious power at

---

* Budapest.

this time of year – buildings damaged, trees uprooted, hailstones big as sparrows' eggs. I experienced it six years ago, when we marched through this very valley against the usurper Maximus. It'll slowly gather force throughout the night and tomorrow build up to a full storm, blowing right in the faces of Arbogast and Eugenius. Ride to Theodosius' tent, Magnus, and tell the Emperor what I've just told you.'

On receiving this intelligence, Theodosius, who was on the point of ordering a retreat, stayed his hand. All transpired just as Gaius Valerius had predicted, and the following day Theodosius went on to win a glorious victory. Eugenius was captured and executed, Arbogast committed suicide, and Theodosius assumed the throne of a reunified empire. And Gaius Valerius acquired an unofficial *agnomen* or title, bestowed on their commander by the men of the Primani Legion: 'Boranus'.

In our innocence, Magnus, we thought that with Theodosius' great victory, a new era of peace and security had been ushered in. How wrong we were! The following year the mighty Emperor was dead, and our hopes crumbled as the Western Empire reeled beneath a barbarian onslaught: the terrible Gothic Wars in which half our armies perished; the crossing of the Rhenus by German hordes; and now the fall of Africa to the Vandals.

But let us not dwell on such disasters. Rome will rise again, and go on to achieve even greater glories; of that I am convinced. As Rutilius says:

No man will ever be safe if he forgets you;
May I praise you still when the sun is dark.
To count up the glories of Rome is like counting
The stars in the sky.

And take Claudian:

To Roman laws, submission Bactria shows,
The Ganges pale 'mid captive borders flows;
And Persia, at our foot with humble air,
Spreads costly ornaments and jewels rare.

> Your course to Bacchus'* utmost limits bend;
> From pole to pole your Empire shall extend.

I share with Symmachus his conviction that the conquest of new territories should be the empire's continued aim, for surely it is Rome's ordained mission to let the world share the blessings of her civilization. But for an *ordo renascendi* – a rebirth of Rome – to take place, two things must happen. The West must purge itself of Germans, illiterate barbarians who can never assimilate with Rome. And we must return to the worship of the old Gods. For let us not forget that Rome's present troubles began when the temples were closed, and the Altar of Victory removed from the Senate. Also, by making men's priority the life to come, Christianity saps their commitment to preserve the empire.

Thank the Gods I still have my library, and am not so reduced that I cannot afford to buy the occasional book. I prefer the old writers (not surprisingly, you're probably thinking!), Caesar, Sallust, Tacitus, *et al.*, but won't deny there are some moderns not without merit: Ausonius, Ammianus Marcellinus, Claudian, Rutilius Namatianus, and a few others. (As for the gloomy rantings of Jerome, Augustine, and their Christian ilk, of them I have nothing to say.)

And so, Magnus old friend, I pass my days here in the pursuit of *otium*** and the tending of my acres, like some impoverished latter-day Horace. It needs but the presence of a congenial guest to make my lot a not unhappy one. I send this by the hand of a friend who is travelling to Arelate on business. He has generously offered to extend his journey to Tolosa† (assuming the Visigoths grant free passage to a Roman), and will, I hope, return with your reply. Farewell.

Written at Tolosa in the Visigothic Settlement of Aquitania, in the consulships of Bassus and Antiochus, V Kalends Oct.‡

---

* Africa's. The god Bacchus was associated with the Libyan goat, symbolic of wine. By extension, Libya becomes a metaphor for all Africa.
** Leisured scholarship.
† Toulouse.
‡ 27 September 431.

76

Magnus Anicius Felix, once tribune in the Primani Legion, senator; to Gaius Valerius Rufinus 'Boranus', formerly commander of the Primani Legion, decurion, greetings.

What a joyous surprise to receive a letter from my old commander, though I am saddened to learn that Fortuna has not smiled on you. Whatever the reason for your difference with the authorities, I cannot believe it could justify their persecuting one who has given such distinguished service to the state. Though now domiciled outwith the sphere of Roman jurisdiction, I am not without friends in the Senate (of which I am still nominally a member), and would gladly write to them on your behalf. Your old tribune would deem it an honour to extend what help he can.

Here, things are less dreadful than you seem to imagine. I retired from the army to manage the family estate in Aquitania – just in time for the Gothic occupation! However, I was pleasantly surprised to find that our new masters, far from being the uncouth savages we Gallo-Romans had feared, were generally courteous and fair in their dealings with us. In my own case, the Gothic noble who commandeered my villa paid me a not unreasonable sum, given that he could have evicted me without any compensation, had he been so minded. I suppose their lengthy sojourning within the Roman Empire prior to being granted a homeland, has rubbed away their rougher edges. Many of their leaders copy Roman dress and manners, and wish their sons to learn Latin. Which has been most opportune for me: I have inveigled myself into Theoderic's court circle at Tolosa, where I have found ready employment dinning *amo, amas, amat* into tow-headed youngsters.

Also, I am high in King Theoderic's favour. When he discovered that I alone among his entourage could play backgammon (which he loves), he was overjoyed. So now several times a week we have a game – which I am always careful to lose. That's a trick I learned from you, Gaius Valerius, who were so skilled in the management of men and horses: 'Always make friends with the leader of the pack,' you said. Sound advice. Now here's an interesting comment from a 'barbarian' for you to mull over. Theoderic himself once said to me, 'An able Goth wants to be like a

Roman; only a poor Roman would want to be like a Goth.'
All things considered, life for me could be a lot worse.
Indeed, I think it much to be preferred to that of many
living in Roman Gaul, reduced to penury by the exactions
of the tax-collectors.

You'd be surprised at how 'Roman' everything remains
in Aquitania. After the initial shock of learning to adjust to
alien rule, things have settled down, and relations between
Goths and Romans are comparatively harmonious. This
despite the fact that the Romans generally affect to look
down on their 'guests', for being (in their view) uncultured
boors. The Goths, who make up only a small proportion
of the total population, live under their own laws, and let
us keep ours. Trade, though reduced, still carries on; mosaic
workshops thrive, and the potteries of Burdigala* are (unfortunately) booming, flooding the market with hideous grey-
and-orange Burdigalan ware.

Though many smaller properties – mine, alas, included –
have been confiscated, the great fortified villas have been
(wisely) left alone. You should see Burgus, the vast estate of
Pontius Leontius, head of Aquitania's leading family. Bath-
houses, weaving-sheds, its own water-sources, splendid
mosaics, even a private chapel with murals illustrating themes
from Genesis. Anyone who thinks they're anyone in Aquitania
– Goths included – would kill for an invitation from the
Leontii. So you see, Gaius, good old Roman snobbery remains
alive and well here!

But now, my old and much esteemed commander, I
must speak my mind concerning certain points you raised
in your letter. I realize that in so doing I risk destroying
whatever *amicitia* exists between us. I am prompted only
by the high regard in which I hold you, and by concern
for your happiness. If this sounds presumptuous coming
from one who was once a junior officer under your
command, I beg forgiveness. I recall your advice to young
tribunes reporting on a battle situation: 'Tell it as it is, not
how you think I would like to hear it.' That precept I shall
now apply.

* Bordeaux.

78

First, regarding your sentiments regarding the Germans, and your prescription that we get rid of them. How do you propose that this policy – even supposing it were desirable – should be accomplished? Repatriation? Extermination? The plain fact is that the Roman government in the West is far too weak to have any hope at all of enforcing either of these 'solutions'. The Germans are here to stay, and Rome would be wise to accept it. Properly treated, the Germans could be a tremendous asset to the empire. Though admittedly lacking in refinement, they are, with few exceptions, brave and honourable; they admire *Romanitas* and, if encouraged to assimilate, would in time, I believe, make model Roman citizens. But how does Rome treat them? With hostility and contempt. Intermarriage between Romans and Germans is forbidden; the wearing of furs and trousers in Rome is declared illegal; Germans are treated as heretical untouchables because their Arian form of Christianity differs somewhat from our own. Such attitudes are purest folly. They will succeed in turning a formidable minority, who at present wish for nothing more than friendship, into dangerous enemies. Having lived among Germans for some thirteen years now, I think I can speak with some authority.

You say that Rome should return to the old gods, and imply that by abandoning them we incurred their wrath, and were punished for that apostasy by the barbarian invasions. If that is so, why has the Eastern Empire, which is if anything more Christian than the West, been largely spared? In any case, it is far too late to attempt to restore the Pantheon. Do you seriously think that anyone believes in Jupiter, Juno, and the rest any more? If Julian tried, and failed, to reverse things seventy years ago, what chance is there of doing so today?

You say you believe that Rome will rise again. With all my heart I hope that you are right. But she will do so only if men see clearly whence her troubles stem, and, instead of taking refuge in comforting illusions, are willing to take radical measures to deal with them. To think otherwise is to indulge in culpable self-deception. As for the notion that Rome should contemplate annexing new territories, when she cannot even retain those she already has . . .! Tact alone restrains me, Gaius, from expressing what I think, except to say that such opinion is unworthy of you.

There – I have said too much already, and fear in doing so may have given mortal offence to one whose good opinion I value above most others'.

Your kind invitation to visit you is much appreciated. If you would still find me welcome as a guest, nothing would give your old tribune greater pleasure than to come to the Villa Fortunata. It would be good to fight the Frigidus again over a flagon of Falernum. Here, alas, the only drink is German beer or Massilian vinegar. Farewell.

Sent by the hand of the bearer who brought yours.

ELEVEN

All pagan practices, whether public or private, are to be banned
                                    Edict of Theodosius I, 391

Shock gripped Titus, as he drew rein at the entrance of the Villa
Fortunata. The gate drooping drunkenly from a single hinge, and
the glimpse of untended weed-choked fields beyond, told their own
story. Something was wrong, terribly wrong. As he rode slowly
down the grass-grown drive, Titus spotted in the distance a figure
bent over a plough drawn by two draught-mules. Tethering his
horse to a tree, he walked towards the ploughman. The man was
old, dressed in a dirty, worn tunic, his thin shanks wrapped in mud-
spattered cloths. The plough halted as it struck a rock, and the old
man bent down to try to remove the obstruction. Something familiar
in the set of his head struck Titus . . . It was his father – ploughing
his own land, like a latter-day Cincinnatus.

He joined the struggling figure, gently pushed aside the blue-
veined hands with their bleeding cracks and swollen knuckles.
Gripping the boulder, he wrenched it free with a single vigorous
heave.

Gaius, his cheeks covered in a three-day growth of stubble,
stared at his son with rheumy eyes. 'Titus!' he exclaimed in a
breaking voice. 'I – I hoped you'd come. But . . .'

'But you were too proud to ask,' rejoined Titus, his heart
seeming to fill his chest. 'Oh, Father, what am I going to do about
you? Come here.' He extended his arms, and father and son
embraced.

They separated, and looked at each other with moist eyes. 'You
lead the mules,' said Titus, a lump rising in his throat. 'I'll take
the plough-stilts. We'll finish this furrow-length, then go to the
house. There's much for us to talk about.'

'. . . and if that's how the empire rewards its loyal subjects, there's
something rotten at the heart of Rome,' said Gaius. His account

of the hardships he had suffered since their last meeting, nearly eight years before, had been a long catalogue of injustices, and confirmed all that Titus had heard from friends of the family. With mingled rage and pity, he looked round the familiar *tablinum*: the scrolls thick with dust, cobwebs festooning the room's corners. The house-slaves had all had to be sold, leaving a single freed-woman to deal with all the domestic tasks. It was persecution by petty-minded officials, the bishop and mayor in particular, that had reduced his father to these present straits.

'I began to think about your views concerning Germans,' Gaius went on, 'and decided that, after all, perhaps there was some-thing in what you'd said. It would seem they have virtues which our ancestors once possessed, but which modern Romans have abandoned for the most part. As you know, I correspond with a wide circle of friends from the curial class to which I once belonged. One of them lives in Aquitania, the part of Gaul assigned to the Visigoths as their homeland. Instead of being evicted from his villa without compensation, he received a sum of money from its Gothic occupier. How many Romans would have done the same, had the position been reversed? And his case, apparently, is far from unique. Perhaps his Christ God, which now is also yours, is worthier of adoration than the old gods of Rome.' Gaius paused and, for the first time that Titus could recall, looked abashed. 'And now,' the older man went on, 'regarding your marriage to Clothilde: if it is not too late, accept the blessing and apologies of a foolish old man.'

'Gladly, Father,' replied Titus, experiencing a rush of huge relief and joy. 'But do not say "foolish". Soon, I hope, you'll see your grandson.'

'Let us drink to that. You can't imagine what pleasure it would give me.' The old man recharged their beakers with Falernian from the last of the cellar's amphorae. 'Now, you wished for my advice concerning Aetius.' Some of the old steel entered Gaius' voice as his eyes locked with his son's. 'End your service with him. For the basest of reasons, he has betrayed Rome and done her irreparable harm. You worry that leaving him would smack of breaking faith? But such a man, by his actions, has forfeited all claims to loyalty. Your duty is to Rome, not to the man who has weakened her. If you wish to serve anyone, it should be Boniface.'

'But it was Boniface who let the Vandals in. Surely—'

'Granted, he was guilty of a huge misjudgement,' Gaius interrupted. 'But he has a noble heart, and wishes above all to make
amends. He served under me once as a young tribune, you know,
and was one of my bravest and most conscientious officers. I
believe he is the only man living who can save Rome in her
present crisis.'

Riding towards Tremeratae, the market town which bought the
Villa Fortunata's produce, Titus reviewed the measures he'd
adopted in the past few days to improve the estate's (and his
father's) fortunes. He'd called a meeting of the tenants, the *coloni*,
and made a radical proposal, which he'd already discussed with
Gaius, and to which the old man had gratefully assented. Let
the estate be run in the Egyptian manner, with all, including
Gaius, sharing in the profits, and some of the surplus being
ploughed back. That way, everyone would benefit and the estate
remain viable. He'd hired some of the tenants to give the house
a thorough cleaning and refurbishment (including the unpleasant
task of clearing out the hypocaust), and drawn up a duty rota to
maintain the work on a permanent basis. The plan was received
with enthusiasm and, after a *conductor* or foreman had been
chosen, was formally adopted.

Now, Titus thought as he entered the town, time to settle
scores with the bishop. Tremeratae, though not a city, had its
own see, like many other even smaller places. Bishop Pertinax,
despite being disliked by most of the *curiales* or leading citizens,
had been foisted on Tremeratae by the metropolitan bishop in
Mediolanum, at the end of Honorius' reign. Owing to the unfortunate rule which laid down that bishops, once appointed, could
not transfer to another see, Tremeratae was stuck with an unpopular bishop; while Pertinax, ambitious and energetic, felt increasingly frustrated by having to preside over what he no doubt
considered to be a rural backwater. One of the new thrusting and
intolerant breed of clergy that had come in with the Theodosian
reforms, Pertinax saw it as his vocation to root out paganism in
all its manifestations. That he pursued his goal with fanatical zeal
was, Titus thought, partly due to the bitterness he felt about his
career being stalled.

As a result of Pertinax's campaign, pagan practices – even acts as apparently innocuous as making offerings to images, burning incense, or hanging up garlands – quickly disappeared, at least overtly. Except in the case of Gaius, who accordingly bore the full brunt of the bishop's displeasure. The carrying out of the consequent restrictions placed on him fell to the mayor, a genial weakling who had once been Gaius' friend, but who now, for the sake of a quiet life, found it expedient to conform with the new order.

Titus' knock at the gatehouse of the bishop's palace was answered by a beefy manservant.

'You have an appointment?' he said, in answer to Titus' request to see the bishop. He looked Titus up and down with bored indifference.

'Just tell him the son of General Rufinus wants to see him.'

'Get an appointment.' The porter began to close the gate.

Titus' hand shot out, gripped the other's elbow, and squeezed. The man gave a gasp of pain and his face whitened.

Pushing him aside, Titus strode through the vestibule into the atrium, followed by the protesting porter. The sound of a raised voice coming from behind a closed door, alerted Titus.

'. . . seen lighting a lamp before an image of Serapis.' Uttered in strident tones, the words carried clearly. 'Think yourself lucky that you're getting off with a heavy fine. Next time, it'll be gaol.'

Titus burst into the room. Seated at a desk, a richly clad personage confronted a shabby townsman – a carpenter from the wood-shavings adhering to his tunic.

'I tried to stop him, Your Grace,' whined the porter, 'but he . . .' He tailed off as Titus turned towards him and began to raise his hand.

'Out,' snapped Titus. Then, turning to the tradesman, he said more mildly, 'You too, I'm afraid.' The porter slunk out, followed by the carpenter.

'How dare you!' exclaimed the seated man, his face reddening with anger. 'What is the meaning of this outrageous intrusion?'

Pertinax was nothing like the lean, burning-eyed ascetic whom Titus had imagined. He was a plump, sleek figure in early middle age, dressed in the fashionable finery of a Roman noble, rather than the simple vestments of a cleric.

'General Rufinus – Gaius Valerius Rufinus. I'm his son.'

'If you wish to see me, make an appointment with my secretary,' said the bishop. 'Now, kindly leave.'

'I'll leave when I'm ready, you greasy tub of lard,' grated Titus, stepping forward and grabbing the other by the front of his expensive dalmatic. He jerked the bishop to his feet. 'And that will be when you've given me some answers. My father's been reduced to penury, thanks to you. I want to know why.' He released his grip on the bishop, who slumped back in his chair.

Pertinax licked his lips nervously, cowed by Titus' menacing manner. 'He – he brought it on himself,' he protested. 'I was only enforcing the law, which I'm duty bound to do.' As he spoke, his fat, ringed hand slid surreptitiously along the edge of the desk towards a hand-bell – then retreated when Titus gave a warning shake of the head.

'Your duty? To persecute a defenceless old man for the terrible crime of venerating the old gods? You're going to have to do better than that.'

'A law of the Augustus Theodosius the First, passed on the twenty-fourth of February in the thirteenth year of his reign, is unequivocal,' declared Pertinax, a note of shrill defensiveness creeping into his voice. '"All pagan practices, whether public or private, are to be banned." How else was I supposed to act?'

'By showing a bit of humanity and compassion, that's how. Scripture says, "Jesus was moved with compassion toward the people, because they were as sheep not having a shepherd." A fine shepherd you are! My father was guilty of nothing worse than refusing to give in to petty officialdom. You didn't like that, did you? So you decided he had to be taught a lesson.'

'When laws are broken, examples must be made.'

'Your sort make me vomit!' spat Titus. 'Sheltering behind words on parchment, to justify bullying those who can't hit back. Gaius Valerius is worth twenty of you. He was saving Italy from the Goths when your pedagogue was leading you to school.'

Titus glanced round the richly furnished room, with its profusion of ornaments and plate. He picked up a beautiful porphyry miniature group, showing Orpheus with his lyre soothing a lion and a wolf.

'Put it down!' cried the bishop in alarm. 'It's priceless.'

'It's pagan,' responded Titus. 'You of all people shouldn't be keeping such things. Oops!' And he dropped the miniature, which shattered on the mosaic floor. He strolled over to an array of silverware on a low table. 'Tut, tut,' he said in mock dismay, examining a chased goblet. 'Look: Diana with her bow; and here's Apollo. Surely this must be Venus? And what's this? Cupid lurking in the bushes?' Crumpling the goblet in his fist, he shook his head disapprovingly. 'It really won't do, you know.' And pursued by a frantically pleading Pertinax, he progressed around the room, smashing carvings, stamping on gold and silver vessels or hurling them against walls; anything was fair game, provided it had a pagan motif.

His tour completed, Titus advanced towards Pertinax, who scuttled behind his desk.

'Feels different when the boot's on the other foot, doesn't it?' sneered Titus, looming over the cowering cleric. 'You oily hypocrite. Listen – and listen well. As of this moment, you'll leave my father alone. If I ever hear that you've done him the slightest injury in future, I'll be back. That's a promise. Then this' – he indicated the wreckage in the room – 'will seem like a gentle game of *harpastum** at the baths. All right?'

The bishop nodded.

'Good. I'm glad we understand each other.' As a parting gesture, Titus lifted a brimming wine-jug from the desk and emptied its contents over the bishop's head. Then, turning on his heel, he strode from the room.

In the atrium he was confronted by a row of servants armed with staves. Something in his look and bearing, however, made them fall back, and he left the palace unmolested.

As he rode back to the villa, his elation began to evaporate. He was in deep trouble, he realized. If, as he had already decided to do, he acted on his father's advice concerning Aetius, he would be forfeiting the protection of the most powerful man in the Western Empire. As if that were not enough, he already had the Empress's hand against him. Soon, she might be joined by Pope Celestine; Pertinax was said to have his ear. 'Well, David had only a sling,' he reminded himself, 'but he prevailed against Goliath.'

---

* A ball game involving passing between players.

TWELVE

Nothing is to your interest that forces you to break your promise
Marcus Aurelius, *Meditations, c. 170*

Mansio Felix, nr. Arelate, Province of Viennensis, Diocese of the Seven Provinces. The year of the consuls Bassus and Antiochus, Nones III Oct.* [Titus paused to remove a hair, caught in the split of his reed pen's nib, then continued.] By the light of a guttering oil-lamp, I'm updating the family archive in the euphemistically named 'Happy Inn' – an over-priced fleapit run by the private sector's travel and transport network. This operates in parallel with the Imperial Post, an institution which still creaks along, despite the unsettled times.

Following our little 'talk', I was pretty sure that Bishop Pertinax wouldn't be troubling my father in the immediate future. But I wasn't taking any chances. More than anything, Gaius needed a long spell of rest and care; when I suggested that he might like to meet his grandson sooner rather than later, he readily concurred. Accordingly, I escorted him to the Burgundian village between Basilia and Argentorate Stratisburgum,** where Clothilde and Marcus live with her father's family on their farm. Clothilde has become like a daughter to him, and he dotes on little Marcus; he'll need watching, or he'll spoil the boy! I left him arguing happily with father-in-law about the respective merits of Roman wine and German beer; I suspect he secretly rather likes the latter.

From the Burgundian Settlement in Upper Germany, I travelled to Arelate. Unlike the Rhenish provinces ceded to 'barbarians', Provence seems little changed by the invasions;

* 5 October 431.
** Basle and Strasbourg.

87

villas – though now more resembling fortified villages than estates – still exist, the towns seem not un-prosperous, vine-yards and olive groves are in good heart. Tomorrow I press on into Aquitania (assuming the Goths permit me), where I intend to seek out Aetius and formally request my discharge from his service. I owe him that at least – although it would be easier (and perhaps safer?) just to abandon my duties in Ravenna, and sneak off without a word.

Trying to master his apprehension, Titus waited outside the command tent at Aetius' field headquarters near Tolosa in the Visigothic Settlement. According to the pair of Roman soldiers on sentry duty outside the tent, the general was in conclave with certain Visigothic chiefs, thrashing out peace terms following the tribe's failed attempt to capture Arelate and expand their terri-tory eastwards.

About two hours later, the nobles filed out, looking chastened and sullen. Titus was astonished at their appearance. Unlike the Burgundians, who clung to Teutonic fashions such as long hair and trousers, these men were totally Roman in their dress, with short hair, and shaved faces. Only their great stature and blond colouring betrayed the fact that they were Germans.

After being announced, Titus was told to enter the tent. This proved to be in two parts: a front area hung with maps – clearly a planning and briefing 'room' – and a curtained-off section at the rear.

'Come,' said a familiar voice from within. Titus pulled aside the curtain and entered what was clearly the general's private office. Seated at a desk littered with scrolls and writing para-phernalia, Aetius looked, Titus thought, untypically drawn and strained.

'Tiresome fellows at times, these Visigoths,' Aetius observed. 'They were given Aquitania – the best land in Gaul – for their own homeland by Constantius twenty-one years ago, so you'd think they'd be satisfied, wouldn't you? But no, they get greedy from time to time, and have to be slapped down. Still, their King Theoderic and I get on well enough – or perhaps I should say we share a working misunderstanding; provided he knows I'm keeping an eye on him, he keeps them in line. Most of the time, that is. Well, Titus Valerius, what brings you here? A palace revolution in Ravenna? Valentinian wanting to cut loose from mother's apron-strings? He must be, what, all of twelve by now?'

There was no point in beating about the bush. Swallowing nervously, Titus announced, 'Sir, I wish to be discharged from your service.'

Aetius regarded him quizzically for a few seconds. 'Oh you do, do you? And what's brought this on, may I ask? Let me guess – something to do with rumours you've been hearing about myself and Boniface. Right?'

'All you have to do is deny them, sir. Then I'd be more than happy to withdraw my request.'

'How very generous. There's just one little fact that appears to have escaped your notice, Rufinus. You were under orders to stay in Ravenna and prepare a report. I don't recall releasing you from your duties. Technically, that makes you guilty of desertion – assuming there's a *status belli* between myself and the imperial government. I can assure you Placidia thinks there is. I could have you arrested. To quote Marcus Aurelius, "It never pays to break faith." He should have added, "with someone more powerful than yourself."'

'But given my suspicions, sir,' Titus protested, 'don't you think I am justified—'

'Oh, spare me the rest,' Aetius snapped. 'Honour . . . betrayal . . . the cause of Rome . . . et cetera, et cetera. Brutus would have been proud of you.'

'Such things are hardly unimportant, sir, Titus cried, nettled. 'Look what you've achieved yourself in Gaul: containing the Franks in Lower Germany, and persuading them to become Rome's loyal allies; forcing the Visigoths to keep within their bounds; cementing peace with the Burgundians. Why treat Boniface as an enemy, sir? Together, you could have made Rome strong again, like Claudius "Gothicus" and Aurelian, or Diocletian and Constantine.'

'You've missed your vocation, Rufinus,' said Aetius drily. 'You should have been an orator. I'll tell you what is important. Survival. You don't honestly think that what I'm doing in Gaul is for the glory of Rome, do you? If so, you're an even bigger fool than I imagined. It's a dog-eat-dog world at the top, and only the strong last the pace. Like Julius Caesar before me, I'm building up a power-base in Gaul, as a safeguard against my political enemies

– no need to spell out who they are.' Aetius scribbled something on a scrap of parchment, and handed it to Titus. 'Here's your discharge. I haven't forgotten that you saved my life once; I reckon this evens the score.' He studied Titus appraisingly. 'You should have stuck with me, you know. You're still young – twenty-six, twenty-seven, is it? I could have made something of you, but on your own you'll never amount to anything. I see you dying – for Rome, of course – in a squalid little skirmish against the barbarians, in some God-forgotten corner of the empire. Well, as you can see' – he waved at the clutter on his desk, then bent over a document – 'I've a peace to negotiate. Close the curtain on your way out.'

Seething with resentment at the manner of his dismissal, Titus yanked the curtain to, with a jerk that almost tore it from its rings. For just a moment, when Aetius had given him his diploma, Titus had thought he glimpsed a crack in the persona of weary cynicism, a shadow of regret behind the general's eyes. Obviously, he had been wrong.

As he marched to the tent's entrance-flap, his eye was caught by a codex lying amid a jumble of papyri on a table. It was beautiful, its visible cover, of ivory, exquisitely carved to represent a mythological scene. On a sudden impulse, Titus picked it up and opened it. The waxed boards were blank save for a brief and enigmatic inscription on the first. It read: 'His Philippi – the fifth milestone from A.'

THIRTEEN

Set up in the reign of the Emperor Flavius Valerius Constantinus;
five miles from Ariminum
Inscription (conjectural) on the fifth milestone from
Rimini, on the Aemilian Way

Titus rode across Ariminum's five-spanned bridge of white
marble, past the triumphal arch erected by Augustus to mark the
junction of the Via Flaminia and the Via Aemilia, and headed
north-west up the latter.

Southwards, the Via Flaminia hugged the coast for twenty miles,
before turning inland bound for Rome. This was Italia proper:
parcelled neatly into farms and villas, studded with little towns,
overshadowed by the Apennini Mountains. Northwards, bounded
on the south by the Aemilian Way, stretched the vast alluvial
wetlands of the Po basin, the old province of Cisalpine Gaul, which
still in some ways felt unlike Italia, almost foreign.

Solving the cryptic inscription in Aetius' codex hadn't been
difficult. 'His Philippi' could surely only refer to a decisive contest
between Aetius and his arch-rival Boniface; that historic field had
witnessed Mark Antony and Octavian smash the forces of Brutus
and Cassius. 'The fifth milestone from A'? 'A', while theoretically
applicable to any of a thousand places, probably referred, Titus
decided, to somewhere not far from Boniface's headquarters in
Ravenna. Titus reasoned that Boniface, having taken a mauling
mentally as well as militarily in Africa, would instinctively want
to remain close to his base, like a hurt animal. Aetius would realize
that, and intend to bring the battle to his rival, in such a way as
to secure an advantage for himself.

Working on this theory, 'A' could mean (moving north to south
in an arc round the head of the Adriatic) any one of the following:
Aquileia, Altinum, Ateste, Ariminum, Ancona. Titus conjectured
that Ariminum,* being nearest to Ravenna, was the most likely.

* Rimini

He had already examined the terrain around the fifth milestone from Ariminum on both the Popilian Way – the coast road from Ariminum to Aquileia – and the Flaminian Way. On the former, he had found himself in a bleak wilderness of salt-marshes, dunes, and lagoons – a most unsuitable venue for a battlefield. On the latter these features were replaced by terraced cultivation – again, hardly ideal for the deployment of forces. 'The fifth milestone', on whichever road it was, must be in an area which guaranteed Aetius tactical superiority, and to which Boniface must be persuaded to bring his men. The only other road out of Ariminum was the Aemilian Way, so that must be the best option. Autumn was now well advanced. Winter rains and freezing Alpine winds meant that Aetius would not be engineering a confrontation before spring at the earliest, which gave both sides a breathing-space in which to make preparations. Though Boniface didn't know it yet, his preparations could well be shaped by information stemming from Titus' investigations.

Walking his horse along the soft verge of the arrow-straight Aemilian Way, Titus reached the fifth milestone in a little over an hour. A cylindrical column of limestone on a square base, it bore the inscription '*IMP. CAES. FLAV. VAL. CONSTANTINO: AB ARIMINO M. P. V.*'

He consulted his road-table, a chart showing sections of the Way in 'ribbon' style, and noted the salient features of the surrounding landscape. A small stream, the Uso, flowed through a culvert beneath the road. (The next crossing – of the famous Rubicon, – lay a mile or so ahead.) To the north of the road stretched a vast expanse of reedbeds. Beside the corresponding area on his chart appeared the word '*cuniculi*': drainage channels. To the south, the terrain was unreclaimed marshland. The road was virtually a causeway over a swamp.

Depression swept over the young man. Despite its proximity to the Rubicon (whose weight of historical association might be calculated to attract Boniface), of the three possibilities this looked the least promising. In fact, from a tactical point of view, none of the sites made any sense at all – prompting the suspicion that 'A' must represent somewhere other than Ariminum. Rain began to fall, adding to Titus' gloom. Within seconds it was sheeting down, soaking through the thick wool of his cloak, bouncing off the road, gushing into the side-ditches. As he turned his horse's head for the return journey, Titus became aware of a loud gurgling: rainwater rushing through those drainage channels. Realization burst upon him. His hunch had played off: this was indeed the spot selected by Aetius for Boniface to meet his Philippi.

FOURTEEN

The everlasting hills do not change like the faces of men
Tacitus, *Annals, c.* 110

When Titus appeared at the west gate of Ravenna's imperial palace and requested an interview with Boniface, he was met with a polite but firm refusal. 'Sorry sir,' replied one of the guards. 'We're under orders not to admit you.'

'But it's of vital importance I see the Count,' insisted Titus. 'The only reason I'm debarred is because I used to work for Flavius Aetius. I've now left his service.' He produced the parchment Aetius had given him. 'Look, here's my certificate of discharge, signed by him. Just show it to someone in authority, and repeat what I've told you. I don't mind waiting.' With feigned absent-mindedness, he began playing with a *tremissis*, a small gold coin worth a third of a *solidus*, part of the diminishing funds he had saved from his pay while serving Aetius.

'See what I can do, sir,' said the guard, palming the coin with a conspiratorial wink. He summoned a temporary replacement from the guardroom, and set off through the gardens for the main buildings. Half an hour later he re-appeared, accompanied by an official. 'You're to go with him, sir.'

Titus followed the man through the gardens, along a wide passage between the four central blocks, then down a long peristyle and through a portico into the imperial apartments – they were familiar from that long-ago encounter with the Empress and her son. The official opened a door and ushered Titus into a hallway, empty save for two burly Nubians wearing slaves' short, sleeveless tunics. The click of a key turning in the lock behind him, told Titus he had walked into a trap.

He knew instinctively that resistance was futile, that these men were trained athletes whose skills would outmatch his own, but nevertheless he put up a fight. As the Nubians closed on him, he gave the leader a kick in the solar plexus which would have felled a normal opponent. It was like kicking a tree trunk; the man merely grunted and came on. Titus' second blow – a neck-breaking jab with the heel of his hand against the other's chin – produced a similar reaction. Then his arms were seized and wrenched behind his back. The pain was excruciating. Realizing that just a little more pressure would break them, Titus surrendered and allowed himself to be led from the hall. He was marched down a corridor into a large pillared chamber, in which were seated the Empress Galla Placidia and her son, Valentinian. A sulky-looking lad of twelve or thirteen, Valentinian was tall and strong for his age. He had inherited the long nose and fine grey eyes of his grandfather, the great Theodosius, but the weak chin and petulant mouth were those of his imperial uncle, the feeble Honorius.

'Is it arrogance or merely stupidity that causes you to persist?' asked Placidia in a glacial voice. 'You become tiresome. Not content with once assaulting the Emperor, you have attacked a bishop in his palace, so the Pope informs us, and then have the temerity to demand an audience. Somehow, you have survived the measures we took to have you silenced, and have cheated the Ferryman. That wasn't warning enough, it seems. Do you really think that *this* will make a difference?' And she held up Aetius' document discharging Titus.

'Mother, I have a suggestion,' Valentinian lisped, his tone eager.

Placidia's expression softened. '*We* have a suggestion,' she corrected mildly. 'Yes, Flavius?'

'An attack on our person was foiled by these two loyal servants, who intercepted and killed the would-be assassin before he could reach us. Clever, don't you think?'

The Empress smiled indulgently. 'Well, it would save a lot of bother, I suppose. Very well.' She nodded to the Nubians.

One wrapped his arms round Titus in a vice-like grip. The other took Titus' head between his hands, and began to twist. Terror flooded Titus as he tried to fight the pressure. It was no good; his head turned inexorably – in a few seconds, barring a miracle, his neck must break.

In a pain-filled haze, he was dimly aware of Valentinian staring into his face, murmuring, 'Blink for me.'

A miracle happened. The door opened and in walked a huge and familiar figure: Boniface. 'My apologies, Your Serenities, I didn't mean to—' He broke off as he took in the scene.

'Help me!' Titus managed to croak.

Looking both astonished and concerned, Boniface raised his hand in a commanding gesture. Relief swept through Titus as the pressure on his neck eased.

'Would someone please explain?' said Boniface in puzzled tones.

'This man was trying to kill me,' said Valentinian sullenly.

'It's not true!' cried Titus desperately. 'You remember me from Africa, sir? I brought you a letter from Count Aetius.'

'That's right, so you did,' said Boniface. He gestured to the slaves, who released Titus and stood aside. Turning to the Empress, he said placatingly, 'Aelia, my dear, there must be some misunderstanding. I know this young man. He may have served the traitor Aetius, but . . . a murderer? Surely not. In my youth I fought under his father against Radogast the Goth. A finer soldier than General Rufinus would be hard to find.'

'It was you I came here to see, sir,' declared Titus, gingerly feeling his neck. 'I no longer serve Aetius. Look: the Empress holds in her hand my official discharge.'

'Aelia?' queried Boniface, his tone friendly yet holding a hint of reproof.

The Empress shrugged, conceding defeat. 'Oh, very well,' she said. 'It's probably best we let you deal with him. You'll be doing us a service by taking him off our hands – we were beginning to find him a trifle tedious.'

'So you've left Aetius,' said Boniface, when he and Titus were ensconced in the Count's own suite of rooms within the palace. He shot Titus a keen glance. 'You may be interested to know that I received a letter from Aetius the other day, suggesting we hold a parley next year, at—'

'—the fifth milestone from Ariminum,' broke in Titus excitedly, 'on the Aemilian Way.'

'Now, how in the name of Jupiter did you know that?' asked Boniface, visibly impressed.

'Well, sir, it goes back to a meeting I had with one of your old soldiers, a disabled veteran called Proximo.'

He held back nothing, but told of his conversation with Proximo and the attempt on his life; the discussions with his father; the confrontation with Bishop Pertinax; the stormy meeting with Aetius; finally, his investigations from Ariminum. 'It was those words, "His Philippi",' he finished, 'that made me realize Aetius intends springing a trap.'

'Well, thanks to you, I can start planning how to unspring it,' said Boniface. 'Proposing a parley near the Rubicon,' he murmured reflectively. 'Cunning. It shows he understands my fondness for historical conjunctions. A weakness, I admit – and one he was clever enough to exploit. I'm grateful to you, extremely grateful.' He looked at Titus appraisingly. 'So, young man, you wish to enter my service, you say. I'm flattered, of course. But after my – shall we say – less than distinguished record in Africa, I'm rather puzzled as to why you should wish to.' And he gave a self-deprecating smile which Titus found oddly touching.

'My father believes in you, sir. Let's just say I trust his judgement.'

'In that case, welcome aboard, Titus Valerius. Tomorrow we'll swear you in as one of my *agentes in rebus*, then you can start being useful straight away. I have a little job that I think would suit your talents.'

The five horsemen trailing Titus spurred their mounts from a plod to a walk – the speediest gait possible on the steep, east-ward-facing foothills of the Apennini mountains. Titus smiled as he did likewise, welcoming the chance of a little excitement in what had looked to be an uneventful assignment. His horse, a pure-bred Libyan, had been supplied by Boniface from the palace stables. It came from tough, fast, tireless stock, and he was confident it could out-distance his pursuers. As far as he could tell at a distance of several hundred paces, their horses were chunky Parthians, sturdy and reliable, but not to be compared in speed and endurance to North African breeds.

Who were these men? wondered Titus. Their horses looked like Roman cavalry mounts, suggesting their riders were soldiers. Perhaps from a faction opposed to Boniface, who had seen Titus leave the palace? Brigands on stolen army horses? Brigandage was a growing problem: many peasants and workmen, driven to desperation by excessive tax demands, were leaving the fields and cities for the outlaw life.

Meanwhile, nothing could dampen Titus' euphoria on this glorious late-autumn day. All his troubles seemed to be evaporating. The rift with his father was healed; Gaius was recovering his health and well-being in the bosom of his new German family; and the running of the Villa Fortunata was back on a sound footing. Titus was the father of a strong and healthy son. Lastly, thanks to Boniface, Placidia's vendetta was over; and Titus had exchanged service with a self-seeking schemer, for honourable employment in the cause of Rome. Despite his elation however, he couldn't stifle his sadness that Aetius, his lost leader, had proved to be an idol with feet of clay. But Titus had come to terms with changing that allegiance, and felt that his hard decision had been justified.

Boniface had entrusted him with the delivery of two messages, one each to the garrison commanders at Placentia and Luca.* The first was to be given strict instructions (backed up by written orders from the Count) to allow Aetius free passage through Placentia on the way to his meeting with Boniface at the fifth milestone from Ariminum – whenever that should happen. The commander at Luca was to be handed a sealed letter from Boniface. The Count had emphasized to Titus that the contents were of vital importance, and must on no account be allowed to fall into the hands of a third party.

After completing the first part of his mission, Titus had stopped overnight at an inn in Placentia. The following morning he retraced his steps along the Aemilian Way for a dozen miles then, as instructed, turned to the right, off that broad and arrow-straight highway on to a side road leading to the village of Medesanum. He paused to consult a sketch-map which Boniface had had prepared for him. His route, north–south to Luca, struck obliquely across four rivers – the Tarus, the Parma, the Entia, the Secies** – and the spurs dividing them, each spur higher than the last until the main crest of the Apennini was reached. On the far side of the watershed, in Etruria,† the route then followed the valley (known as the Garfagnana) of the River Sercium, all the way to Luca.

Barring the Garfagnana, the route was, Boniface had warned him, a hard and testing one: rugged and remote, traversed only by mule tracks. But it was the most direct and quickest way to

* Piacenza and Lucca.
** The Taro, Parma, Enza, and Secchia.
† Tuscany.

reach Luca from Placentia, and it was a matter of great urgency that the commander at Luca receive his missive as soon as possible. At the conclusion of his briefing, the Count had said in tones of resigned sadness, 'Your role, Titus, is preferable to mine. To paraphrase Tacitus: yours to cross steep mountains, but at least they do not change; mine to deal with men, who are inconstant.' Titus had no doubt that he was referring to the perfidy of Aetius, the 'friend' who had deceived and then betrayed him.

Boniface was right about the route being hard. It entailed a stiff climb of several miles and fifteen hundred feet, up hillsides clothed with trees and scrub, with cultivation giving place to pasture. At the ninth hour Titus reached Medesanum, a scatter of small stone houses grouped around a church and a *taberna*. During the ascent Titus had become aware of being followed, so, stopping at the inn just long enough to rest his horse and swallow some bean soup, he pushed on towards his next objective, the little town of Fornovium on the far side of the Tarus. He would be easier in his mind once the width of a river was between himself and his pursuers.

Instead of a conventional river flowing between banks, Titus encountered a wide plain of dazzling rocks and sand, with beyond it the huddle of buildings that was Fornovium. Was this the Tarus? he wondered in amazement. There was no bridge, but the few narrow rivulets winding through the bed looked easily fordable. As he was about to urge his horse forward, he was stopped by a shout from a shepherd tending his flock nearby. The shepherd, a tall mountaineer with kindly eyes, explained that those innocuous-looking *rami* were treacherous: many people, unaware of the danger, had been drowned while attempting to cross. Titus gratefully accepted the man's offer to show the way. Testing the ground with his crook before each step, the shepherd preceded Titus across the first stream, which rose neck-high in the deepest part. Leading his horse, Titus followed, and was surprised by the unexpected power of the icy current; he kept his footing with difficulty on the shifting boulders of the bed. The second stream proved impassable where first encountered – it was dangerously deep and fast-flowing – so Titus and his guide followed it upstream for nearly a mile to where an 'island' stood above the river-bed.

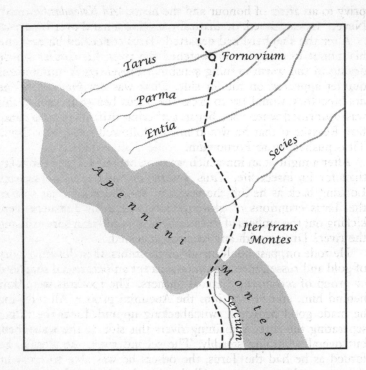

Here, the shepherd located a ford by an ingenious trick which greatly impressed the young courier. Lobbing stones in succession into mid-stream, the shepherd noted the difference between splashes until he located shallow water. Where it was deep, the stone sank with a hollow 'plump', the displaced water rising in a vertical spout; where shallow, both sound and splash were more diffused. Thus, slowly and with circumspection, the remaining five channels were negotiated, and at last the two men stood dripping on the farthest bank.

After thanking the shepherd, and rewarding him with a handful of *nummi*, Titus appealed to him not to show the way to a group of five riders, should he happen to encounter them. He, Titus, had dared to court the daughter of a rival family, he explained, for which temerity her relatives had vowed to pursue and kill him. The shepherd's eyes sparkled with delight at being made

privy to an affair of honour and the heart. '*Ad Kalendas Graecas*!*
Never!' he exclaimed, dramatically placing a hand over his heart.

After the shepherd had departed, Titus concealed himself and his mount in a copse, and watched the river, his clothes slowly drying in the warm evening sunshine. Presently, the mysterious quintet appeared on the far side. Dusk was not far off, and he doubted they would try to cross the Tarus before morning: this was confirmed when they began gathering driftwood for a camp fire. Reassured that he would not be followed until after dawn, Titus pushed on to Fornovium.

After a night at an inn which was notable less for its hospitality than for its insect life, Titus was in the saddle before sun-up. Looking back as he left the town, he spotted on the far side of the Tarus eruptions of glowing dots where his pursuers were kicking out the embers of their fire. How would they fare crossing the river? Drown with any luck, he chuckled.

He rode on, past noble stands of chestnuts, their leaves a glory of gold and russet, meeting no one except an occasional shepherd or group of *carbonarii*, charcoal-burners. The foothills were now behind him, and he was into the Apennini proper. All morning he made good progress, switchbacking up and down the ridges separating the three remaining rivers this side of the watershed, but overall climbing steadily. The second river, the Parma, he forded as he had the Tarus; the others he was able to cross by rickety wooden causeways. All the time he checked his route by sightings of a strange rock looming on the southern skyline, a vast square column thrusting up from a sloping base.**

Early in the afternoon – about the eighth hour he reckoned – Titus came to the mouth of a deep and silent valley, hung with enormous woods and sloping upwards to where it was closed by a high grassy bank between two peaks. This bank, he felt, must be the central ridge of the Apennini, the watershed beyond which lay Etruria and journey's end.

An hour later, Titus dismounted on the crest. Looking back, he surveyed with a quickening of the pulses, all the Aemilian plain, the old province of Cisalpine Gaul, unrolling northwards

---

* 'To the Greek Kalends', a Roman proverb, roughly equivalent to our colloquialism 'When Hell freezes over' (see Notes p.430).
** Known today as Castelnuovo, from the nearby town of that name.

from the mountains' base, and on the far horizon a line of sharp white clouds. But they were motionless, and he soon realized they must in fact be the Alpes. Far below and miles away, five crawling dots told him the pursuit had not been abandoned. He was not worried; all being well, by dusk he'd be in Luca, his mission safely accomplished.

Crossing the watershed marked by a line of cool forest, Titus heard on every side the noise of falling water, where the Sercium, springing from twenty sources on the southern slope, cascaded down between mosses and over slabs of smooth, dark rock. A glade opened, giving a view down the Garfagnana, whose western wall was a high jagged massif, with cliffs and ledges of a dazzling whiteness. Snow, thought Titus at first. But no: these must be the mountains of Carrara, quarried for their marble these five hundred years. He rode on, filled with pleasant thoughts of the bath, food, and rest that awaited him at Luca – no doubt to be followed in due course by congratulations from a grateful Boniface for a task well done.

Titus had begun to relax when his horse suddenly checked and stumbled. Titus dismounted and examined its legs, but could find no damage. Then his eye caught the glint of metal a few paces behind; it was a *solea ferrea*, a broad iron cavalry horseshoe. He quickly checked his horse's hoofs, and found that the off front shoe had been cast, while a rear shoe was so loose that it would likely have come off within another mile. Cursing the imperial farrier who had done such an evil job, Titus realized that the game might well be up. To ride on would be to lame his horse to no avail, for his pursuers must now inevitably overtake him. Nor could he expect to fare any better on foot; in this steep-sided valley, here clothed with grass instead of sheltering woods, he was as effectively trapped as a penned steer. Relieving his mount of its harness and saddle, which he concealed in bushes (a futile gesture, he admitted), he left it to graze and, for want of a better alternative, trudged on downhill, his saddlebag containing the precious missive slung over a shoulder.

He had gone perhaps three miles when he came to a strange and solemn place, a veritable 'town' of cone-shaped tumuli. Etruscan tombs from a thousand years before? Feeling like a hunted animal run to earth, he entered a tunnel which opened out of one of the tombs. As a hiding-place it was hopeless. His pursuers had only to spot his horse to know that its rider could not be far away. Still, at least the narrow entrance meant they could not surround him but must come at him singly. At least he would go down fighting.

So this was how his bright dreams were to end, Titus thought bitterly: in failure, and death at the hands of unknown killers. All he could do was ensure that Boniface's message to the commandant at Luca remained secret. He removed the parchment scroll from his saddlebag and tore it into tiny pieces which he proceeded, with some difficulty, to swallow. Gulping down the last fragment, he looked out of the tunnel's entrance and saw, with a sinking of the heart, five distant riders moving down the valley. When the distance had closed to a hundred paces, he could see them clearly at last: five soldiers, their leader a giant of a man.

Five against one: despite his fighting skills, those odds were too great. But at least he could try to take one or two with him. Drawing his sword (as an *agens in rebus*, he had been issued with uniform and weapons), he backed a few feet into the tunnel. While he waited, inconsequent details of his surroundings registered in the dim light filtering from the entrance: strange wall-paintings showing dancing-girls, boar-hunts, wrestlers, musicians, dead souls led away by good or evil spirits.

Footsteps sounded outside. A series of questions as to the purpose of his journey was fired at Titus by his unseen hunters. Ignoring the temptation to bargain for his life, Titus maintained a stubborn silence. If he had to die, he would die with honour.

A pause, then laughter sounded outside the tomb: Titus determined grimly to inflict maximum damage before he went down. Then a familiar voice called out, 'The game's over, Titus. You can come out now.'

His brain in a whirl, Titus emerged to find a smiling Boniface standing there. 'Well done, Titus Valerius,' said the Count. 'You gave us a good run for our money. We can all go home now.'

'But . . . my mission, sir? The messages?'

'The first, to the commander at Placentia, was genuine. The second was a subterfuge.'

'And the horseshoes were loosened, I suppose?' Titus felt anger begin to stir inside him.

'You suppose correctly; the deed was done when you stopped at Placentia.' Boniface shrugged, and smiled apologetically. 'The second message was intended to be confidential. So naturally you didn't read it. Ah, did you?'

'Of course not.'

'Well, if you had, you'd have found it was a poem by Catullus. What did you do with it, by the way?'

'I ate it, sir.'

Boniface stared for a moment, then gave a shout of laughter, in which he was joined by his four men. The fury and resentment that had begun to build up in Titus abruptly dissolved, and he found himself joining in. It was less amusing when he and his saddlebag were searched, but he knew it was necessary.

In a gesture oddly reminiscent of Aetius' after Titus had saved him from the *catafractarius*, Boniface grasped Titus by the arm. 'Don't be angry, my young friend,' he said. 'In my position, I have to be sure that those who serve me can be trusted. I'm glad to say you passed my little test like a true *agens*.

FIFTEEN

Before the battle, Aetius provided himself with a longer spear
Count Marcellinus,* *Chronicle*, fifth century

'Placentia, that's the rendezvous.' Aetius rapped the tip of his staff against the map, on the red circle at the northern end of the Aemilian Way. 'I, with the Visigoths and Roman contingents shall take the Julian Augustan Way along the coast to Nicea, then north-east to Placentia. Litorius, you'll head north from Arelate, up the Rhodanus valley to Lugdunum,** and await the Frankish and Burgundian federates. As soon as they arrive, press on eastwards to the rendezvous via the Mons Matronae Pass† and Augusta Taurinorum.‡ There's a good secondary road and a station refuge, Druantium, at the summit of the Cottian Alps. Our forces will meet at Placentia not later than the Ides of June. Further briefing when we get there. Right, gentlemen, I think that's all. Any questions?'

The officers – Romans with a sprinkling of Germans – were silent for a minute. Then a lone voice called out, 'Sir, is the wine in Italy any better than the vinegar we get in Gaul?'

'Much better,' Aetius assured him amid the general laughter. 'If that's all, to your posts. We march in an hour.'

The officers filed out. Aetius sank gratefully on to a folding stool. God, he felt tired. Dealing with barbarians was enough to wear out an Alexander or a Caesar. It wasn't that they were difficult to beat; apart from Hermann's destruction of Varus' legions back in the reign of Augustus, the only pitched battle they'd ever won against Rome was Hadrianopolis, fifty-four years ago. And that only happened because the Eastern Emperor hadn't waited for

---

* Not to be confused with Ammianus Marcellinus, the fourth-century soldier and historian.
** Rhône valley; Lyon.
† Genèvre Pass
‡ Turin.

Gratian's Western army to join up with him. Then he remembered the recent African disaster. Well, that was entirely due to Boniface panicking; inviting in the Vandals, and then losing his nerve. If he'd really wanted to serve Rome, he should have done the decent thing and fallen on his sword, the moment he received the summons recalling him to Italy. Ferociously brave the Germans undoubtedly were, but they lacked patience and discipline. Properly led and supplied, Roman troops could thrash them every time. It was the Germans' raw energy, resilience, and sheer persistent aggressiveness that eventually began to grind you down. Like this recent trouble with the Visigoths. They wanted to be part of Rome but, like unruly children, kicked over the traces when conditions were imposed. Still, under Roman officers they made effective soldiers. Which was why, this time, he would at last be able to finish Boniface.

'You look tired, sir,' said a voice behind Aetius, echoing his reflections. 'You should get some rest.'

'Litorius, you still here? Didn't see you.' Aetius accepted the proferred cup of wine. 'Thanks. Was there something you wanted?'

'May I speak frankly, sir?'

'When people say that, it's usually to tell me something I don't want to hear,' sighed Aetius. 'Oh, very well, then, if you must.'

Count Litorius, Aetius' second-in-command, pulled up a camp stool beside the general. 'I'm concerned about you, sir,' he said solicitously. 'You can't continue like this – you're wearing yourself out. You've more than enough to cope with, keeping the barbarians in check in Gaul, without embarking on a civil war in Italy.'

'I'm touched,' sneered Aetius. 'You'll have me crying next. What do you suggest I do? Extend the hand of brotherly love to Boniface?'

'Something like that, sir,' said Litorius earnestly. 'Why not? Together, the two of you could cure some of Rome's most pressing ills.'

'You're beginning to sound like Titus, my former aide,' observed Aetius in wry tones. 'It's too late to make things up with Boniface. Once, perhaps, we could have worked together, but since Africa—' He broke off and shook his head. 'He blames me for what went wrong, and is never going to trust me again. He and Placidia won't rest until they've seen me crushed. Which isn't going to happen, by the way.'

'I should think not, sir!' declared Litorius. 'Your plan will see to that. But once you've dealt with Boniface, I beg you to set yourself an easier pace. Rome needs you.'

'I doubt Placidia would agree,' said Aetius drily. Draining his cup, he rose and clapped Litorius on the shoulder. 'You're getting to be like an old mother hen, Count. I appreciate your concern, but after Boniface there's still Gaul to keep an eye on, Spain to be cleared of Suebi, Africa to re-conquer, perhaps one day even Britain. However, if the federates in Gaul start causing trouble, I can always call in my friends the Huns to whip them into line.'

'The Huns . . . mightn't they in turn become a threat to Rome?' said Litorius doubtfully.

'Hardly. A mob of primitive shepherds. Against disciplined Roman troops backed by Roman-led federates, they wouldn't stand a chance. Right, my friend, time to inspect the troops.'

Marching six abreast, freshly scoured helmets and corselets glittering in the June sunlight, square and dragon standards fluttering and flapping bravely, Aetius' Roman bodyguard swung down the Via Aemilia. Behind, without regard to formation, tramped the Visigoth levies, flaxen-haired giants without armour, carrying spears and round shields. In the van, headed by Aetius and his staff, rode the cavalry, keeping to the grassy belts verging the paved road-surface. The force crossed a stone bridge over the little Rubicon, and halted after a further mile or so, in sight of a squat stone column beside the Uso brook – the fifth milestone from Ariminum. On the far side of the Uso, Boniface's troops were drawn up: the imperial army, consisting of the Western survivors of the African expedition, supplemented by household troops. On either side of the Way, stretched dreary marshland: reedbeds to the north, swampy levels to the south.

'Look, Litorius, there's Boniface in that ridiculous antique armour of his,' Aetius chuckled. 'That lanky beanpole beside him is his son-in-law Sebastian. And there, by all the saints, is young Titus Rufinus, the ungrateful renegade. I should have hauled him before a military tribunal while I had the chance.'

'You can see why they call Boniface "the fighting general",' observed Litorius. 'He seems ready for action – personally.' He smiled. 'Best not get too close, sir. That long spear of his looks pretty businesslike.'

With a trumpet flourish, a herald cantered out from Boniface's lines and drew rein before Aetius' command group. Unfurling a scroll, he declaimed: 'Boniface, Count of Africa, Patrician, Master of Soldiers, both Horse and Foot – in the name of the Augustus Valentinian the Third, Most Noble One, twice Consul; and of the Most Holy Empress Mother in Perpetuity, the Augusta Galla Placidia; to Aetius, Count, Master of the Horse in all the Gauls; gives greetings, and requires to know, under this solemn parley, what are his wishes concerning . . .'

'Ever the stickler for correct procedure,' Aetius, shaking his head, chuckled to Litorius. 'Well, now he's in for a little surprise.' And with a wink to his second-in-command, he signalled his trumpeter. But before the man could raise the instrument to his lips, flames suddenly appeared at various points in the reeds; during the herald's harangue, some of Boniface's men had moved on to the verge, and were now proceeding to toss blazing torches into the head-high vegetation.

Written at Ariminum, in the consulships of Aetius and Valerius, II Nones Jul.* Titus Valerius to Gaius Valerius Rufinus, greetings.

Honoured Father, I write in haste and sorrow, sending this by the hand of one who leaves for Gaul tonight. By the time you read this, I should myself be on my way to join you, for it is no longer safe for me to remain in Italia, within range of the Augusta's malice. Boniface is dead, slain (some say by the hand of Aetius himself) in a battle fought near here yesterday. Under cover of a prearranged meeting between them, Aetius planned to ambush Boniface; however, we had discovered his intentions, and were able to turn this knowledge to our advantage. (As you know from previous letters of mine, I took your advice and left the service of Aetius for that of Boniface.)

At the point where the meeting was to take place (near that fateful stream the Rubicon), a great expanse of reeds adjoined the road. These beds were criss-crossed by a network of *cuniculi* drainage channels – potential cover for an army (which in fact is exactly what they became), the tall reeds providing perfect concealment. It transpired that the night

---

* 6 July 432.

before the meeting, Aetius had dispatched a federate advance force to take up position in the *cuniculi*. Knowing this, we fired the reeds, which were tinder-dry after weeks of scorching weather. Father, it was dreadful: within moments the reedbeds had become a roaring inferno, incinerating the poor wretches hiding there. I shall carry their screams in my head until my dying day. A few charred horrors struggled to the causeway, and were cut down; surely a merciful release from a lingering death in agony. A terrible, perhaps indefensible, way to make war, you may think. Yet what choice had we? It was Aetius, by his treachery, who forced our hand.

With half of Aetius' force destroyed, the outcome of the battle was never in doubt. But our victory was robbed of any triumph by our leader's death. Rumours are flying thicker than snow in January, that Aetius cut his way through our van and killed Boniface in a hand-to-hand fight. I cannot confirm or deny the truth of this, for I was too busy relaying messages during the fray to witness what happened. But I find the story scarcely credible: two modern Roman generals engaged in single combat – like Homeric heroes in the Trojan War! Yet I suppose it *may* be true. Aetius is a driven man. Fury and despair at the ruin of his plan may have pushed him to the verge of madness, prompting him to desperate action. And Boniface, ever careless of personal safety, was never averse to adopting a heroic role. Also, many swear to have seen the incident. But you, Father, more than most, know how it is with soldiers. When Constantine declared he'd seen a vision of Christ's cross in the sky, within an hour half the army swore they'd seen it too!

This was indeed a black day for Rome. Despite his blunders in Africa, I believe that Boniface alone had the stature and the vision to heal the Western Empire's wounds, and make it strong again. Who is left to steer the ship of state? Placidia? Valentinian? Then is the vessel dismasted and heading for the reefs! What now? Aetius' star has surely fallen. Should he escape, he will be outlawed, his life and property forfeit. His only course then will be to seek refuge with his friends the Huns. As for myself, I will make for Upper Germany with all speed, calling at the Villa Fortunata on my way, to check that all is well. My love to Clothilde and little Marcus. God willing, Father, I shall see you soon. Farewell.

SIXTEEN

He possessed the genuine courage that can despise not only
dangers but injuries
Renatus Profuturus Frigeridus, *Eulogy of Aetius*, fifth century

Head held high, the lead bull stared at Aetius with coldly hostile little eyes. The huge creature presented a formidable sight. Powerfully muscled, its head and fore-parts covered in a dense, shaggy mat of brown hair, it towered a full seven feet at the crest of the massive hump that rose behind its neck. This was the wild ox known to the Romans as *bonasus*, and to the barbarians variously as *Wisent*, *Bisund*, or *bison* – the largest and most powerful animal in Europe. Behind the leader walked the herd, shrouded in the dust-cloud stirred up by twelve thousand hooves.

Aetius had known real fear only a few times in his life; now was another of those moments. Licking his lips, he looked to Attila, next to him in the line of dismounted Huns, willing his friend to give the signal that would, he hoped, halt the herd's advance. But Attila was much enjoying seeing him sweat, Aetius thought furiously, as the other grinned at him. (The stop-line's mounts which, even when ridden by such master horsemen as the Huns, would panic and bolt in face of a bison herd, had been tethered some distance away.)

At last, to Aetius' enormous relief, when the leader was barely ten paces away, Attila raised his long whip and cracked it with a deafening report. All down the line, whip-cracks and shouting broke out. The herd-bull halted, snorting and pawing the ground; behind him the herd milled uncertainly, filling the air with sharp grunts. Attila raised a hand, then, followed by the others, took a step forward. Slowly, step by step, to the accompaniment of shouts and snapping whips, the line began to advance. Suddenly, the bull turned and, lowering his great head, lumbered away on a course parallel to the line of Huns. Gradually, the whole herd wheeled round and took off after its leader. The earth began to tremble as the great beasts broke into a gallop, their hoofs lifting to head-level, reminding Aetius of the high-stepping gait of the imperial white horses used on state occasions or the now-banned pagan processions. Swiftly retrieving their mounts, the Huns galloped in pursuit, overtaking the herd and riding along its flank, to ensure that it maintained its direction.

As, beneath him, Bucephalus settled into a mile-eating stride, the events of the past few weeks unrolled themselves in Aetius' mind.

Defeat by Boniface, followed by disgrace, outlawry, and flight from Italia – all that should, by any calculation, have resulted in overwhelming rage and shame. Instead, once into Pannonia and across the River Sava, Aetius found to his surprise that his chief feeling was one of liberation, of an oppressive burden having been lifted from him. For a time, at least, he was freed from the strain of alternately placating and cajoling the German federates in Gaul, of plotting to stay one jump ahead of Placidia in Ravenna, of campaigning against a powerful rival. Pannonia was safe territory, which he'd forced a reluctant Placidia to cede to his friends the Huns, as a consequence of his coup following Iohannes' abortive usurpation.

He'd followed Tiberius' road from Istria, north-east through a deserted landscape studded with ruined villas and abandoned forts, past the long, long Balaton lake and the wooded slopes of the Bakeny Wald, to Aquincum on the Danubius – the old imperial frontier. On the way, the only signs of life had been occasional sightings of the nomads' flocks and herds. At Aquincum, now virtually abandoned to squatters, he'd hired a boat to take himself and his tiny entourage across the river to where began the vast prairieland of the western steppes, part of the Huns' domain, which now extended from the Sava to the Mare Caspium.

Meeting a party of Huns, who seemed in some strange way to be apprised of his presence, he and his followers were conducted eastwards to the Hun 'capital' near the foothills of the Transylvanian Alpes, in what had once been the Roman province of Dacia – abandoned these hundred and fifty years. This settlement was in fact a mobile camp, its centre a prefabricated wooden palace, which could be dismantled and re-assembled as the nomads switched pasture. Aetius noted considerable changes since he had last solicited the Huns' help seven years previously. Clans had coalesced into tribes, tribes into confederacies. These, three in number, had recently become a single confederacy under the rule of Rua, the uncle of Attila, Aetius' old friend from his youth as a hostage with the Huns. Hierarchical trends were emerging in what had been a society of equals: chiefs styling themselves 'nobles', and their families becoming a quasi-aristocracy; a hereditary dynasty in process of forming; a permanent Council of influential leaders beginning to displace the assembly of all adult males.

Attila's father, Mundiuch, the brother of Rua, had led one of the three former confederacies, which made Attila a strong candidate to succeed Rua. Should he become ruler, Attila might prove a barbarian version of Plato's philosopher king, reflected Aetius with some amusement, for he had always displayed an unfortunate trend towards kindness and consideration. These qualities might be liabilities in a ruler – especially if that ruler's subjects were savage barbarians like the Huns, who above all respected strength and a leader's power to enforce his will. Attila had confided to Aetius his intention, should he become king, to end the practices of stoning to death a warrior suspected of even the slightest degree of cowardice, and of killing off the aged. Aetius had argued that, brutal though they might seem, such traditions helped to keep a nation successful and vigorous – like animal packs or herds, where only the strong survived, or the ancient Spartans who exposed new-born infants if sickly or deformed. Attila, though he paid courteous attention to this reasoning, had seemed unconvinced.

To Aetius' appeal for help to reinstate him, Rua – recalling that previous assistance was rewarded with gold and Pannonia – had been sympathetic. A decision would be taken in Council, which consisted (though now only in theory) of all adult males, assembled on horseback.

Meanwhile, all activities had been suspended for the duration of a great bison drive. As well as being an exciting diversion, if successful this would provide a welcome supplement to the Huns' staple diet of goat-flesh and mutton. The herd had been spotted grazing near the Danubius but heading away from the river, near the famous Iron Gate gorge. The plan was to turn the herd back towards the Danubius, then stampede it over steep bluffs overlooking the water. The task of turning the herd was a dangerous privilege reserved for the boldest and most experienced. Once the bison were headed in the right direction, the main body of Huns would join in the chase, containing the herd on the flanks and at the rear.

Racing alongside the galloping bison, Aetius whooped aloud in sheer release of tension. Like boulders surfacing in a river in spate, the humps of the great beasts rose and fell above the whirling dust-pall enveloping them, while the drumming of their hoof was a thunderous tattoo. Suddenly, Aetius was aware that ahead the horizon appeared to have foreshortened. The bluffs! With the other horsemen, he peeled away to the side, while the doomed herd charged on, its vanguard now aware of the peril but, driven on by the mass of animals behind, unable to stop.

Drawing rein on the lip of the drop, Aetius watched in awed fascination as the bison hurtled over the edge in a brown water-fall, their bodies spinning and tumbling to crash far below on the beach bordering the river. Further upstream, where the bluffs gave way to sloping banks, the Huns descended to the river and galloped back to where the bison lay in heaps and windrows, many kicking feebly and uttering hoarse cries. Swiftly and effi-ciently, the hunters set about the task of dispatching and butchering, then loading the pelts and meat on to packhorses.

Faintly through the din Aetius heard a cry. He looked up and saw a young tribesman struggling in the water: in all the confu-sion and violent activity, he must have overbalanced near the edge. Then things began to happen, in a sequence which somehow, in retrospect, seemed inevitable. Attila rode into the river and urged his horse towards the Hun, who was in the grip of a powerful current carrying him into midstream. Cursing Attila for his misplaced altruism which, for obvious political reasons he himself must be seen to support, Aetius raced along the beach towards a skiff drawn up on the shingle. He dragged it to the water, jumped in, pushed off with an oar and began to row towards Attila, whose horse, with the swimmer now clutching its bridle, was trying to fight its way back to shore. But the current was too strong; the horse with its double load ceased making headway, and started to move downstream.

Suddenly, a cross-flow seized the skiff and swept it into the middle of the river. Pulling with all his might, Aetius managed to intercept the group as it was about to bob past him. Attila scrambled from the saddle into the boat, then both he and Aetius grabbed the third and hauled him over the side, leaving the horse to be carried helplessly away. Attila then picked up one of the poles lying on the floorboards and stationed himself at the stern, commanding Balamir, the young tribesman, to do likewise at the bow. 'Keep her nose into the current,' he called to Aetius above the noise of rushing water. 'Our lives depend on that.'

'Why don't I just try to row us to the bank?'

'Too late – the current's got us. We'll have to try to ride the river through the Iron Gate.'

'Is that risky?'

Attila laughed grimly. 'Does iron sink? Pray to your triple-headed god, my friend; no one's yet been known to get through the Iron Gate. Alive, that is.'

The bluffs on either hand changed to towering walls of naked rock which, closing in, compressed the channel to a width of little more than a hundred paces. The river became a raging torrent on which the little boat was borne along like a twig. Fighting panic, Aetius strove to keep the bows parallel with the current; should the skiff be buffeted sideways, it would immediately start shipping water. High up on the rock face to his right, Aetius glimpsed the rotting remains of cantilevered planking – put there three centuries before to widen the road carved out of the cliff by Trajan's artificers, he realized inconsequently. And there was the *Tabula traiana*, the emperor's great rock-cut inscription showing shipping regulations for the Danube.

Such fleeting observations were forgotten as an ominous booming filled the air. Ahead, fangs and ledges of rock broke the surface of the river, which was transformed into a seething chaos of whirlpools and eddies. Next moment they were in the mael-strom, fighting desperately with oars and poles to keep the boat on course and from smashing against boulders.

'We're through!' shouted Aetius exultantly as they emerged, miraculously unscathed, from the boiling turbulence into a calmer stretch, where the river became a smoothly speeding millrace. But Attila pointed ahead, and Aetius saw that the river disappeared in a wall of spray. Seconds later, half blinded by spray and deafened by the crash of falling water, he gasped in horror as the skiff slid over the lip of a cataract.

Down swooped the boat in a sickening rush, to smash into the plunge pool at the bottom. It surfaced groggily, half full of water, but there was no respite for baling; plucked downstream by the savage current, the fragile craft was swept down a series of rapids. Time after time it hurtled towards rocks, disaster being averted only by the heroic efforts of Attila and Balamir, their poles bending like bows with the pressure of fending off.

Then suddenly the ordeal was over. The boat shot from the final rapid and whirled round a bend into a broad and placid reach. Thanks to a combination of nerve, luck, judgement, and the skill of the Danubian boat-builders, they were through the Iron Gate.

At their next Council assembly, the Huns unanimously supported Rua's proposal that they provide Aetius with military backing towards his restoration.

Aetius hummed the soldiers' song 'Lalage' as he made the familiar journey from the imperial palace back to his re-requisitioned head-quarters near Ravenna. The meeting with Placidia had yielded all he'd planned for. Humiliated and furious, the Empress had been forced to climb down and accede to his demands that he be promoted to the rank of Patrician, and made Master of both Horse and Footsoldiers – in fact Emperor in all but name. The newly created Master chuckled to himself as he urged Bucephalus into a canter; with a huge force of Huns at his back, she'd had little choice. It would, he supposed, have been simple enough to depose Valentinian and assume the purple himself. But it was more prudent to leave that odious youth on the throne; that way, constitutional stability would be preserved, while the real power was wielded by himself.

Now he could concentrate on furthering his plans. These were simple: to take whatever steps were necessary to consolidate his position as master of Gaul, as Magnus Maximus had so nearly done before him, and Carausius had succeeded for a time in doing in Britain. With Boniface gone, his allies the Huns behind him, and Ravenna in his pocket to provide a screen of legitimacy, there was no one in the empire strong enough to stop him. Forget all that high-sounding rhetoric he'd spouted to Litorius about recovering Africa et cetera. That had been intended merely to preserve his persona of 'Saviour of the Republic'. Actually, the empire was probably doomed; it was only blind fools like Boniface who refused to face that reality. Best to salvage what you could, before the ship of state struck the rocks.

Angrily, Aetius tried to suppress inner voices which urged a different course, the voices of his father, Gaudentius, a distinguished cavalry commander who had devoted his career to the service of the Empire; of his gentle mother from a noble Roman family which, in a cynical and degenerate age, continued to uphold the worthy standards of an earlier time; of Titus Valerius, who had left his service in disgust; of Boniface, good man and well-intentioned patriot, whose downfall and death he had brought about. 'Rome has made you what you are,' they said. 'Can you then act as though you owe her nothing?' With an effort, Aetius willed himself not to listen, and, as if obedient to his command, they fell silent. For the moment. But they would return, he knew with a feeling almost of guilty dread. As surely as the sun was going to rise next morning, they would return.

Later in the year that he became 'Lord of the West Romans' (as writers began to style him), the one thousand, one hundred and eighty-seventh from the founding of Rome,* Aetius heard that Rua had died, and that Attila had succeeded to the throne of the Huns.

* 433.

PART II

CONSTANTINOPLE
AD 434–50

SEVENTEEN

Their savage custom is to stick a naked sword in the earth and worship it as the God of War
Ammianus Marcellinus, *The Histories, c.* 395

Crowning its huge timber plinth, the Sacred Scimitar glittered in the pale spring sunshine. Looking at the shining blade, Attila smiled to himself as, accompanied by his guide, a one-eyed, smiling little Greek, he rode out of the Hun camp at the start of his long journey to the north-east. Years previously, the sword had been gifted to him by a herdsman who had dug it from the ground after one of his heifers cut its leg on the sharp point hidden in the grass. Attila had laid the thing aside and forgot it until, on becoming co-ruler with his brother Bleda, he had considered its potential as a symbol to enhance his kingship. For the sword possessed a strange quality which, in the eyes of unsophisticated nomads, gave it magical powers. Though made of iron, it never rusted.* When cleaned after its removal from the earth in which it had lain for unknown decades, it was as bright and unblemished as though it were fresh from the swordsmith's forge, an appearance it had retained ever since. Traditionally, his people had worshipped a naked sword stuck in the ground. The Sacred Scimitar, imbued with both ancient custom and magic power, could, Attila realized, be valuable in building his personal legend.

Attila's production of the scimitar had created an effect beyond his expectations. After a trial period, in which it was exposed to the elements and observed not to rust, it was accepted by the Huns as a manifestation of their warlike god Murduk, and deemed to bestow on its owner semi-divine status. This, Attila thought,

---

* Probably through an accidental admixture, during its making, of chromium, a metal whose ore exists abundantly in Hungary, and which today is the vital ingredient in the manufacture of stainless steel.

must give him a considerable advantage in the power struggle which he saw developing between himself and Bleda.

Since becoming king, a plan for his people's destiny had begun to form in Attila's mind: a vision of a great nation whose homeland would span the vast steppes extending between the empires of the Romans and the Chinese. In order to survive, and not, like innumerable nomad peoples in the past, flourish briefly, only to be absorbed or annihilated by the next westward-advancing wave, a nation must develop written laws, and institutions. Without these things, Attila believed, there could be no long-lasting stability. Rome had lasted for hundreds of years, China for thousands; with a viable constitution, and the energy of its teeming population productively channelled, there was no reason why the Hun Empire should not outlive them both. Was there? And who better than his friend Aetius, now ruler of the West Romans, to help him build the foundations for such an empire?

But Attila knew that his brother, unless kept in check, would compromise his vision. Jealous, vindictive, insatiably ambitious, Bleda made up in cunning what he lacked in intelligence. It was inconceivable he would co-operate with Attila in the furtherance of his plan. Therefore he must be sidelined. Two things should help to ensure that: Attila's possession of the Sword of Murduk; and, if his current journey bore sweet fruit, the immense boost his prestige could receive. If the fabled sage and seer Wu Tze were to predict favourable auguries for Attila's reign, that would confer on the king an authority decreed by Fate.

'Callisthenes of Olbia' – it has a certain ring, you must agree. You won't have heard of me, of course. Yet. But you will, you will. And why is that? I hear you ask. The answer, my friends, is because I have decided to cast in my lot with that of one who I predict will prove to be the greatest man the world has ever seen – to wit, Attila, nephew of the late King Rua, and now joint ruler of the nation of the Huns. Lest you be tempted to dismiss my claim as mere sounding brass and a tinkling cymbal, let me explain.

I am what you might call a man of business (a definition I prefer to 'merchant') from a long line of traders settled in Olbia, a Greek outpost city near the north coast of the Pontus Euxinus,* now in the Huns' domain. My family were among the original settlers when Olbia was founded, a century and more before the Graeco-Persian Wars. The place was set up with the sole purpose of commerce, in which activity it was extraordinarily successful, establishing trading links throughout the Scythian world** and beyond – to India and China. One of my ancestors, another Callisthenes, was chief supplier to Alexander the Great (not, I hasten to add, the Callisthenes who paid with his life for daring to criticize the Macedonian's adoption of Persian regalia and mores). He ensured a constant flow of supplies, not only for Alexander's army but for the flood of scientists, settlers, officials, and artisans that followed in its wake to consolidate his empire – the same categories of men that Attila will himself need when he implements his Great Plan.

You see, since choosing me (on account of my contacts throughout Scythia, and – though I say it myself – unrivalled knowledge of its peoples, tongues, terrain, and climate) to be his guide on his present journey to consult the seer Wu Tze, he has confided to me something of his ambitions. An Empire of the Steppes, bridging the realms of Rome and China: a virtually empty land providing a splendid opportunity for the eastern expansion of his people. What the Germans, in their drive to claim new territories within the Roman frontiers, call *Völkerwanderung*. What a man! What a vision! But to turn that vision into reality, he will need to build upon the vast network of trading links and multifarious interest groups that permeate Scythia. In other words, he will need me.

But that is for the future. This present journey of some two thousand leagues (or, if you prefer, six thousand Roman miles) to the shores of the Baikal lake, involving the crossing of six mighty rivers – the Borysthenes,† the Tanais,‡ the

---

* The Black Sea.
** 'Scythia' was an imprecise term, implying roughly the whole of the steppe region.
† The Dnieper.
‡ The Don.

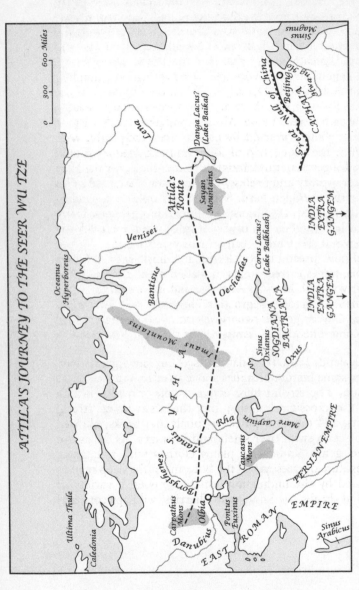

ATTILA'S JOURNEY TO THE SEER WU TZE

* The place names are, as far as possible, taken from Ptolemy's World Map (SECOND century), supplemented in one or two cases from Ortelius' *Theatrum orbis terrarum*. Some names, e.g. Danga Lacus (Ortelius) for Lake Baikal, are conjectural. Both Ptolemy and Ortelius show a large lake in roughly the right area for Lake Baikal, but this may be guesswork – although of a higher category than the 'Here be dragons' variety. Where the ancient name can't be traced, the modern form (e.g. R. Lena) is used.

Rha,* the Bantisus,** the Yenisei, and the Lena – might seem to the ordinary traveller an immense and daunting undertaking. But to a Hun, and to a Greek acquainted with the region, it is nothing. For it follows all the way a fine and level road, greater by far than any the Romans ever made. A road a thousand miles wide and paved with grass, extending all the way from Old Dacia† to China: the Highway of the Steppes. Rivers apart, there are only two natural obstacles, the Carpathus and Imaus Mons,‡ and they both easy to surmount, both traversed by passes. Travelling light, with remounts, the round trip of four thousand leagues should take no longer than three months, four at most, for the Hun horses are sturdy and tireless, able to cover a hundred miles a day, more if ridden hard. Such a trip's only to be undertaken from May to August, the northern steppes being gripped by winter in the other months, when the cold – at least beyond the Urals – can be really terrible.

And now, preamble concluded, I, Callisthenes, a Greek of Olbia, trader extraordinary, traveller, natural philosopher (and, if you will, both an Aristotle and an Arrian to Attila's Alexander) begin this chronicle, *The Attiliad, a Scythian Odyssey*, in the twenty-seventh year of the reign of the second Theodosius, Emperor of the East Romans.¶

XVII Kalends Junii.¶¶ Today crossed our third great river, the Rha some hundred leagues above its entry into the Mare Caspium. The stream here above a mile in width, which made the crossing lengthy; but the absence of strong currents, and the abundance of shoals and banks, allowed our horses to swim over safely and in stages. As far as eye can see, gently undulating plains clothed with rich grass, and destitute of trees; yet in the bottoms of the deep ravines concealed by the undulations of the steppes, a variety of trees and shrubs – willows, wild cherries, wild apricots, and

* The Volga.
** The Ob.
† Romania.
‡ The Urals.
¶ 434.
¶¶ 16 May.

others. For several days have noticed large mounds of earth up to forty feet in height. Ancient tombs?

Soon after our river crossing, encountered a band of nomads travelling with their wagons, the men riding, the women and children in the wagons, together with their flocks and herds. Found them courteous and hospitable, as are all steppe peoples who, though very warlike among themselves, are invariably kind to strangers. Invited by them to share a meal, a pottage of onions, beans, and garlic, with horse-meat, lamb, and goat, cooked in a great bronze cauldron. Tunny and sturgeon (dried) also offered as side dishes, but declined. To drink, wine and the ubiquitous *kumiss*, or fermented mare's milk. Men's garments – close-fitting tunic and trousers (convenient for riding and therefore universal in the steppes, and even copied by the imperial cavalry of China). Their women wear long dresses and a tall headdress covered with a veil. Clothing of both sexes ornamented with colourful designs, cut out separately then sewn on to the garment, much jewellery displayed, especially gold. Clear skies. Weather very hot.

In this one band alone is displayed a wide variety of tints: hair red, fair, and black; skins white to olive; eyes blue, green, brown, black. Regarding these differences, which show clear intermingling of races and may in part be explained by polygamy being general among the nomads, they seem quite indifferent. (A lesson here, perhaps, for Romans, for whom intermarriage with Germans is forbidden.) Indeed, though diverse in blood, the peoples of the steppes show a remarkable uniformity of culture and, though all have their separate tribal languages, can communicate with each other easily enough in a bastard Persian, which serves as a common tongue. On their departing, presented them with some beads of amber from the shores of the Mare Suevicum* (from our store of trade goods for just such occasions), which pleased them greatly.

Post Scriptum.

Everywhere we've passed, Attila spoken of with interest and respect, proof that his reputation as a leader is already

* The Baltic.

to be reckoned with. (We travelling incognito as traders, Attila not recognized for who he is, though his presence and gravity of demeanour never fail to impress all we meet, that here is a man of consequence.) Have heard reported many supposed 'sayings' of Attila, which amuse him greatly (the only times I've observed him to smile), some of which I here set down:

A wise chieftain never kills the Hun bearing bad news, only the Hun who fails to deliver bad news.
Great chieftains never take themselves too seriously.
Every decision involves some risk.
Huns only make enemies on purpose.
Never appoint acting chieftains.
Some have solutions for which there are no problems.
Every Hun has value – even if only to serve as a bad example.
Suffer long for mediocre but loyal Huns; suffer not for competent but disloyal Huns.

IV Nones Junii.* Made camp on the shores of the Cham lake, halfway between the Irtish and Bantisus rivers. Though hot by day, the nights now very cold. (The reason I think may be this: as we approach the centre of this vast continent of Asia, so the land, becoming ever further from Ocean, is no longer warmed by its winds; also, as we progress, our direction being north of east we trend away from the temperate lands, towards the Boreal. If Ptolemy is correct, we should now be near the latitude of Ultima Thule.**) Rivers here have gravelly bottoms, and from constant changing of their beds have formed strange abandoned banks and islands, marooned in the midst of dry land! We now encounter fewer parties of nomads (some for the first time displaying the Mongol cast of feature) and, though always from a distance, more wild animals than formerly – elks, bears, wolves, bison, wild horses. Stands of timber, mainly pines, birch, and larch, more and more commonly seen. The steppe in places carpeted with sanfoin and wild thyme

* 2 June.
** Probably the Orkneys or Shetlands, though some have speculated Iceland.

which, with the increasing frequency of trees, helps to break the monotony of the endless sea of grass. (I've heard that these vast steppes can, in some travellers, induce a weariness or sickness of the spirit.) Abundance of francolin and pheasant, a number of which Attila (like all Huns a superb marksman with the bow) shot – a welcome change to our usual fare of dried flesh. These delicious seasoned with salt, which the nomads obtain from the many salt lakes hereabouts, and which they're willing to trade for trinkets – mirrors, needles, and the like.

Attila much given to contemplation. As we ride, he observes everything around him with a hunter's eye, distinguishing an eagle from a buzzard when to me both are mere dots in the sky, yet all the time thinking deeply, as evidenced from the penetrating questions he continually shoots. Why, think you, Callisthenes, does the sun appear to move round the earth? What makes objects fall? Why do things appear smaller with distance? Why does a stone acquire more force the further it drops? Which shows that, in addition to possessing a supreme gift of leadership, Attila has a deep and penetrating mind.

That notwithstanding, I remind myself he is still a savage – an unlettered barbarian without recourse to written store of knowledge, and so limited by memory and observation to everything he can know or recall. Can a barbarian, however noble his vision, ever transcend such limitations? Ever react to, or plan against, what is not in the present? Construct a water-clock or understand Pythagoras? I venture to think that Attila might indeed discover the power to snap the bonds of barbarism, and escape the tyranny of the immediate. For he seems *aware* of such restrictions, and that surely must be half the battle to free himself of them. A man who cannot read, provided he has the will and can command the influence, may at least surround himself with those who can, and thus provide himself with access to learning.

XII Kalends Julii.* Arrived today at the shores of that great inland sea, the Lake of Baikal or Bai-Kul (which the Mongols

* 20 June.

call Dalai Nor or 'Holy Sea') enclosed by high, fir-covered hills. Since crossing the Yenisei river ten days ago, the country much changed – a chain of tall mountains always on our right hand,* and the grassy plains much interrupted with hills and forests. Several days of heavy rain (from the proximity of mountains?); plagued by mosquitoes. Since the Yenisei, all the natives of Mongol race – Calmucks, Buryats, Ostyaks – in appearance so resembling the Huns that they take Attila for one of themselves, and seem surprised he does not comprehend when they address him in their own tongue. Which is surely proof that the belief of some natural philosophers, that the Huns originated from a region to the north of China, is correct. These people all herders of reindeer, which they also ride sitting on their necks or shoulders, the animals' backs being not strong enough to bear a man's weight. They introduced us to a drink called *chai*; this comes in the form of a cake a little of which, broken off and infused with boiling water, is drunk with a lump of butter. Somewhat bitter, but refreshing and much to be preferred to *kumiss*.

A curious incident occurred as we pitched camp on the banks of the Lena, not long before we reached the lake. We were struck by hearing a low, pleasing, musical note, repeated time after time and issuing from beyond a nearby rise. Investigating, we observed a great bear standing on his hind legs and, with his forepaw, bending then releasing a broken-off bough projecting from a tree, whose vibrations caused the sound. (Which proves that the myth of Orpheus charming the beasts with his lyre was based on true observation – namely, that animals are not indifferent to music.) Seeing us, the bear made off; Attila and I then tried in turn to bend the branch, but could not move it.

For many days have observed quantities of huge bones littering the ground: rhinoceros and elephant, but from animals of a size far exceeding that of any members of those species known today. Which leads me to speculate: did the Creator fashion such creatures (which in respect to size are so different from their modern counterparts)

---

* The Sayan Range.

on the Fifth Day, along with the other beasts? Or could they be the ancestors (as Empedocles – who held that forms are constantly changing from an inferior to a more perfect state – seems to imply) of today's rhinoceroses and elephants, grown smaller through the ages? And is it heresy (by challenging Holy Writ) to raise such questions? I trust not; after all, the Schools of Athens are still permitted to discuss all matters freely, whether or not they touch on the Divine Logos.

Tomorrow, Attila sets out for the abode of the sage Wu Tze, to ask (myself interpreting) what the Fates portend – as the Greeks of old, before embarking on any great enterprise, sought out the Delphic Oracle.

Excursus:* Terra Nova?

The nomads here tell of a land beyond Ocean to the east, not further than a four moons' journey north-eastwards to its nearest point, where it's separated from the end of Asia by a narrow strait of only ten leagues' width, in which are three islands. This, the local people, who are called Inuit, cross with ease in their canoes, paddling from island to island, as we would cross a river using stepping-stones; also, when the sea's frozen, on sleds drawn by dogs, but then with more difficulty on account of the ice being hummocky, not smooth. Could this be that lost island of Atlantis of which Plato wrote in the *Timaeus* and the *Kritias*, and which was spoken of (although I think on hearsay) by Pliny, Diodorus, and Arnobius? Lucian, in his *True History*, speaks of an island eighty days' sail westwards of the Pillars of Hercules, but this has generally been dismissed as imagined. The Celts believe in a Land of the Dead beyond the Western Sea, which they call Glasinnis or Avalon (the Hesperides or Isles of the Blessed, of our Greek forebears?); these things however pertain rather to Legend than to Geography.

Atlantis, then: substance or mere shadow? And, if more than fabled, could it be related to the land visited by the

---

* Digression: a favourite device of classical authors, wishing to expand on a topic not necessarily connected with the main narrative. A famous example is Ammianus Marcellinus' 'Excursus on the Huns', in his *Histories*.

Inuit? Had but the modern Hellenes the same spirit of enquiry and adventure as that Greek of old, Pytheas,* then might we know the answer ere too long.

And now, for the moment, Callisthenes must lay aside this his chronicle, as translating for both Attila and Wu Tze will take precedence over other matters.

With anticipation not unmixed with doubt, Attila drew near to the abode of the holy man Wu Tze. Reputedly over a hundred years old, the famed seer was a native of China, whence, so ran the story, he had travelled as a child with his father as part of a mission to the court of the great Constantine, when Rome was still the mightiest power in the world. On the journey home, the party had been captured and enslaved by Alans. The young Wu Tze, however, had impressed his masters by exhibiting a rare gift: an apparent ability to contact the world of spirits and dead ancestors. Released from bondage, he developed this talent through following a regime of contemplation and rigorous disciplines, gradually acquiring a status of pre-eminence among the shamans consulted by the nomads of the plains.

After dismounting, and hobbling their horses and remounts, Attila and Callisthenes approached the shaman's felt tent, or yurt. Attila had made the pilgrimage with the intention of gaining from the sage a prediction of what the future held regarding his Great Plan. Although totally cynical about the supposed magical properties of the Sacred Scimitar, he shared with all his race a belief in the existence of the spirit world, and reverence towards individuals who professed to be able to make contact with it. He had had some doubts about the wisdom of leaving Bleda behind as sole ruler during his absence, but, with no great enterprise afoot involving the Huns, Bleda could do little damage. And the cachet that he, Attila, hoped to gain as a result of receiving favourable omens from Wu Tze, and of making contact with the spirits of his dead father and uncle – Mundiuch and the mighty Rua – must surely far outweigh the effects of any spiteful slander his jealous brother might spread.

Before he reached the entrance to the yurt, a high-pitched, bell-like voice from inside called, 'Enter Attila. You are welcome.'

* A Greek navigator who, in the time of Alexander, sailed round the north of Britain, perhaps as far as Iceland, and explored the Baltic.

Attila started; how could his presence have been known in advance? Travelling incognito, he and his Greek guide had encountered on the journey only the occasional band of nomads, who could scarcely have had time or opportunity to spread word of his coming, even if they had discovered his identity.

Callisthenes following, Attila entered the yurt. The interior, heated by glowing charcoal in a bronze brazier of Chinese design, was pleasantly warm, in contrast to the keenness of the air outside. To Attila's surprise, there was none of the usual shamanistic clutter – skulls, bones, dried animal parts, and so on. The tent was furnished, richly if simply, with nomad rugs, Chinese calligraphic scrolls, and a small square altar of dark wood. Wu Tze himself was a tiny figure, encased in a long tunic of soft deerskin, and high felt boots. Abundant white hair hung to his waist, framing a face whose skin was smooth and semi-transparent, like parchment, and of much the same colour and texture. It was as though the long passage of the years had refined and condensed his body, instead of inflicting on it the normal ravages of age.

'You both have journeyed far and must be tired,' said the shaman (the Greek translating) in those strange musical tones, after Attila had presented him with a bale of fine furs and expertly cured skins. 'Tomorrow, Attila, you will tell me the purpose of your visit. But now, when you have seen to your horses and your gear, you and your companion must sleep; first, some refreshment.' And he pressed on both a simple but sustaining meal of dried reindeer flesh and barley cakes, washed down with *kumiss*.

Next morning, after a sound sleep on a bed of furs, Attila, the Greek beside him to translate, accompanied Wu Tze on foot on a search for a species of mushroom which would, the shaman explained, help to induce the state of heightened perception essential for making contact with the spirits. Attila felt filled with energy and confidence. On this bright, tingling day, it was joy just to be alive. Impatient enthusiasm to begin to implement the grand scheme for his people swept through him. He had no illusions about the magnitude of the task. He was, he knew, essentially the unlettered leader of a shepherd people – in Roman eyes, a savage, a barbarian. But he had the vision, the strength of purpose, and the will to learn, to make his plan succeed. After all, Philip of Macedon had been little more than the tribal chieftain of an obscure barbarian nation; yet his son Alexander had created an empire to rival that of Rome. As they tramped uphill towards the treeline through meadows of coarse grass, the vast expanse of Lake Baikal unrolled itself beneath them, reflected light from its surface seeming to fill the air with limpid radiance.

Attila asked the shaman if he could foretell what the future might hold for him as co-ruler of the Huns.

'Understand that I cannot of myself foretell anything,' replied the sage, who, despite his great age, set a pace Attila found hard to match. 'I am a mere vessel, to be filled by whatever messages come to me from the spirit world. Nor can I explain their meaning. That is for the recipient to discern for himself, or, if he cannot, to wait for their fulfilment, when their meaning will surely become clear.'

They entered a stand of timber, outrider of the *taiga*, the great forest belt bounding the steppes, to the north. Here, they located the mushrooms, large red discs with white warts, thus easily visible. Soon, they had filled a small basket, after which they returned to the yurt. The shaman proceeded to burn a sweet-smelling substance on a bronze dish placed on the altar. Then, after preparing and consuming some of the mushrooms, he began to gyrate slowly round the inside of the tent, all the while beating a circular drum made of deerskin stretched on a wooden frame. The fumes from the altar and the insistent rhythmic drumbeat combined to make Attila feel drowsy . . .

He started awake. Several hours must have passed, for no sunlight filtered into the tent, which was dimly illuminated by glowing coals in the brazier. Wu Tze had put aside his drum (the cessation of its thumping must have been what had aroused Attila), and was sitting cross-legged on the floor, his shiny black pebbles of eyes seemingly focused on some distant object. Suddenly, in a flat sing-song, he began to speak: 'I see a wild ass running over the plains, and an eagle flying above it. Together, they attack and put to flight a wild boar. Now the ass pursues another eagle, wounding it before it can fly away. But the wounded eagle turns on the ass, which leaves it to attack the first eagle. This eagle is now joined by the boar, and together they put the ass to flight.' He paused for a few seconds, then went on, 'The vision fades. There is no more.'

Wu Tze stirred and, shaking his head, appeared to come out of his trance. He turned to face Attila. 'Whatever I have related is for you alone to interpret,' he said in his normal voice. 'I have no memory of it, and even if you were to describe it to me I would be unable to explain its meaning.' He looked at Attila intently, and said gently, 'But this much I *can* tell you. I feel you have a great heart and a powerful mind, Attila. But I sense also there are violent passions – anger, will, ambition. These things are not in themselves necessarily harmful; directed properly, they can work towards the good. All things turn on the struggle between two opposing forces, the dark, negative Yin, and the bright positive Yang. Let your Yang rule your Yin, and you will achieve great things. But should it be the other way round, I fear for the consequences. We have a saying in my country: "Happy the people who are governed by a strong ruler and a kindly sage." You will be a strong ruler Attila; of that I have no doubt. But will you also be a kindly sage?'

When Attila and Callisthenes reached the Hun camp, Attila was accosted on the outskirts by Balamir, the young Hun he had rescued from the Danube. He seemed agitated. 'Sire, you are back none too soon!' he said urgently. 'Things have been happening which you should know about.' He hesitated, as if unsure how to proceed. 'Forgive me, Sire, but they concern your brother. I – I fear it may not be my place to inform you.'

Bleda. He might have known his brother would cause trouble the moment his back was turned, Attila thought furiously. Temporarily dismissing Callisthenes with grave courtesy, Attila turned to the boy. 'You may speak freely, Balamir. A loyal friend has nothing to fear from telling Attila the truth – however unwelcome it may be.' He had formed a liking for this youth who, in gratitude to Attila for saving his life, had appointed himself an unofficial guard and page.

'The day after your departure, Sire, Lord Bleda called a full meeting of the Council,' Balamir began. 'He proposed that the peace treaty with the Eastern Empire, which was interrupted by the death of King Rua, be immediately resumed.'

A slow-burning rage began to build in Attila. How dare Bleda summon the Council in Attila's absence, and without his agreement? It was a calculated insult – worse, a naked bid to undermine him. The proposed resumption of the treaty was, Attila suspected, a mere pretext for extortion.

The background to the treaty was complex. The Boii,* with some lesser German tribes who had recently submitted to Hun suzerainty, had revolted and asked the Eastern Emperor for protection. Theodosius, exhibiting the folly of a weak man trying to appear strong, had agreed, and the rebel tribes had entered into a formal alliance with the East Romans – who quickly discovered that they had roused a tiger. Outraged by this provocative act, Rua had demanded in the most forceful terms that the East retract its agreement with the rebels. Realizing that their attempt to play off one set of barbarians against another had badly miscarried, Theodosius and the Senate of Constantinople backed down with unseemly haste, and sued for peace. Negotiations were set in train but, on the death of Rua, were suspended.

'How did the Council vote?' asked Attila heavily, knowing in his heart what the answer would be.

'When Lord Bleda suggested that a condition of the treaty should be that the East pay for its presumption in gold . . .' Balamir trailed off uncomfortably, the implication of his unfinished sentence only too clear.

Gold. It would prove the ruin of his people, thought Attila despairingly. In the past indifferent to the 'yellow iron', whose softness made it useless for any practical purpose, the Huns had recently become obsessed with it. Once they had made the momentous discovery that gold could command power and possessions without limit, they couldn't, it seemed, get enough of it. Bleda had sown the seed of an idea in their minds: that the Eastern Empire could prove a milch cow for the precious stuff. Like greedy children who come across an unguarded peach orchard, they would become difficult to govern and direct, their minds preoccupied by the easy acquisition of riches, which in the end would avail them little. Unless he could nip that temptation in the bud, the task of realizing his dream – the forging of his people into a great nation, for which he needed the help and friendship of the Romans – would prove immeasurably harder. At one stroke, it seemed, Bleda might have dealt his plan a fatal blow.

* Bavarians.

EIGHTEEN

All fugitives will be returned, the annual subsidy doubled, safe
markets established for the Huns, and Rome will make no alliances
with anyone at war with the Huns
Priscus of Panium, *Byzantine History*, fifth century

Whips in right hands, reins in left, Attila and Bleda, flanked by
their seconds, faced each other across the forest clearing. Attila's
attendant was young Balamir, Bleda's a middle-aged warrior of
hulking physique. Raising his hand, the latter called out, 'No
weapons other than whips; no strikes on the face; the contest to
continue until one surrenders.' He glanced at each opponent, who
nodded in turn; then his hand swept down.

The long lash of the whip trailing behind him, Attila circled
the glade, never letting his eyes leave his brother, who matched
his movements as though their mounts were connected by an
invisible axis. Bleda was afraid, Attila could tell: there was sweat
beading his unhealthily plump features, and a nervous grin had
replaced his habitual crafty smirk. Also, he was out of condition
and beginning to run to fat; since becoming joint ruler, Bleda
had felt free to indulge a gluttonous trait. Despite being physi-
cally at a disadvantage, Bleda had had no choice but to accept his
brother's challenge to a duel. A refusal, if broadcast, would have
branded him a coward – a fatal tag for a Hun, especially if he
were a ruler.

Fighting with whips required expertise (acquired only through
long and arduous practice), courage, and cool judgement. Each
flick, because it could not be quickly repeated, had to count –
hopefully forcing one's opponent to retreat, or landing a blow.
Blows could inflict wounds varying from angry weals to frightful
lacerations.

Slowly tensing his right arm, Attila judged his moment carefully, then struck. The whip-lash buzzed through the air like an
angry viper, to smack against Bleda's shoulder, ripping away a

strip of clothing and skin. Bleda shouted in surprise and pain; he riposted, but not quickly enough, allowing Attila to weave aside, then send his lash snaking across to land a second blow, this time across Breda's rib cage. The duel continued, the long lashes hissing, coiling, and snapping. Attila's superior skill enabled him to score hit after hit, while avoiding Bleda's clumsier strokes.

Attila had no wish to cause Bleda serious injury, merely to teach him a lesson for his presumption, and to force him to disclose certain information he was keeping from Attila. Balamir had said that subsequent to Bleda's Council meeting, but prior to Attila's return from his pilgrimage, he had several times observed Bleda engaged in earnest conversation with leading members of the Council. At Attila's request, the young Hun had, at some risk to himself, managed to eavesdrop on one further such conversation, by listening outside Bleda's tent under cover of darkness. The voices had been too low for him to glean much, but it had sounded as if they were discussing conditions to be imposed on the Eastern Empire, regarding the peace treaty the Council had voted to resume. Excluding Attila from these secret deliberations – by which the terms of the treaty would become set firm – was an insult not to be borne; hence Attila's challenge to his brother.

Bleda was tiring, his strokes becoming wilder and more desperate. Fear and hatred showed in his eyes; and something else, which Attila could not immediately read – a look of cunning calculation? Too late, Attila saw his brother nod imperceptibly; then he felt his whip tighten against its stock and resist his pull. Whirling round in the saddle, he saw that Bleda's burly second had gripped the lash by the middle. Even as he looked, the accomplice wound the tail section round his waist, to provide an anchor. Balamir flung himself at the man, only to be knocked senseless by a massive blow to the temple. A sudden stinging pain across his nose and cheeks, accompanied by a loud crack, made Attila turn towards Bleda. His brother's apprehensive expression had changed to a triumphant leer, as he drew back the whip to deliver a second stroke. The first, had it landed two inches higher, would have blinded his opponent.

Attila reacted with lightning speed. His horse, trained to interpret and obey the smallest signal, backed swiftly in response to the pressure of his master's knees. With enough slack now to wield it, Attila smashed his whip-stock into the face of Bleda's second.

Howling with pain, the man released the whip and staggered back, clutching his shattered jaw. So quickly did all this happen that when Attila turned back to his brother, the latter's whip hand was still moving back. Naked terror showed in Bleda's face; he struck out frantically. Ignoring the pain, Attila took the blow on his forearm, then grabbed the lash and, with a violent wrench, tore the whip from his brother's grasp. Flinging it to Balamir, who was picking himself up gingerly from the ground, Attila snarled in a voice thick with rage and contempt, 'Watch, brother. Watch – and learn what happens to a traitor when he crosses Attila.' Unhurriedly and systematically, he began to hunt the injured man with his whip.

Screaming, pleading for mercy, Bleda's accomplice stumbled about the glade, vainly trying to escape the terrible whip, which snapped and sang, laying flesh open to the bone with every cut, and gradually reducing him to a tattered scarlet horror. Eventually, he swayed, seemed to stiffen, then with a loud cry flung up his hands and collapsed, as his heart stopped beating.

'Play me false again, brother,' Attila grated, 'and I swear I'll kill you, too. Now, tell me the terms that you and your friends in the Council have decided to impose upon the East.'

The setting for the signing of the treaty with the Eastern Empire, near the city of Margus in the Eastern province of Upper Moesia, was tranquil and beautiful: a grassy plain surrounded by tall mountains clothed in forests of oak, beech, and chestnut. Attila and Bleda, with a sizeable retinue consisting of armed warriors and the leading members of the Hun Council, all mounted, confronted the Roman delegation from Constantinople. The latter, perhaps hoping to flatter and mollify the Huns, and thus secure more favourable terms, had proceeded from Margus to the meeting-place on foot. The Roman party was made up of two ambassadors, Plinthas, a general of barbarian origin but of consular rank, and the *quaestor** Epigenes, a wise and experienced statesman; a clutch of secretaries and officials; and a number of young Germans from important families, fugitives who had sought refuge in the Eastern Empire when the Huns conquered their homelands. This last group looked distinctly apprehensive.

* Magistrate.

Epigenes, a tall and dignified man clad in the robes of his office, opened the proceedings. 'Welcome, Your Majesties,' he said with a smile, addressing Attila and Bleda. 'My master, Theodosius, the second of that name, Emperor of the East Romans, fourteen times Consul, Calligrapher,* bids you welcome and trusts you are in good health. He sends you word that it is his sincere wish that the good relations formerly existing between our two peoples can be re-established, and that the unfortunate, ah, misunderstanding that arose concerning your German conquests, and the fugitives therefrom, be put behind us and forgotten.'

Bleda opened his mouth to answer, but Attila silenced him with a look, and made reply: 'A misunderstanding, Roman, which will cost your master dear. As to forgetting, that will happen only when we have received full reparation from your government for forming an alliance with our rebellious German subjects, and for affording refuge and protection to those of them who fled.'

'That is fair,' conceded Epigenes. 'The Emperor is willing to make reasonable compensation for any wrongs we may have done you. We would know your terms.'

'One: the right of our people to trade freely on your side of the Danubias,' stated Attila roughly. 'Two: a fine or ransom of eight gold pieces for every Roman captive who escaped from us. Three: your Emperor to renounce all treaties with the enemies of the Huns. Four: an annual contribution of seven hundred pounds' weight of gold to be paid us by your government. Five: all fugitives now under your protection to be returned.'

Gasps of astonishment among the Huns, and of consternation from the Romans, greeted this declaration. 'Seven hundred pounds – that's twice what the Council and I decided!' protested Bleda. 'They'll never pay it – they can't; they haven't the resources. And fines for escaped prisoners, the return of the fugitives – what will that gain us? We're better off without them; anyway, how could they begin to track down and identify prisoners? This is folly, brother. We could end up with nothing.'

Privately, Attila worried that Bleda might be right, and that this might be pushing the Eastern delegates too far. But to reverse any

* An astonishing title, bestowed on Theodosius on account of the beautiful handwriting he displayed in transcribing religious books.

damage Bleda had done his reputation, he had little choice but to come up with some radical proposals. These, in terms of financial gain for the Huns, must be a clear improvement on any conditions thought up by Bleda and the Council. They must also demonstrate that Attila not only could act independently of his brother but was the dominant sibling.

'This is intolerable!' snarled General Plinthas, his hand moving to his sword-hilt. 'That unwashed savages should dictate such terms to Romans – it's an insult to the majesty of the Empire.'

'Excuse him, my lords,' broke in Epigenes hastily. 'His manners have been formed in camps not courts.' He paused, then went on, a note of pleading in his voice. 'But his rudeness is perhaps understandable. These are indeed heavy terms. Too heavy, I think.'

'His manners are of no consequence,' said Attila indifferently. 'You think our terms heavy? Perhaps you would prefer to see your cities in flames, and your people massacred or enslaved.'

'You would have us sail between Scylla and Charybdis!' exclaimed the *quaestor* bitterly. He fought for composure, then continued more calmly, 'Permit us to return to Constantinople, to put your terms to the Emperor. My authority, I fear, does not extend to accepting such conditions.'

Attila, who had been prepared for such a reaction, considered his response carefully. If he allowed the Romans to return to Constantinople without having signed the treaty, negotiations would drag on and on, because Theodosius – flattering himself that he was playing a masterly political game of cat and mouse – would procrastinate endlessly. The Eastern Empire was wealthy; to pay the subsidy demanded would hurt, certainly, but could surely be managed without emptying the imperial coffers. To safeguard his reputation with the Huns (and therefore preserve the viability of his Great Plan for his people) Attila must convince the Roman ambassadors that they had no choice but to sign the treaty. Now. And to achieve that, he must provide them with an object-lesson which would leave them in absolutely no doubt as to his utter determination and capacity for ruthlessness in pursuit of his aims. This, although it had cost him much agony of spirit, he was also prepared for.

'If parting with gold distresses you,' he suggested, unable entirely to prevent the scorn from showing in his voice, 'perhaps parting with the fugitives would cause you less concern.'

'Betray those we are sworn to protect? Never!' shouted Plinthas. 'That would be to make a travesty of Roman honour. We spit on such—'

'Hush, friend,' interrupted Epigenes, laying a hand on the general's arm. 'We have no choice, shameful though it is to have to admit it.' Turning to Attila, he declared heavily, 'Take them; they are yours.'

On Attila's signal, Hun warriors surrounded the young Germans and removed them from the Roman group. 'What shall we do with them, Lord?' the escort's leader asked Attila.

'Crucify them,' ordered Attila, his voice impassive.

'No!' roared Plinthas, making to draw his sword. Several of his own party restrained him forcibly, though he continued to struggle and protest.

Some of the Huns swiftly felled trees and constructed rude crosses, while others dug pits to secure their bases. The unfortunate youths were bound by wrists and ankles to the beams, and spikes were driven through their hands and feet, pinning them securely to the wood.

In a horrified silence broken only by the curses of Plinthas and the cries of the victims, the Romans watched as the crosses with their human burdens were hauled upright, then dropped into the holes prepared for them. Attila willed his face to remain a stone-like mask, while rage and pity warred within him. Rage that his brother's folly had forced him to this action; pity for the young men sacrificed. He told himself that only an act of spectacular cruelty, calculated to spread terror throughout the Eastern Empire, would persuade the Romans, those masters of prevarication, to accept his terms without delay. And such a demonstration was also necessary to prove his authority to the Huns, after Bleda's attempts to weaken it.

It worked. The Huns immediately began to show him awed respect, far exceeding anything they accorded Bleda. That same day, in the lovely flower-starred meadow where the condemned fugitives groaned upon their crosses, the Romans signed the treaty.

That night, alone in his tent, for the first and last time in his life Attila wept. What was it Wu Tze had said to him? 'You will be a strong ruler, but will you also be a kindly sage?' Well, he had shown he could be strong. To survive, and therefore to have any hope of implementing his vision, he had had to demonstrate that strength in an act of graphic brutality. As for being a kindly sage, perhaps that was a role no barbarian leader, however much he wanted it, could aspire to. Through no fault or wish of his own, the iron, he felt, had begun to enter his soul.

NINETEEN

He [Attila] alone united the realms of Scythia and Germany
Jordanes, *Gothic History*, 551

'Aetius, old friend, welcome!' exclaimed Attila. The Roman general had just arrived in the Hun camp, accompanied by his son Carpilio, now grown into a tall, well-built young man. 'It's good to see you, Flavius,' Attila declared warmly, 'and you, too, Carpilio. You still have my gift, I see.'

'I'll never part with him sir,' replied Carpilio, proudly, patting the neck of his beautiful Arab steed. 'I've named him Pegasus for his speed and courage. You remember, sir, how he stood against the bear?'

'How could I forget?' murmured Attila dryly.

'To what do we owe the honour of this visit?' asked Attila, when he and his guests were ensconced in his private quarters within the wooden royal palace.

'I come to ask a favour, old friend,' said Aetius. 'A very great favour. Twice in the past, the Huns have come to my assistance. Would they stand by me a third time, perhaps even a fourth?'

'We were amply rewarded on both those occasions, I recall,' said Attila, re-charging the Romans' wooden cups with millet beer. 'Why should we not help you again?'

'This time, payment may have to be deferred,' said Aetius with a rueful grin. 'The West's coffers are all but empty – I have to pay my field army in Gaul in kind. The loss of Britain, Africa, and part of Hispania, has decimated our revenue from taxes, and the federate Germans settled in Gaul are exempt from paying tribute.'

'But you have something to offer as security?' said Attila, giving an oily leer and rubbing his hands, in imitation of a Syrian moneylender.

'Only the Western Empire,' replied Aetius wryly. 'Or what's left of it. Oh, and Carpilio here has volunteered to stay behind as your hostage.'

'Well, let us call the Empire an "ultimate surety",' laughed Attila, 'and Carpilio is welcome to remain as our honoured guest. I hardly think we'll be calling in those particular assets.' He added with apparently careless generosity, 'Pay us when you can, Flavius. Your word is pledge enough. But tell me, why do you need our help?'

'My problem concerns Gaul. The German federates – Franks and Burgundians in the east, Visigoths in the south-west, – were, in theory, originally allowed to settle in the Empire on condition they would fight for Rome if called upon. In reality, of course, they just marched in and took the land; we weren't strong enough to stop them. However, the government of our late lamented Honorius patched up a face-saving understanding with them which has, on the whole, held. They know that in a pitched battle my army will beat them every time – and that keeps them in check. But my soldiers can't be everywhere at once, in the event of trouble breaking out on several fronts. Also, as I've mentioned, pay is a constant worry, to say nothing of replenishing inevitable wastage of men and supplies. Then there's the Bagaudae.'

'The Bagaudae?'

'A brigands' movement centred in Aremorica* in north-west Gaul, also active in Hispania. It's made up chiefly of disaffected peasants and smallholders who've been taxed beyond endurance, and as a result have taken to a life of banditry. Their numbers have been swollen by fugitive slaves and army deserters. Their leader in Gaul is one Tibatto – a sort of latter-day Spartacus. They're well organized, with their own courts and a quasi-military government of sorts. If the Bagaudae in Gaul were to start a full-scale revolt, I'd be hard pressed to cope.'

'I can see you hardly have your troubles to seek,' mused Attila. 'What you're asking for, then, is Hun backing to help suppress the federates, and these Bagaudae should they break out, if your field army can't manage on its own?'

'Exactly. Are you willing to provide that backing – in return for payment at a future date, if necessary?'

'Just so. A poor friend he, who would not help another. And we two, Flavius, go back a long way. Consider the bargain sealed.'

* Brittany.

And, in the Roman manner, he extended his hand. Aetius, his heart full, reached out and took it.

During his return journey to Gaul (minus Carpilio), Aetius pondered the implications of what his friend had said about his own intentions. Attila was expanding his territory north-westwards to the Oceanus Germanicus, Mare Suevicum* and Scandia**, thus adding to his realm all Germania outwith the Roman Empire. As he could field up to half a million mounted warriors at short notice, this ambitious project was not as formidable as it might seem. The plan was music to Aetius' ears; at one stroke, the threat of further invasion by German tribes was cancelled, which would enable him to concentrate on pacifying Gaul.

Attila had also confided to Aetius his dream of establishing a great and lasting Empire of the Huns, extending eventually to include all the steppe peoples, and had asked Aetius for advice and help in setting up institutions which would provide 'Greater Scythia' with the necessary continuity and stability. In this connection, he had introduced Aetius to his Greek factotum, one Callisthenes, a garrulous little merchant with a single eye, who claimed a vast web of contacts throughout the whole steppe region. Inclined at first to dismiss the Greek as an empty amphora, in the course of several conversations with him, Aetius revised his opinion, conceding that the man, despite his boastful manner, was in all likelihood extremely competent in his field, and also genuinely devoted to Attila's interests. Such an ally would be invaluable in helping Attila realize his vision.

Aetius thought the plan stood virtually no chance of succeeding, even with a leader of Attila's stature. The Huns, despite rapid social change in the recent past – they now had a hereditary monarchy, an aristocracy of sorts, an economy beginning to be based if not on money, at least on bullion – were too primitive, too freedom-loving and nomadic, to be constrained by laws, taxes, cities, roads, et cetera. But Aetius could not bring himself to disillusion his friend. So, despite his reservations, he had promised to send Attila a team of jurists and administrators to help him start implementing the great design.

* The Baltic.
** Scandinavia.

Although sceptical about its chances, Aetius had been touched and profoundly moved by Attila's vision. That an unlettered barbarian could conceive such a noble project put him, Aetius, to shame, and made him reflect on his own narrow ambitions. Compared to Attila's, they suddenly seemed sordid and petty. Was he really content to be merely a successful warlord, with Gaul as his fief, pulling up the drawbridge while all around him the Western Empire crumbled? After all, did he not owe the Empire an act of reparation? It was his selfish rivalry with Boniface, he at last admitted, that had resulted in the loss of Africa – a potentially fatal blow to the West. With Gaul stabilized by means of Hunnish help, and, he hoped, the federates in time integrated as Roman citizens – a status the Visigoths were already aspiring towards, surely it was not impossible that the lost territories of Britain, Africa, and Galicia in Spain, could be recovered. Their resources and revenue from taxes, could then pump fresh blood into the arteries of Empire.

Why, only six years ago,* Germanus, a former officer of his father's who had turned churchman and become Bishop of Autissiodorum, had shown what could be achieved in Britain, long abandoned by the legions. Sent by Pope Celestine to combat the Pelagian heresy, Germanus had stayed on to organize resistance among the eastern Britons, against a Saxon–Pict alliance. Inspired by the warlike bishop, the British host had raised a mighty cry of 'Alleluia!' and had so demoralized the enemy that they turned and fled without a blow.

The West *could* be made whole again, and Rome perhaps begin a new revival, as in the days of Diocletian and Constantine. It was a task, Aetius knew, which called not only for military reconquest but for a rekindling of patriotic spirit. That would necessitate the rooting out of official corruption, and a fairer distribution of the tax burden. An enormous challenge, certainly – but, given dedicated leadership, surely not an impossible one. The voices of conscience that had so often troubled him in the past suddenly returned – this time with a message not of condemnation but of hope. '*In hoc signo vince*,' they seemed to say, echoing the words of Constantine, when he saw his vision of the Cross: 'In this sign shalt thou conquer.' But what sign?

* In 429; Autissiodorum is now Auxerre.

Then it came to him. Attila's unselfish ambition to build a 'Greater Scythia' – *that* was the examplar he had been vouchsafed. Like Paul on the road to Damascus, Aetius felt that he had been shown a new and worthier path to follow. He arrived back in Gaul filled with optimism and renewed energy. The iron had begun to leave his soul.

TWENTY

They put out a smokescreen of minute calculations involved
in impenetrable obscurity
Edict of Valentinian III against corrupt financial officials, 450

'I've a friend who works in the Treasury at Ravenna,' Synesius, a rising lawyer, said musingly to Flaccus, son of a small landowner. The two young men were in the *calidarium* or hot room of Verona's last functioning bath-house. Flaccus, who had just come into a legacy, was consulting his friend about finding a profitable way to invest some of it. 'For a small consideration,' Synesius went on, 'I daresay I could get him to pull some strings. I happen to know that the post of *canonicarius* – financial overseer – for the land tax from First Belgica is about to fall vacant. It's in the gift of the Praetorian prefect. If your application were successful, the prefect would naturally expect some, ah, "compensation" shall we call it?'

'But . . . isn't that illegal?' exclaimed Flaccus in shocked tones.

'Don't be naive,' sighed Synesius, rolling his eyes. 'Of course it's illegal; I thought everyone knew that. But as long as those in the system turn a blind eye, who cares? Pass that strigil, would you? Thanks. Honestly, you'd think they could manage to lay on a slave or two to scrape you down. Cutbacks – that's all you hear about these days. Well, shall I contact my friend?'

Written at Ravenna, the Treasury, in the consulships of Areobindus and Aspar. Nones Aprilis.*

My dear Synesius, your *sponsio*** much appreciated. I have seen the Praetorian prefect re your friend's application, and he says to tell him that the *suffragium* or going rate for the post is a hundred *solidi*. Of course, your friend will still have

---

* 5 April 434.
** 'Backhander'.

146

to present himself for interview, but that should just be a formality. What's termed 'general merit' (*id est*, good birth, education, and loyalty) is more important than financial aptitude. Anyway, he'll have a small staff of clerks to deal with technical matters.

A hundred *solidi* may seem a largish sum to secure the appointment, so you should point out to your friend that, if he uses his imagination and initiative, he can expect to recoup his outlay at least fourfold during the two years the job will be his. The post does carry a salary: virtually nominal, but then you could hardly expect otherwise, could you?

By the way, in order to arrange my meeting with the prefect, I had to proceed via the *tractator*, his intermediary with the relevant provincial governor. So you'll appreciate that I had to grease a few extra palms. Which alas made quite a dent in the *sponsio*. The things we do for friends! Do you know Rufio's wine shop in Verona, near the amphitheatre? Well, if you were feeling generous, an amphora of Falernian (or Massic at a pinch) despatched by wagon, wouldn't go amiss . . .

'This is nothing short of naked robbery!' shouted the governor of First Belgica. He flung down on his desk the last of the rolls containing the revised assessments for the province's land tax, which Flaccus had presented for his inspection. The two men were in the *tablinum* of the governor's fortified villa overlooking the River Mosella. The room commanded a view of a blighted landscape: ruined vineyards, abandoned villas, fields reverting to scrub and swamp, the results of insecurity caused by recurring Frankish raids. The same landscape that, a mere two generations before, the poet Ausonius had described as smiling and fruitful.

Flaccus shrugged and spread his hands. 'Blame the times,' he said mollifyingly. 'The state must collect the *iugatio** if the army's to be paid. And without the army all this'– he indicated the countryside outside – 'would soon be part of the *barbaricum*.' Rather to his surprise, he had quickly grown a thick skin in the execution of his job. After all, a man had to look out for himself,

---

* land tax.

especially in these uncertain times, and especially as the post was only for two years – not much time in which to set himself up. Besides, it wasn't as though he had to live with these people.

'But in some cases there's a thirty-per-cent increase!' protested the governor. 'How can that possibly be justified?'

'Well, let's look at some examples,' said Flaccus in reasonable tones. 'Take this village, Subiacum. When we re-surveyed it, we found that several hundred productive *iugera** had been omitted in the returns for the past five Indictions.** The tax equivalent has to be made up – plus, I'm afraid, the interest owed.'

'"Productive", you say! Look, I *know* the place. That was poor-quality land hardly worth the trouble of ploughing. It went out of cultivation when the owners fled to escape the tax-collectors. Now there aren't enough *coloni* left to work it, so it's become "deserted land".'

'But not officially. It's not listed as such in the records, you see. All land, unless it's taken out of registration, must be taxed.' Flaccus assumed his most sympathetic smile. 'Nothing personal, you understand. And then a number of *coloni* in Subiacum owe tax arrears. They claimed they didn't – well, they would, wouldn't they? – but when asked for proof, they couldn't produce receipts.'

'But no one thinks to keep receipts – especially not poor, uneducated farm labourers.'

'That's hardly my responsibility,' countered Flaccus smoothly. He shook his head regretfully. 'Believe me, if I could ignore these lapses, I would. I'm just—'

'I know, "doing my job",' interrupted the governor bitterly. He gave Flaccus a searching stare. 'Have you people the least idea how much misery and hardship the land tax causes? To say nothing of all these extra charges you seem able to discover.'

'Times are hard. We must all make sacrifices.'

'Some more than others, I daresay,' retorted the governor, glancing significantly at Flaccus' well-nourished frame and expensive *byrrus*, or hooded cloak. 'Don't worry, you'll get your tax,' he sneered. 'The full amount. But only because the decurions, the poor overworked town councillors, who alone keep the

---

* The *iugerum* was the basic Roman unit of land measurement. One *iugerum* = ⅟, of an acre.

** Roman financial years.

machinery of state from seizing up, have to make up any short-fall out of their own pockets. No wonder they're leaving in droves, seeking promotion or simply taking flight.'

'They can always appeal, you know.' Flaccus injected a note of helpful concern into his voice. 'The courts of the Praetorian prefect and the finance minister are expressly charged with hearing such complaints.'

'And much good would that do them,' snapped the governor. 'They aren't rich enough to afford court expenses and tip the judge.' He gathered up the rolls on his desk. 'Well, don't let me keep you. After all,' he went on with heavy sarcasm, 'you have your job to do.'

TWENTY-ONE

Men live there under the natural law; capital sentences are
marked on a man's bones; there even rustics perorate and
private individuals pronounce judgment
Anonymous, *Querolus* (the Protestor), fifth century

In that vast and dreary landscape, the three men looked like
crawling dots, the only moving things in an expanse of soggy
bottom land, intersected by sluggish tributaries of the lower
Sequana.* They had met by chance south of Samarobriva** three
days previously, and, discovering that they had all forsworn Rome
and had a common destination, had decided to travel together
for mutual security.

The eldest, a spare man in his fifties whose careworn features
bore the stamp of authority, had quickly emerged as their leader.
His once fine but now travel-stained dalmatic hinted at curial
status. He it was who, when the party discovered it was being
followed by hunting dogs – lean shaggy brutes of British ancestry
– had cajoled and bullied his companions into outrunning pursuit
through unimaginable thresholds of pain and exhaustion, until
they could throw off the scent by crossing running water.

The youngest was a rangy lad of eighteen, whose chapped
hands and incipient stoop denoted a farm labourer. A pus-stained
bandage concealed the wound where his right thumb had been.
His gentle face had the stricken expression of a dog whose master
has unexpectedly kicked it.

The third man, who could have been any age between thirty
and fifty, had eyes bleared from much close stitching, and a palm
calloused from the pressure of a cobbler's awl. He had the slack,
desperate expression of one whom circumstances had conspired
to break.

* The Seine.
** Amiens.

For days, the trio struggled westwards through the wetlands, where possible following broken causeways, more often splashing knee- or waist-deep through morasses. As recently as the reign of Gratian, this land had been fertile and well-drained. Now, thanks to depopulation resulting from the combined effects of a crushing land tax and growing insecurity, it was fast reverting to its pristine state – to swell the Register of Deserted Lands in the archives of Ravenna. But at last the ground began to rise, allowing swifter progress, and, ten days after they had met, when they were down to their last scraps of stale bread and rancid pork, they crossed a height of land to find the streams now flowing westwards and to see, in the far blue distance, their goal: the granite hills of Aremorica.

Looking around, Marcellus, the eldest of the trio, saw that the glade in which they had been resting was now fringed by men: nut-brown stalwarts, dressed in an assortment of skins, patched homespun, and the tattered remnants of army uniform or civilian Roman dress. A tall man, whose silver neck-torque and air of command suggested he was the leader, stepped from the ring and addressed the fugitives. 'Welcome to Aremorica. You travel light, I see; business or pleasure?'

An educated voice, Marcellus noted. 'We flee the tyranny of Rome,' he replied, holding the other's gaze. 'We were hoping to start a new life among the Bagaudae who, we've heard, respect freedom and justice – unlike the Roman government.'

'Freedom and justice,' repeated the tall man wryly. 'Noble concepts, but perhaps expensive luxuries when times are hard. Still, we do our best. Our motto is:

> "If each gives what he is able,
> Then all can share a common table."

It seems to work.' He grinned, and added disarmingly, 'Well, most of the time it does.'

'So you are Bagaudae?'

'Bandits? That's what the Romans call us. We prefer the name "Free Aremoricans". Once, we were Roman citizens like you. But, also like you, finding Roman rule oppressive and unjust, we removed ourselves from it and set up our own republic, here in the far north-west.' He surveyed the group appraisingly. 'You'll understand that before we can accept you you'll have to prove you can make a useful contribution to our society. We can't afford to carry passengers. First, however, we'll give you a good meal, which you certainly look as though you could do with.'

For some hours, Marcellus and his companions were escorted along woodland paths. Several times they saw by the side of the track a grim signpost: a stout pole bearing a wooden placard and surmounted by a skull. On asking what they signified, Marcellus was told, 'They're the heads of our executed criminals, with a notice of their sentence.'

Eventually, they arrived in a large clearing containing a dozen long huts, of rough but workmanlike construction. Around them, noisy children played and women cooked. Carrying farming implements, men were filing into the clearing – from nearby fields or plots, Marcellus assumed.

'The capital of my own little fief,' declared the Bagaudae leader. 'We Free Aremoricans are a very loose society, with lots of little communities like this one, each with its own headman and elders. There's an overall Grand Council, and a President – one Tibatto. Also a code of laws that all must subscribe to.'

'And if the laws are broken?'

'Small matters are settled at community level. Major transgressions are dealt with by courts appointed by the Council. Now, my nose tells me supper's almost ready. Come and eat.'

After a welcome and plentiful meal of game pottage, washed down with tart beer, the newcomers were summoned to a meeting of the elders in the largest hut. Here, they were requested to give an account of themselves, in turn. 'My name is Marcellus Publius Bassus,' began the eldest, 'decurion of the imperial city of Augusta Treverorum, in the province of First Belgica.'

It was the time of the Indiction again, the first of September, the beginning of the fiscal year when the annual budget had to be made up and balanced, from the collection of taxes.

In his office in Augusta's vast brick basilica, built a hundred years before by Constantine, Marcellus – one of the councillors responsible for collecting the revenues within the city's fiscal catchment area – groaned aloud. Once, he reflected sadly, men of good family had competed eagerly for the honour of serving the community. But that was back in his great-grandfather's time, before Diocletian had ushered in an era of grim austerity and crushing taxes, to save a sinking empire. Now decurions were mere agents of an oppressive government, required to carry out its more unpopular policies – squeezing money taxes and levies in kind from their fellow citizens, helping to manage imperial mines and estates, and drumming up recruits for the army. Most of the money went to pay for the army, which, ironically, seemed less and less able to protect citizens from barbarian incursions.

Every year the task became harder and more repugnant. But there was no way out, Marcellus thought grimly. Men like himself, owners of twenty-five Roman acres, were compelled to serve as decurions. But not the very rich – senators and knights – who, to add insult to injury, always found ways of evading or postponing paying tax, which left those least able to pay, the poor, to shoulder the bulk of the burden.

This year, the collection of the revenue was going to prove even more difficult. The harvest looked to be the worst in a decade, and a particularly destructive raid by a Frankish war-party (the latest in a long series), had left a swathe of smoking villages and blackened fields in its wake. A compassionate man, Marcellus hated the business of extracting money from poverty-stricken peasants and artisans; for many of them, payment of the standard seven *solidi* might spell financial ruin.

A servitor appeared in the doorway. 'They're here, sir,' he announced nervously. (Marcellus' temper was notoriously short at Indiction time.)

'Well, send them in then, send them in,' Marcellus barked.

Into the office filed two groups of rough-looking men: the *susceptores* responsible for collecting the normal dues, and the *compulsores* charged with enforcing payment of arrears.

'Here's your list.' Marcellus handed a scroll to the *susceptores'* foreman, distinguished from his fellows by a patched and grubby dalmatic. The man nodded and led his team out.

'And here's yours.' Marcellus glared at the leader of the second gang, a brutal-looking thug appointed by the provincial office. 'Just remember,' he grated, 'that like yourselves these people are Roman citizens. They're to be treated with restraint and consideration. If I hear there's been any . . .' Marcellus trailed off in impotent frustration: any threat he made would be an empty one. Failure to collect outstanding dues meant that the shortfall would have to be made up from his own purse and those of his fellow decurions. A blind eye had, perforce, to be turned to methods of extraction.

'Persuasion?' With an insolent grin, the foreman completed Marcellus' phrase. 'We'll be as gentle as lambs, won't we, boys?' he continued, turning to his men, who responded with a chorus of ironic assent. In a significant gesture, some touched the cudgels in their belts.

When the last of the *compulsores* had trooped from the office, Marcellus found that his hands were shaking and his heart was thumping in his chest. A wave of helpless fury swept over him. He felt ashamed – and dirty.

Apprehension gnawed at Petrus the cobbler, making it difficult for him to concentrate on his work. Spraying nails from his mouth, he cursed for the third time that morning, as his hammer struck his fingers instead of the nail he was driving through the sole of the shoe on his last. Replacing the dropped 'sparrow-bills' between his lips, he tried once more to focus on his task. It was no good. The dread that had been building up relentlessly for weeks before the Indiction, seemed to have formed a permanent cold lump in his stomach. The tax-collectors would be arriving at any time, and he could pay them but a fraction of their seven *solidi* – to say nothing of the arrears he owed from the previous Indiction. That none of this was his fault would, he knew, make no whit of difference to the agents of the tax officials.

For most of the last year, by drastic scrimping and saving, and working far into the night by flickering lamplight until his eyes ached, Petrus had managed to earn enough *nummi* – the little copper coins worth seven thousandth of a *solidus* – to cover both amounts owed. Then the Franks, ferocious yellow-haired giants, came rampaging through the district. Fondly, he had thought his hoard – in sealed bags, or *folles*, each containing a thousand *nummi*, and buried inside a jar beneath the earthen floor of his workshop – would be inviolate. But with practised efficiency, the raiders had forced him to disclose it, by the simple expedient of holding his wife's feet to an open fire. Though superficial, the burns had turned septic; a week after the Franks had gone, she had died from blood-poisoning, leaving behind Petrus and their twelve-year-old daughter.

'Let him go,' sighed the *compulsores*' leader in disgust. 'He's telling the truth. Seems the Franks did take his savings.' Reluctantly, his men released Petrus – minus three teeth, and with a broken nose.

The foreman cast an expert eye around the workshop. 'Take the tools and stock,' he ordered. 'They'll fetch something at auction. Then strip the house.'

Petrus' pleas – that without tools he could no longer earn a living and would therefore be unable to pay future tax – were ignored. His few pathetic possessions – an iron cauldron, a bronze skillet, some sticks of furniture and kitchen crockery – joined his work gear on the gang's cart. Then one of the *compulsores* appeared in the workshop, dragging a weeping girl. 'Look what I found hiding in the privy,' he announced with a lascivious leer. 'Skinny as a plucked chicken and a bit on the young side.' He grinned at the foreman. 'But not too young, eh?'

The foreman shrugged and said carelessly, 'Go on, then.'

Helpless in the grip of his tormentors, Petrus roared and wept, while his daughter was raped by all the gang in turn.

'Think of it as part payment in kind,' sneered the foreman, as they departed.

Hours later, Petrus was roused from his stupor of misery and helplessness by an ominous creaking from the living-quarters adjoining his workshop. He rushed into the room and saw his daughter's body gyrating slowly, suspended from a roof beam.

Numb with grief, Petrus buried her in the weed-choked yard behind his cottage. Then, making a bundle of a spare tunic and a stale loaf, all that the tax-collectors had left him, he set out for the west. In Aremorica, so he'd heard, men lived freely and paid no taxes. Now without family or means of livelihood, it seemed he had but one option: to seek a new life beyond the reach of Rome.

Awkwardly, young Martin hefted the axe in his left hand and raised it above his right, which was pressed flat against the log, with thumb extended. His mouth dried, and a red mist seemed to form before his eyes. He could feel his pulses racing. Twice he laid down the axe, his courage failing him at the last moment. Suddenly, he heard the distant calls of searching *bucellarii*, the private retainers whom the landowner, like most Gallic magnates, employed in these times of insecurity. Realizing that if he didn't act now, he might be leaving it too late, Martin gritted his teeth and swung the blade down with all his strength.

From the moment he could walk, Martin had been put to work on the estate where his parents laboured as humble *coloni*. He had always hated the back-breaking drudgery of farmwork, and at every opportunity slipped off to the woods bordering the fields, to study the wild creatures and plants there, to fish, or just to dream. He longed above all to enter a monastery like those he had heard of in far-off Caesarodunum and Limonum,* founded sixty years before by his namesake Martin, who had been a peasant before enlisting in the legions. In such a community his knowledge of plants and animals might, he hoped prove an asset. But when he had asked the landowner for permission to follow his vocation, he had been curtly informed that a recent edict of the Emperor specifically forbade such a thing. He was *adscriptus glebae* – tied to the land – and tied he would remain.

Which left only one avenue of escape from his present lot, the army, an alternative which for a gentle dreamer like Martin, held even fewer attractions than the life of a *colonus*. Like all magnates with large estates, the landowner was required by law to provide recruits for the service, on an ad hoc but fairly regular basis. Invariably, the ones selected were his least useful tenants, so it should have come as no surprise when the steward told Martin to present himself at the estate office the following morning, to await the recruiting-agents. But Martin *was* surprised. Surprised and appalled. The thought that (from the landowner's view) he was an ideal recruit had never occurred to him. His only recourse, he realized with horror, was to amputate a thumb, preferably the right one – the standard way to render oneself ineligible for service.

Martin stared in shock at the severed thumb lying on the ground, then at the raw, gaping wound on his hand, where bone gleamed

* Tours and Poitiers.

briefly white before vanishing in a tide of blood. Without the thumb, it no longer resembled a hand; more the clawed forefoot of an animal. Pain and nausea clubbed him; before fainting, he managed to staunch the bleeding with a pad of spiders' webs secured with a bandage, both of which he had ready.

He stirred into consciousness, saw he was surrounded by *bucellarii*, one of whom was shaking him. He was dragged to the steward's office where, besides that official, were three soldiers in undress uniform of undyed linen tunics, with indigo roundels on the hems and shoulders. Their height and flaxen hair suggested they were Germans, and therefore unlikely to have any local sympathies. Martin saw the steward pass a purse to their *circitor*, the one in charge.

When Martin displayed his thumbless hand, the *circitor* laughed and shook his head. 'Another *murcus*,' he declared, not unkindly. 'You've lost your thumb for nothing, lad. We've orders now to take anyone, mutilated or not. Two *murci* equals one sound recruit.' He pointed at Martin, then at the purse in his hand. 'Two *murci*,' he chuckled.

On the way to the town where his escorts were billeted, they crossed a bridge over a fast-flowing tributary of the Mosella. Martin seized his chance and threw himself over the parapet into the water. He was swept away by the current and carried a mile downstream before he managed to struggle ashore.

Coughing water from his lungs, Martin orientated himself from the sun's position. Motivated more by instinct than a reasoned plan, he began to plod westwards through a sodden waste of osier beds and boggy scrubland. He could hardly return to the estate, not after good money had been paid to be rid of him and spare the landowner the need to provide a second – and sound – recruit. Besides, that would be the first place the recruiting agents would look. Somewhere to the west – how far he didn't know – he'd heard there was a land called Aremorica. A place where men were free and equal, where there were no landlords or *coloni*, no laws tying workers to the land. A place of refuge for a poor, desperate outcast? Well, there was only one way to find out.

When all the tax returns were in and he'd had time to study them, Marcellus, as senior decurion, called an emergency meeting of all the councillors of Augusta Treverorum, to be held in the basilica. The yield in cash and kind was risible – barely half the amount the government demanded, worse by far than for any previous Indiction.

'Well, gentlemen, what's to be done?' said Marcellus, after announcing the results to a shocked curia. 'That's what we're here to decide. I'm open to suggestions.' After having faced up to and absorbed the sheer enormity of the problem, he felt strangely calm.

'How – how could this have happened?' exclaimed the newest member of the Council, a portly, youngish man; his face was ashen and he trembled visibly.

'I think it's been coming for a long time,' replied Marcellus gently, 'but we chose not to see it. This year we've been caught out by a particularly unfortunate combination of circumstances, any one of which alone would have caused us a serious problem. Coming together, their effects have been catastrophic. A terrible harvest, devastating barbarian raids, the field army unable to help because of being tied up in Aquitania and Italia: all that has put an unprecedented strain on taxpayers already hard put to it to pay their dues. The result – predictably in hindsight – has been mass flight to Aremorica or to the landlords of great estates. In the latter case, in exchange for binding themselves over to serfdom, the fugitives will at least be protected from barbarians and rapacious tax-collectors.'

'Disgraceful!' shouted an elderly decurion. 'They should be brought back, flogged, and branded. What's the empire coming to, I'd like to know?'

'A premature end, if we adopt *your* solution,' snapped Marcellus. 'Look, I accept that the government needs money from taxes to pay the army. But the burden's unfairly loaded on to the poor. If the rich could be made to pay in proportion to their wealth, and corruption stamped out among the tax officials, we'd be halfway to solving the problem.'

'No doubt,' put in another councillor in a world-weary voice. 'But we'll have a heat-wave in January before that happens. Meanwhile, we have the little matter of making up the shortfall. Paying it out of our own purses will drive many of us to the wall.'

The meeting dissolved into hubbub, some decurions declaring that they would be ruined, others speculating that they might be forced to pawn the family silver, or sell property in Italia or other parts of Gaul.

Eventually, Marcellus called the meeting to order: 'Gentlemen!' The authority in his voice stilled the uproar. 'If I may make a suggestion, there is a precedent for tax relief being granted to provinces which have suffered from barbarian invasion. For example, in the nineteenth year of the reign of our late Emperor, Honorius, the taxes due for the Suburbicarian provinces of Italia were reduced to one-fifth. I shall write today to the provincial governor, presenting our difficulties as cogently as I can, and requesting that he put our case before the Consistory in Ravenna. Even allowing for the imperfect functioning of the imperial post, I think we may expect a reply within a month. I suggest, therefore, that we meet again whenever that arrives, and review the situation.'

But even before the last of the decurions had left the basilica, Marcellus had quietly made up his mind that he himself would not be present at that meeting. There would, he suspected, be no remission from Ravenna. Valentinian's inefficient administration lacked the will or competence either to reform its tax-gathering machinery, or to make adjustments to ease the financial burden on hard-hit communities. He would no longer, he decided, serve a government that was prepared to crush the poorest of its citizens in order to maintain itself. He would this very day leave for Aremorica, and with luck begin a new life among the Bagaudae. (A widower, whose children had long left home, he had no ties.) Rome, its resources stretched to the limit to retain control in Gaul,had virtually abandoned any pretence of ruling what was still officially the province of Lugdunensis III.

Marcellus had no illusions as to the momentousness of his decision. For a man of his age and position to abandon the life he knew, and take his chance among the outlaws, would test his strength and courage to the utmost. But strangely, as he walked home through streets still bearing the scars of the last barbarian sack of twenty years before, to prepare for his journey, he felt a lifting of the spirit, as though an oppressive burden had been lifted from him.

When the last of the fugitives, Martin, had finished telling his story, the three were sent outside the Council hut to await the elders' decision.

'Let the decurion stay,' pronounced the leader. 'He is old, beyond working in the fields, but he has integrity and wisdom. He would be an asset in helping us run our community. I suggest we also keep the cobbler. His spirit may be broken, but that hardly affects his practical skills – skills we are in sore need of. Are we all agreed so far?'

There was a general murmur of assent.

'Good. The boy, however, is a different matter. He is young and strong, but his self-inflicted wound severely curtails his usefulness. Also, someone who is prepared to cut off his thumb to avoid military service shows a lack of moral fibre.'

'Are we to send him away, then?' asked an elder.

'That would not be wise. The lad is a liability – to himself as well as to us. If we let him go, he might become a security risk by turning informer to the Romans.' The leader paused expectantly, but no voice was raised in dissent. 'That's settled, then.' He nodded at a burly member of the group. 'See to it. Make sure there are no witnesses, and that the body won't be found.'

TWENTY-TWO

The poor are being robbed, widows groan, orphans are trodden down, so that many seek refuge with the Bagaudae
Salvian, *On the Government of God*, c. 435

Tibatto raised his arms and a hush spread throughout the ruined amphitheatre, its tiers close-packed with humanity from every part of north-west Gaul between the Liger and the Sequana.* If the vast crowd could be characterized by one single factor, that factor was diversity. The majority were *coloni*, peasants and small-holders dressed in patched or ragged tunics; there were also many whose once-fine dalmatics betrayed their curial status; others bore on their arms the brands of slaves or conscripts, the latter distinguishable from the former by the callus under the chin from the knot securing the cheek-pieces of a helmet; here and there a cobbler or tailor with hunched shoulders, a smith with brawny biceps. All, whatever their origins, had this in common: they now belonged to the huge and growing class that officialdom had proscribed as *perditi*, criminals and outlaws, to be hunted down and exterminated without distinction and without pity.

Tibatto stood in the president's box from which senators, and once the would-be emperor Magnus Maximus, had opened the games, and surveyed his audience. A bald, powerfully built figure, with strong yet sensitive features, the outlaw leader had a presence which commanded attention and respect. His background was a mystery. Some said he had been a soldier, others a judge; he had been a senator who, disgraced, had changed his name, a wealthy merchant who had lost his fortune, a courtier fallen from favour, et cetera, et cetera.

'Friends and fellow Gauls,' he began, speaking in a clear, resonant voice, the voice of an educated man, but one who had the common touch, 'for five hundred years, ever since Julius Caesar

* The Loire and the Seine.

161

placed it on our necks, we have endured the yoke of Rome. It has been a heavy yoke, grown more and more oppressive, and at last become intolerable. None of you here present is guilty of wrongdoing – unless it is a crime to refuse any more to pay unjust taxes or render services grown too demanding. The poor toil yet starve, their earnings eaten up by rents and levies, while the rich pay nothing. We are forced to choose between death from hunger and a life of robbery. What choice is that? "Bagaudae" bandits – that is what Rome calls us. But it is Rome which has forced us to become so.' Tibatto paused, and looked around the ranks of rapt faces, then went on, his voice rising to a passionate shout. 'As Rome has rejected us, so shall we reject Rome. Let us throw off the yoke of our oppressors. Rome grows weak and is beset by enemies. Our time is at hand; be ready for the signal. When it comes, rise and strike – for Gaul and freedom!'

Silence. Then, scattered at first, gradually merging in a solid roar, from all over the amphitheatre voices took up the rallying-cry, 'For Gaul and freedom!'

'"*His rebus confectis, Caesar cum copiis magnis in fines Germanorum progredit*",' Marcus read from the scroll, slowly but without stumbling. It was his daily Latin lesson with Gaius Valerius.

'Good,' said Gaius warmly. 'Splendid. Now, the translation?' Little Marcus was proving an apt pupil. He had a quick mind and, unusually in one so young, an ability to concentrate and persevere until he succeeded in whatever task he set himself – damming a stream, climbing a tree, or teasing out the meaning of a Latin sentence.

Gaius was happy. He had adapted well to living among his daughter-in-law's extended family, coming to like these Germans for their frank, open ways and genuine hospitality. Helped by his grandson, he was picking up German and could now converse fairly easily. Less and less did he miss the refinements of a Roman lifestyle – baths, plumbing, central heating, elaborate meals. In fact, the spartan conditions of a simple hut (Titus had ordered one especially constructed for his father, a typical oblong *Grubenhaus* with sunken floor) rather appealed to him, as being closer to the austere standards of his heroes from the great days of the Roman Republic: Regulus, the Scipios, Cato the Censor, et cetera. One luxury, however, he did permit himself: books.

Titus had arranged for a consignment to be sent from the Villa Fortunata, which was prospering under the system Titus had initiated. (In fact, Titus was there at the moment, supervising a land-drainage project.)

'"*His rebus*" . . . "By these things"?' offered Marcus, in German, his mother tongue. He looked at his grandfather hopefully, then frowned and shook his head. 'No, that's not right.'

'Ablative absolute?' Gaius prompted.

'Of *course*,' the boy acknowledged. He scrutinized the passage. 'I've got it now. "Having completed these matters, Caesar advanced into the territory of the Germans."'

'Rather risky to do that on his own, wouldn't you think?' said Gaius solemnly.

'Forgot. "*Cum copiis magnis* – with large forces". There, finished.' He looked at Gaius with a triumphant grim. 'Was that all right, Grandfather, and can I go and play now?'

'The answer's yes on both counts. Off you go, and don't be late for supper. Your mother's grilling those trout you caught yesterday.'

At the hut's entrance, Marcus paused and looked back. 'Grandfather, if Julius Caesar was Roman, why would he attack the Germans? You're Roman. Father's Roman, Mother's German, Grandfather Vadomir's German. I thought the Romans and the Germans were friends.'

'Bless you, boy,' laughed Gaius. 'And so they are. Romans and Germans get on fine. Julius Caesar lived a long time ago. Things have changed since his day.'

But had they really changed? Gaius wondered, when the boy had gone. When he had first come to live in the Burgundian Settlement, he had felt that a genuine rapport was possible between the Gallo-Romans and the new settlers, which boded well for the future. After all, the Gauls themselves had strenuously rejected Rome at first, and look at them now – more Roman than the Romans. On a personal level, he had experienced nothing but kindness and hospitality from his German hosts, and was finding it easier to adapt and integrate than once he could have imagined possible.

Of late, however, he had begun to wonder if perhaps a change of attitude was taking place among the Burgundians. It was nothing he could put his finger on: a shade more abruptness on the part

163

of local Germans in their dealings with him, a touch less warmth in their greetings. With the exception of Clothilde, wife of Titus and mother of little Marcus, his German in-laws, though still friendly, sometimes seemed stiff and awkward in his presence, almost as if they should not be talking to him. Gaius told himself that he was imagining things, that any perceived change of mood was not directed at him personally, but probably resulted from a poor harvest followed by a hard winter; the newest of the grave-rows outside the village had lengthened markedly during the cold season just past. His soldier's instinct, however, told him not to relax his vigilance – just in case. In case of what? But to that he had no answer.

'Sorry, Mark, Father says I'm not to play with you any more.' Hariulf, the blacksmith's son and Marcus' best friend, hung his head and scratched the earth apologetically with a bare toe.

'*Komm zurück, Junge,*' called the blacksmith, appearing in the doorway of the forge.

'I'd better go back,' muttered Hariulf. Avoiding Marcus' eyes, he turned and shuffled back towards the smithy.

Disconsolately, Marcus wandered off through the scatter of thatched longhouses which made up the village, passed through one of the entrances of the surrounding timber palisade, then struck out over the common pasture to the edge of the forest. This made the fifth day in a row that Hariulf had avoided his company. On the other days he'd made excuses; but this time-he'd actually been forbidden. Why? Except for that time when he'd crossed the stream on a fallen tree, and Hariulf had followed him and fallen in, Marcus hadn't got his friend into any scrapes. It just didn't make any sense. Well, in the absence of a playmate, he would visit the otter's holt he'd discovered in a hollow tree by the river. With luck, he'd be able to watch the cubs playing with their mother.

A sudden sharp blow on his back made him turn. On the ground lay the stone that had struck him. Two boys, the swine-herd's sons, stood facing him twenty paces away. Oafish and stupid, they tended to pick on boys younger or smaller than themselves. '*Schwarzkopf! Schwarzkopf!*' they taunted, alluding to the dark hair Marcus had inherited from his Roman father, which marked him out from fair-haired German boys. '*Blöde*

Römer.' One still had a stone in his hand, and now threw it. Easily dodging, Marcus grabbed the stone on the ground, hurled it, and had the satisfaction of seeing it smack into his assailant's knee. The boy yelled in surprise and pain, then both rushed at Marcus.

Marcus raced into the forest, hoping to throw them off among the trees. Naturally agile and fleet of foot, he began to draw ahead, diving into a thicket when he was sure that he was out of sight and earshot of his pursuers. A short time later, snapping twigs and rustling undergrowth told him they were heading in his direction. The sounds grew nearer, stopped close to where he was sheltering. Marcus crawled to the edge of the coppice and peered out. A few paces off, the swineherd's sons were talking. Marcus strained to hear their words.

'We've lost him,' said the elder. 'Let's go back.'

'May as well, I suppose,' agreed the other. 'Though I don't like letting him get away with hurting my knee. Roman pig. Anyway, he and the other Romans have got it coming to them. I overheard Father talking about a meeting of the tribe's leaders on the night of the coming full moon. At the Wotan Stein. They're going to be told about a plan to—'

'Sssh, *Dummkopf*,' interrupted the elder angrily. 'We're not supposed to know anything about that, never mind talk about it. Come on, let's go.'

Marcus counted slowly to a thousand, before leaving the thicket and heading for home.

From the ruined watchtower built back in the time of Marcus Aurelius as part of the Rhenish frontier defences, Gaius looked down on the moonlit scene. A vast and growing crowd was assembling on the floor of the huge chasm, its walls seamed with crags and precipices, with here and there a lofty pine sprouting from a crevice where soil had gathered. This was a natural fault, a titanic gash in the rocks which, so ran the legend, was the result of a blow from Wotan's sword. In the centre of the space loomed a massive rock, the Wotan Stein, on which stood Gundohar, King of the Burgundians: a gigantic figure, majestic in embroidered cloak and richly decorated *Spangenhelm*, the conical segmented helmet favoured by German warriors who could afford it. The whole wild scene put Gaius in mind of one of those German legends featuring gods and warrior-heroes, engaged in epic battle set in some grim rock-girt wilderness.

Gaius had listened with mounting concern to Marcus' account of the conversation he had overheard in the forest. The meeting at such a charged spot as the Wotan Stone, with its association with heroic German myth, might have a military significance, especially in the context of veiled threats against Romans. The Burgundians might now be Christians (although only recently converted, and of the heretical Arian persuasion) and officially allies of Rome. But these constraints might well be skin-deep. The old general knew from experience how readily the German fighting spirit could flare up, and once aroused make them ferocious opponents. Even now, the Visigoths – the most Romanized of the German tribes, after tramping round the empire for nearly two generations before being granted a homeland – couldn't be trusted to remain at peace. On the other hand, the meeting at the Wotan Stone might be nothing more than a festive or ritual gathering, the boys' chauvinistic words concerning Romans mere childish boasting. Still, his vague feelings of a cooling of attitude towards himself on the part of the Burgundians – something now apparently extended to his grandson – couldn't be ignored. Gaius had decided that the only thing to do was to attend the gathering in secret, and learn for himself what was afoot.

He had said nothing about his intention to Marcus' mother, Clothilde, or to the boy himself, merely stating that he had to go on a short journey. Then, exchanging his dalmatic for a coarse woollen tunic and the once-despised trousers, he had pulled on stout rawhide boots, flung a cloak over his shoulders, and, early in the morning of the day before the meeting, set off, carrying a satchel of provisions prepared by Clothilde. It was a full day's journey to the Wotan Stone; arriving shortly before sunset, Gaius had taken up position in the old watchtower, before settling down for a night's sleep prior to his vigil.

Before the King had uttered a dozen words, Gaius felt a thrill of horror as his worst suspicions were confirmed.

'Burgundians, are we sheep, meekly to obey the Roman shepherds?' Gundohar began, in a growling shout. 'Thirty years ago, I led you across the frozen Rhenus to claim our present homeland by right of conquest. Our nation since has prospered and multiplied, and now we need more land – land to the west and the north that is there for the taking. The Romans say we must be satisfied with what we have. But Rome has grown too soft and weak to stop us. If they lack the spirit or the power to defend what they claim is their territory – land which they themselves once seized from the Gauls – they no longer deserve to hold it. I say to you, let us take it for ourselves.'

A roar of approval greeted his words. When the acclamation had subsided, Gundohar continued: 'Let us choose the moment of attack to our advantage. My spies tell me that the Visigoths in Aquitania intend shortly to invade Provincia. More importantly, the Bagaudae in the north-west are planning a general uprising, to begin on the fifteenth day of May. Let us strike on that same day. Rome will then have two enemies to fight at the same time, perhaps even three if the Visigoths march. Weak, her forces divided, Rome can surely never stand against our warriors. Their dead will be our gift to the raven and the wolf. Return now to your homes, and send out the summons for all men aged sixteen to sixty to assemble here in arms upon the day.'

Long after the last man had departed from the scene, Gaius struggled to resolve an agonizing dilemma. The Ides of May – only four days away! His immediate thought was that he must return home with all speed to warn Clothilde that, as the wife of a Roman, she might be at risk in the upsurge of anti-Roman feeling that would accompany the rising. And Marcus, as the son of a Roman, would be in even greater jeopardy. Also, in the event of a Roman counter-attack, the Burgundian Settlement would become a war zone, with perilous consequences. There was still time for Clothilde and Marcus to flee the Settlement and reach the safety of the province of Maxima Sequanorum, under Roman administration, before the fatal day; but only if he set out immediately to warn them of their danger.

And there lay the rub. The nearest Roman garrison, Spolicinum on Lacus Brigantinus (coincidentally, the fort where Titus had once served as a clerk) lay many miles to the south-east – too far for Gaius to warn them in time, were he first to make a journey to alert Clothilde. With a heavy heart, the old soldier realized where his first duty lay: he must set out for Spolicinum at first light, even though it meant abandoning his daughter-in-law and grandson to an uncertain fate. The thought that his exemplars – those iron men of Rome's heroic age – would have taken the same course without hesitation was little comfort. But, like that Roman (or was it Spartan?) matron who would rather have seen her son's body brought home on a shield than that he should shun the battle, he must be strong. In a mood of sombre resolution, Gaius began to plan his route to Spolicinum.

TWENTY-THREE

At daybreak, when loth to rise, bear this thought in mind:
I am rising for a man's work
                                        Marcus Aurelius, *Meditations, c.* 170

Forced to think the unthinkable, Gaius acknowledged to himself
that the impending crisis – simultaneous risings by the
Burgundians, the Bagaudae, and the Visigoths – was one of
the most serious Rome had ever faced. Conceivably, it might deal
the Western Empire – already terribly weakened by the loss of
Africa – a blow from which it could not recover. Always in the
past, the times had thrown up a man of sufficient stature to meet
the challenge of external danger: a Scipio to match Hannibal, a
Marcus Aurelius to hold the line against the Quadi along the
Rhenus and Danubius, an Aurelian to wipe out the Alamanni
sweeping into Italia, a Boniface to crush the Moors in Africa. But
now, with Boniface gone, who was there in the West capable of
dealing with the present danger? Reluctantly, Gaius was forced
to face the unpalatable truth that the answer was the man who
had first betrayed then destroyed Boniface: Flavius Aetius. Well,
so be it. A great leader need not necessarily be a good man, more's
the pity. After all, Julius Caesar's path to greatness had been stained
by treachery, bloodshed, and deceit.

With the fate of the West hanging in the balance, his choice
of route to Spolicinum was of crucial importance. He had two
options. The first was to head south-west down the Rhenus valley
to Basilia from his present position south of Argentoratum, then
follow the Rhenus which now turned sharply east, to the southern
shore of Lacus Brigantinus on which the fort was situated.

The advantage of this route was that it was easy: it followed
top-grade military roads built when the Rhenish salient was of
vital strategic importance. That frontier might now be abandoned, but roads of such quality would still be serviceable. There
were, however, two disadvantages. The route, at least as far as

Basilia, lay in the broad fertile valley of the upper Rhenus, thickly studded with Burgundian settlements. With the rising imminent, anyone suspected of being Roman would be at risk. (Even before its proclamation, the ordinary tribespeople seemed to have been aware that something was brewing, hence the anti-Roman feeling Gaius had sensed.) The other disadvantage was the route's length: forming two sides of a triangle, it must measure at least two hundred miles, an impossible distance for someone of Gaius' years to cover on foot in four days.

The second option was to cut south-east across country to Lacus Brigantinus in a straight line. By following this third side of the triangle, the distance would be almost halved, representing an average daily stint of about thirty miles – feasible although demanding, especially for an old man. This route, apart from being much shorter, had the great advantage that it was known to Gaius – although from thirty-three years previously. To counter the lightning advance of Alaric's Goth host into Raetia, Stilicho had summoned Roman troops from wherever they were stationed in the West, even including the Twentieth Legion in Britain. Gaius' unit, then stationed on the Rhenus, had made a forced march to the threatened province, over the same route that he now intended to take. The terrain was punishing, a densely wooded mountain-chain which the Germans called the Schwarzwald.* The way was navigable, using certain mountain peaks as landmarks, and threading certain valleys; Gaius just hoped he could remember them. The area was however sparsely inhabited, so security shouldn't be a major problem. With a touch of gallows humour, Gaius reviewed his plan in military fashion.

1. *Objective*
   The Roman fort of Spolicinum on Lacus Brigantinus.
2. *Aim*
   To warn (within four days) Spolicinum's garrison about the risings of the Burgundians et alii.
3. *Means*
   i Manpower: one retired general, reasonably fit but aged.
   ii Rations: bread, salt beef, and beer – enough to last

* The Black Forest.

several days. (Clothilde has been generous with her
provisioning.)

iii Weapons: lacking. (Except in areas troubled by
Bagaudae, Roman civilians are forbidden by law to carry
them.)

iv Base and communications: non-existent.

v Route: south-east across the Schwarzwald from the
Rhenus to Lacus Brigantinus. Distance approximately
100 miles.

Gaius woke in the grey dawn, chilled and stiff after his second
night in the watchtower. Feeling every one of his seventy-seven
years, he rose gingerly from the bed he'd made from last autumn's
fallen leaves, and flexed the stiffness from his joints. What was it
Marcus Aurelius (one of Gaius' heroes) had said about getting up
at dawn? 'When loth to rise, bear this thought in mind: I am
rising for a man's work.' Very appropriate in the present circumstances, Gaius thought wryly. Shivering beneath his cloak, he ate
some of the food Clothilde had provided, washing it down with
beer from a leather flagon. A robin whirred down from a gap in
the roof, and perched on a fallen beam beside him. Its feathers
fluffed up against the cold so that it resembled a tiny red and
brown ball, it hopped closer, regarding Gaius hopefully with a
bold, bright eye. Smiling, he tossed it some crumbs, and they
partook of breakfast together.

Somewhat cheered by the visit of his feathered guest, which
– had he still really believed in the old gods – might have seemed
a good omen, Gaius left the watchtower and took stock of the
terrain. To the west, in Gaul, rolled the long line of the Vosegus
Mountains, their crests glowing in the sun's early rays. Eastwards,
across the Rhenus in Germania, loomed the forbidding mass of
the Schwarzwald, covered in dark firs, except where isolated peaks
broke through the dense pelt of vegetation. Spring had come late
that year, and patches of snow speckled the high summits. At the
foot of the bluff on which he stood flowed the Rhenus, its broad
valley, once chequered by vineyards and fertile farms, now
reverting to scrub, the sites of villas marked by roofless ruins and
weed-choked fields. In their place had sprung up isolated hamlets,
each a score or so of thatched huts encircled by a palisade and
surrounded by an untidy jumble of arable plots and pasture.

'*Sic transit gloria mundi*,' or, more appropriately, '*gloria Romae*,' thought Gaius sadly, as he made his way down to the river. For a few *nummi*, he was able to persuade an early-rising farmer to row him across the river, and was pleased that neither his appearance nor his German aroused any curiosity. In a few hours, heading south-eastwards by the sun, he had crossed the flat valley-bottom and reached the foothills of the Schwarzwald.

He paused to rehearse the key features of his route, aware that any miscalculation could be disastrous. He tried to create in his mind a map of the Schwarzwald: a great triangular massif, narrow at the top or northern end, wide at the base demarcated by the Rhenus where the river turned eastwards, and bisected by a chain of mountains running north to south. He combed his memory for the landmarks he must locate to have any hope of tracing his route. Separating the foothills from the massif proper there was, he seemed to remember, a stream called the Gutach, after crossing which he must surmount the steep western flanks of the chain, where it would be fatally easy to become lost in the tangle of

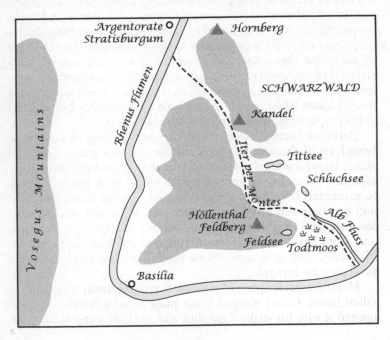

valleys that seamed the slopes. Once the height of land was reached, the worst would be over. An ancient trackway, the Hohenweg, followed the ridge, whose main summits were the Kandel and the Feldberg, to a deep ravine called the Höllenthal, running west to east and leading to the valley of the River Alb which debouched into the Rhenus upstream of Lacus Brigantinus.

Reassured at finding the Gutach more or less where he remembered it, Gaius forded the stream at a point where the channel braided. Then, in order to avoid those treacherous ravines, he struck up one of the lateral spurs that ran down from the mountain-chain like ribs projecting from a backbone. Tall, dense-packed, rising from a mossy carpet studded with ferns and berry-bearing plants, the pines closed round Gaius, enshrouding him in a twilight world suffused with a not unpleasant smell of resin and damp mould.

Gradually the slope steepened, at times becoming precipitous; on these pitches Gaius could make progress only by gripping branches and hauling himself bodily upwards. His breath became a series of tortured gasps, his leg-muscles, unaccustomed to this sort of punishment, seemed on fire with pain. More and more frequently he was forced to halt and rest his trembling limbs, while he sucked air into burning lungs. Navigation, by the angle of the slope and occasional glimpses of the sun, was virtually reduced to guesswork. Not until he had climbed above the tree-line and reached the summit chain, a matter of ascending some four thousand feet, would he be able to check his bearings by getting a sighting on one of the landmark peaks.

Darkness found him still on the westward-facing slopes. To be benighted in the forest at high altitude was not good. Cold and attack by wild animals presented real risks. However, most large animals – bear, bison, and wild boar – had been hunted almost to extinction by gangs supplying animals for the Roman Games, and had only recently begun to recover. Lynx and wildcat were less rare, and capable of inflicting serious damage, but were shy, and dangerous only when threatened. Which left wolves. Normally, they gave man a wide berth, but they might attack if prompted by hunger.

Making separate piles of dry wood, ranging from tiny twigs to fallen limbs, Gaius scraped some punk from a hollow log and ignited it with his strike-light flint and steel. Blowing steadily on the smouldering tinder until it burst into flame, the old soldier fed it from the fuel he had prepared, until he had a vigorous blaze going. Gratefully, he huddled close to its cheering warmth.

Ribs showing through its matted coat, the old wolf that had been trailing Gaius, halted when it saw the fire flare up. Fires meant danger, searing pain, light that dazzled and confused. He lay down on his belly, eyes fixed on the figure crouching with hands extended towards the flames. He was content to wait, knowing from experience that, come the dawn, the man would kill the fire and begin to move again.

The wolf had seen the passing of twelve winters, none more bitter than the last. He was a huge animal and in his prime had been magnificent, with a glossy pelt of thick grey fur, shading from near-black to whitish on the belly. A successful pack leader for many years, he had fathered many strong cubs, all from the same dam. Then, four winters previously, his life had changed traumatically. His mate had fallen to a hunter's spear; he pined for her, his leadership had lost its edge and he had been ousted by a younger rival. Forced to hunt alone, he had subsisted well enough until last winter when the red deer and the roe, his staple prey, had become scarce because, unable to dig through the crust of hard-frozen snow to browse on the underlying vegetation, many had died or migrated. He had been reduced to hunting small rodents. Once, in desperation, he had tried to steal the bait from a hunter's trap; hunger had made him careless, and he set off the deadfall, which collapsed, maiming a forepaw. Now, lame and starving, the wolf had suppressed his instinctive fear of man and, in order to survive, was prepared to hunt and kill this member of their kind. The man, he sensed, was old and weak. He should be easy prey.

Gaius slept in brief snatches throughout the long, long night, tending the fire in the intervals between. As the first grey light filtered through the branches, he kicked out the embers and continued on his way. Gradually, he became aware of a faint booming sound. The noise grew louder, the earth began to tremble, and suddenly, entering a glade, he found himself confronting a mighty waterfall crashing and foaming down hundreds of feet in seven wild leaps from platforms of granite. The Falls of Triberg, he remembered, with a lifting of the spirit;

he was now not far below the height of land. He pressed on; soon the trees thinned out, giving place to grassy slopes with here and there an isolated stand of mountain pine, and at last he stood on the summit ridge.

The weather was crisp and clear, so that even distant tops – the Herzogenhorn, the Belchen, the Kandel – stood out sharp-etched against the sky. Anxiously, he scanned the horizon to the south-east, and there it was, his main landmark: round-topped and bare, towering above the other peaks: the Feldberg. Spent but enormously relieved, the old general sank down and unbuckled his satchel. The worst was behind him. With the going now comparatively level, he should tonight reach the Höllenthal below the Feldberg; and tomorrow should see him through that narrow valley to the Alb, and then the Rhenus. The back of the journey would then be broken, and he could expect to reach Spolicinum on the fourth day as planned.

Having breakfasted, Gaius set out feeling much refreshed, and still uplifted in spirit; provided the weather held, allowing him to keep the Feldberg and the Kandel in view, navigation should no longer be a problem. Especially as there was now a clear-marked ridgeway track to follow, the Hohenweg. In contrast to the previous day, the going on the tops was superb, being firm gravel or springy turf. From the Kandel, fantastic views unrolled around him: the Vosegus and Mons Jura ranges and the distant rampart of the Alpes, while below, set off by the forest's sombre green, tarns gleamed like turquoises. Then, at some point in the afternoon, his soldier's instinct told him he was being followed. Turning, he saw some fifty paces behind him a huge wolf, long of leg and muzzle, gaunt to the point of emaciation, its fur dull and staring, lips drawn back in a snarl baring rows of vicious fangs.

Gaius experienced a moment of gut-churning fear. Clearly, the wolf had only one purpose in its mind, and he was in the poorest position imaginable to resist attack. He was remote from habitation; he had no weapon, not even a stick. Above all, he was old, lacking the strength to fend off an attack – something the wolf would have sensed instinctively, reinforcing its determination and aggression. Yet there had to be something he could do; there always was, even in the most desperate situation – as he had learnt during years of hard campaigning.

Then it dawned on Gaius that he was not, after all, entirely without means of defence; these grassy tops, studded with granite outcrops, were littered with stones of every shape and size. Even the heaviest stone, with only the power of an arm behind it, wouldn't suffice to counter an attack by a savage wolf, but arm-power could be assisted. Propelled by a sling, a tiny pebble acquired enough force to kill. Think man, think. He had it! Dumping the contents of his satchel on the ground, Gaius hastily refilled it with stones, then hefted it by the carrying-strap, testing its weight and swing. Now he had a truly formidable weapon, the equiva-lent of the gladiator's ball-and-chain.

The wolf attacked suddenly, coming at Gaius in a weaving rush. He swung the weighted satchel, missed, tried to dodge but felt the slashing teeth rake his thigh. Had its damaged foreleg not slowed the wolf's impetus, it would have inflicted serious injury instead of merely a nasty gash. Twice more it charged, coming in from the side, gaining in confidence as its teeth ripped the man's flesh. Both times Gaius' improvised weapon missed its target, mainly because of the difficulty in co-ordinating timing and balance to deliver an effective sideways blow.

Nevertheless, he knew that if he could hold on, and shut his mind to the pain and loss of blood, his chance would come. So far, the wolf had been probing for weaknesses, testing his reactions. Sooner rather than later, in order to finish the contest, it must launch a frontal attack. Gaius now had the feel of his weapon; could he but land a solid blow, the odds might tilt in his favour.

On its fourth attack, the wolf came in for the kill, charging straight at Gaius and, when a few paces distant, springing for the throat. But Gaius was prepared. Already whirling the satchel round his head to build up impetus, he timed his blow sweetly. As the huge animal hurtled through the air towards him, the bag, with the full impact of its massive weight, slammed into the crea-ture's head with a meaty crunch. The animal collapsed on the ground, its head and neck horribly missapen. Gaius swung the satchel in a second tremendous blow, and crushed the beast's skull like a stove-in barrel. A shudder rippled through the wolf's body, then it lay still.

Reaction hit Gaius. He swayed, as blackness seemed to gather before his eyes. But he must not faint, he told himself; he must find the will-power and the strength to keep going and complete his mission. His wounds were bleeding copiously, so he tore strips from his tunic to make bandages, and managed to staunch the worst of the bleeding. Emptying the stones from his satchel, he replaced them with the provisions scattered on the ground. Though his stomach rose against it, he made himself eat in order to keep his strength up. Then, slowly and painfully, he resumed his journey, forcing himself gradually to increase his pace, in an effort not to lose time.

He reached the Höllenthal just as the sun was setting, and in the semi-darkness managed to clamber down the ravine's steep and craggy nearer wall to its floor, aware that, in his weakened state, a night spent on the exposed tops might see him perish from the cold. Too tired to gather fuel for a fire, he passed the hours of darkness in a fitful doze, shivering beneath his cloak.

Next morning, he pressed on eastwards through the Höllenthal. The name, which meant Valley of Hell, was apt, he thought, oppressed by the savage chaos of rocky turrets that loomed on either side. The ravine narrowed, became wilder, the fantastic spires and crags of its containing walls seeming to defy every law of order and possibility. Then, with a welcome though almost shocking suddenness, the grim scene changed to one of beauty. The valley broadened, the grisly cliffs fell back, replaced by gentle slopes of green studded with groves of beech and starred by flowers, while the air was filled with birdsong and the chirring of grasshoppers. This, Gaius recalled, was called the Himmelreich, the Kingdom of Heaven.

The rest of that day passed in a dreamlike blur. He seemed to have crossed a threshold, beyond which pain and tiredness were scarcely felt. After skirting a marshy tract, the Todtmoos, or Dead Man's Swamp, he joined the Albthal, a desolate valley lined with firs and beech growing between grey outcrops of granite. At times the Alb was a gently rippling stream, at others, where the valley twisted and steepened, a mountain torrent swirling round bends and crashing against rocks in cascades of spray. In these stretches, Gaius could proceed only with the utmost difficulty, clinging precariously to moss-grown crags and overhanging branches, as he worked his way along banks whose slopes at times approached the vertical. Then suddenly, far below him through a gap in the trees, he glimpsed a mighty river, slow-moving, majestic: the Rhenus! And those wooded slopes fringing the farther side were the Roman province of Maxima Sequanorum.

By now totally exhausted, Gaius staggered and stumbled the last few miles, reaching the Rhenus late in the afternoon. Shortly afterwards he was picked up by a state barge carrying timber and building stone, bound for Felix Arbor, a fortress on Lacus Brigantinus to the east of Spolicinum. At sunset, the barge put in at a landing-stage on the Roman side for the night, and the following morning rowed slowly upstream and entered the lake. Some hours later, Gaius was helped on to the pier serving Spolicinum, where some off-duty soldiers volunteered to take him to the commandant. He was delirious and very weak, but his mind cleared long enough for him to convey the news about the risings in Gaul.

As a personal favour, he asked that a messenger be sent to his son at the Villa Fortunata, and this was readily granted. Calling for a diptych, he scratched a brief letter to Titus, then tied the cords and gave it to the bearer. Gaius lingered for a few more hours, while the fort's surgeon fought to save his life. But the old soldier's heart had been overtaxed and he had lost too much blood. He died murmuring lines from Namatianus' poem of farewell to Rome: ' "*Te canimus semperque, sinent dum fata, canemus: hospes nemo potest immemor esse tui.*" '*

---

* 'Thee we sing [O Rome], and shall ever sing, while the fates permit; no guest of thine can be forgetful of thee.' This noble poem was penned in 410 – ironically, the very year in which, a few months later, Rome was taken and sacked by Alaric.

TWENTY-FOUR

*He [Aetius], uniquely, was born for the salvation
of the Roman Republic*
Jordanes, *Gothic History*, 551

'*Unconquered Eternal Rome, Salvation of the World*', ran the inscription on the coin that Aetius, awaiting the arrival of his officers at his headquarters in Provence, absently rolled between his fingers. The obverse showed Valentinian in armour dragging a barbarian by the hair, the reverse a winged figure representing Victory. (Officially it was an angel, but the symbolism was obvious.) Aetius smiled at the irony of the coin's message. Did those idiots of *procuratores* who ran the mints at Rome, Mediolanum, and Ravenna, really think that such fatuousness fooled anyone?

The officers began to file into the command tent. When all were seated, Aetius took up his position beside a large campaign map of Gaul, supported on an easel facing his audience.

'Serious news, gentlemen,' he announced briskly, 'just arrived by fast courier from Raetia. It seems that trouble's breaking out in Gaul on three fronts. First, Aremorica.' With a pointer he circumscribed a large area in north-west Gaul. 'The Bagaudae have risen in revolt against the big landowners and the Roman authorities in general. Second, the Burgundian Settlement.' The pointer indicated a strip of territory along the upper Rhenus. 'The tribe's broken its boundaries and is invading the Belgic provinces. Thirdly, our friends the Visigoths in Aquitania.' The wand rapped south-west Gaul. 'Up to their old tricks again; hoping to expand their territory eastwards. It seems they're preparing to invest Gallia Narbonensis. Any questions, gentlemen, before I go on?'

'How do ve know all sis?' asked a German cavalry commander.

'It's thanks to General Rufinus, whom some of the older ones among you may remember. Apparently, he was able to spy on a convention of Burgundian leaders, and overheard their king telling them what I've told you. He then covered over a hundred miles on foot through rough country, to bring the news from Gaul to Spolicinum fort in Raetia. Got mauled by a wolf on the way, and died later from wounds and exhaustion. Rome owes that brave old man a debt, gentlemen. Thanks to him, we've learnt about the situation early enough to be able to take effective counter-measures.'

'And those are, sir?' This anxiously from a middle-aged *protector*, or senior officer.

'I was coming to that. You're probably thinking that, with just one field army to cope with three major insurrections simultaneously, we'd be hopelessly overstretched.'

'Well, wouldn't we?' interrupted a tough-looking duke. 'Putting it bluntly, sir, I don't see how we can cope. If it was just the Bagaudae on their own we had to deal with, we could manage – they're a rabble of slaves and peasants. But these wretched federates, the Burgundians and Visigoths, they're a different matter. In my opinion, we'd be well advised to sue for peace and, for the time being, grant them the land they want.'

'If you'd allow me to finish,' Aetius protested mildly, 'I was going to add that our field army won't have to fight on its own. Reinforcements have been promised and should be arriving any day.'

'Household troops from Italia, I suppose,' sneered the duke. 'Much use they'll be. Parade soldiers who spend more time polishing their kit than campaigning.'

Aetius raised his hands in exasperation. 'You've a short memory,' he sighed. 'Who was it helped me – twice – in the recent civil wars in Italia? The Huns, my friend, the Huns. That was in Rua's time. Now, their new king, Attila, who's an old and loyal friend, by the way, has sworn assistance. His word is even more to be trusted.'

A stir of interest swept round the tent. Faces which, following Aetius' original announcement, had registered shocked concern now showed relief and eagerness.

'Here, then, is what we do,' continued Aetius. 'Marcus, my old warhorse, remember how you held the Huns in check while I scouted Aspar's lines?'

A grey-haired duke grinned in recollection. 'Aspar son of Ardaburius – the Alan general who cramped our style in that

Ioannes business? Hard to forget it, sir. Tremendous fellows in attack, your Huns. But nearly impossible to hold on a leash.'

'Well, this time I've an easier job for you. The Visigoths, bless their hearts, have decided to oblige us by laying siege to Narbo Martius*. But, as we know, like all barbarians they're hopeless when it comes to siege operations. Shouldn't be too difficult for you to keep them pinned down with Roman troops, until I can send a force of Huns?'

'I'll enjoy it, sir,' declared Marcus, rubbing his hands. 'A series of hit-and-run raids to harass them and disrupt their supplies, while they blunder about with siege contraptions which fall to bits or fail to work. Why, we could even besiege the besiegers. Pen them in and starve them, by throwing up a circle of earthworks around their positions – as Stilicho did against Radogast and his Goths at Florentia. I should know; I was there.'

'Excellent. That's the Visigoths taken care of, then. Now, the Bagaudae. Litorius, I recall you did a first-rate job guarding our retreat after the Battle of the Fifth Milestone. Would it be beneath you to deal with the bandit revolt?'

'Absolutely not, sir,' rejoined the count. 'I'm no Crassus, who felt soiled by taking on Spartacus and his slave army.'

'Splendid. You'll need a large force. The rising will affect a huge area – about a quarter of Gaul. Take half of what's left of the field army, after Marcus has had his pick, and I'll send you half the Huns. When you've crushed the Bagaudae, you can join forces with Marcus against the Visigoths. Myself and Avitus** here' – he nodded to a tall officer with patrician features – 'will move against the Burgundians with the remainder of the Romans and the rest of the Huns. Right gentlemen,' he concluded brightly, looking round the rows of faces, 'that covers everything, I believe. Begin your preparations immediately. We march tomorrow.'

Spolicinum Fort, Province of 2nd Raetia, Diocese of Italy [Titus wrote in the *Liber Rufinorum*]. The year of the consuls Flavius Theodosius and Flavius Placidius Valentinianus,

---

* Narbonne.
** From a distinguished Gallo-Roman family, Avitus rose to become Prefect of Gaul in 439, and briefly (455–6) Western Emperor.

Augusti, their fifteenth and fourth respectively, VIII Calends June.*

I was at the Villa Fortunata when my father's letter arrived with the terrible news of the Burgundian rising et cetera. Fearing for the safety of my dear Clothilde and Marcus, I rode with all speed to Spolicinum (which seems little changed since I was last here twelve years ago) as it lies on the most direct route to the Settlement. Here, I was told the sad tidings that Gaius Valerius had died soon after writing to me. He is buried in the soldiers' cemetery outside the fort. In my grief, I found comfort in the knowledge that he had given his life in the service of Rome. He could have wished for no better end. I have left some money, together with instructions, for a gravestone bearing this inscription:

GAIUS VALERIUS RUFINUS: COMMANDER OF THE
PRIMANI LEGION: 77 YEARS OF AGE. HE LOVED ROME
AND SERVED HER WELL. HE IS LAID HERE.

In his letter, Gaius begged me to consider re-entering the service of Aetius, who, he believed, is the only man who can deal effectively with the crisis in Gaul. I had thought my break with Aetius irrevocable, but *tempora mutantur*, as they say. I will consider my father's plea. Whether Aetius would take me back is another matter, and I could be putting myself at risk in approaching him; he might bring me before a military court for switching my allegiance to Boniface.

Tomorrow, I leave for the Burgundian Settlement via the valley of the upper Rhenus. The roads, I am assured, are still in good repair though now outwith Rome's direct administration. I leave this journal here at Spolicinum for safe keeping, for I fear there will be little leisure or security where I am bound for.

From their position on a Pannonian hilltop, the two royal brothers watched as the Hun cavalry set out for Gaul. Soon, individual warriors disappeared in the dust-pall stirred up by sixty thousand

* 25 May 435.

horses – a vast greyish-yellow cloud which filled the plain and rolled swiftly towards the western horizon.

'Well, brother,' I hope you think it's worth it,' snarled Bleda. 'That's a tenth of our fighting force you've just lent out. And for what? So you can improve your standing with your Roman friends, I suppose?'

Attila studiedly ignored his brother – as he could afford to, ever since he had stamped his authority on the Huns, by his conduct at the Treaty of Margus. It was pointless trying to explain his ambitions to a coarse buffoon of limited vision like Bleda. The Empire of the Huns was now vast, approaching in extent that of the Romans. It stretched from Scandia to the Mare Caspium, uniting for the first time in history, the Teutonic peoples of Germania and the nomads of the steppes. A great achievement, surely? Perhaps; but only if it contained the seeds of permanence – like Greece or Rome. Otherwise, it might fall apart and vanish as quickly as it had arisen. In a vague yet passionate way, Attila yearned for something more satisfying than power and plunder. He wanted greatness for his people, so that in future ages men would speak of Attila not as they would of the cruel tyrant Gaiseric, whose African kingdom was surely transitory, but as they did of Alexander or Caesar, whose legacies survived even to this day. Which was why he needed the help and advice of Aetius and, if possible, the friendship of the Romans. (And that would now be hard to secure, Attila conceded. After Margus, his name throughout the Eastern Empire had become a byword for ruthlessness and terror.)

Although Attila would never admit it, Bleda had a point. The Council, and the Huns generally, would expect rewards for the massive investment they had made in backing Aetius. In the past, such credit had been handsomely repaid. But with the West now weakened and imperilled, could that still be guaranteed? Attila could only hope that it could.

'I see a wild ass running over the plains, and an eagle flying above it. Together, they attack and put to flight a wild boar.' Unbidden, the words in which the seer Wu Tze had described the first part of his vision, rang in Attila's brain. Suddenly, the meaning of the words was clear: the wild ass of the plains must represent the Huns; the eagle was the symbol of imperial Rome; the wild boar was a favourite emblem among the Germans, standing for courage and ferocity. In other words, the Huns and Romans would join together to defeat the Germans – exactly what was beginning to develop! Awe tinged with dread rose in the King. What did the rest of the vision mean? Angrily, he shut his mind against further speculation. Attila would be the master of his own destiny.

When Titus reached the village where his family lived, he found it semi-deserted. Under Chief Vadomir, Clothilde's father, all the able-bodied men had left to join the host of King Gundohar, which had headed north to claim more land for the tribe. Rumours had filtered back of fighting with the Romans, but whether skir-mishing or pitched battles was unclear. His joy at being reunited with Clothilde and Marcus was clouded by awareness that, should things go against the Burgundians, the village might become the scene of fighting or the target of raiding-parties. That night, when both were spent after passionate lovemaking, made more intense by long separation and the present ambience of insecurity, Titus mentioned his fears to Clothilde.

'Come away with me,' he added on sudden impulse. 'You, I, and Marcus, travelling as a small group, could easily make it to Roman-occupied Gaul. My horse can carry you and Marcus, and we can ride and tie.'

'And leave my family and my people, at this time of peril for them?' She sat up below the furs that covered their bed, and gently traced her husband's features with her hand. 'Darling, my heart urges me to do as you suggest. But . . .'

'But your conscience tells you otherwise,' Titus completed the sentence. 'I understand,' he said bitterly. 'At least, I think I do.' He gazed at her in the faint illumination from the embers of the cooking-fire. Her face, serene and relaxed after love, and framed in heavy coils of flaxen hair, had never looked so beautiful. He was filled with an aching love, and a fierce longing to protect her and their child.

'As my husband, you could command me and I would have to obey,' she said. 'But that would not be the Titus I married, the man I know and love.'

'I can't bear the thought of harm coming to you!' exclaimed Titus in anguish, knowing that the price of forcing his family to flee would be the loss of her respect and, in the end, her love. 'What must I do?' he cried, more to himself than to Clothilde.

'What would Gaius Valerius have done, my love?' she murmured gently, planting a kiss on her husband's brow.

All at once Titus' doubts and inner conflict cleared away. Gaius would have stayed – as he, Titus, must. It was the right, the *Roman* thing to do.

'My people need a leader,' said Clothilde, seeming to sense her husband's change of mood. 'Darling, you could be that leader. The men left behind are old and weak, and they are also, being Germans, by nature fierce and quarrelsome. Without someone to guide them, they would argue among themselves and nothing would be done to prepare against attack. If the Romans came, they would rush out against them with what makeshift arms they could collect, and all be killed. Then it would be the turn of the women and children. But you, my dearest, are young and strong. You have served among the Romans and know how war is managed. It might take persuasion, perhaps even knocking heads together, but the villagers would listen if you put a plan to them. If an attack came from regular Roman troops, you as a Roman might be able to negotiate peaceful surrender terms. Alan or Frankish federates fighting under Rome's banner would be a different matter.'

'But the Franks are Germans like yourselves. Surely they would be more likely to spare the village.'

'Not so. There is little fellow feeling between the German tribes. We may mostly be tall, fair-haired and blue-eyed, speak variants of the same tongue, have once all worshipped the same fierce gods, but that's as far as it goes. To a Frank, a Burgundian is almost as much a foreigner or a potential enemy as a Roman. And federate troops, whatever tribe they may belong to, are notoriously undisciplined. Believe me, if the Franks come, rape and slaughter will be the village's likely fate. If the Alans – who are not even Germans but of eastern origin – such a fate will be a certainty. But no more about such things for the present. Now we should sleep, my love. But first, let us pray to Christ, who is both your Lord and mine. He will surely guide you through every trial in the days ahead.'

Titus looked round the circle of old men, women and children gathered in the open space before the village meeting-house. Most looked indifferent, some even hostile. 'My name is Titus Valerius

Rufinus,' he announced in German. 'Thank you for agreeing to hear me. I think you all know who I am – the husband of Clothilde, Vadomir's daughter.'

'And a Roman,' growled an ancient greybeard. 'I fought against Gratian and the first Theodosius, and one lesson I learnt was never trust the Romans. Both those emperors broke treaty after treaty with our people. I say the Romans are a perfidious race. Why should we listen to you, who are one of them?'

'Yes, I am a Roman,' responded Titus, keeping his tone mild and friendly. 'By accident of birth. But my only concern at this moment is to protect my family, and – if you'll let me – help you to protect yourselves. Will you at least allow me to try?'

He sensed the villagers' mood alter subtly as a result of his appeal. There followed some whispered discussion, in which an elderly uncle of Clothilde seemed to be swaying the argument in Titus' favour. Then the previous speaker, apparently the dominant figure in the assembly, spoke again – this time in a less bellicose voice. 'Very well, Roman, tell us what we should do.'

'Our first line of defence must be the palisade,' said Titus, relieved that he could now take charge. 'I'm assuming that all weapons will have been taken by the fighting men. So we must improvise. Scythe-blades fixed to staves, pitchforks, billhooks, axes, sledgehammers – they all make effective weapons, especially bill-hooks. That will be the task of the men. I'm putting you in charge,' he said to the graybeard. 'All right?' The other smiled sardonically but nodded.

'Should the palisade be carried,' Titus continued, 'we will retreat to the village's strongest building, the meeting-house behind us here. The most vulnerable part of it will be the thatch, so the women and girls must fill every kettle, pail and cauldron – anything that holds water. Clothilde, will you organize that?' A look of mutual love and trust flashed between husband and wife, assuring Titus that that particular task was in safe hands.

'Now, you boys and girls,' Titus concluded. He held up a small gold coin which gleamed enticingly in the late-spring sunshine. 'This *tremissis* goes to the one who collects the biggest pile of stones by sunset.' He looked round the assembly, and felt a sudden rush of affection for these rough and simple but essentially good people, who had entrusted him with their protection: grey-haired ancients in furs and homespun; women in sleeveless dresses, a few with bright shawls or neckerchiefs; tow-headed children with dirty faces and bare feet. A tiny army, of which he was commander. A little flock, whose shepherd he had become. 'Right, everyone,' he said with a grin, 'let's get started.'

After days of anxious waiting, the attack came suddenly. Titus had posted lookouts close to the forest verge. Shortly before noon, one came running with the news that he had spotted horsemen approaching through the trees. A horn was sounded to recall the other sentries and warn the villagers. All came hurrying into the central space before the meeting-house.

'You all know what to do,' Titus said quietly. 'Men and young-sters over twelve, proceed now to your stations at the palisade. The rest go inside the meeting-house. 'We'll join you if the fence falls.'

Looking out over the empty fields surrounding the defences (the cattle had been brought inside the village), Titus was aware of his heart thumping violently. Soon he might be fighting for his life. Against fellow Romans, he suddenly realized. What did that make him? With an effort, he suppressed the thought. He was defending his family – as any man would, whatever the circum-stances. And that was all that mattered.

This was his first command: he suddenly felt a huge weight of responsibility pressing down on him. Had it been arrogant presumption to persuade these people to appoint him their leader? His experience of war was limited to being present at two minor battles in which, strictly speaking, he had not even been a fighting soldier. Well, it was too late now for doubts; besides, Clothilde – one of the most perceptive people he knew – seemed to have every faith in him.

At least the palisade was strong. Composed of stout ten-foot logs driven deep into the ground, with an earthen fighting-platform behind, it presented a formidable barrier. Its main weakness was that its perimeter was too extensive for his scant force to guard effectively. The best he could do would be to concentrate his defenders at whatever points came under attack. A simple system of horn-blast signals to control basic movements had been worked out and rehearsed. Fingering the Chi–Rho amulet the subdeacon in Ravenna Cathedral had given him all those years ago, he offered up a prayer to God.

Titus started. At the edge of the forest where, moments before, there had only been a distant line of trees, a fringe of riders had materialized. About two hundred strong, they began to advance at a slow trot across the intervening fields. As they drew nearer, Titus began to make out details: stocky powerful men on big ill-conformed mounts; the yellowish skins, slitted deep-sunk eyes, and flat beardless faces of the riders, all of whom were armed with bows. These were not Romans, they were Huns.

'Keep close to the fence!' shouted Titus, and the warning was passed around the ring of defenders. The Huns, increasing their pace to a canter, then a gallop, fanned out to form an extended line, then, wheeling, began to race round the palisade, discharging arrows in a high trajectory so that they fell close behind the barrier. But, by following Titus' advice and keeping their bodies pressed close against the wall of stakes, the defenders escaped injury. All save one who, rashly raising his head above the parapet, took an arrow in the throat and fell back, fatally wounded.

Their initial foray completed, the Huns regrouped, then split into several parties which positioned themselves at various points around the fence. Ordering his defenders to assemble opposite these concentrations, Titus, with his own detachment, anxiously watched the nearest group of Huns. Half rode forward whirling noosed ropes round their heads, the rest drawing their bows to give covering fire. The ropes snaked out and several running nooses fell over the tops of two adjoining posts in the palisade; the tough hide ropes tautened as the Huns' mounts backed. With several horses pulling against each post, they were subjected to tremendous strain, which must eventually uproot them.

From the piles assembled at various points along the fighting-platform, Titus and his men hurled volleys of stones at the ropers – dangerous work, for even momentary exposure above the fence attracted a salvo of arrows. Nevertheless, they succeeded for a while in keeping the Huns at bay, some slashing at the ropes, while others discouraged fresh attempts to noose the posts, by maintaining a barrage of stones. But when five of his men had been shot dead and three wounded, Titus realized that the position had become untenable, and ordered the signal blown for a retreat to the meeting-house. Carrying their wounded, the defenders streamed back to the great hut and joined the women and children inside. The leather flap which served as a door was now removed. It would hardly deter an assault, merely hinder observation by the defenders.

To carry the building, the Huns would have to dismount and try to force the doorway. Choosing ten of the strongest men, Titus waited with them against the wall on either side of the doorway. Through the entrance, he watched the Huns make short work of breaching the palisade, then assemble close in front of the meeting-house.

A knot of dismounted Huns with drawn swords suddenly rushed the doorway. Titus ceased to be aware of anything except what was happening immediately in front of him. A barrel-chested Hun came at him, swinging a vicious cut at his head. Titus blocked the sword with his billhook, felt a numbing shock as his arm absorbed the impact. The man was pushed up against Titus as more Huns pressed in from behind, preventing either man from wielding his weapon. A rancid stench from the man's unwashed body and filthy skin garments filled Titus' nostrils; glittering with ferocity and malice, the Hun's deep-set black eyes glared into his. Knowing it was risky, but that it was the only way he could gain an advantage, Titus leapt back, creating a gap between himself and his adversary. The man stumbled forward, tried to parry Titus' billhook. Too late; the bill's vicious blade slashed down, sinking deep into the angle between the man's neck and shoulder. Bright arterial blood fountained from the wound, and the man sank to the ground.

Filled with a kind of battle-madness, Titus swung and hacked with the bill at the press of Huns pushing through the entrance. A truly fearsome close-quarters weapon – more than a match for a sword – the billhook cleared a bloody path in front of Titus . . . Suddenly there were no more Huns, and he was standing gasping in the doorway beside the five other survivors of the attack, all wounded, some severely. Looking down, Titus saw that he had a deep gash in his thigh, besides several cuts. Dead and dying Huns littered the entrance – testimony to German courage and fighting ability, even among old men too advanced in years to join the host.

The graybeard who had originally questioned his authority, nodded approvingly at Titus. 'You did well – for a Roman,' he grunted.

The dying Huns were dispatched, while the women attended

to the injuries of the Burgundian wounded, and replacements were chosen to make up the numbers defending the doorway. Two more Hun attacks were beaten back, each time with the loss of several defenders. With a sinking heart, Titus, himself now weakening from loss of blood, realized that arithmetic was in the Huns' favour and that, if the attacks continued, the Huns must soon storm the meeting-house.

But the Huns, no doubt unwilling to expend more lives than necessary, resorted to a different tactic. Fire-arrows were shot high in the air, to fall vertically on to the thatched roof. This, despite having already been liberally doused with water, began to smoulder in several places. As smoke began to curl down from the rafters, a chain of vessels containing water was passed up a ladder through a gap in the thatch, to a volunteer on the roof. Flames started to break out in the smoking patches, to be doused by the brave fire-fighter. However, he was soon picked off by Hun archers who climbed on to the roofs of nearby huts. Another volunteer barely made it to the roof before suffering the same fate. By now the thatch was ablaze in so many places that any further attempts to extinguish the fire were clearly doomed. The hut filled with choking smoke and blazing thatch began to fall inside, leaving the villagers with no alternative but to leave the building and sell their lives as dearly as possible.

Resolving that they should all die together, Titus looked around in the smoke and confusion for his wife and son. As, with a swelling heart, he called Clothilde's name, a roof beam collapsed in a shower of sparks and lumps of blazing thatch.

'Titus!' An agonized cry from Clothilde enabled him to locate her – pinned beneath the blazing roof beam, which Marcus was flailing at with his tunic in an attempt to beat out the flames. Titus joined the boy in his efforts and in a few moments they succeeded. With Marcus doing his best to assist, Titus strained to lift the massive timber; but to no avail. Desperately, he shouted for help – then realized that, apart from the three of them, the hut was empty. Screams and shouts from outside cut through the roar and crackle of the flames, as the villagers died, skewered by Hun arrows.

Then, above the din of slaughter and conflagration, there sounded a trumpet call, high, clear, and piercing. The unmistakable sound of The *lituus*, the Roman cavalry trumpet! Hope flared as Titus renewed his calls for help. Roman treatment of rebels could be uncompromising, but they would surely not stand by and let a family die like trapped rats.

Two men entered the hut. For a moment, Titus' heart leapt; then he saw that they were not Romans but Huns. One rushed at Titus while the other advanced on Marcus with sword upraised. With a cry of anguish, Titus flung himself at his son's assailant, dimly aware as he did so of a third figure entering the hut. Then a blinding flash exploded in his skull and blackness overwhelmed him.

Titus opened his eyes, and was aware of a dull, thumping pain in his head. He was lying in a cot, one of a long row inside a tent; most of the beds' occupants were bandaged. For a few moments he struggled to recall the past; then memory came flooding back – the Hun attack on the village, the desperate last stand in the meeting-house, Clothilde trapped beneath a roof beam in the burning hut . . . He sat up, ignoring the shaft of agony that shot through his head, called desperately to a passing *capsarius*.*

The man hurried over, glanced at the disc suspended round Titus' neck. 'Titus Valerius Rufinus?' Titus nodded, and the man went on, 'You're in an army hospital near Argentorate Stratisburgum. There's someone wants to see you; asked to be informed the moment you came to.' And he hurried off, returning a short time later accompanied by a man in general's uniform. A familiar, stylishly distressed uniform – that carelessly tied neckcloth and battered cuirass. It was Aetius! The general's hair was now streaked with silver, Titus noted, his face deeply etched with lines which had not been there at their last meeting.

'General, Clothilde and Marcus? Can you tell me what happened to them?'

Aetius knelt by the cot and clasped Titus' hand. 'Your son is safe,' he said. 'He's being cared for by a local German family. They'll be bringing him to see you.' Aetius paused, then continued in tones of quiet compassion. 'Your wife is dead, Titus. I'm truly sorry to be the bearer of such heavy tidings.'

'What happened, sir?' whispered Titus.

* Medical orderly.

'I was there,' said Aetius. 'When your village was raided, the fighting was officially over. Gundohar had already surrendered, and the Burgundians been granted generous peace terms – which means, of course, that you can't be charged with aiding rebels, if that's any comfort. The Huns who attacked you were a stray marauding band; one of several, I fear. After the peace agreement, I travelled round with a heavily armed detachment cracking down on looting, and abuse of civilians by undisciplined units. Unfortunately, I arrived just too late to save your village. The Huns made off as soon as we approached, but I found two in the meeting-house who hadn't noticed our arrival. Probably intent on a spot of private plunder or mopping up. One, who was about to run through your little boy, turned on me but wasn't quick enough to stop a thrust below the breast-bone. Before the other could attack me, he was struck by falling débris from the roof – as you were yourself.'

'And Clothilde?'

'I tried, of course, to shift the beam, but it was hopeless. It would have taken several strong men to move it, and there was no time to summon any of my soldiers – the roof was on the point of falling in. She implored me to kill her. Her lower body was crushed beyond any hope of her recovering – even had she been freed – and I could not let her perish in an inferno. So I . . . I did what was necessary. As you yourself would have done.' Aetius paused, then, his expression bleak, said, 'But I could not blame you if you were now to hate me.'

Titus brushed away tears, collected himself with an effort. 'The opposite is true, sir. I hope I'm Roman enough to appreciate that what you did was an act of mercy, carried out because it was the right thing to do. For that I'll always be grateful – as I'm grateful that you saved my life and my son's.'

'I made Marcus leave the hut before—' Aetius broke off, then continued quickly, 'Then I dragged you out. I was only just in time – the roof collapsed as we got clear. You took a nasty blow on the head and you've lost a lot of blood, but the doctors say that with rest you'll make a full recovery.' There was a short silence, then Aetius asked in friendly tones, 'Well, Titus Valerius, what will you do now?'

'Probably return to Italia with Marcus, sir, and manage the family estate.'

'That, in my opinion, would be a waste of your talents. I have another suggestion.'

'Sir?'

'Come and work for me again. Rome needs loyal servants as never before. Especially if they happen to be the son of Gaius Valerius Rufinus, whose heroism may have saved Gaul. No need to decide anything now. I'll come back for your answer in a day or two.'

Titus recalled his father's final letter, in which he'd recommended just such a course as Aetius was suggesting. Also, Titus felt that in some subtle way Aetius had changed, and was perhaps no longer the ruthlessly ambitious soldier/politician he had once been. He made up his mind. 'No need for that, sir,' he said. 'If you're willing to have me back, I'll be glad to serve you again.'

Aetius smiled and took his hand. 'Then welcome back, Titus Valerius, "thou good and faithful servant", as the Scriptures say.'

TWENTY-FIVE

A race of uncivilized allies [the Visigoths] bids fair to bring
Roman power crashing to the ground
Sidonius Apollinaris, *Letters*, after 471

'Congratulations, Count,' his young second-in-command said to
Litorius as, accompanied by the mixed force of Huns and Romans,
they forded the Liger near Caesarodunum* and headed south, out
of Aremorica. 'It'll be a long time before those scoundrels raise
their heads again.'

'A bloody business, Quintus,' sighed Litorius, shaking his head.
'The Bagaudae had to be crushed, of course. But still . . .'

'Don't say you're going soft, sir?' jibed Quintus, with the affectionate familiarity born of months of shared campaigning. 'They
challenged Rome and got what they deserved. And so did those
Burgundians. General Aetius was too easy on the Burgundians the
first time; when they rebelled again, he really taught them a lesson.
Killed – how many was it? Twenty thousand? – then marched off
the survivors to captivity in Sapaudia.** We should mete out the
same treatment to the Visigoths.'

'Everything's in black and white to you young fire-eaters,'
laughed Litorius. 'If only things were that straightforward. I met
Tibatto, you know,' he went on musingly, 'after he was captured,
and before we separated his head from his shoulders. Crucifixion,
as for Spartacus, would have been more appropriate, I suppose;
but of course that was abolished by Constantine a hundred years
ago. By no means your ordinary rabble-rouser. Quite cultured,
actually. Quoted Tacitus to me: "They create a desert and call it
peace."'

'Who's "they" sir?' asked Quintus, mildly puzzled.

'Don't they teach the young the classics any more?' exclaimed

---

* Tours
** Savoy.

Litorius in mock outrage. ' "They" refers to the Romans, in a speech put into the mouth of Calgacus, leader of the Caledonians at the Battle of Mons Graupius, by Tacitus in his *Histories*.'

'We beat them, didn't we?'

'Well, we may have won that particular battle, but the Caledonians threw us out eventually – back in the reign of Septimius Severus, just over two centuries ago. The first time that had happened in the whole empire; perhaps it marked the turning of the tide for Rome.'

'Look on the bright side, sir,' said Quintus cheerfully. 'The tide may now be turning the other way. Once we've dealt with the Visigoths, Gaul will be fully back under Roman control.'

'You're probably right,' responded Litorius, brightening. 'After all, we crushed the Bagaudae, didn't we? Perhaps we can crush the Visigoths, too.'

'No "perhaps" about it, sir,' replied Quintus stoutly. 'And it'll be good to see the south again – feel the sun, breathe upland air, smell the shrubs and pines, see olive groves and vineyards once again, taste some decent wine instead of your piss-thin northern beer.'

They rode for some miles in silence, then Quintus suggested, 'Like me to check on the column, sir?'

'Yes, do that.' Litorius sounded both relieved and grateful.

'Column' was a euphemism for the vast, amorphous horde of Huns that formed the bulk of the army, thought Quintus, as he walked his horse to the top of a hillock from which he could view the force. He was worried about his commander. Litorius was a decent man and, in normal circumstances, a good soldier, but suppressing the Bagaudian revolt seemed to have taken a heavy toll on him. Some of the things that had taken place had been pretty stomach-turning, Quintus admitted: that quarry near Lexovium* where thousands of rebels and their children had been corralled, to become targets for Hun archery practice; the mass executions in the Sequana**, with prisoners roped together in groups and stones tied to their ankles . . . But that was war – horrible things happened, and you just had to grit your teeth and get on with it. Perhaps the count was suffering from *fastidium*, squeamishness, a condition

* Lisieux.
** The Seine.

brought on by exposure to prolonged bloodletting on campaign. If so, that might impair his judgement, potentially putting his own men at risk.

On several occasions, Litorius had tried to restrain the Huns – with embarrassing lack of success: they ignored him, responding only to their own commanders. Outside the walls of towns and the great estates, they had raided and slaughtered indiscriminately. That was one thing if you were putting down renegade peasantry, but if they continued in that vein once they had left Aremorica, there would be serious friction with the Roman authorities. The strain of heading a 'dirty' campaign, one in which his control had proved at best tenuous, had had a destabilizing effect on Litorius. At times he had seemed rashly over-confident, once, for example, leading a scouting-party into an ambush, from which it had extricated itself only with difficulty; at other times he had been cautious to the point of timidity, more than once allowing concentrations of Bagaudae to escape. Quintus hoped that, when faced with the formidable Visigoths, Litorius' nerves and skill would not desert him.

The army pushed on, past the milestone marking the centre of Gaul and into the plateau of Arvernum:* a strange region of lava deserts and extinct volcanoes shaped like cones or domes, the whole area seamed by valleys of contrasting greenness, which provided welcome fodder for the horses. Where the River Dor** joined the Elaver† the army picked up the Via Rigordana – once a Gallic trackway leading to high summer pastures, now the main Roman road to Nemausus through the Cebenna.‡

Like a swarm of locusts the host rolled south, past Tigernum Castrum¶ above a spectacular gorge, then climbed through successive zones of woodland: oaks and chestnuts, birch and beeches, finally a belt of pines debouching on to a series of undulating plateaux spotted with shallow reed-lined lakes and bathed in a

* The Auvergne
** River Doré.
† River Allier.
‡ Nîmes; the Cévennes.
¶ Thiers, in Puy de Dôme.

strange pearly light. The route then led through an unearthly landscape of volcanic peaks, fantastic humps and spires of black lava looming above wooded gorges and sculpted cliffs, some resembling titanic water-organ pipes. At Revessium*, where the Via Rigordana crossed the Via Bolena linking the Elaver and upper Liger, the army came in sight of the mighty outrider of the Cebenna. Round and bald, its approaches sprinkled with the rare white groundsel, the mountain's summit marked the southern limit of Arvernum, and formed the watershed of the Oceanus Atlanticus and Mare Internum**.

The Huns, having had licence to pillage at will in Aremorica, became a serious nuisance in Arvernum. Complaints about their depredations were brought to Litorius almost daily by outraged landowners and magistrates. The local inhabitants – descendants of the fierce and volatile Arverni, whom Julius Caesar had quelled only with difficulty – were not the sort of people to suffer wanton spoliation meekly. Most plaintiffs the Roman commander managed to placate with apologies, promises of reparation, and on occasion compensation from his own purse. One incident however, was to have consequences both immediate and far-reaching.

As the army passed Avitacum, the estate of Senator Avitus – who was fresh from helping Aetius in the Burgundian campaigns – a servant remonstrated with some Huns who were carelessly trampling terraces of vines. Typically, they ignored the man, but when, with misguided courage, he persisted, one of the Huns, displaying an almost casual contempt, drew his sword and killed him. Quintus reported the matter to Litorius who shrugged wearily, remarking, 'These things happen, Quintus. I can't be everywhere.' He sent an aide to fetch a purse of gold and told the man, 'Take this to the servant's family with my regrets.'

But the matter did not end there. An hour later, Avitus himself came spurring up and drew rein right in front of Litorius, forcing him to halt. 'Keep your money, Count,' he snapped, throwing the purse on the ground. 'It's tainted. I'll provide for my man's family myself.' He went with cold anger, 'Is this how you keep discipline among your troops? If so, small wonder the barbarians despise us.'

* St-Paulien, in Haute Loire.
** Mediterranean Sea.

'The Huns are not the easiest of people to control, Senator,' replied Litorius, flushing.

'Aetius can manage them. If you cannot, perhaps another should be commanding here. I demand that you point out the guilty man.'

Litorius could hardly refuse. Accordingly, the army was halted and, there being no shortage of witnesses – Romans as well as Huns – the murderer was soon identified. Avitus rode up to him and addressed him briefly in Hunnish, presumably asking if he had killed the servant. The Hun, astride his horse, made no response except to smile insolently.

Suddenly drawing his *spatha*, Avitus cut at the man, who barely managed to swerve aside, his complacent smirk changing to an astonished scowl. Quickly unsheathing his own sword, he parried a second blow. Wheeling round each other in a display of masterly horsemanship, the two antagonists cut, thrust and parried, their blades ringing and sparking, while the nearest troops watched in delighted fascination. It was soon evident that Avitus was the more skilful swordsman; the fight had lasted only a few minutes when, with an expertly timed feint, he caused the other to open up his guard. In a flash the *spatha* plunged between the Hun's ribs. As he slid dying from the saddle, Avitus wheeled his mount without a word, and galloped back the way he had come.

The incident galvanized Litorius. His mood-swings and passivity were replaced by an alert yet calm decisiveness. Suddenly, he seemed to be everywhere at once, inspecting, admonishing, encouraging. Among the Roman troops, discipline and morale which had taken a knock in Aremorica, began to recover; the Huns, clearly impressed by Avitus' demonstration of Roman authority, caused no further trouble.

After crossing the Cebenna, the army descended upon Provincia: fertile, urbanized, thoroughly Roman. At Nemausus, it swung south-west following the great military road leading to Narbo Martius. Twenty miles from that city, as the army pitched camp for the night on the north bank of the River Rauraris,* Litorius sent for his second-in-command. 'Tomorrow, Quintus, the army rests,' he said, adding water to wine in a

---

* River Hérault.

silver mixing-bowl. 'Not because they need to, but to await the arrival of supply wagons.'

'Supply wagons?' repeated Quintus, who had long ago learnt that deferential curiosity could be an aid to advancement.

'Loaded with flour. The campaign's Praetorian prefect of supplies has assured me the wagons are scheduled to arrive any day, from state storehouses in the provinces of Viennensis and the First Narbonensis.'

He handed Quintus a brimming goblet. 'Only Massilian, I'm afraid – best I could get. The plan is this. Those poor devils in Narbo Martius are starving; no food's got in for months. According to a scout who managed to get through the Gothic lines the other day, they're on the point of surrendering. If we can get the flour in, that won't happen and Narbo will be saved. Aetius is on his way from Burgundy; our joint forces will far outnumber the Goths, and they'll have to raise the siege. However, we can't afford to wait for Aetius. We must deliver the flour now.'

'Just one point, sir,' Quintus said delicately.

Litorius raised his eyebrows.

'How do we get the flour through the Goths' entrenchments? With an army the size of ours, they're bound to get word of our coming and prepare to resist. Also, wagons are slow, cumbrous things, not easy to defend.'

'You said one point, Quintus,' Litorius chided gently, recharging their goblets. 'I make that two.' Eyes shining with enthusiasm, he began to pace the tent. To answer both: one, the Goths won't get word of our coming because we'll approach silently, by night; two, using cavalry we'll dispense with the wagons to get the flour through – each horseman will carry behind him two sacks of flour. The scout has prepared a sketch-map showing where the enemy lines are weakest; that's where we'll strike. Marcus' men have been primed to guide us in. Well, what do you think?'

'It's a brilliant plan sir,' conceded Quintus, before continuing more dubiously, 'but risky, if you ask me. Night operations are tricky things – so much can go wrong. Given perfect planning, preparation, and discipline, it *could* work, I suppose.'

'It *will* work,' affirmed Litorius, adding with a smile, 'thanks to you.' He placed a hand on the other's shoulder. 'My dear Quintus, I have complete faith in your ability to ensure that those details you've just mentioned function smoothly. 'So you'd best get started. But finish your wine first.'

Wakened by a distant sound, the Goth sentry blearily opened his eyes. Guiltily, he stared about him in the grey half-light at the familiar scene: the tracery of scaffolding surrounding Bishop Rusticus' half-rebuilt cathedral showing above the great North Gate in Narbo's walls; the arches of the aqueducts striding above the clumsy earthworks thrown up around the city; the pole of a battering-ram, abandoned after its protective shed had been shattered by rocks dropped from the walls by the defenders; a rickety siege-tower, stuck in the space between the walls and the trenches, its wheels sunk to the axles in the soft ground. The man listened; he could hear it clearly now: a low rumbling like distant thunder, growing steadily louder. Then it dawned on his sleep-fogged brain what it was he was hearing – cavalry! Grabbing the horn suspended by a baldric from his shoulder, he blew a warning blast.

Too late. As the nearest Goths stumbled from their tents and shelters, a tide of mailed Roman horsemen swept up and over the entrenchments, and fell on the besiegers in their path. The fight was short and bloody. Taken by surprise while the bulk of their army still slumbered, the Goths in the path of the Romans fell swiftly to the chopping *spathae* that rose bright silver in the morning rays, swept down, then rose again; but this time red. Their preliminary task done, the cavalry formed two outward-facing lines in front of the North Gate, creating a clear passage for the Huns who followed, each galloping warrior with two sacks of flour tied behind his saddle.

To the cheers of the besiged, the North Gate swung open to admit the Huns. For two hours, the Roman cavalry, reinforced by Marcus' troops, threw back wave after wave of Goths, while the Huns poured into the city like a river in spate. When the last Huns were inside, the cavalry followed, fighting every foot of the way as they backed through the entrance. Then the valves of the gate were slowly pushed shut against a howling press of Goths, and the great securing bars dropped into their holding-braces. A few Goths who had pursued the cavalry too closely found themselves trapped inside and were cut down without quarter.

'Congratulations, Count – a brilliant operation,' Aetius told Litorius. They were in Aetius' tent outside Narbo, ten days after the relief of the city, and the day after he had arrived at the head of his Huns and smashed the Gothic host. (The survivors had retreated to their assigned homeland, leaving eight thousand corpses behind them.) 'Your relief of Narbo is an object lesson in the two key principles of war, innovation, and what I call "operational command". The successful general is one who is not afraid to apply original ideas and who, while overseeing general strategy, trusts his subordinates to use their own initiative and implement details on the ground. You have truly shone regarding both these points.'

'Thank you, sir,' acknowledged Litorius, flushing with pleasure. 'But, as I've said, much of the credit must go to Quintus here, my second-in-command. The overall plan to get flour to the besieged may have been mine, but the execution was largely his doing.'

'An excellent example of operational command in action,' said Aetius with a smile. 'Well done, Quintus. Promotion's in order, I think. "Duke Quintus Arrius" – it has a certain ring, you'll agree. Don't worry,' he laughed, turning to Litorius. 'He won't be usurping your position. I'm putting you in sole command here while I make a trip to Italia. A little bone to pick with our beloved Empress. You'll be acting Master of Soldiers pending my return.'

'*Magister militum!*' breathed Litorius. 'This – this is more than generous, sir.'

'Hardly that, Count. "Sensible" is the word I'd use. Those Visigoths are hard nuts to crack. They'll need close watching to keep them in their place. But I know I'm leaving the task in capable hands. You'll earn your title, never fear.'

TWENTY-SIX

You cannot serve two masters, God and mammon – in other words Christ and Caesar

Paulinus, Bishop of Nola, *Letters, c.* 400

'Gaius says . . .' Quoting from the famous jurisconsult's *Institutes*, the defending lawyer continued to demonstrate why his client not only was innocent of the charge against him but was in fact the injured party.

'Ah, but Ulpian maintains . . .' countered the prosecutor.

'Gaius . . .'

'Papinian . . .!'

'Paulus . . .'

'Ulpian . . .?'

'Modestinus . . .'

And so it went on, the two trading legal precedents like sparring gladiators exchanging blows. The case, a dispute concerning alleged land encroachment, had dragged on inconclusively throughout the afternoon. The judge was an overworked decurion appointed by the provincial governor (of Second Narbonensis in the Seven Provinces) as *defensor civitatis* to deal with minor jurisdiction. He was impatient to wrap up the case and avoid an adjournment to the following day. It was already late: entering the courtroom within the great basilica of Nemausus, a slave began to light the lamps.

'And what does Papinian say?' asked the *defensor* wearily, turning to Crispus, the legal assessor. All magistrates – busy men usually too swamped with other business to be learned in the law – had an assessor, always a trained lawyer, to act as legal referee. In cases where a clear verdict could not be arrived at, the recently enacted Law of Citations, which called on the authority of the five leading jurisconsults, was invoked. If they disagreed, the Law decreed that the majority should carry the day; if there was a tie – as in the present case – Papinian was to have the casting vote.

'Well, what *does* Papinian say?' repeated the *defensor* in exasperation when, after a longish pause, Crispus had made no reply.

But the assessor, a young barrister trained at Rome, hadn't heard the question. Crispus was preoccupied by something that had recently begun to worry him to the point of his being almost constantly in a state of terror: the fate of his immortal soul.

Unusually for a Christian, Crispus had been baptized in childhood, when he had fallen ill and been expected to die. Most Christians postponed baptism until their death-beds, leaving them free to sin until the last minute, when the rite would wash away all sin, thus ensuring that their purified souls would enter Heaven. Once baptized, any subsequent sins could be expunged by doing penance. But this could happen only once; further sins were unredeemable, and those who died in sin could expect to go to Hell. Even if one were careful to avoid committing obvious sins like adultery and fornication, it was very difficult, unless one became a hermit or a monk, for an ordinary citizen – especially if he were engaged in public service such as the army or the law – to avoid becoming contaminated by sin. 'Those who acquire secular power and administer secular justice cannot be free from sin,' one pope had declared.

All this, while vaguely troubling the sensitive and imaginative lad as he grew to manhood, remained at the back of Crispus' mind, existing only as an abstract set of concepts; besides, he comforted himself, there was always penance to fall back on in old age, when presumably both temptation and opportunity to sin would have largely evaporated. And so, although concerned at a subliminal level about the spiritual danger inherent in adopting the profession, the young man had embarked on a career in the law. Committed and conscientious, he had risen swiftly, becoming an assessor at an age when most of his contemporaries were struggling to master the *Responses* of Papinian. And his life might well have continued in that vein – busy, fulfilled, only occasionally troubled by vague fears concerning the hereafter.

But a few weeks previously he had experienced a traumatic epiphany which brought those fears surging to the surface, and made them burgeon and expand to the point where they threatened to dominate all his waking thoughts. In the middle of the Sunday service at Crispus' church in a village outside Nemausus, a stranger had invaded the building, a gaunt, wild-looking fellow with a shaven head and wearing a black robe. This was one of a new breed of cleric that could be seen tramping the roads singly or in pairs: a vagrant monk. Roughly elbowing aside the priest, he faced the congregation and began to speak. The angry protests and the priest's remonstrations died away as the man's eloquence and sheer power of personality began to grip his audience.

'I have a simple message for you,' the monk declared. 'You wish to save your souls? Then you must renounce the world and its temptations, abandon earthly pursuits. Why?' He glared round the congregation with burning eyes, and his voice rose to a shout. 'Because to embrace the world is to risk incurring sin, and to die a sinner is to enter Hell!' Then his voice quietened, became mild, reasonable. 'How many of you, thinking it no sin, keep a concubine or visit the theatre, watch wild-beast fights in the arena and chariot races in the circus? You may not realize it, but in so doing you have endangered your immortal souls, for all these things are sins. I daresay most of you attend the baths – not in itself a sin, I grant.' Again his voice rose. 'It is, however, an indulgence which can stimulate the carnal appetites, and tempt you to the sin of fornication. As is indeed the marriage bed itself; better by far for husband and wife to suppress desire and live in mutual chastity. Have you been a soldier? If so, you may have committed the sin of murder – for such is any killing, even of an enemy. Are you a lawyer or a magistrate? Then are you almost certain to have sinned, for which of you can truly say that all your judgments have been just? And if, in passing judgment, you have condemned a man to death, you are guilty of murder as surely as if you had killed him by your own hand. I tell you, the only certain way to enter Heaven is to—'

'Enough!' interrupted a member of the congregation, bolder than the rest – they, including Crispus, were both cowed and fascinated by the monk's performance, almost as though they were under a spell. 'Have you no care for the welfare of the state?' continued the speaker, a ruddy-faced decurion. 'If we were to heed your advice, what would happen to the empire? Who would defend us from the barbarians were soldiers to lay down their arms? Where would Rome find the sons and daughters she so desperately needs in these times of crisis, if we practised celibacy? What you advocate is tantamount to treason. I'm minded to report you to the governor and have you arrested for sedition.'

'You are welcome to try, my friend,' responded the monk with gloating scorn. Such was the veneration in which holy men were held, that any attempt by the secular authorities to curb their activities might easily provoke a riot. 'You all accept that sinning leads to Hell,' he went on, as his opponent bit his lip and fell silent. 'But have you any concept of what Hell is truly like?'

In a dramatic gesture, the monk thrust out a hand above a candle burning on the altar. For several seconds, apparently unperturbed, he held it just over the flame; a horrified gasp arose from his audience as a smell of singeing flesh pervaded the building. Removing his hand, the monk declared, 'Even I, schooled as I am in mortification of the flesh, can endure the pain for but a fraction of a minute. And if one little candle can inflict such pain, think of the agony you must endure when you are thrust into Hell's fiery furnace. An agony, moreover, which will never end.' His tone took on an edge of chilling menace. 'Imagine the everlasting torment, the screams, the writhing of your bodies, which can never be consumed by the flames that sear them. A minute of such torment would seem like an eternity. Yet ten times ten thousand years would pass without release from anguish, to be repeated endlessly for all time. Weighed against your soul's salvation, what can matter worldly things? Choose Christ or Rome – you cannot serve them both.'

Shaken and afraid, Crispus stumbled from the church. Most of the monk's hearers, he suspected, would strive for a week or two to follow his advice, then lapse back into worldly ways. Perhaps from time to time they might experience a thrill of guilty terror as they made love to a mistress, or cheated on a sale, or bet money on a charioteer; but the fear of Hell would soon recede to the back of their minds, especially as the majority would not yet have been baptized – thus holding an insurance against the risks of sinning.

How he wished he could be like those others, but he knew he wished in vain. His nature was less coarse-grained than that of most, or, put another way, more sensitive and impressionable, therefore more vulnerable. It was as though that monk had got inside his head and unloosed a Pandora's box of terrors, which could never be put back. True, he still had one more chance of absolution: penance. But suppose he should fall victim to a fatal accident, or be taken sick with a swiftly fatal disease before he could perform the required act of penitence? The monk's horrifying depiction of Hell kept returning to his mind, and he was powerless to exorcise it. 'Choose Christ or Rome – you cannot serve them both.' The cleric's message held a stark and dreadful warning which, however much he might wish otherwise, he knew he was compelled to heed.

Crispus was vaguely conscious of someone shaking his shoulder. As though emerging from a trance, he became aware of his surroundings: the courtroom dimly illuminated by flickering oil-lamps, the *defensor*, looking both concerned and irritated, leaning forward in his chair, flanked by the two lawyers and their clients. A servitor handed him a beaker of water.

'Are you unwell?' enquired the *defensor* with some asperity. 'If so, we could I suppose, adjourn proceedings for today.'

Crispus blinked and shook his head. 'No, I'm all right, sir,' he mumbled apologetically. 'A sudden headache; it's gone now.'

'Good. Then perhaps we may proceed. To refresh your memory: we seem to have reached an impasse in this case, and to settle it we require to know how Papinian would find.'

With an effort, Crispus forced himself to recall the details of the case. A had accused B of filching some of his land while he, A, was absent on business, by altering the boundaries – a charge which B denied. Witnesses for both parties had been called and the weight of evidence for each claim, supported by reference to the standard authorities, compared. The result had been finely balanced, hence the need to consult Papinian in order to obtain a decisive verdict.

During the progress of the case, Crispus had become convinced that B, who had come over strongly as greedy and unscrupulous, had bribed at least one witness, and was guilty as charged. He was also certain that Papinian favoured A's claim. And – something which was potentially extremely serious for B – during the hearing it had been established beyond doubt that B had made certain intimidating statements to A concerning the disputed property. Did these remarks constitute a threat of force or injury? No, according to two of the subordinate jurisconsults. Yes, according to the remaining pair: an opinion which was, Crispus knew, supported by the supreme authority, Papinian.

The trouble was that B would then be guilty not just of

misappropriation, but of *latrocinium*, robbery. The *defensor* would then be obliged to refer B to the criminal courts, which would almost certainly mean an extended wait in gaol before B came to trial. Conditions for remand prisoners were notoriously appalling; many died before they could appear in court. If that should happen to B, Crispus, in the Church's eyes, would be guilty of the mortal sin of murder, with all the peril that implied for the salvation of his soul.

Smarting with shame for traducing the ethics of his profession, Crispus heard himself solemnly pronounce a total fabrication: 'According to Papinian, in cases involving possession, where the validity of competing claims cannot be determined in favour of either party, the disputed property shall be equally divided between the claimants, according to the decision of an impartial arbiter.'

'So you wish to join our little brotherhood?' the Abbot of Lerina* asked the nervous young man standing before him in the Superior's Lodging. A kindly and perceptive man, the abbot regarded Crispus with a mixture of curiosity and concern. From the cut and quality of his dalmatic, he was clearly from the upper middle class, a stratum of society not noted for supplying recruits for the monastic life. There were exceptions – notably the ex-senator Paulinus of Nola – but they were rare. This young man, in contrast to the confidence displayed by most of his kind, had a troubled look which spoke of inner turmoil.

'With all my heart, Father,' Crispus replied, with desperate eagerness.

'I have to warn you that the life is hard,' cautioned the abbot, 'one that you may not find easy to adapt to, and for which your life to date has not, perhaps, prepared you. I must be satisfied that your calling is sincere. You'd be surprised at how many try to enter the monastic life in order to escape the retribution of the law, or simply to be assured of life's basic necessities.' He looked appraisingly at Crispus. 'Tell me, my son, why it is you would become a monk.'

'I wish above everything, to live a life free from temptation to sin.'

* Lérins.

'Well, there is certainly little enough to tempt you here,' confirmed the abbot with a smile. 'But you are young to wish to leave the world.' Rising from his throne, he placed a hand on Crispus' shoulder and turned him to face through a window. 'Look: over there, across that little strip of sea, is Grinnicum*: the stir and bustle of a busy city, beautiful women, the excitement of the Games, song and laughter, rich food and fine wines, poetry, music, the theatre. Are you really ready to abandon these things? Here, on this barren island, you will find only solitude, work, and prayer.'

'And communion with God, through avoidance of sin?'

'That too, perhaps, should He bestow His Grace,' conceded the abbot gently, moved by the young man's sincerity. 'Very well, I shall accept you as a postulant. If your commitment remains firm, in a little while you will enter upon your novitiate.'

Sobbing with relief and gratitude, Crispus fell to the ground and kissed the abbot's feet.

* Cannes.

TWENTY-SEVEN

There are men who shun the light and call themselves monks;
because of their fear they shun what is good; such reasoning is
the raving of a madman

Rutilianus Namatianus, *On His Return*, 417

Valentinian's eyes widened in delight as, carried by two slaves, the architect's model was placed on a plinth before him. Made of wood coated with plaster to simulate marble, it represented a triumphal arch, with panels showing in relief victorious Roman cavalry riding down fleeing Burgundians and Visigoths. For the record, a few Huns, squat and uncouth, had had to be included. But the message above all was that this was a *Roman* triumph, masterminded by none other than the Emperor himself, whose gilded effigy held the reins of the quadriga surmounting the whole. It was Aetius who had actually conducted the campaigns, Valentinian conceded to himself, but then that's what generals were for. After all, when people thought of the conquest of Britain, it was Claudius, not Aulus Plautius, whom they remembered.

'Magnificent!' breathed the Emperor, walking round the model, admiring the artistry with which terror or resolution had been rendered on the faces of barbarians and Romans respectively. It would of course be erected in Rome (which he much preferred to provincial little Ravenna surrounded by its foggy marshes) and outdo in size and splendour the arches of Titus and Constantine.

There was unfortunately one tiresome matter to be negotiated before the project could go ahead: funding. The Treasury officials were bound to prove their usual difficult selves; but with his mother's help they could probably be persuaded.

In a reception chamber of Ravenna's imperial palace, the Emperor and his mother – the Augusta Galla Placidia – enthroned, confronted the two chief financial ministers, the *comites rei privatae* and *sacrarum largitionum*, the Counts of the Privy and Public

Purses respectively. Between the two groups stood the model of the projected Arch of Valentinian.

'It can't be done, Your Serenity,' said the Privy Purse, shaking his head regretfully. A thin, intense man, he had the manner of an anxious schoolmaster. 'The expense for such a capital project would be enormous – far exceeding any surplus from the rents of imperial lands. Surplus did I say?' The man gave a weary smile. 'Serenity, there *is* no surplus. The income from your patrimony is barely enough to cover the expenses of your household. In fact, even as I speak, the wages of the secretariat are considerably in arrears.' He coughed discreetly. 'If I might presume to suggest, a certain, ah, "readjustment", shall we call it, of the palace budget would help to balance the books. Last week's banquet for the Eastern Empire's ambassadors on the publication of the Theodosian Code, for instance. Snow to cool the wine, brought from the Alpes in baskets by relays of runners; pigs' testicles from Provincia; dormice stuffed with larks' tongues . . . A trifle excessive, perhaps? Oysters, pork, and hare, obtained locally – at a fraction of the cost – would surely have sufficed.'

'I see,' sneered Valentinian. 'To save a few *tremisses*, you would have us serve distinguished guests sausage from Bononia* garnished with prime Ravenna cabbage, and washed down with that Mantuan vinegar they call wine. Cato the Censor would have approved, I'm sure.' He turned to the other count, a thickset florid man. 'If the Privy Purse is too mean to let us celebrate our victories, perhaps the state will prove more generous.'

'Your Serenity, forget this folly,' declared the Count of the Public Purse brusquely. 'The Treasury needs every *nummus* it can wring in taxes, just to pay the army in Gaul.'

'You dare address your Emperor thus!' shrieked Valentinian, spittle flying from his lips. 'I'll have you dismissed, banished. A life among the goats of Cephalonia might cure you of your insolence.'

'Aside from the fact that Cephalonia now falls within the jurisdiction of the East,' rejoined the count smoothly, quite unperturbed by the emperor's outburst, 'what would that achieve?' The count was secure in the knowledge that, without the backing of Placidia and Aetius, Valentinian's threat was an

* Bologna.

empty one. Even mighty emperors like the first Valentinian or Theodosius the Great, had been unable to bully or manipulate (beyond a limited extent) a bureaucracy grown all-embracing, powerful, and quasi-independent, since its virtual creation under Diocletian. Nor, despite sustained efforts, had they been able to rid the system of its greatest evil: endemic corruption. This, combined with the disbursement of salaries for the army of tax and administrative officials, accounted for a serious erosion of funds reaching the Treasury.

'Perhaps Your Serenity does not fully appreciate just how parlous the situation has become,' the count continued. 'Apart from Italia, Provence, and central Gaul, there's nowhere left *to* tax. Africa and Britain are both gone. Hispania's in turmoil from encroachments by the Visigoths, the Suebes' occupation of Gallaecia, and Bagaudian resurgence. The federates are exempt from levies, and it'll be years before Aremorica recovers sufficiently to—'

'But Uncle Honorius had *his* arch,' said Valentinian, cutting short the minister and turning to his mother.

'Yes; finished just in time for the sack of Rome as I recall,' chuckled the Public Purse. 'The Goths – any who could read, that is – must have been amused by the inscription: "Subdued for all time – the Goth nation." To build another might be tempting Providence.'

'My royal half-brother perhaps could not really afford such an expensive monument,' said Placidia soothingly to Valentinian. She turned to the Count of the Public Purse. 'Could we not settle for a compromise: triumphal games in a refurbished Colosseum? That wouldn't empty the coffers, surely?'

The ministers exchanged glances, a reciprocal nod confirming mutual acceptance of this olive branch. 'Well, I suppose it *might* be managed,' said the Count of the Patrimony grudgingly. 'It'll mean economies,' and he glanced meaningfully towards Valentinian.

'And an overhaul of the tax net,' took up the other minister, 'to ensure that no one who can pay slips through the meshes.'

'Who, pray, *is* escaping their fiscal obligations?' demanded Valentinian.

'Apart from mass desertions by decurions and *coloni* to the great estates and, until their revolt was crushed, to the Bagaudae of

Aremorica,' the count replied, 'we have these monks – a huge and growing class of parasites, whose priority is not to save the empire but to save their souls. Also, quite apart from the fact that they make no contribution to the state in dues or labour, their vow of celibacy is causing the population to diminish, thus further reducing the tax base and eroding recruitment for the army.'

'Then we must stop the rot!' exclaimed Valentinian, pleased to have found a target on which to vent his disappointment. 'I'll have the Senate ratify an edict forbidding anyone to enter the monastic life without permission.' He looked at Placidia, seeking her approval. 'A good idea, Mother?'

'A splendid one,' confirmed the Empress warmly, casting an indulgent glance towards her son.

'I would remind Your Serenities that such legislation has already been enacted,' put in the Public Purse tartly. 'It states that no one can leave the land on which they work, to become a monk, without their lord's permission – which is to be granted only in the most exceptional of circumstances.'

'Then the edict isn't working!' shouted Valentinian, stamping his foot. 'It must be renewed, extended, with the harshest penalties for non-compliance.'* He glared at the others. 'Who would be an Emperor?' he cried. 'My subjects disobey me, my ministers defy me, even the Augusta fobs me off with honeyed words. Sycophants, traitors – get out, the lot of you! Out! Out!'

Alone at last in the chamber, Valentinian, his features convulsed with fury and frustration, hurled the model from its plinth, to shatter on the marble floor.

* The frequency with which imperial legislation in the late Western Empire was re-enacted, with increasingly dire threats of punishment, shows how weak the central government was becoming.

TWENTY-EIGHT

*The proud Litorius directed the Scythian horsemen
against the ranks of the Goths*
Sidonius Apollinaris, *The Panegyric of Avitus*, 458

Praetorium of the Master of Soldiers, Ravenna, Province of
Flaminia and Picenum, Diocese of Italy [Titus wrote in the
Liber Rufinorum], in the consulships of Flavius Placidius
Valentinianus, Augustus (his fifth), and of Anatolius, Ides
Nov.*

Aetius came close – so very close – to achieving what he
had set his heart and mind on: the re-establishing of Roman
ascendancy in Gaul. Then the joint Prefectures of Gaul and
Italy would have become the base for launching the reconquest of the lost dioceses in Spain and Africa, and even
perhaps the recovery of Britain. With Roman rule firmly
restored, the burden of taxation redistributed on a fair basis,
corruption rooted out, and revenue efficiently utilized, an
era of stability could have been ushered in. Then, following
the pattern of client kingdoms in the past, the federate tribes
would, in a generation or two, have become absorbed into
the life and culture of the Roman Empire, and become loyal
Romans: as Hispani, Gauls, Britons, Illyrians, et alii had
done before them. Alas, it was not to be.

Yet even as recently as the summer of last year it all looked
so promising. The Burgundians, after rebelling a second time,
were crushed so completely (their King, Gundohar, was killed)
as to pose no further threat to Rome. The Bagaudae had been
put down with appalling but effective severity, thus securing the
return of Aremorica to the Roman fold. The Visigoths had
been hurled back from Narbo Martius with heavy loss and were
now licking their wounds, with a commander of proven skill

* 13 November 440.

213

and experience, Litorius, keeping watch to make sure they stayed within their bounds. And, at least to my mind, something even more important than any of these had begun to take place, something intangible yet vital: a feeling of common purpose among the Roman troops. They had faced fearful odds – and won; and that experience had forged them into something like a band of brothers, united under a charismatic and inspiring leader. Wishful thinking? To some extent, perhaps. But a spark *was* there, and, if circumstances had not conspired to extinguish it, might have rekindled a flame of patriotism, not only in the army but among ordinary citizens. It is not impossible that Narbo could have become another Zama, where Scipio finally crushed Rome's arch-enemy, Hannibal.

That summer, the only cloud on the horizon was the non-arrival of pay for the troops, Huns, as well as the Roman field army. Hence Aetius' visit to Italia to find out the cause of the delay. At the time of his departure (with myself in tow), he was not seriously concerned; it seemed to be just another example of the inefficient administration of Valentinian – now an obnoxious youth of twenty – or rather of his mother, Galla Placidia. Aetius had submitted his returns, all scrupulously itemized and costed, to the Praetorian prefect, and had no reason to suspect that they would not be met in full.

By this time I had fully recovered from my injuries. Marcus I had entrusted to the care of a married couple, *coloni* on the family estate, good people unblessed with children of their own. As for me, I had returned to my old position on Aetius' staff of *agens in rebus*, a flexible term officially meaning a courier, but which could be extended to cover roles in diplomatic missions, investigative work, or even spying. It felt good to be back in uniform – pillbox cap, military belt, and long-sleeved tunic with indigo government roundels sewn on the hips and shoulders. (Owing to government cut-backs, the tunic was of undyed linen instead of scarlet wool.)

Once in Ravenna, Aetius entrusted me with the task of locating the missing funds. In my innocence I imagined this would be a reasonably straightforward matter. I was in for a shock. Investigating the *Sacrae largitiones*, the imperial finance ministry, would have made threading the Cretan labyrinth seem like child's play. I was passed from one department to another, interviewing a series of *numerarii*, or financial officials, and in turn their assistants, accountants, and paymasters; then separately scrutinizing the records of the various *carae epistolarum*, the officials in charge of financial correspondence. However, armed with a writ from Aetius, I was permitted to follow up my chain of investigation without obstruction, and, after ten days of the most mind-numbingly tedious and complex work I've ever undertaken, at last discovered what had happened to the missing funds.

And a sorry tale it was. The money had been 'diverted' (id est, peculated) along with other revenue, towards implementing a scheme of monstrous folly on the part of Valentinian: the refurbishment on a massive scale of the Colosseum,* followed by the most lavish games (wild-beast hunts et cetera, but of course no gladiatorial combats) to be staged in the Flavian Amphitheatre for a generation. And the reason? To celebrate the triumph of *Valentinian* for the victories in Gaul! As if the credit for those hard-won campaigns somehow belonged to the Emperor rather than his Master of Soldiers. (Shades of Claudius and the conquest of Britain.) The vanity, jealousy, and self-delusion of Valentinian and his scheming mother, which this act of insane extravagance illustrates, simply beggars belief. But the Emperor, I hear you cry, wouldn't wittingly jeopardize the security of the empire just to gratify his envy and resentment of the man who ruled it in his name. Well, if you think that, all I can say is, you don't know your Valentinian.

That this was a major setback for Aetius, there was no denying. Still, the money to pay the army could have been found somehow: if necessary by raiding the *res privata*, the Emperor's private income, derived from royal estates, bequests, confiscation of common land and pagan temple property, et cetera. As Patrician and Master of Soldiers, Aetius certainly had the power (if not the authorization) to do this. But then all such considerations were pushed into the background as the thunderbolts started falling.

* In 438, one of the last major public works projects carried out in the Western Empire.

First came the shocking news that Gaiseric had captured Carthage, the capital of Roman Africa, and seized the remaining grain-producing areas. Four years earlier, when the crisis in Gaul erupted, Aetius had – in order to avoid trouble breaking out in his rear – agreed a deal with Gaiseric by which the Vandals accepted federate status. Now, with the taking of Carthage and the adjacent territories, any hope of accommodation between Rome and the Vandals evaporated. Gaiseric went on to declare himself monarch of an independent kingdom, dating his regnal years from this event. Africa was torn away from the empire altogether, and the last of its grain supplies to Rome cut off.

But worse was to follow. No sooner had we learnt of the final fall of Africa, than a letter arrived for Aetius from Avitus in Gaul, containing terrible news.

Titus sighed as he searched through the jumble of papers in Aetius' office at his headquarters near Ravenna. Promotion within the courier service to the rank of *curiosus*, or inspector for the imperial post, meant that one of Titus' tasks was to check the warrants of those using it. Locating the documents in the chaos to which the Master of Soldiers regularly reduced the *tablinum* could be a time-consuming business. Presiding over the clutter were bronze busts, one at either end of the office, of Valentinian and Placidia. They had replaced an earlier bust, of Boniface, and had been installed for the same reason: 'Know thy enemy'. Typically, Aetius was marching up and down the room, consulting then discarding papers, while dictating to the unfortunate scribe who was trying to keep pace with him and simultaneously take down the message.

A slave entered and announced that a courier had arrived from Gaul with a letter requiring the general's immediate attention.

'Tell him to wait,' replied Aetius, then, 'Gaul, did you say? No, better send him in.'

Idly, Titus broke off his search to watch, while Aetius unfurled the scroll the dusty messenger handed to him, and began to peruse it. Suddenly, the general's face blanched and he swayed on his feet. 'Tell Avitus I'll make all speed to join him!' he cried hoarsely. Dismissing the courier, also the scribe, he stood in the middle of the room staring at the letter and muttered, 'I should have seen that this might happen.'

'Bad news, sir?' ventured Titus.

'What's that?' said the general distractedly, looking up. Seeing Titus, he exclaimed, 'Disaster! It seems Litorius may have lost us Provincia. Listen to what Avitus says.

'"I felt that the man had become dangerously unstable, – perhaps some of the things he had to do in Aremorica had affected him. You'll have heard, of course, about the incident on my estate. That in itself wouldn't have indicated that the count was unbalanced, only that he had difficulty controlling the Huns – admittedly, not an easy task. But when Quintus, his second-in-command, came to me privately and confided his doubts regarding Litorius (not from disloyalty – Quintus is the most faithful of subordinates – but out of genuine concern), I became seriously worried. Then came his brilliant relief of Narbo Martius. We were all tremendously impressed, and I began to think that I had judged the man too hastily. (Although in hindsight, there was, I think, an element of reckless bravado about the operation; it could so easily have gone badly wrong.) All things considered, when you appointed him commander-in-chief during your absence in Italia, I allowed my fears to become lulled. After all, the task you entrusted to Litorius was scarcely a demanding one. The Visigoths had been badly mauled and wanted nothing more than to be left to lick their wounds. Litorius, as I distinctly recall you making clear to him, was to be a vigilant policeman, nothing more.

'"So when the count announced that he intended to invade the Goths' homeland, granted them under treaty by Constantius, and invest their capital, Tolosa, I was thunderstruck. I tried to reason with him, pointing out that it was folly to pick an unnecessary quarrel with a tribe who appeared to have learnt their lesson, but who, if provoked, might still prove dangerous. But he wouldn't listen, declared that the only thing barbarians understood was force, and that he was going to treat the Goths as you had treated the Burgundians. He ignored the fact that you destroyed that tribe only when they broke out a second time. I think that his success at Narbo may have gone to his head, creating the delusion that he was invincible.

'"Anyway, he marched with the Huns to Tolosa. (Fortunately, I managed to persuade him to leave the bulk of the Roman field army behind, with myself, as a rearguard.) When he got to Tolosa – you won't believe this, he conducted a full-scale pagan sacrifice,* complete with augurs examining the entrails and predicting victory! What the Huns made of it I can't imagine, and any Romans present must have thought he'd taken leave of his senses. Did *you* know the man was a closet pagan? I certainly had no inkling. When I heard about it, I became convinced that the man's mind had become unhinged. I added my voice to that of King Theoderic's emissaries – bishops, no less – pleading with Litorius that he accept their peace proposals. But he rejected them, with the predictable result that the Goths became desperate.

'"With nothing to lose, they launched a night attack on the count's camp, which in his rashness and over-confidence he'd neglected to fortify or appoint sentries to guard. Prepare yourself my dear friend, for what I must now tell you. Litorius has proved a second Varus, who led his legions into an ambush, resulting in their annihilation. The Huns were wiped out almost to a man, and Litorius himself taken; whether he is still alive, I have no means of knowing. The situation here is critical. The Goths, now full of confidence and clamouring for revenge, are preparing to invade Provincia. Whatever business you have in Italy, I urge you to abandon it. Collect what troops you can, and march for Gaul immediately. I am strengthening the walls of Arelate and, with the field army, will try to hold the line until you join me."'

Rolling up the letter, Aetius stared at Titus bleakly. 'Sixty thousand Huns – lost,' he whispered, and Titus saw in his eyes a flash of something he had never seen before: despair. Suddenly, the general looked shrunken, old.

But only for a moment. Squaring his shoulders, Aetius announced crisply, 'I must prepare to leave for Gaul. Meanwhile, you, Titus, will go to Attila as my emissary. Travel by imperial post to the frontier, then buy the fastest horse you can. Explain to Attila exactly what has happened, sparing no details – he'd see through any excuses or cover-ups straight away. Tell him that I'll do all in my power to repay in full the debt I owe him, and assure him that I'll come in person as soon as I have settled things in Gaul. Perhaps we can still save something from the wreck. If it is to survive, the West must continue to have Hun help. All right?'

---

* The last time an official pagan sacrifice was ever held.

'Of course, sir. But . . . wouldn't a letter from you carry more weight?'

Aetius shook his head. 'Attila is a barbarian, remember. They distrust and despise parchment promises. Believe me, personal contact is now our only hope of mending bridges.' He gripped Titus by the shoulder and gave a wan smile. 'Do you best, Titus. Once you saved the life of a Roman general. Now your words to Attila could save Rome itself.'

'. . . and promises to come himself, Your Majesty, as soon as he has finished dealing with the Visigoths,' concluded Titus. He could feel his heart thumping and sweat break out on his palms, as he waited, standing to attention, for Attila's response. At the other end of the reception chamber in the King's timber palace, Attila, clad in a skin robe, was seated on a throne-like wooden chair: a stocky, powerful figure with an enormous head, whose very stillness, like a wound-up ballista, hinted at enormous reserves of stored energy. His flat Mongol features remained impassive.

'Tell your master, the Patrician, Flavius Aetius,' Attila said at length, in his deep, guttural voice, 'that I will not see him. It is finished between us. I trusted him, put the flower of my army at his disposal. And how does he repay me? By contriving their destruction. You say he swears to make good the debt he owes me. How, then, does he propose to give me back my sixty thousand warriors? By sowing dragon's teeth perhaps?' He gave a bitter laugh. 'I had thought Aetius to be that rare thing among Romans, a man of honour whose word was good. Now I see his promises are worthless, like those of all his race. For the sake of the friendship that was once between us, I will allow his son Carpilio, my hostage, to return with you. Go now, Roman, and tell your master this: should we meet again, it will be as enemies, not friends.'

When Titus and Carpilio had departed, Attila rode out of the encampment alone, to nurse his fury and sorrow. Fury that his trust had been betrayed, sorrow for the ending of an old and valued friendship; both fury and sorrow for the loss of so many fine warriors, and the collapse of his vision of a Greater Scythia. If he and Aetius had been the only players in the game, perhaps their friendship could have survived. Perhaps. But, with the

Council to answer to, that was no longer an option. Especially as Bleda could be guaranteed to exploit the crisis to the maximum, in order to undermine his brother's position. Attila's credibility was on the line; once the disaster of Tolosa became generally known, recriminations and divisions in the Council, with discord and disunity spreading like a cancer through the nation, would inevitably follow. Unless . . .

In a flash of intuition, Attila realized what he must do. At this critical juncture, what was needed above all was decisive leadership – leadership which he alone could supply. If he could no longer give his people greatness, he could at least give them what they lusted after. Gold. And the source of that gold? The empire of the Romans.

His powerful mind teeming with plans and ideas, Attila returned to the palace. Which empire to attack, East or West? He would spare the West – he perhaps owed Aetius that much. Besides, the West's treasury was depleted, half its territory ceded to German federates who paid no tribute. Whereas the East was wealthy beyond computation, its cities populous and rich, its churches and cathedrals crammed with treasure. And the time was ripe for an assault on the Eastern Empire. Its Emperor, Theodosius II, was weak and irresolute. And the East was distracted on two fronts. It was involved in a campaign against the Persians on its eastern frontier; and its remaining legions had been sent to Sicily, to help the West recover Africa from Gaiseric. In fact, the Vandal King, that implacable enemy of Rome, had already sent emissaries to Attila, proposing a Vandal–Hun alliance: a suggestion which Attila, hoping to establish good relations with the Romans, had so far ignored. But now such an offer seemed uncannily fortuitous. He would dictate a letter to Gaiseric, agreeing to the pact. He sent for Orestes, his young Roman secretary.[*]

While he waited, the words in which Wu Tze had described the second part of his vision suddenly rang in Attila's head: 'Now the ass pursues another eagle, wounding it before it can fly away.' As before, when he had sent his Huns to help Aetius, the meaning became clear. The wild ass of the plains was the Huns, the another eagle the Second Rome: the Huns would attack and harm the Eastern Empire. A chill foreboding gripped the monarch, even

---

[*] Father of the last West Roman Emperor, Romulus Augustus (see Notes p.434).

as he insisted to himself that the seer's prediction was merely coincidence.

. . . and so Fortune, who only a short time ago smiled on Aetius [Titus wrote, tying up the threads of the entry in his journal], has now spun her wheel against him. In a twinkling, all his hard-won gains have been put in jeopardy. Gaul, which had seemed secure, is again under threat: the Visigoths, their power so nearly broken, are once more strong and ambitious, with eyes fixed upon Provincia; the Franks are encroaching in the north-east.

Money is the crying need – cash to pay the troops, to replenish supplies, arms and armour. Man for man, the Roman field army remains more than a match for its enemies, but for lack of cash is gradually eroding away. And the treasury is empty. Africa, once the jewel in the imperial crown, whose grain and tribute once filled Rome's stomach and her coffers, is now totally lost (although a joint East–West expedition for its recovery is now preparing in Sicilia).

Most serious of all has been the slaughter of the Huns at Tolosa, through the folly of Litorius (who, Rome has learnt, has been put to death by his Goth captors). As a result, Aetius has lost the friendship and support of Attila, his oldest and most powerful ally. And without Hun help the West is dangerously weakened. If they should ever turn against us . . .

One bright ray shines through the gathering clouds: Aetius and Theoderic, King of the Visigoths and son of the mighty Alaric, have become reconciled. When the Roman army and the Goth host confronted one another, following Aetius' return from Italia to Gaul, the two generals decided that a bloody encounter whose issue was uncertain was not in the interests of either. Avitus arranged peace terms which have been accepted by both sides.

Boniface and Litorius: these two may prove to be Aetius' Nemesis. Had he not made an enemy of one and put his trust in the other, Africa and Gaul, whose fate may decide that of the West, would today be secure within the empire.

TWENTY-NINE

They [The Huns] gallop about inflicting tremendous slaughter;
what makes them the most formidable of warriors is that they
shoot arrows from a distance
Ammianus Marcellinus, *The Histories, c.* 395

'Three across, two down, Gallus,' the soldier called to his comrade.
They were *limitanei*, despised frontier troops, on lookout duty on
top of a small fort that formed part of the defensive chain along the
Eastern Empire's Illyrian frontier. Half a mile away stood a hilltop
signal station, visible to the stations on its left and right, and to
the intervening forts. It consisted of a timber scaffold, with apparatus for raising and lowering long beams, four on each side; on
a clear day, these could be seen over a distance of several miles.
At night or in misty conditions this system was replaced by one
of timed flares synchronized with gradations on a water-clock; on
the flare being extinguished, the final mark was noted by the
recipient, who then consulted a table of messages corresponding
to the gradations.

Gallus checked the reference chart, a square board divided into
sixteen smaller squares, each marked with a letter of the alphabet:
A–Q. Four squares across and two down, that was 'M'. He consulted
the message table: 'M: hostile cavalry approaching, strength
maximum.' That was odd; and alarming. Incoming messages almost
always referred to tiny isolated groups of Huns, Goths, or Sarmatians,
who had crossed to the Roman side of the Danube, and were 'A:
small mounted party passing, armed', 'B: small foot party passing,
armed', or 'C: nomads with herds, passing'. Large concentrations
of warriors were rare. 'Hostile' was a first, as was 'maximum'. 'Sure
you got the signal correctly, Paulus?' he called.

'See for yourself.'

Gallus crossed the keep's flat roof and mounted the steps to
the battlements. He looked towards the signal station. Sure
enough, the distant installation, which resembled a giant rake

with upward-pointing tines, showed three upright arms on the right side, two on the left, starkly silhouetted against the sky.

Any doubts concerning the accuracy of the message were about to be dissolved. 'Domine!' breathed Paulus, pointing. Five miles or so ahead, stretching to right and left as far as the eye could see, a shimmering wall of dust, dotted with winking points of light, was rolling swiftly towards them. There came to their ears a sound like the distant booming of breakers, which swiftly grew to a thunderous drum-roll. Now, they began to make out figures in the dust-cloud, skin-clad warriors with flat yellowish faces, bows slung on back and swords on hip, mounted on huge, ugly horses.

Like a tidal wave breaking on a reef, the horde of Huns crashed against the line of forts – strongholds which had held firm against Alaric's Goths – pausing only long enough to overwhelm the defenders and torch the interiors before sweeping south, leaving a row of blazing shells, like beacons, in their wake.

On the roof of their tower, Gallus and Paulus, joined by comrades from below, strove desperately to dislodge the grapnels that showered over the crenellations. As well try to keep back the tide with a broom; no sooner was one hook removed than two more came thudding on to the walkway. Powerless to hold back the mass of Huns that swarmed over the parapet, they died where they stood. Blazing bales were hurled into the keep's interior from the trapdoor in the roof, forcing those guarding the gate from inside to open it – and meet the fate of those above.

In the basilica of Sirmium,* the mighty Illyrian city which had been the headquarters of the first Valentinian in his campaigns against the Germans, and where the great Theodosius had been proclaimed Emperor, there was an air of near-panic among the decurions assembling for an extraordinary meeting of the council. When all were seated and after the ritual acclamations had been made, the president, a chubby figure with a blandly beaming face, ascended the rostrum. He was immediately greeted by a barrage of questions: 'Is it true that the Huns have taken Singidunum** . . . Are they heading this way? . . . What's the army doing? . . . Have the *limitanei* really been wiped out?'

---

* Mitrovica, in Kosovo.
** Belgrade.

The president raised his arms and gradually silence spread throughout the great hall. 'Fellow decurions,' he declared, assuming his most reassuring smile, 'it is indeed unfortunately true that Singidunum has fallen.' Uproar. 'However,' he continued, when the hubbub had died down, 'it was to a large extent the citizens' own fault. They kept no watch and were consequently taken by surprise. They had allowed their defences to fall into disrepair, and they made no effort to treat with the enemy. We in Sirmium, however, are in an infinitely stronger position. Our walls, the strongest in Illyria, are virtually impregnable. We've had ample warning, so we can strengthen any weak points and maintain a twenty-four-hour lookout. Also, I propose that we select a certain number from among our inner committee, the *principales*, to meet the Hun leaders and negotiate with them. We know how much they love gold. If we present them with valuable gifts, and promise a handsome subsidy to boot, I have every confidence they will leave Sirmium unmolested.'

Privately, the president intended to make quite sure that any delegation to the Huns would be headed by himself. For he had decided, as a personal insurance policy, to take a leaf out of the Bishop of Margus' book. Just in case the projected negotiations failed. The bishop had provided the Huns with a pretext for their invasion. They alleged that he had plundered certain burial sites of their kings, north of the Danubius, removing valuable grave-goods. When, in order to appease the Huns, the Roman authorities had been about to hand the bishop over, the wily cleric had stolen a march. Making a secret deal with the Huns, he opened the gates of Margus to them, in return for his life being spared and a substantial reward. Whereupon Margus, the city that six years earlier had witnessed an important treaty with the Huns, was given over to fire and sword.

As anything that offered hope of averting a visitation by the Huns was what all the councillors wanted to hear, the president's suggestion was eagerly seized upon, and a deputation quickly appointed, headed, with general consent, by the council's president. Soon afterwards it was reported that the Huns had been sighted approaching the city; the delegation prepared to head for the main gate. But as they left the basilica, they were surrounded by an angry, frightened crowd. Word of the plan – which had perhaps been overheard by an eavesdropping janitor on duty in the basilica – had leaked out. The ordinary citizens of Sirmium, who had long ago lost the right to elect the council, suspected that the delegates were preparing to effect a sell-out in order to save their own skins. These suspicions were reinforced when, as a result of the deputation being jostled and rough-handled, some of the intended gifts came to light.

What had started as a heated demonstration soon flared up into a full-scale riot – something deeply feared by all Roman councils, whose authority was backed up by an often inadequate police force. Sirmium had only the night watch and a skeleton garrison of superannuated *limitanei*; both, on this occasion, conspicuous by their absence. Through some malign alchemy, the truculent crowd was transmuted in a twinkling into a raging mob which, after beating up the delegates and robbing them of the gifts intended for the Huns – thus effectively destroying any hopes of buying them off – proceeded to storm the basilica and give chase to the departing councillors.

At the first sign of trouble, the president, streetwise and cunning, had darted for cover behind a row of stalls. Now, under cover of the fighting and confusion, he slipped into a side alley and made his way to the city walls. Removing a massive key from under his dalmatic, he unlocked a postern gate and stepped outside the ramparts – to find himself confronted by six mounted warriors: from an advance party sent to reconnoitre the environs of the city, ahead of the main Hun force. Switching on his most ingratiating smile, he moved towards the riders, holding aloft in one hand the postern key, and in the other a heavy bag which chinked.

The first arrow transfixed his stomach, the second his throat, cutting off his screams of agony. Within seconds, he resembled an oversized pincushion which twitched briefly on the ground, then lay still. Picking up the key and the bag of *solidi*, one of the scouts galloped back to report to his captain while the others, laughing, resumed their circuit of the city.

Despite its massive fortifications, Sirmium held out against the Huns for an even shorter time than Singidunum. Within an hour of their first being sighted, the city, like a rock in an angry sea, was surrounded by a swirling horde of Huns. With a courage born of terror, the citizens, using improvised weapons – kitchen knives, gardening-tools, even prised-up cobblestones – strove to stem the flood of Huns that threatened to engulf the ramparts, as ladders and grapnels thumped against the battlements, and siege-towers, constructed under the direction of captured Roman engineers, were wheeled against the walls. For a time, they succeeded in keeping the enemy at bay. Infected by a mood of febrile triumph, they redoubled their efforts, hurling ladder after ladder crashing to the ground, each scattering its load of Huns, or fighting with such desperate fury that even the ferocious savages who had gained a footing on the walkway were daunted.

But their optimism was premature. Suddenly, the defenders found themselves embattled on two fronts, as Huns who had infiltrated the city through the unlocked postern poured on to the ramparts from the staircases on the inside face of the walls. The Sirmians' new-found confidence evaporated as suddenly as it had arisen, and they began to throw down their weapons in droves; in a few minutes all had surrendered.

The inhabitants were assembled on a plain near the city and divided into three parts. The first class consisted of the garrison and men capable of bearing arms. They were massacred on the spot by Huns who, with bended bows, had formed a circle round them. The second class, consisting of the young and attractive women, and skilled tradesmen such as smiths and carpenters, were distributed in lots. The remainder, being neither useful nor a threat to the nomads, were turned loose – many to perish of starvation in the fire-scorched wasteland to which the Huns had reduced northern Illyria. Emptied, the city was looted of anything of value, then systematically demolished, with a thoroughness which almost justified a saying that was already gaining currency: 'The grass never grows where the horse of Attila has trod.'

In furious impatience, Aspar, son of the great Ardaburius, veteran of the campaigns against Ioannes (successful) and Gaiseric (unsuccessful), and now commander of the joint East–West army assembled in Sicilia for the reconquest of Africa, paced the colonnade of his headquarters in the Neapolis district of Syracusa. For perhaps the tenth time that morning, he looked down at the Great Harbour, crammed with the expedition's warships, hoping to spot the arrival of a fast galley – one must surely soon bring word from Constantinople. News of Attila's onslaught on Illyria had arrived weeks before. The expedition had immediately been suspended, but the expected imperial missive ordering it to return to the capital, to counter the Hun threat, had so far failed to arrive.

The Romans were letting Gaiseric run circles round them, Aspar thought, in frustration mingled with contempt. The combined naval and military armament of both empires had been ready to move against the Vandal tyrant. And Theoderic, King of the Visigoths, in a bizarre reversal of his recent anti-Roman operations, had been burning to lend his support to the expedition! (His daughter, married to Gaiseric's son, was suspected of involvement in a plot to poison the Vandal king, and had been sent back to her father by Gaiseric – minus her nose and ears.) But Gaiseric, as cunning as he was cruel, had stolen a march on the Romans and their new Goth friends by forming an alliance with Attila, who had promptly obliged by invading the Eastern Empire.

If only he could be given a free hand, Aspar fumed. There was that business over the usurper Iohannes sixteen years ago, for instance. He'd just about had Aetius stalemated, and could have gone on to beat him if he hadn't been summoned back to the East over a trifling border dispute with Persia. Then there was that chaotic shambles in Africa, when the Vandals had been allowed to destroy the joint forces of both empires, because the commander-in-chief, Boniface, had lost his nerve. Had the command been his, Aspar told himself, the result would have been very different. (Of course, the fact that he was an Arian had all along probably blocked any chance of his being appointed Master of Soldiers.) And now, when the safety of the Eastern Empire's northern dioceses depended on getting an army there as quickly as possible, here he was stuck in Sicilia, while Attila ravaged Illyria at will.

It was all the fault of Arnegliscus, the new Eastern Master of Soldiers, thought Aspar bitterly. Ambitious, brutal, and slow-witted, Arnegliscus had murdered the previous *Magister militum*, a fellow German, and usurped his post. He'd have had no difficulty in persuading his imperial master, the weak and pliable Theodosius, that he'd done so to forestall a plot against the Emperor, say. And the fact that he was supported by the circus faction of the Greens (the people's party) would have put Theodosius under extra pressure to confirm him in the post or risk provoking a riot. By the time that ponderous Teutonic mind had got round to deciding that something should be done about the Huns, Attila would probably be battering at the gates of Constantinople.

Being a fair-minded man, however, after a little reflection Aspar reluctantly admitted that he was being less than just to Arnegliscus. He was allowing frustration and impatience to colour his assessment of the man. Coarse-grained and limited the German might be, but the very fact that he had become Master of Soldiers showed that he at least possessed two sterling qualities, leadership and courage. Otherwise, the legions would never have accepted him. For the same reason, he could hardly be considered stupid: fools did not become top generals. Nor, as Aspar could testify from personal experience, did paragons of gentle forbearance. In the dog-eat-dog world of Roman power politics, Arnegliscus might have been compelled to eliminate his predecessor in order to forestall his own assassination by one who feared a rival. As for his embroidering the truth in order to influence Theodosius, well, hadn't every successful general and politician been compelled to play that game, from Pericles to Constantine and beyond?

Suddenly, Aspar's pulse began racing. Oars flashing in the sunlight, a fast galley shot from behind the islet of Ortygia and raced towards the entrance of the Great Harbour. Backing water with a stylish flourish as it neared the mole, it shipped oars and glided gently to its moorings. Surely this, at last, must be the ship bringing the orders for the expedition to return to the Golden Horn. The Alan general waited expectantly for a messenger to arrive, and, sure enough, a little later a *biarchus* was ushered into his presence. The man handed Aspar a sheaf of scrolls. The general scanned each briefly, with growing impatience and concern: fodder returns for the new cavalry barracks at Nicomedia; a complaint about the quality of a batch of javelin heads from the state arms factory at Ratiaria; a plea for a diploma of discharge on behalf of a standard-bearer claiming disablement . . .

'You're quite sure there's nothing from the palace?' he asked.

The *biarchus* looked in his satchel and shook his head. 'Sorry, sir. Wish I could say different. There's not a soldier in the empire but wishes you and the army were back home.' He added anxiously, 'Er, best forget I said that, sir.'

'Said what?' smiled Aspar. He suddenly came to a bold

decision; this farce had gone on long enough. 'What's your ship's next destination?'

'Cyrene, sir.'

'No it isn't. Tell the captain I'm requisitioning his vessel to take me immediately to Constantinople.'

'Yes, *sir!*' With a delighted grin, the man saluted and hurried off to deliver the general's command.

Theodosius, the second of that name, Emperor of the East Romans, the Calligrapher (of all his royal titles, the one of which he was most proud), laid down his pen from the task in which he was engaged: copying, in beautiful Rustic capitals, Jerome's *Third Attack on the Pelagian Heresy*. 'Will it do, sister?' he enquired anxiously of the handsome but dowdily dressed woman in her early forties who had just entered the *scriptorium*.

'I'm sure the monks of my new monastery will be impressed,' sighed Pulcheria wearily. She went on with a hint of impatience, 'There are, however, also worldly matters which have a claim on your attention. I would remind you, brother, that the generals have been waiting more than an hour.'

'Oh dear, as long as that?' murmured the Emperor contritely. 'Well, we'd better see them, I suppose.' He rose from the writing-desk; two slaves dressed him in a purple robe and slippers, then placed the imperial diadem on his head. Meekly, he followed his sister, the Augusta, along a succession of corridors to the audience chamber. This was a grand colonnaded affair, overlooking the jumble of splendid but asymmetrical series of buildings, cascading downhill towards the Propontis,* that made up the rest of Constantinople's imperial palace.

The two men who bowed low, 'adoring the Sacred Purple', at the entry of the royal pair were very different in appearance. Aspar, the Alan general, was slight, with delicate aquiline features and olive colouring. The other was tall, of massive build, with shoulder-length yellow hair and fair skin, a magnificent specimen of manhood. This was Arnegliscus, the Master of Soldiers. Their dress pointed up the contrast between the pair. Aspar's simple military tunic and leggings still bore the marks of travel, for he had come straight from the docks on the Golden Horn. The German

---

* The Sea of Marmara.

was got up in the full regalia of a Roman general, complete with silvered cuirass and bronze-studded *pteruges*, leather strips protecting the shoulders, and the lower body from waist to knee.

Theodosius and Pulcheria seated themselves on thrones. 'Aspar,' declared the Emperor, 'we are displeased that you have taken it upon yourself not only to return to Constantinople without our permission, but to commandeer a naval vessel, thus preventing it from transacting important business in Cyrene.' Striving for stern censoriousness, Theodosius succeeded in sounding merely peevish. He turned to Pulcheria. 'His presumption is inexcusable, do you not agree?'

'Let us hear what he has to say, before we judge him,' replied the Augusta. 'You may speak, Aspar.'

'Your Serenities must excuse me if I speak in plain terms,' began the Alan. 'The situation as I see it is approaching crisis. Our army is absent and divided – half on the Persian frontier, the rest in Sicily. Meanwhile Attila is rampaging freely throughout Illyria, destroying cities, massacring or enslaving the people. It makes no sense that our troops are not here. As a matter of the most urgent priority, I say we must recall both forces without further delay.' All at once, Aspar realized that any appeal to reasoned compromise would probably fail. To make sure it was his view that prevailed, he was first going to have to daemonize the big German. Reluctantly switching to attack mode, he went on, 'Frankly, I am at a loss to understand why the Master of Soldiers has not done this already.' Despite having an Asiatic contempt for petticoat politics, Aspar was thankful for the presence of Pulcheria. Strange, he thought, that each half of the empire was run by a strong-willed woman controlling a weak Emperor. But where Pulcheria was sensible and decisive, Placidia was inept and devious; where Theodosius was merely ineffective, Valentinian was vicious and a liability.

'Arnegliscus?' invited Pulcheria.

The commander shrugged. 'Come the autumn,' he said slowly, 'Attila must return to his meadows beyond the Danubius. Already his horses grow thin; he has all but exhausted the pastures of Illyria.'

'And next year?' sneered Aspar. 'Having discovered that the empire provided such easy pickings, do you really suppose that Attila will fail to return? Or that he won't keep coming back year after year – until the empire takes a stand? Or is it perhaps that Arnegliscus is afraid to match himself against the Hun?' In fact, as Aspar well knew, Arnegliscus was no coward; few Germans were. But if it took a confrontation to unblock the log-jam of inactivity, so be it.

The German rose to the bait. 'Anyone who says Arnegliscus is afraid, lies,' he growled.

'Fine words!' retorted Aspar. 'But words are cheap. Let us see if you dare match them with fine actions.'

An angry flush suffused the German's cheeks. 'Perhaps now is not the time for action,' he countered, his tone defensive and his blue eyes flashing with resentment. 'To confront Attila at this moment is to risk the destruction of our armies. I say let the Huns ravage Thracia, Dacia and Macedonia.* Poor, thinly populated, in the last resort they are expendable. It is the wealthy east and south – Asia Minor, Syria, Palestine, Egypt, Libya – that we must safeguard above all. To attack them, Attila must first take Constantinople. And that he cannot do.'

Privately, Aspar was forced to concede that what Arnegliscus said had much to recommend it. The mighty walls of Constantinople could withstand the worst assault that Attila could hurl against them, and, with the capital inviolate, the security of the Eastern Empire's heart was guaranteed. But abandon Illyris Graeca** to the fury of the Huns? Unthinkable. Wasn't it? For the first time, Aspar was assailed by a creeping doubt regarding the wisdom of taking the field against the Huns – at least until the armies of the East had developed effective tactics against the terrible archery of the nomad hordes. But it was too late to row back now.

'So you would have the army sit safe behind the ramparts of Constantinople,' he sneered, 'without lifting a finger to help, while Attila's savages wreak havoc and destruction throughout Illyria, Thrace, and Macedonia? To settle for a shameful policy of appeasement – that is the coward's way.'

'Enough!' said Pulcheria sharply. 'Rather than fight among ourselves, we should be planning how to deal with our common foe. Aspar is right. Things must not be allowed to drift any further.

* The Balkan provinces.
** The Balkans (region).

Let us recall our legions from Sicilia and the east; the situation on neither of these fronts is critical, and anyway operations can be resumed when the present danger is past.' She turned to Theodosius. 'Agreed, my lord?'

'Oh, very well,' assented the Emperor testily. Then, as if to avoid giving the impression that he was passively yielding to pressure, he sat up erect on his throne and announced loudly, 'It is our word and our command that the African Expedition and the troops now serving on the Persian frontier be immediately recalled to Constantinople, and that they be put in readiness to march against the Huns. You, Arnegliscus, will be in overall charge, with Aspar as your second-in-command.'

Surveying the Roman dispositions from a low hill behind the cavalry wing on the army's left, Aspar was overwhelmed by uneasiness. The terrain was hot, barren, and dusty; in the distance, the Thracian trading-port of Kallipolis* huddled beside the blue waters of the Hellespont. A splendid opportunity to check 'the Scourge of God', as Attila was becoming known, had been squandered by the folly of the Emperor.

Following the recall of the troops from Sicilia and the Persian front, Aspar, with Arnegliscus' agreement, had bought time by arranging a truce with Attila, through promising the return of fugitives, also paying part of the arrears of tribute fixed by the Treaty of Margus. Time which he had made good use of to begin to hammer the two halves of the army into a disciplined, united force capable of taking on an unfamiliar and terrible enemy. But, to Aspar's fury, these solid gains had been needlessly thrown away. With a false confidence inspired by the return of the legions, Theodosius had forced Aspar to renege on his promises to the Hun king. By order of the Emperor, fugitives were not after all to be returned, nor was any further tribute to be paid. Predictably, Attila had been enraged, and had responded by launching a strike to the east: taking Ratiaria (an important state arms factory and the base of the Danubius fleet), Naissus, Serdica**, and Philippopolis. With the Huns now dangerously near his capital, Theodosius had ordered a reluctant Arnegliscus

* Gallipoli.
** Niš, Sofia.

to take the field against them. Unsurprisingly, the half-trained army had suffered two reverses. Pressed ever eastwards by the victorious Huns, it had been outflanked by Attila and now, its retreat cut off, had been forced into the Chersonesus of Thracia, the narrow peninsula bounding the northern shore of the Hellespontus.*

Never was a position more hopeless, thought Aspar despairingly, looking at the way Arnegliscus had drawn up the army. The infantry were arranged in a solid block twenty-five ranks deep, with a cavalry wing on either side. The formation resembled a plump partridge, a partridge ready for plucking. The two engagements with the Huns so far had been running skirmishes rather than full-scale encounters. Now, boxed into the Chersonesus, the Romans had no choice but to fight a pitched battle. What on earth was Arnegliscus' tactical thinking? By concentrating his men in a solid mass, the German presumably imagined he was maximizing their effectiveness. That might have made sense in the days of the Macedonian phalanx, but against a highly mobile and – in terms of numbers – vastly superior enemy, armed moreover with long-range weapons, it was suicidal folly. Ultimately, however, the blame must lie largely with himself, Aspar admitted, with a sick feeling of guilt. If he hadn't overridden Arnegliscus and persuaded the Empress to take the battle to the Hun . . .

Arnegliscus had positioned the Roman force on open ground facing the direction the enemy must approach from, with the supply wagons some distance to the rear. What he had failed to grasp was that there *was* no rear. He was inviting the Huns to employ their most successful tactic: to move round behind their opponents and encircle them. Unless something was done, the Battle of Kallipolis would prove to be another Hadrianopolis. Well, he, Aspar, wasn't going to stand by and let disaster overtake them, without first putting some suggestions to his superior. Dispatching a galloper to summon Areobindus, the commander of the cavalry on the right wing, Aspar spurred over to Arnegliscus' command tent behind the infantry. Dismounting, he strode inside.

Arnegliscus was seated at a table strewn with maps and documents; there were also a flagon and goblets. He stared at Aspar

* The Dardanelles.

with some irritation, but retained enough manners to offer the general some wine.

'Thank you, but I prefer to keep a clear head,' retorted Aspar. 'I have several suggestions that must be made.'

'"Must"?' growled Arnegliscus, his blue eyes widening. 'You forget yourself, I think.'

'Yes, "must", snapped Aspar. At that moment, Areobindus, a tall German with hair cut short in the Roman fashion, entered the tent. 'As things stand,' Aspar pressed on, 'you face almost certain defeat. Your flanks are exposed, therefore the Huns will surround you. The infantry are packed together in a solid mass, a formation far too deep to allow the rear ranks to help those in front.' He turned to Areobindus. '*You* can see that, surely?' he appealed.

'Aspar does have a point, sir,' Areobindus observed tactfully. 'Our front would become more effective if you were to expand it; eight ranks are quite sufficient to give staying power. May I also suggest that the wagons are brought up closer to the line? They would then be protected and could, if occasion arose, be deployed to form a protective screen. Left where they are, they will certainly be looted and destroyed.'

'Above all, you must protect the flanks,' urged Aspar, his heart sinking as he noted a look of stubborn defensiveness settle on Arnegliscus' face. 'Only a mile from here, there's a steep-sided valley, not too broad for our troops to span. Our flanks would then be secure.' Actually, what he was suggesting was, Aspar knew, a desperate enough alternative; to form an unbroken front across the valley would mean stretching the Roman line perilously thin. But almost any plan would be preferable to the present arrangement.

'I had thought guarding the flanks was the duty of the cavalry,' said Arnegliscus sourly. 'I must have been mistaken.'

Areobindus stiffened and an angry gleam appeared in his eye. Determined not to be drawn, Aspar said coolly, 'I shall ignore that, sir. Another thing. The men have been standing in the sun for hours. They're hot, thirsty, and demoralized. Issue them with food and water, and give them permission to stand down until the enemy's sighted. They'll fight better rested and on a full stomach. Also, a few words from yourself might help to raise their spirits.'

'Very well,' conceded Arnegliscus, 'it shall be done. And I shall extend the line as you suggest. Also the wagons will be brought up closer to the rear. These things are only sensible, I grant. But I see no need for other change. The army stays where it is.'

Further argument was pointless, Aspar realized. He glanced at Areobindus, who shrugged resignedly. 'On your head be it,' Aspar said to Arnegliscus. 'If the year of the consuls Maximus and Paterius* is remembered in Rome's annals for another Cannae, Rome will know whom to blame.' Saluting, he left the tent, mounted, and rode back to his station.

A murmur passed along the Roman lines as a galloping scout hove into sight. A little later, the commanders assembled in front of their units to announce that the enemy was close; and that from this moment on the men were to maintain silence, observe orders, and keep position.

A bank of what seemed like mist or smoke had appeared on the horizon. Extending on either hand to the limit of visibility and growing taller by the second, it rolled swiftly towards the waiting Romans. A distant murmur changed to a steady pattering, which in turn became a rumbling roar. The earth began to tremble. Now dots could be made out in the dust-cloud, dots which rapidly grew into galloping riders.

'Right, boys, let's have the *barritus*,' called a *primicerius*. 'Make it a good one.'

Clashing their lances against their shields, the Romans gave their battle-cry, beginning on a low note and swelling to a deafening shout. It was intended to raise morale when the line confronted a charging enemy, but this time the *barritus* wavered and died away as the Hun formations, instead of engaging the Roman front in a head-on attack, split and wheeled when just beyond javelin range, to pour past the army's flanks in two enormous masses and reunite behind its rear. Now the Romans found themselves encircled in a vast whirlpool of horsemen, who began to shoot their arrows.

In a continuous blizzard, the shafts arced high in the air, to plunge down on to the Romans. The front ranks, the only men issued with both helmets and mail coats, and with enough room to raise their shields, remained comparatively unscathed. But the

* 443.

soldiers in the middle, helmeted but lacking body-armour, and so close-packed they were unable to use their shields to protect their upper bodies, began to suffer terrible punishment. The cavalry wings did their best to keep the Hun archers at bay, charging time after time to drive them back. Barring scouts and skirmishers, the Roman horse consisted of heavy armoured cavalry, virtually invulnerable to arrows, and more than a match for their opponents on an individual basis. But when outnumbered on a huge scale their effectiveness was severely limited.

Once, in an attempt to come to grips with the enemy, the trumpets on the Roman side sounded the advance. But the encircling Huns merely kept pace with the advancing Romans, whose formations began to lose cohesion and to take even more casualties. When the halt was eventually sounded, the Roman infantry had been reduced to a panic-stricken rabble, desperate to flee or to engage their tormentors, but unable to do either. Taking turns to peel away and breathe their horses, the Huns were able to maintain a constant barrage, which exacted a terrible toll. Throughout that endless afternoon, the Roman ranks thinned steadily, which by a grim irony benefited the survivors, who now had room to raise their shields and protect their torsos. Only the coming of darkness brought respite to the beleaguered army.

Tortured by thirst and wounds throughout the long night, the Romans awaited the dawn with dread. But the rising sun showed only an empty plain. The Huns had gone.

To his captains, Attila's decision to spare the shattered remnant of the Roman army smacked of commendable contempt for a negligible foe. How could they guess that it stemmed from self-disgust? Attila's stock could now stand hardly higher. To his people he was a conquering hero, who had brought them plunder beyond imagining and made their name feared throughout the world. But to Attila himself it was all a hollow triumph, like those apples of legend which turned to ashes in the mouth. This was not what he had wanted for his nation. Any hopes now of creating a Greater Scythia were dashed for ever; he had sent home the team of advisers Aetius had provided. Posterity would remember Attila not as a second Caesar or another Alexander, but as the Scourge of God, the barbarian who had loosed death and destruction on a scale never before witnessed.

THIRTY

*We knew not whether we were in Heaven or on earth; for on earth
there is no such splendour or such beauty*
Report of the envoys of Prince Vladimir of Kiev,
on Constantinople, tenth century

'Gold, more gold . . . Let us send envoys to extort rich gifts . . .
They are pressed by enemies on all sides – Persians, Isaurians,
Saracens, even black men from Axum in the farthest south, so they
cannot refuse us anything we ask . . . Gold, gold . . .' From all
over the assembly, convened to determine Hun policy towards
Eastern Rome, arose excited demands, inflamed by avarice and
arrogance deriving from overwhelming victory, to extract more
and yet more tribute from the Romans following their crushing
defeat in the Chersonesus. After that battle, peace terms had been
negotiated with Anatolius, military commander for the diocese of
Oriens, terms which were vastly harsher and more punitive than
those of Margus, but which the East had been in no position to
refuse.

Savages, thought Attila, surveying his Council with weary
contempt. Short-sighted barbarians. In wishing to impose such
humiliating conditions on the Eastern Romans, his people were
forgetting the cardinal rule of nomad society: you did not destroy
a beaten enemy, you assimilated or befriended him, becoming in
the process more powerful yourself. The Huns were changing he
thought sadly. Gold and grass – or rather the lack of it – were
now the new determinants. Gold had made them greedy; and in
extending their conquests so far westward, the Huns had at last
run out of steppe. With no more grasslands to the west of them,
and too little in their present homeland to sustain their herds
indefinitely, the old free nomadic life was ultimately doomed. All
the more reason then to find accommodation with the Romans,
rather than bleed them white.

Trapped in his role of mighty conqueror, the terror of his

enemies and bounteous provider to his people, Attila assured the Council that a series of embassies would be sent to Constantinople, ostensibly to oversee the implementation of the treaty. In addition, the intention was to intimidate the imperial court into appeasing their conquerors by presenting the ambassadors with valuable gifts, symbolic reminders of their own weakness and the Huns' supremacy.

'Saiga!' cried the groom to Uldin, pointing to a cluster of faraway dots moving slowly across the dusty plain. This land had once been part of Dacia, a province abandoned by the Romans these hundred and seventy years. To recognize the antelope at such a distance, the lad must have eyes sharper than a hawk's, thought Uldin admiringly. Though not yet forty, Uldin was already an elder of the Hun Council, elected for his shrewdness, good sense, and ability to relate to people – even Romans. It was for these qualities that Attila had chosen him as one of the first envoys to be sent to Constantinople, a mission from which he was now returning. Some way off rode the other envoy, a taciturn man who preferred to keep his own company. Behind, surrounded by the grooms, pages, and translators of the ambassadorial retinue, rocking and rolling over the steppe, came the supply-wagon, part of its load consisting of valuable gifts from the imperial court.

And none more valuable than that loping beside him as he rode, thought Uldin with pride. While in Constantinople, he had one day seen in the gardens of the imperial palace a strange animal being walked on a leash by its keeper. With its tawny black-spotted fur, cat's head, and long tail, the creature somewhat resembled a leopard, but the exceptionally long legs and deep chest were those of a coursing dog. His curiosity aroused, Uldin had asked the handler, an elderly Goth who, it transpired, had survived the Great Expulsion of his race in the previous reign, about the animal. The man had replied that it was a *youze* or *chita* from Persia, much prized for hunting on account of its speed. 'I call him Blitz,' the man said, 'which in my tongue means "lightning".'

So taken with the creature was Uldin that, when the time came to depart, he had begged the emperor that he be permitted to forgo all other presents, if only he could have Blitz. Theodosius had demurred, but his sister, the Augusta Pulcheria, had overridden him, generously waiving the suggested condition and presenting Uldin with the cheetah in addition to his other gifts.

In the early stages of the thousand-mile journey back to Transylvania, Uldin had taken time to get to know Blitz, talking to and hand-feeding him. The attention was rewarded with affection, the animal often choosing to accompany him during each day's ride, and sleeping next to him at night.

Now, feeling his blood begin to stir with the anticipation of the chase, Uldin dismounted and slipped a leather hood over the cheetah's head. After attaching a long leash to Blitz's silver collar, he swung himself back into the saddle, and, calling to the groom to follow, headed for the saiga herd. Covering the ground at a fast tripple, he detoured somewhat to the flank in order to stay upwind of the antelope, which would stampede at the slightest hint of danger.

Two hundred yards from the edge of the herd, Uldin dismounted and threw the reins over the horse's head as a sign to it to stay still. Unalarmed, the antelope continued to graze. Pale brown above, creamy-white below, the males alone bearing lyre-shaped horns, the saiga were distinguished by a grotesquely inflated nose. Removing the leash and holding the cheetah by the collar, Uldin slipped the hood from its head. Immediately, the animal tensed and pulled against the restraining grip.

'Go, Blitz,' Uldin whispered, and released the collar. The cheetah crept towards the saiga, undulating over the ground as it took advantage of every bush and unevenness for concealment. Warned at last by a sentinel antelope, the herd suddenly took off at a lumbering gallop, but were swiftly overhauled by their pursuer – a streaking tawny blur as it accelerated to an incredible speed. Selecting a victim, the spotted cat bowled it over with a blow of its paw, ripped open its throat, and proceeded to suck the blood spouting from the severed arteries.

'Well done, my Blitz!' cried Uldin in delight, as he cantered up. Enticing the cheetah from the kill with a strip of meat he had ready in his saddlebag, Uldin signalled to the groom to gut the carcase, prior to removing it to the wagon. He thrilled with the anticipation of seeing the admiring envy on the faces of his fellow Huns, passionate hunters all, when he showed off the cheetah's skills. His one fear was that Attila might himself take a fancy to Blitz. As a gesture of courtesy, he would have to offer the King the presents he had received. But Attila was a just and open-handed monarch; surely he would not deprive a favoured councillor of the one gift he prized above all the rest. Would he? With something akin to surprise, Uldin acknowledged to himself that to part with Blitz would cause him real distress.

'It's a leopard!' Uldin's wife screamed in consternation when, followed by a train of grooms bearing the presents from Byzantium, and accompanied by Blitz, Uldin reached his home on the outskirts of Attila's royal village. (As he had hoped, the Hun king had graciously disclaimed any royal right to the gifts, save for one, a cup supposedly made from the horn of a unicorn, which was said to possess the valuable property of changing colour when charged with any liquid containing poison.)

With some difficulty, Uldin managed to persuade his wife and extended family that Blitz was *not* a leopard, displaying, instead of that feline's vicious temperament, a gentle affectionate nature and a fondness for being petted. (Few Huns, the younger ones especially, had ever seen a leopard. But folk-memories from the tribe's long sojourn in Asia, of a fearsomely dangerous animal capable of disembowelling a man in seconds with its raking hind claws, were still strong.) After Uldin had arranged a race over a short distance, in which Blitz left his mounted competitors standing, any lingering hostility towards the cat evaporated.

As the pointer on the clepsydra's float reached the mark designating the hour, a tiny gilded bird above the escape cistern opened its beak and gave forth a gurgling trill. 'Aaah!' gasped Uldin's father, his eyes shining with rapture. 'It is indeed a princely gift. Thank you, my son.'

Uldin smiled to himself. His attempt to explain the function of the water-clock, a wondrous contraption of bronze and ivory, had failed completely. The measurement of time, in any form more sophisticated than noting the position of the sun, was a concept beyond the old man's grasp. But that did not matter; he was captivated by the machine's beauty and seemingly magical movements. To his kinsfolk packed inside the family yurt, Uldin distributed, to gasps of wonder and delight, the other treasures he had brought. There were silks, silver mirrors, and jewellery for the women and girls; and for the males, daggers with jewelled hilts, silver horse-trappings, and golden drinking-vessels. The gifts presented, and great platters of roast meat and bowls of *kumiss* circulating, the questioning began concerning the wonders of the great city.

'Can Constantinople be taken?' demanded a fierce old warrior.

'Not in a thousand years, uncle,' declared Uldin.

'Why?' came back the other belligerently. 'Viminacium, Margus, Singidunum, Sirmium – these and many others fell to us.'

'Agreed, uncle,' conceded Uldin, fondling Blitz's head. 'But we took them with the help of captured Roman engineers, who could show us how to make and use siege-engines. Constantinopolis is built on a promontory, surrounded on three sides by water with fast-flowing currents and rip-tides which make it difficult to attack from the sea, an option hardly open to ourselves in any case. On the landward side, it is sealed off by a great wall running north and south.'

'Walls can be scaled.'

'Not these walls, uncle. You have not seen them or you would not ask. Compared to them, the defences of Sirmium were like a brushwood fence. They are immensely tall and thick, studded with mighty towers with platforms for catapults, so that every approach is dominated by a field of fire. Any attacking force would be half destroyed before it reached the rampart's base.'

'And is the city big?' asked a wide-eyed boy.

Uldin nodded gravely. 'Yes, son, it's big. Very big.'

'Bigger than our royal capital?'

Uldin smiled. 'This town would fit twenty times inside it and still leave room. As for numbers . . .' Uldin struggled to find a simile to convey the reality of half a million people. 'As many as the flocks and herbs that graze the pastures around us.'

Uldin sensed that his hearers were impressed, his known probity ensuring that his remarks would not be dismissed as boastful exaggeration.

'What is it like, this city?' asked a young matron shyly.

'It is more splendid and beautiful than you can imagine,' replied Uldin with some feeling. 'There are five great gateways through the wall, from the northern and southernmost of which two wide streets, both called Mesé – after passing through the western suburbs where are great cisterns, a mighty aqueduct, and many monasteries and churches – come together in a great open square called the Amastrianum. The heart of the city lies beyond the Amastrianum, at the eastern end of the peninsula – almost a city within a city, you could say. Here are the great imperial palace, the barracks of the Emperor's guard, the offices of his ministers, the huge Church of the Holy Wisdom, and the Hippodrome where chariot races are held. Here you will see the very heart of the city's heart, the kathisma or emperor's box, a building in itself, crowned by four mighty horses in bronze.'

'From what you tell us, Uldin, it would seem that the citizens do not keep herds or flocks,' observed his father, 'and that not many of them are warriors. So what, apart from chariot racing, do they find to talk about.'

Uldin paused, aware that his answer could lead him into a verbal labyrinth, and wishing he possessed the skill to argue like a Greek. 'Well, Father,' he began, recalling the passionate theological debates he had overheard everywhere in the East Roman capital and which the translators had explained to him, 'when not discussing trade or business, they converse mostly about their god.'

'What is he like, this god of theirs?'

Uldin groaned to himself. An intelligent and by nature an enquiring man, he had, as a senior member of the Hun Council, seen as one of his obligations the need to acquaint himself to some extent with the mores and beliefs of the Romans. But how to explain an abstract concept like the Trinity to his fellow tribesmen? Their deity, Murduk, the god of war, was symbolized by Attila's Sacred Scimitar on its plinth, and was, therefore, something tangible and visible. They could also hear him; for was it not his voice that spoke whenever thunder rumbled in the sky?

'They believe he is one god, yet at the same time three – a father and his son, together with a being called the Holy Ghost.'

'I shall remember that, next time I barter for a yearling foal,' declared one tribesman gravely. 'As you all know, the price for such a horse is three heifers. The vendor will of course complain when I offer in exchange a single cow. I shall reply, however, "This is a Christian cow, my friend; it may look like one beast, but really it is three."'

When the laughter had died down, Uldin pressed on gamely, but with a growing sense of futility. 'The Holy Ghost – who is god as well – fathered a child on a woman called Mary. The child, called Jesus – who is also god – after he was grown to manhood was put to death for his teachings by the Romans. Although they now believe in him, at that time they thought he was a danger to the state. Today, they worship him when they meet together in their churches, the houses where their god lives.'

'But you said there were many churches,' objected a shepherd. 'How can their god live in them all at once, even if he can split himself in three?'

Uldin shook his head. 'I do not know,' he confessed, giving a weary smile. 'It is a mystery.'

'What do they do, these Christians, when they worship their Jesus?'

'A shaman in a white robe speaks some words of magic over bread and wine, turning them into Jesus' flesh and blood.'

'If it works the other way, we should have one of these shamans next time a beast is slaughtered,' whispered a boy to the friend beside him. 'Think of all that blood turned into wine!' (Their muffled giggling was swiftly quelled by a stern look from an elder.)

'And what happens to this flesh and blood of Jesus?' enquired a grey-haired Hun with skin as brown and corrugated as a walnut.

'They eat and drink it.'

Exclamations of revulsion broke out around the yurt. 'Then are these Romans cannibals,' someone declared. 'They call us savages, but we do not devour the flesh of men.'

'The Christians call the change "transubstantiation", Uldin pressed on lamely, aware that his audience was baffled, and that he himself was treading water. 'By this they mean – at least I think they do – that, although the bread and wine continue to *look* like bread and wine after the shaman has pronounced his magic, in some way known only to their god, they have really—'

'Enough,' interrupted Uldin's father gently, laying a hand on his son's arm. 'Let us leave these matters for the Romans to untangle, if they can. Look, you have sent poor Blitz to sleep.'

THIRTY-ONE

The fair-haired races are bold and undaunted in battle; they calmly
despise death as they fight violently in hand-to-hand combat
Mauricius, *The Strategikon*, sixth century

'Sitting ducks, sir,' called Constantius to Aetius cheerfully, as he
splashed through the ford across the Phrudis,* to join the rest
of the general's cavalry, who had dismounted and were having a
scratch breakfast of *bucellatum*, the hard biscuit carried on
campaign as emergency rations. 'The Franks are all drunk as
pigs, snoring their heads off – even the guards. They obviously
think there isn't a Roman soldier within a hundred miles.'
Swinging down from the saddle, he accepted the biscuit and cup
of wine that Aetius handed him. 'Thanks, sir. You know, I think
we could take them,' he said, shooting the general a shrewd
glance. 'We may be only light cavalry, but we'd have the advantage of surprise, and . . . Well, let's just say I don't think we'll
get another chance as good as this.' He took a pull at his wine
and grinned disarmingly. 'What do you say, sir? Are you game
for it?'

From Constantius' tone, he might have been suggesting a
spot of hare-hunting on his family's estate in Provincia, thought
Aetius with wry amusement. He liked this dashing young man,
who had turned up out of the blue one day at Aetius' camp,
with half a dozen tough-looking *bucellarii* in tow. In a take-it-
or-leave-it way, he had offered his services, and Aetius had taken
him on for a trial period, as a tribune with an acting commission, pending confirmation by the Consistory. Apart from hinting
that he was *persona non grata* in his home district (because of a
scandal involving the seduction of a local senator's wife),
Constantius divulged nothing of his background, beyond stating
the obvious: that he was from a wealthy family of land-owning

* The Somme.

aristocrats. Beneath the light-hearted insouciance, there was, Aetius suspected, a tough and self-contained young man, worldly-wise beyond his years. A superb horseman and natural leader, whom the men seemed to take to immediately, Constantius, along with his hard-riding retinue, had soon proved useful.

With fast-moving light cavalry units of the field army, Aetius was endeavouring to discover what the Franks were up to. Officially federates, under King Chlodio they had recently broken out of their assigned territory along the lower Rhenus, and were reported to be pushing west through the province of the Second Belgica, towards the Phrudis. After his scouts had told Aetius that they'd sighted a large party of Franks encamped by the hamlet of Vicus Helena near Nemetacum,* Constantius had volunteered to carry out a solo spying mission on the band in question. Acting alone, he argued, he would be able to get close to the Franks and observe their dispositions in detail.

He had been as good as his word.

'Strength?' enquired Aetius.

'Hard to be exact – their tents and shelters are spread over a wide area. Between five and ten thousand, I'd say.'

'Distance?'

'Not much over twenty miles. Flat water-meadows all the way – An easy three hours' ride.'

'Is it a war-party?'

'That wasn't my impression, sir. Seemed more like a festive outing, like a picnic on a grand scale.'

'A picnic! Come, Constantius.'

'No, seriously, sir, it looked as if they're preparing a big cele-bration. They're dressed up in their best outfits; there are several pavilion tents, and the place is crawling with cooks and scullions. And' – Constantius paused, then went on slowly – 'this may be significant. There's one really big, brightly coloured pavilion, flying a flag.'

'Chlodio?'

Constantius shrugged and smiled. 'Well, it just might be we're in luck, sir.'

*Arras.

'Then what are we waiting for? Get yourself a fresh horse; I'll pass the order for the *bucinator* to sound "Saddle up".'

Theudebert was happy. With a full heart, he looked round the long trestle table at his fellow Franks: resplendent in their best and brightest tunics, close-fitting like their trousers; some wearing gold arm-rings or neck-torques, gifts from King Chlodio for loyal service or outstanding courage. He himself, in recognition of his years and many valorous deeds when of fighting age, was seated only three places from the King's right hand. The old days were coming back, he thought, his eyes misting with nostalgia as his mind drifted back nearly sixty years to when he was a young warrior.

They were good days, days of fighting and feasting, of hunting and adventure. In his first battle – against the Alamanni, when he was sixteen – he had possessed only a shield and spear. That day, he had killed his first man and taken his fine *Spangenhelm*, complete with cheek-pieces and ring-mail neck-guard. Then, as the years passed and his fame and prowess as a warrior grew, he had acquired other gear: a *francisca* or throwing-axe, a mail shirt, a horse, a lance, and, best of all, a pattern-welded sword of finest iron edged with steel, the gift of King Marcomir.

Then Stilicho, the Vandal who led Rome's armies, had come down the Rhenus and wooed the Franks with fair words, persuading them to become allies, *foederati* of Rome, in exchange for a strip of land on the Roman side of the river. Land which the Franks could have taken anyway, so weak had Rome become, the old warrior thought in disgust. And much good had taking the *foedus* done his people. True to their promise, the Franks had fought valiantly but in vain, to stem the flood of Vandals, Suevi, and Burgundians that had poured across the frozen Rhenus and into Gaul. They had lost many fine warriors, but, what was worse, were then expected, under the terms of the *foedus*, to settle down and till the soil as peaceful farmers, a shameful thing for proud warriors, an occupation fit only for women and weaklings.

But now, King Chlodio, like a true Frank, had gathered around him a mighty *comitatus*, a sworn following of adventurous young men, and had led his people out of their assigned territory in the Second Germania, and into Roman Gaul. Ah, the glorious days of fighting and plunder that had followed! Swords which had grown rusty in their scabbards had drunk blood again. Tornacum and Cambracum* had fallen to their warriors, yielding a rich harvest of gold and silver vessels, glass bowls, hoards of *solidi* . . . He had been too old to fight himself, of course, but he had shared in the glory of his sons, who had presented him with jewelled cups, and – his most prized possession – a wonderful drinking-horn of clearest glass.

To celebrate his victories and the marriage of his son, the king was holding this splendid feast, the tables spread in the shelter of a hill, along the banks of a pleasant stream. A young scullion offered Theudebert wine; he sent the lad for ale to fill his drinking-horn. Wine was for women and Romans, he thought scornfully, as he reached to carve himself a slice of venison from the haunch further down the table. Ale was the only fit drink for a warrior.

Suddenly, a mass of horsemen in Roman helmets appeared as if from nowhere and swept along the rows of tables, overturning them and slashing at the guests. With their weapons put aside out of respect for the occasion, the Franks fought back bravely with anything to hand – knives, struts wrenched from trestles, even jugs and trenchers. Grabbing a spit, old Theudebert hurled it like a lance at a charging cavalryman, saw the wicked point pierce the soldier's eye and emerge from the back of his skull, between the helmet rim and the lacings of the neck-guard. As the man toppled from the saddle, another horseman cut at the Frank; the *spatha* bit deep into Theudebert's neck, severing the carotid artery, which spouted blood in scarlet jets. In his last moments of conscious-ness, the old man's thin veneer of Christianity, scarcely two gener-ations deep, slipped away. This day I shall feast with fellow warriors in Valhalla, he thought joyfully, for I will have died in battle.

The fight was soon over. To avoid further slaughter of his *comi-tatus*, who would fight to the death to defend their liege lord, King Chlodio raised his hands in surrender, calling on his men to do the same.

Helmet under arm, Aetius stepped forward and addressed the king. 'In view of your people's record of loyal service to Rome, Chlodio, I am prepared – this once – to offer you the *foedus* a second time. Will you take it?'

Chlodio, a tall, impressive figure with long fair hair, dressed

* Tournai and Cambrai.

in white tunic and hose with a green cloak, looked the general up and down with an air of calm insolence. 'Your terms, Roman?'

Aetius shook his head in reluctant admiration of the Frank's coolness. He recalled that in virtually identical circumstances the first Valentinian had burst a blood-vessel and died. 'You're hardly in a position to bargain, Chlodio,' he answered mildly, 'as I think you realize. My terms are these. Withdraw all your people beyond the Scaldis.* That river, together with the Mosa,** will henceforth be the boundary between the Franks and the Romans. Should any Frank be found without authorization west of that line, or south of Arduenna Silva,† he will be put to death on sight. Also, you must swear never again to take up arms against the Romans, and to fight for Rome when called upon. Do you so swear?'

Chlodio inclined his head slightly. 'I do,' he declared, in tones which suggested he was conferring a favour on the victors.

'In that case, you may remove your dead. But everything else remains on the battlefield, as legitimate spoils of war. As from the first hour tomorrow, we grant you two days to remove yourselves to your homeland.'

'Congratulations, sir. A splendid victory,' said Constantius to Aetius, as the last of the Frankish wagons rolled away to the east.

'A few more victories like that, and we'll hardly be able to take the field,' said Aetius ruefully. 'Three hundred men dead. We can't afford that sort of loss.'

'But the Franks lost thousands. Surely—'

'The Franks can soon make up their numbers; we can't.' A note of quiet desperation had crept into the general's voice. 'Theirs is a warrior nation. All their young men are potential soldiers, whereas for us it's almost impossible to find fresh recruits. God knows how much longer we can pay or equip our troops, let alone feed them. The treasury in Ravenna's bankrupt – really bankrupt this time. Fitting out the recent abortive African expedition has emptied the coffers.'

'As bad as that, sir?' murmured Constantius sympathetically. 'I hadn't realized. Still, the situation in Gaul's well under control.

* The Scheldt.
** The Meuse.
† The Ardennes.

The Burgundians and Visigoths, and now the Franks, have been taught a lesson and kept within bounds. Gaul's still Roman.'

'But for how long? If the federates were to break out again . . . Rome is like a man crossing a frozen lake in spring. At any moment the ice may shatter and the man drown. If only we still had the Huns to help us.'

'Can't they be persuaded?'

Aetius shook his head. 'I scarcely think so,' he replied sombrely. Then the germ of an idea flashed into his mind. Perhaps, just perhaps . . . The young man beside him could charm the birds off the trees. If anyone could succeed in talking Attila round, Constantius could.

A *centenarius* who had been supervising the burial detail, approached and saluted respectfully. 'All ready, sir.'

'Come, Constantius. We must commend their souls to God.' As the two officers turned to leave the battlefield, Aetius stooped and picked up something from the ground, a drinking-horn, beautifully fashioned from glass. Miraculously, it had not broken. He handed it to the young tribune. 'I wonder whose it was,' he mused. 'Keep it as a souvenir, my friend, a memento of your first battle.'

Praetorium of the Master of Soldiers, Ravenna, Province of Flaminia and Picenum, Diocese of Italia [Titus wrote in his journal], in the consulships of Flavius Theodosius, Augustus (his eighteenth), and of Albinus, Ides IV Aug.*

With Gaul quiet again after the Frankish scare, Aetius has returned to Italy, leaving Avitus – now Prefect of Gaul – to keep an eye on the two Gallic dioceses. Aetius feels his presence is needed in Ravenna, where he can more easily watch the situation in Africa. With the expedition for its recovery postponed, Gaiseric is flexing his muscles once more; the only barbarian with a fleet (of captured Roman vessels), he has seized the Baleares and Sardinia, established a beachhead in Sicilia, and is now threatening Italia itself.

Money to maintain the army is now the crying need, but all sources are exhausted. So desperate has the government become that it has this year invented a new tax on trade, the *siliquaticum*, a payment of one twenty-fourth on sales.

* 10 August 444.

Hoping to make up the shortfall of recruits by attempting to revive his alliance with Attila, the Patrician has sent a young tribune, one Constantius, to the King, to make overtures on his behalf. I must admit to having reservations. Constantius has admirable qualities: he is brave and resourceful, as he proved at the Battle of Vicus Helena against the Franks; he has tact, charm, self-confidence by the bucketload, and is from a good family, and therefore able to mix easily with the great – all attributes which make him (in theory) an excellent choice for an ambassador.

So why do I have doubts? I just have a feeling that, for all his charm, Constantius will always put his own interests above other priorities. In view of the importance of his undertaking (which could, it is no exaggeration to say, decide the survival of the West), I voiced my fears to Aetius. But he laughed them off good-naturedly. I believe he thinks I'm jealous of Constantius – in case his mission to Attila succeeds where mine failed, I suppose. Well, we can only wait and see what transpires.

THIRTY-TWO

*A man who is base at home will not acquit himself with honour
as an ambassador abroad*

Aeschines, *Ctesiphontem*, 337 BC

Most unusually for him, Constantius was nervous. As he donned his best dalmatic for the interview with Attila, he began to regret having stolen the expensive gifts intended for the King. But the opportunity to raise sufficient cash to pay off his gambling debts, and come to an accommodation with the senator whose wife he had seduced, had been just too tempting – even if the amount paid by the Syrian moneylender in Arelate was but a fraction of the real value of the goods. Still, he could now return to his home and hold up his head again among his family and peers. And he had kept back one or two of the less valuable items, such as the glass drinking-horn Aetius had found on the battlefield of Vicus Helena. Worthless trinkets like that would probably impress a savage like Attila far more than an exquisitely patterned silver dish – or so he had managed to convince himself. Now, with the meeting imminent, he was less certain.

He set out from his quarters in the Hun capital, a vast, sprawling village of tents, with here and there a crudely built wooden mansion belonging to a noble. An astonishing sight – ridiculous, almost shocking in its incongruity – was a huge stone building in pure Graeco-Roman style, which towered above the flimsy roofs of felt or canvas like a war-galley among fishing-boats. This was the Baths of Onegesius, designed by a Greek architect enslaved during Attila's invasion of the Eastern Empire and now a freedman in the service of Onegesius, one of Attila's favourites. As he picked his way through the tangle of filthy lanes that passed for streets, Constantius became surrounded by a noisy crowd of children. During the three weeks that Attila had kept him waiting for an audience, he had become enormously popular among the youngsters, by his gift of mimicry and repertoire of tricks. Today, he was a bear. He rushed among the little Huns, roaring and swinging his head from side to side, his hands crooked like claws, while the children shrieked delightedly and pretended to flee in terror.

Reaching the foot of the hill crowned by the wooden royal palace, he shooed away his young following and began to climb. At the top, he paused to regain his breath while taking in the view: an expanse of flat grassland rolling away to the blue Carpathus mountains on one hand, and the glittering loops of the Tisa on the other. Like drifting shadows, the nomads' herds moved slowly across the landscape. At the entrance gate of the palisade surrounding the palace complex, he stated his business to the guards, and was escorted past the houses of Attila's wives to the main building, an impressive edifice constructed of massive beams of smoothed timber, with a colonnade of curiously carved tree-trunks. He was shown into the audience chamber, to find himself alone in the presence of the King.

Clad in a skin robe, Attila was seated on a simple wooden throne. Looking at the still figure, deep-sunk eyes in the huge head glittering with intelligence, Constantius was put in mind of a great beast of prey, at rest but ready at any moment to unleash an attack of deadly, devastating power. He knew at once that it would be useless to pretend that the gifts in his satchel were of value. Burning with shame, he spread them on a table: a pewter chalice set with 'gems' of coloured glass, a bronze enamelled brooch, a small silver paten, the glass drinking-horn.

Bowing low, Constantius announced, 'My lord Aetius, Patrician and Master of Soldiers of Valentinian Augustus, Emperor of the West Romans, sends greetings to Attila, King of the Huns and ruler of all lands and peoples from the Oceanus Germanicus to the Caspium, and trusts he will accept these poor gifts as a token of his regard.' Licking his lips, he added, 'I apologize, Your Majesty, for this tawdry remnant – all that was recovered when our baggage was swept away as we crossed the swollen Tisa.' The lie was the best he could come up with in the circumstances.

'No matter,' observed Attila in a deep voice, adding wryly with a glance at the other's richly embroidered dalmatic, 'I am glad to see your clothing did not suffer. Tell me, Roman, the reason why your master sent you here.'

'Your Majesty, the Patrician has authorized me to say on his behalf that he wishes – in all humility and sincerity – that the friendship which was once between you both, can be restored.'

'By "friendship" he means soldiers,' rumbled Attila. 'What can he offer in return? My informants tell me that the West's coffers are as empty as the skulls of the Romans that yet lie on the battlefield of the Chersonesus of Thracia.

'He feels, my lord, that with your help he could restore the West – recover Africa and Britain, crush the Suebi in Hispania, compel the federates in Gaul to forswear the use of arms and settle down as tax-paying Romans, like ordinary citizens. Then, with peace and security established, and tribute flowing into the imperial treasury once more, the fiscal anaemia presently afflicting the West would be cured. He would be in a position to offer you, as well as the titles of joint Patrician and *Magister militum*, that of co-Emperor with Valentinian, also one half of the revenue from the West's taxes.' His confidence returning, Constantius proceeded, with his natural eloquence and enthusiasm, to paint a vivid and enticing picture of a vast Romano-Hunnish confederacy stretching from the Oceanus Atlanticus to the Imaus Mons,* the greatest political unit the world had ever seen, encompassing in a single whole an empire greater than Alexander's. He was wildly exceeding his brief. Aetius had said nothing about co-Emperorship; Attila's share of the imperial revenues was to be a fifth not a half; the confederacy that had, in Constantius' grandiose description, included the Eastern Empire in its sweep, in fact referred to the West and Attila's dominions alone. But mundane details could always be amended and scaled down later; the essential thing at this moment was to capture Attila's interest.

It was impossible to tell what effect, if any, his words were having. Attila listened impassively, motionless on his throne, his features without expression. 'We will consider Aetius' words,' he pronounced, when Constantius had finished. 'Meanwhile, it is our pleasure that you remain in our capital until further notice.'

Long after Constantius had gone, Attila sat pondering the implications of Aetius' message, his great mind – like some vast and intricate machine devised by Archimedes or Hero of Alexandria – appraising, comparing, evaluating . . . The young man sent by

* The Urals.

Aetius was unscrupulous and self-centred – that much was obvious. His story about losing his baggage in the Tisa was a transparent lie; from the moment of his entering Hun territory, Constantius' every move was observed, and no such incident had been reported to Attila. But the offer he carried from Aetius, though clearly embellished, was worthy of serious deliberation. Perhaps, after all, Attila reflected, his dream of founding a Greater Scythia was capable of being resurrected. It was a tempting prospect; yet dreams were dangerous, for they could seduce and betray you – as he had found to his cost. But without dreams, what was a man? Nothing: a brute, a savage. He would ponder the matter long and hard, and then decide.

Meanwhile, he could make use of Constantius. The young Roman might be a self-serving opportunist, but he was also articulate, amiable, and sophisticated – potentially far more effective as an envoy than the arrogant and uncouth Huns he had been sending to Constantinople, following the Peace of Anatolius. That treaty had been thrashed out with the Eastern Empire the previous year. The terms had been punitive: Attila's tribute had been trebled to the gigantic yearly sum of two thousand one hundred pounds of gold, plus an immediate payment of six thousand pounds of gold; all escaped Roman prisoners to be returned, or ransomed for a heavy fee; and all fugitives to be handed over on pain of drastic retribution. The negotiations had been decided between Attila's representative, Scotta, and Anatolius, one of the East's top generals. Knowing what accomplished procrastinators the Romans were, Attila had sent a stream of envoys to Constantinople to maintain pressure on the East to fulfil its treaty obligations. Personable and persuasive, Constantius might be just the person to infiltrate the court and discover the East's intentions towards the Huns. Attila would dictate a letter to his secretary, Orestes, requesting a meeting between Constantius and Chrysaphius, the wily eunuch who, next to Pulcheria, pulled the strings that manipulated Theodosius.

When Bleda heard that Constantius not only was to be included in the next batch of ambassadors to travel to Constantinople, but was to be granted an exclusive interview with Chrysaphius, he immediately became excited. Leaving his domain north of the Pontus Euxinus, he hastened to his brother's capital on the pretext of visiting one of his wives, who owned a nearby village. For Bleda had himself for some time been carrying on a correspondence with Chrysaphius concerning a plot of potential benefit to both: nothing less than the murder of Attila. For ten years Bleda had lived in his brother's shadow, scorned and ignored at every turn. For someone of his limited yet ambitious character, the rankling humiliation had grown more and more insupportable, until at last his cunning and devious mind had turned to schemes for getting rid of his hated sibling. As for Chrysaphius, being instrumental in bringing about the death of Attila would make him appear as the saviour of the East, and immensely increase his already huge influence and power.

The plot hinged on finding a third person, bold and venal enough to do the deed. For reasons of security, and safeguard against possible betrayal, that eliminated any of the Hun ambassadors. Now, it seemed, in the person of Constantius, the perfect solution might have presented itself. All that Bleda had heard concerning Attila's new envoy seemed to confirm this. Being a Roman, Constantius owed no loyalty of blood or nationality to the Hun monarch. If the rumours that he had misappropriated Aetius' gifts for Attila were true, there was every chance that he would be susceptible to a hefty bribe. And apparently he had performed creditably in a recent battle in which the West Romans had defeated the Franks, so could be expected to have sufficient nerve to carry out the murder. Chrysaphius was a better judge of character than himself, Bleda knew. Let him assess the young man and, if he thought him suitable, put the suggestion to him along with half the 'fee', the balance to be paid on completion of the task. Bleda decided that he would send a letter by fast courier to Chrysaphius immediately. And he would make a point of getting to know Constantius, with a view to assessing the Roman's suitability for himself.

'They say the world is round, Balamir,' said Attila. He had rescued the young man from the Danubius, just before his accession, and ever since then Balamir had been the most loyal and devoted of all Attila's servants; now, ten years later, he was more a companion and confidant than a menial. The two men had reined in on a spur of the Carpathus to breathe their horses, and were contemplating the undulating grassland that rolled away like a sea to the farthest horizon. Attila had chosen to confer with Balamir in this remote spot because there was no possibility of their conversation being overheard.

'Sire, a clever Greek called Eratosthenes, assuming the earth to be a ball, was said to be able to measure its circumference.' From talks with the freedman of Onegesius and other East Roman prisoners of war, Balamir had picked up a considerable amount of knowledge pertaining to Graeco-Roman culture and ideas. (Having a quick ear for tongues, he had acquired a useful smattering of Greek, enough to follow the gist of most conversations.)

'And what was this Greek's measurement?'

'Eight thousand leagues, Sire, I think was what he reckoned. Of course, it may just all be theory. From up here, it certainly *looks* flat.'

'So it does, yet I believe the Greek was right. Have you ever watched a ship come over the horizon? But I was forgetting – you've never seen the sea. Well, then, a wagon approaching over the steppes. First, the tent appears, then the body, last of all the wheels, which wouldn't happen unless it was moving up a curve.'

'It might be curved, Sire, but still not be round. Like, say, an egg.'

'But the earth's shadow on the moon is part of a perfect circle. You see, my friend, by simple observation anyone can know the earth is round. He does not need to be a philosopher or mathematician. What is the secret of my power, Balamir? I will tell you: it is observation. A successful hunter observes his quarry over many months. He learns when it is safe or dangerous to approach, when it is bold and careless as in the rut, when it is cautious and wary, and so forth. Likewise, by observing men I learn their strengths and weaknesses, and thus am able to exploit and control them. What proportion of your Greek's eight thousand leagues would my dominions represent, do you suppose?'

'From Pannonia to the Imaus Mons, Sire, is – what? Perhaps a thousand leagues? An eighth of the earth's circumference – its widest measurement, remember.'

'Now double it. Unless Constantius is lying, Aetius has offered to share with me the rule of the Western Empire. Think of it, Balamir, two thousand leagues. Assuming all is Ocean between China and the Pillars of Hercules, nearly half the known world would come under Attila's sway.'

'A heady prospect, Sire. Even Alexander didn't achieve that.'

'But can I trust Aetius? We were close once; you were there, remember, when we shot the rapids of the Iron Gate. No better friends than Attila and Aetius could anywhere be found. Although our friendship has since been broken, perhaps it is not past mending. I would like to believe him. Yet I do not fully trust his emissary, this Constantius. He and my brother Bleda have been seen much together of late. And where Bleda goes, trouble follows – as the lammergeier follows the flocks. I am going to ask you to undertake something for me. You are free to refuse, for if you accept, you may be putting your life in danger.'

'Did I refuse you, Sire, when once you asked me to spy on Bleda?' responded Balamir hotly. 'There was danger then, as I recall.'

'That's my Balamir,' laughed Attila. 'Forgive me – I should never have doubted that you would agree. Now, listen well; here is what I want you to do . . .'

THIRTY-THREE

The Emperor has promised Constantius a rich wife; he must
not be disappointed
Priscus of Panium [quoting Attila], *Byzantine History*, after 472

This was the life, thought Constantius as, with Attila's other envoys, he approached the capital of the Eastern Empire. His fortunes were riding high: special ambassador to the Court of Constantinople, his stipulated reward a rich and noble wife. He relished the thought of returning in a year or so, wealthy and distinguished, to the home he'd left as a disgraced and penniless adventurer.

The walls of Constantinople came in sight, an immense bulwark extending for nearly five miles between the Golden Horn and the Sea of Marmara, forty feet high, with massive square towers every two hundred feet or so. The variegated courses of white stone alternating with red brick created a dramatic, unforgettable impression on Constantius. He reminded himself that these were not Constantine's original walls, now demolished. Following the general panic that had swept the Roman world with Alaric's capture and sack of Rome nearly forty years before, these ramparts had been erected early in the reign of the present emperor, more than a mile to the west of the old ones, to incorporate the great cisterns and the mass of suburbs that had sprung up in the interim.

Entering the city via the marble Porta Aurea with its four bronze elephants and huge statue of the first Theodosius, the envoys and their retinue proceeded along the main thoroughfare, the Mesé, and through the five forums of Arcadius, Bovis, with the great bronze ox for which it was named, Theodosius, Amastrianum and Constantine, to the imposing complex of buildings comprising the Hippodrome, the royal palace, and the church of the Holy Wisdom.*

---

* The precursor of the present building known as the Hagia Sophia (Holy Wisdom) which dates from the time of Justinian in the following century. It is now a mosque.

Constantius was intoxicated by the profusion of splendid public buildings – baths, porticoes, basilicas, churches, et cetera – and by the heady mix of old and new. Brashly uncompromising structures of the Constantinian and Theodosian dynasties (many embellished with statues 'borrowed' from both empires) clashed with venerable buildings from the time of Septimius Severus, when today's mighty capital was merely the small Greek city of Byzantium.

Installed in quarters in the sprawl of buildings that made up the imperial palace, Constantius revelled in the luxury of Roman living after the privations of his stay among the Huns. What bliss to sleep on a feather bed instead of a pile of stinking pelts, to dine on honey-glazed sucking-pig washed down with wine, instead of greasy mutton accompanied by fermented mare's milk. The days following his arrival were pleasant: relaxing in the baths, attending chariot races in the Hippodrome, flirting with the ladies of the court, and wooing the high-born widow selected as his bride – a congenial task, as she was as beautiful as she was wealthy. The other envoys depended on interpreters to converse with their hosts, but communication was no problem for Constantius, whose education had included the study of Greek. His facility in the language was already reaping rewards in terms of his spying obligations to Attila. From casual conversation and chance remarks overheard, he was gradually compiling a list of names of fugitives and deserters from Attila's jurisdiction who were still being protected by the empire. More importantly, he was discovering that, through the efforts of Nomus, the brilliant Master of Offices, the northern frontier was being unobtrusively re-fortified, and its slaughtered garrisons replenished. Then, on the morning of the sixth day, a messenger from the senior notary's office presented him with a scroll tied with a silk ribbon. Unfurling it, he found that it was from Chrysaphius, inviting him to attend for interview at the eighth hour the following day.

Balamir was making his own preparations to attend the interview between Constantius and Chrysaphius. Quartered, like most of the ambassadorial retinue, with the palace servants, he had made a point of striking up a friendship with a Hun named Eskam, one of the interpreters who translated the speeches of foreign envoys. These men came under the authority of Nomus, with whom Chrysaphius worked closely, so Eskam was in a good position to discover details concerning the eunuch's timetable. With this in mind, Balamir decided to take Eskam into his confidence. He told Eskam that Attila had entrusted him with a difficult and dangerous mission – namely eavesdropping on the interview (which Attila had requested) between Constantius and Chrysaphius – and appealed to his fellow Hun for help. Swayed by pride at being able to help his people's great leader (also by the generous sum that Balamir had been authorized by Attila to pay any accomplice he might need to enlist), Eskam agreed.

Between them, the two Huns devised a bold but simple plan. With funds supplied by Balamir, Eskam bribed one of the eunuch's clerks to find out the place, date, and time for the interview. Such was the universal terror inspired by Attila's name that Eskam was confident there was little risk of the man betraying them. Next, he had the clerk arrange to let Balamir inspect the eunuch's office, at a time when it was unoccupied.

The dominant feature of the *tablinum* was a great bookcupboard, with pairs of folding shutters top and bottom. The upper section, with openwork shutters, contained documents required for frequent reference: returns from the secretariats, the imperial couriers, the palace guards, et cetera. The nether section, with solid shutters, was stuffed with texts which were consulted on rare occasions only, such as the *Codex Theodosianus*, the recently updated compilation of imperial laws. The plan consisted of temporarily removing these seldom-used works, thus creating a space to accommodate Balamir, from which he could listen to the interview unobserved. The wooden slats separating the two divisions were not tightly joined; the interstices would allow him to breathe freely and overhear anything said in the room. It was of course possible that Chrysaphius might decide to consult one of the volumes in the lower compartment – with resulting exposure and disaster. But the clerk assured the two Huns that the risk was so slight that it could be ignored.

Early on the appointed day, before the house-slaves had arrived to clean the office, the bottom section was cleared of its dusty tomes, which were re-housed in a nearby storeroom, then Balamir installed in their place. Making himself as comfortable as the cramped space would permit, he settled down to wait out the long hours before the interview.

When he was shown into Chrysaphius' office, Constantius found himself in the presence of a grotesquely obese figure perched incongruously on a tiny folding stool. From the pear-shaped head with its multiple chins downwards, the eunuch seemed to consist of successive rolls of fat, putting Constantius in mind of a rotund ivory figure in his family home, which was said to have come from China and to represent an Asiatic sage, one Buddha.

'Your Gloriousness,' began the young Roman, bowing, 'I am honoured, more than any poor words of mine can express, that you have condescended to meet one so humble as myself.' Already, he had mastered the absurdly overblown rhetoric without which, it seemed, official procedure in the Eastern court was unable to function. To his surprise, the other cut him short with an impatient wave.

'Yes, yes,' the eunuch snapped testily. 'Tell me,' he went on, shrewd little eyes sunk in their beds of fat shooting an appraising glance at the other, 'is the widow of Armatius – or more to the point, her fortune – to your liking?'

Constantius relaxed, knowing that he was in the company of another man of the world. He seated himself on the stool the minister indicated. 'Very much so, sir,' he replied with a smile.

'She ought to be able to maintain you in the style to which you are accustomed, at least,' observed the eunuch drily. 'But, in addition to acquiring an income for life, perhaps you would not be averse to earning yourself a generous . . . fee?' His gaze flicked over Constantius, probing, assessing. '*Very* generous.'

'How generous is "very generous", sir?' asked Constantius, intrigued. He had been expecting a tedious discussion about implementing the Peace of Anatolius. This unexpected line was far more to his liking.

'Were you to succeed in the task I have in mind, one result would be the holding of the greatest Games ever seen in Constantinople. The amount expended on the Games, obligatory for a senator elected to the consulship, is two thousand pounds of gold. That seems to me, then, the appropriate amount for your reward.'

Constantius' head swam. Two thousand pounds' weight in gold. It was a staggering amount, enough to keep him in luxury for the rest of his life, irrespective of the widow's wealth, which would of course legally become his on their marriage.

'What . . . I mean, how, would I set about earning such a sum?' he asked weakly, momentarily robbed of his self-possession. What possible skill or talent did he possess, he wondered, that could justify that sort of payment?

'It should not be too hard, given your circumstances and experience. You have killed before?'

Constantius nodded, recalling the Franks he had cut down at Vicus Helena.

'And would be prepared to kill again? In cold blood, I must warn you.'

An assassination, then. Sobered, Constantius took a deep breath. It must be a political killing. No private person's death could be worth the vast sum involved. Weighed in the balance against two thousand pounds of gold, a man's life – any man's – must rise in the scale holding it. So long as the victim was not a friend . . . Again, he nodded.

'The man is known to you, and has no reason to mistrust you. You will have opportunities to be alone with him. Dispatching him should present no real difficulty. In fact, your only problem is to choose a suitable opportunity.'

'It's Attila, isn't it?' breathed Constantius.

'Yes, Attila,' confirmed Chrysaphius, 'the Scourge of God. Removing him should not trouble your conscience unduly, and you would be doing the world the greatest service possible for any man. As to repercussions, you needn't worry: there won't be any. Bleda has sanctioned the, ah, "elimination", shall we call it. In fact, he'll probably reward you with a handsome sum in addition to what you'll receive from myself. You are willing, then?'

'Yes,' declared Constantius, all doubts evaporating. Attila meant nothing to him. His one regret was that he would be letting down Aetius, whom he liked and respected. But in this world a man had to look out for his own interests, for if he didn't no one else would. A chance like this would never come again. The only question to be answered was: had he the courage and the resolution to see the matter through? Oh yes. Two thousand pounds of gold guaranteed that.

'Good,' said Chrysaphius briskly. 'Then it only remains to settle the details. You will remain at Constantinople with the other ambassadors for the duration of the diplomatic visit. Behave normally, and do nothing to draw attention to yourself. Carry out any instructions Attila has given you, as if this meeting had never taken place. Now, your payment. Half in advance, the remainder when the job is done. Acceptable?'

'Perfectly.'

'Then the first instalment will be ready for you on the day of your departure, together with mules for its transport. One thousand pounds of gold, half the amount payable by a senator on becoming consul, to hold the Games.' The eunuch paused, his brows knitting. 'I'm sure that's right. Perhaps I'd better check in the *Register of Senators*. I'll fetch it from the bottom of my bookcase.'

'Please – there's no need, sir,' protested Constantius. Now he could afford to show an aristocrat's disdain for such tradesman's haggling. 'Your word is warranty enough for me.'

'Very well,' said Chrysaphius, rising. 'Enjoy the rest of your stay in Constantinople.' The interview was over.

Several hours later, stiff and horrified, Balamir emerged from his confinement. The burden of guarding his appalling secret through the coming days would be a heavy one.

THIRTY-FOUR

You wish not to be deceived? Then do not deceive another
John Chrysostom, *Homilies, c.* 388

'Well done, my special ambassador,' said Attila warmly, when Constantius had related his spying activities in the Eastern capital. 'You have achieved more in these few weeks than all my envoys put together since the peace was ratified. As a token of my esteem, receive this jewel from my hands.' He held out a necklace of massive gold links from which was suspended an enormous ruby, glowing redly as if from an internal fire.

Attila was providing him with the perfect opportunity, Constantius realized. With both hands immobilized by the golden chain, he would be unable to ward off a sudden blow. But, now that the moment had come, Constantius felt his courage and determination start to drain away. At Vicus Helena, when his blood was up in the heat and fury of battle, killing had been easy. But to stab a man in cold blood, and he someone who liked and trusted you, was a very different matter. An additional complication, one which had not previously occurred to him, was that the deed must be done face to face; a monarch's back was never turned to you.

'You seem agitated, my young friend,' observed Attila kindly. 'Is anything amiss?'

'No, Sire,' declared Constantius hoarsely, his throat suddenly constricted. 'I – I was overwhelmed by your generosity.' It was now or never. Palms sweating, heart thumping, he walked down the audience chamber towards the King. Bowing his head as if to await the placing of the chain around his neck, he whipped a dagger from beneath his dalmatic, and drove it against Attila's chest. To his horrified amazement, a numbing jolt shot through his fingers and the dagger rebounded. Attila released the chain, caught his wrist with a grip of iron, and twisted it. As the dagger clattered on the floor, the King shouted, 'Guards!' Armed warriors burst in, and within seconds Constantius was lying prostrate before Attila, hands bound behind his back.

'The mail shirts produced in Ratiaria's arms workshops – which I now own – are of the finest quality. I gave you a chance, Roman,' Attila rumbled, shaking his great head regretfully. 'Had you but kept faith with me and stayed your hand, you could have kept Chrysaphius' gold with my blessing, and returned with your bride to the West, a wealthy man. I know what transpired at your interview with Chrysaphius, you see. Two thousand pounds of gold: did you rate my life so cheaply, Constantius? You could have bargained for five times that price – and received it without question.' He gave a mirthless chuckle. 'You shouldn't have stopped the eunuch looking in his bookcase.'

'You mean it concealed a spy?' gasped Constantius.

'Just so. He who would deceive Attila must serve a longer apprenticeship in treachery than yours, my friend. Have you anything to say which would persuade me that I should spare your life?'

'I was only to be the instrument, Sire,' cried Constantius desperately. 'I knew nothing about the plot before Chrysaphius spoke with me. It was his idea – his and your brother Bleda's.'

'This I know already,' sighed Attila, in the tone of an indulgent landlord reproving a defaulting tenant. 'Tell me something with which I am not familiar.'

'Aetius, Sire, he also wished to have you killed,' gabbled Constantius, clutching at straws. 'That is why he sent me to you.'

'You lie, Roman. Aetius is the last person to want me dead. He needs my soldiers to suppress the federates. Try again.'

'It's true, I swear!' exclaimed Constantius, trying frantically to think of something credible to reinforce his claim. 'He is convinced that when you have finished ravaging the East you will turn against the West. He fears the federates less than he fears the Huns. He says that, while the federates may be unruly and treacherous, at least they do not massacre whole populations and reduce entire provinces to smoking deserts. "If Attila is not stopped, the cities of Italia and Gaul will share the fate of Sirmium and Singidunum" – his very words, Sire.'

It could be true, thought Attila, a terrible doubt entering his mind. How could Aetius know that circumstances had conspired to force Attila to make war on the Romans against his will, or that for the sake of their old friendship he had chosen to invade the East rather than the West? Ignorant of Bleda's attempts to usurp his brother's authority, it was only natural that Aetius would view the invasion of the East as unprovoked aggression, and not what it really was: an act of political necessity, forced on Attila by the pressures of leadership. Any detached military observer must think that it was only a matter of time before the Huns turned their attention to the West.

'I am minded to believe you, Roman,' said Attila heavily. 'Not that anything you have told me will save you. It may, however, comfort you to know that I intend to grant you the same death as your Christ-god. As you hang upon the cross, reflect on these words, which I believe he uttered, "Render unto Caesar the things that are Caesar's".' Turning to the guards, he commanded with weary sadness, 'Crucify him.'

Alone in the audience chamber, a dreadful bleakness of the spirit descended on Attila. He could see it all clearly now. Coldly and with calculation, Aetius had exploited his knowledge of Attila's ambition to create a Greater Scythia. He had sent the persuasive, snake-tongued Constantius, to sell his erstwhile friend a shining dream, the greatest empire the world had ever seen. And Attila, 'the Scourge of God', whose cunning was as legendary as his feats of conquest, had fallen for the ruse. Lulled into a false sense of security he would have dropped his guard, one day to fall victim to Constantius' dagger, had not the Roman's plans been overtaken by the clumsy plotting of Bleda and Chrysaphius.

Well, so much for dreams. He was done with such illusions, which served only to weaken and distract. Henceforth, he would deal only in the solid currency of war. Death and destruction, plunder and tribute – these would be his sole watchwords. The Romans would pay dearly for their perfidy. When the East had been made to render all its dues in full, then would come the turn of the West.

Constantius screamed as the nails were driven between the long bones of his forearms below the wrists, and through his feet. But when the cross stood upright in its socket, he could no longer scream. His body sagged, compressing his lungs so that he began to suffocate. Only by pushing himself upright against the block his feet were nailed to, despite the agony this caused, could he relieve the pressure sufficiently to breathe. But all too soon his weight pulled him down, and the cycle recommenced. Crying weakly for his mother, Constantius began to die.

THIRTY-FIVE

Attila murdered his brother Bleda and took over his kingdom
Count Marcellinus, *Chronicon, c.* 450

Following the return of the envoys from Constantinople, ensconced in his wife's village near the Hun capital Bleda daily awaited news that his brother had been slain; whereupon he would proclaim himself sole ruler of the Huns. He had received confirmation from Chrysaphius that Constantius was both suitable and willing to carry out the deed. So when he received a summons from Attila to attend him in the palace, he was filled at first with trepidation: the plot had been discovered or miscarried, and his part in it exposed. Then, on reflection, he told himself that such a reaction was premature, that in all probability Constantius was simply biding his time, not yet having found a suitable opportunity. If Attila really suspected his brother of being involved in a plot to kill him, instead of a courteous messenger he would surely have sent armed guards with instructions for Bleda's arrest. No, he was behaving as the guilty always tended to do: seeing in every trivial occurrence, proof that their crime had been discovered. In any event, he had no choice but to comply with his brother's request. To ignore it would only be to invite suspicion – most likely needless.

Bleda's fears were further dissipated by his brother's cordial reception in his private chamber within the palace. Attila pressed him to partake of Roman wine and fine peaches from the orchards of Colchis*, while soliciting his views on the deliberations of the Council, the pasturing of the royal flocks and herds, and the implementing of the Peace of Anatolius. At last, reassured that nothing of the plot had come to light, Bleda felt secure enough to risk a casual enquiry about Constantius. 'Your young Roman

---

* Trans-Caucasia. Colchis, the legendary location of the Golden Fleece, was famous for its fruit.

envoy; as I recall, Brother, you entertained great hopes regarding his negotiations with Chrysaphius?'

'Constantius, you mean? Yes, he performed most ably. By the way,' Attila continued, as if recalling something that had slipped his mind, 'I have arranged for you to meet him.'

Bleda was confused. All his assignations with the Roman had been, so far as he knew, outwith Attila's ken. Why should his brother now be setting up a formal concourse? 'For what reason should I wish to see Constantius – or he me, for that matter?' he queried.

'Why indeed?' replied Attila enigmatically, throwing open the shutters of a window. 'Unfortunately, he cannot come to you, but from where I stand he will be able to hear any words you wish to address to him.'

Suddenly afraid, Bleda hastened to the window and looked out. Before him was a grassy enclosure normally used for exercising horses. In the middle of the space had been erected a tall cross, on which a figure writhed and moaned feebly – Constantius.

'Why are you showing me this?' exclaimed Bleda in horror.

'I think you know the answer, Brother. You didn't really expect that Constantius, when confronted with proof of his treachery, would not seek to implicate you?'

'Implicate me in what, Brother?' blustered Bleda, trying to master the terror that threatened to overwhelm him. 'I do not know what he has said about me. But whatever it is, he lies.'

'Spare me your excuses,' said Attila wearily. 'Your plotting with Chrysaphius is known. During the envoys' visit to the East, my spy overheard him discuss with Constantius a conspiracy to have me murdered. Your involvement in the plot was very clear. Also, a recent letter from the eunuch to yourself, establishing your guilt beyond doubt, was intercepted before you received it.' He took from a chest a flask and a strangely shaped vessel, a drinking-horn made of glass. He emptied the flask's contents into the horn, which he placed on a table. 'I give you a choice, Brother. You can die with dignity, in the knowledge that your treachery will remain undisclosed. Or you can face a charge of treason and defend your actions before the Council. I need hardly point out that they will certainly find you guilty, or what the penalty will be.'

Bleda shuddered as the memory of a scene he had once

witnessed rose in his mind: a condemned felon running between two lines of warriors armed with clubs, and gradually being beaten to a shrieking pulp.

'The choice is yours, Brother,' said Attila quietly, moving to the door.

'What is it?' whispered Bleda, pointing to the horn, with its semi-translucent, almost milky contents.

'Hemlock. Compared to crucifixion or the gauntlet, it brings a merciful and, save at the end, painless death. First, you will become weak, so that if you attempt to walk, you will stagger. Then your hands and feet will begin to feel numb, and paralysis spread up your limbs to your body. Finally, your lungs will cease to work and you will die in asphyxial convulsions. A Greek called Socrates was condemned to die by this method. His crime was corrupting youth. An appropriate death for you to share considering your subverting of Constantius. When I return tomorrow, it will be to find you dead or dying, or to have you brought before the Council. It would be pointless for you to try to escape; the room is closely watched. May your last night on earth bring peace, Brother.'

After Attila had gone, Bleda sat staring at the horn in horrified fascination. Several times in the hours that followed, while sunlight slowly bled from the chamber to be replaced by the faint illumination of the stars, and the moans of Constantius came thinly to his ears, he approached the thing with hand extended, only to shrink away in terror at the last moment. Eventually, exhausted by fear and tension, he fell into a fitful sleep, waking as the first grey light of dawn filtered through the windows. Constantius' cries had at last fallen silent. Presumably, he was dead and so at peace. Peace. Even if that was the blackness of eternal night, surely it must be preferable to prolonging his life for a few more wretched hours, which was all he could look forward to if he refused the hemlock. Before his resolution could falter, Bleda grasped the horn and drained it in a single draught. Soon, a not unpleasant tingling began in his toes and fingers, to be succeeded by a creeping numbness . . .

Bleda's death went unlamented. His contribution to the achievements of the dual monarchy had been negligible, eclipsed by the mighty exploits of his brother. Nevertheless, whatever his deficiencies as a ruler might have been in life, in death he was accorded a funeral befitting a King of the Huns. If anyone suspected that Attila had played a part in his brother's death, they remained silent – less, perhaps, from any fear of retribution, than from indifference. Bleda had been neither loved nor respected, and, besides, possession of the Sacred Scimitar conferred on Attila an authority believed to be divine.

Attila was now sole monarch of the Huns, the undisputed ruler of a realm stretching from the Visurgis* in the west to the Oxus in the east; between Scandia in the north and Persia in the south. It should have been a moment to savour. But the knowledge brought him no satisfaction, was as gall and wormwood on the tongue. For his dream of greatness for his people lay in ruins, past any hope of restoration.

* The Weser.

THIRTY-SIX

To Aegidius,* consul for the third time, the groans of the Britons.
Gildas, *The Destruction of Britain*, late fifth or early sixth century

The tempest that had raged over Britain for many days and blown the two sea eagles from their hunting range above the Cambrian cliffs almost to the shores of Gaul, was at last abating. The two great birds swooped and soared among the lessening gusts. Then, finding a field of stable air some thousands of feet above the Fretum Gallicum, the narrow strait between the coasts of Gaul and Britain, they turned north-west and headed for their eyrie, with slow, majestic flaps of their huge wings.

From such a height, the whole of Britain's Saxon Shore, with its chain of forts extending from the Metaris Aestuarium to the Isle of Vectis,** was encompassed by their indifferent gaze: Branodunum, Garannonum, Regulbium, Rutupiae, Portus Dubris, Anderida and mighty Portus Adurni.† For more than a hundred and fifty years, these massive structures had kept at bay the blue-eyed heathen pirates from across the German Ocean. Now, but thinly manned by unpaid *limitanei*, they were failing to hold the line. These second-rate frontier troops were all that remained of the Army of Britain after the usurper Constantine (self-styled the Third) had, more than a generation before, led away the legions into Gaul, never to return.

No longer under the unified command of a Count of the Saxon Shore appointed from Ravenna, the forts had become mere isolated strong-points, between which the Saxon raiders could row their craft unchecked up creeks and estuaries, to ravage far inland. With no Duke of Britain to organize resistance, the hinterland behind the forts was reverting to heath and scrubland, as people fled the land to migrate west or seek shelter behind the

* In error for Aetius; see Notes p.436.
** The Wash to the Isle of Wight.
† Brancaster, Burgh Castle, Reculver, Richborough, Dover, Pevensey, Portchester.

strong walls of the cities. Grass now grew on the splendid roads that had once echoed to the tramp of Roman cohorts; the fox and badger made their lair in abandoned farmsteads, and the mosaic floors of crumbling villas became the hearths of passing war-bands.

On the wrinkled sea beneath the eagles' flight, three dots crept towards the British coast.

'To Flavius Aetius, Patrician, Master of Soldiers in all the Gauls, in his third consulship, greetings. I, Ambrosius Aurelianus, your friend and fellow Roman, humbly ask that you will heed my plea on behalf of the miserable inhabitants of this island: defenceless sheep harried by the Saxon wolves, whose plight—'

Ambrosius threw down his stylus in disgust. Had he really written that? With the blunt end of the instrument he erased what he had written on the waxed tablet. Seeking inspiration, he began to pace the room, an upper chamber of an inn in Noviomagus* which, as *consularis* of the province of Maxima Caesariensis, he had taken over as his headquarters. Ambrosius chuckled to himself. *Consularis* of Maxima Caesariensis! A meaningless euphemism plucked from the imperial past and bestowed on him by Noviomagus' remaining decurions, and implying governorship of an area covering the whole of south-east Britain. In fact, of course, he was nothing more than a successful warlord, whose fief precariously extended from the Fretum Gallicum northward to the Tamesa, and east to west from Cantium** as far as near Sorbiodunum the ancient Hanging Stones.† He supposed he owed his position to a record of proven ability as councillor, then mayor, and latterly resistance leader; also perhaps to the mystique conferred by his senatorial rank, and the fact that he was a Roman from a distinguished consular family – a real Roman, not a Celtic chief with a veneer of *Romanitas*.

He looked northwards over the city's neat grid of red-roofed houses to the chalk ridge‡ swelling on the horizon, the whole

* Chichester.
** Kent.
† Stonehenge near Old Sarum (an abandoned settlement by Salisbury).
‡ The South Downs.

scene bathed in mellow summer sunlight. But that idyllic view masked an uncomfortable reality. Beyond the city walls, where once were only gravel pits and cemeteries, extended a wide belt of cultivated strips; with the rural population crowding into the towns, these had in effect replaced the villas as centres of food production and distribution. And those distant hillsides, once grazed smooth by sheep, were now disfigured by a creeping pelt of furze and bracken.

His reverie was interrupted as a retainer, accompanied by a stranger in the garb of a minor cleric, appeared in the doorway.

'A message for you, sir,' the retainer announced in halting Latin, before retiring. Ambrosius sighed. It was a matter of regret that Britain, part of the empire for nearly four hundred years, was discarding Rome's legacy with unseemly haste. These days, you were lucky to hear Latin spoken in the streets; everyone was reverting to the native British tongue which, prior to the loss of the diocese, had been shunned by anyone with social or political ambitions. Roman dress, too, had been virtually abandoned, as had refinements like bath-houses, central heating, three-course meals, and reading the classics. It was a sign of the times, he thought sourly, that he couldn't even find a secretary with enough command of Latin to take dictation in the tongue of Cicero and Claudian.

Smiling, Ambrosius looked enquiringly at the cleric.

'I come from the Bishop of Autissiodorum, Your Honour,' the man said, 'on whose staff I serve as a humble reader. The bishop, who is on an official visit to Britain, finds himself in your vicinity and wonders if he might avail himself of your hospitality.'

Germanus here in Britain! Ambrosius' mind whirled, delight at the thought of seeing again his old friend and fellow Roman mingling with consternation at the prospect of entertaining such a distinguished guest and his inevitable retinue. This might include, besides priests, deacons, and subdeacons, acolytes, exorcists, readers, and singers.

Dismissing the cleric with a message of welcome for the bishop, Ambrosius began shouting orders to his household to prepare food and quarters. His was a rough-and-ready military establishment, hardly suitable for receiving a high official of the Church; nevertheless, he must do his utmost not to shame his guests. He glanced with dismay at his clothing: baggy British trousers (none too clean) and a rough tunic of chequered pattern. He couldn't greet the Bishop of Autissiodorum – a senator to boot – like that. But he had discarded his dalmatics one by one as they wore out, as being totally impractical for the active soldier's life he led. Then relief flooded him as he remembered his own senatorial toga, packed away years before as something unlikely to be needed again. Smoothing his cheeks with pumice from the last consignment he had been able to obtain before trade with Gaul closed down, he donned the noble, if archaic, garment, carefully adjusting its folds to create an imposing air of gravitas.

'Germanus, old friend!' A lump rose in Ambrosius' throat as he embraced the bishop warmly. 'How long has it been? Seventeen years? Do you remember, on that first visit, after you had confuted the Pelagian heretics, how you led a British host against the Picts and Saxons and routed them by shouting "Alleluia"?' Privately, Ambrosius was shocked by his friend's appearance. When he had last seen him, Germanus still bore the worldly stamp of the provincial governor he had once been. Now he was gaunt to the point of emaciation – the result, no doubt, of a self-imposed ascetic life. Instead of the richly embroidered episcopal vestments Ambrosius had expected, the bishop wore a rusty black robe (a hair shirt showing at the neck), with a leather bag of relics slung across his chest. And his previous bluff geniality of manner had been replaced by a self-effacing meekness.

'That victory was due to the terrain rather than any action of mine,' replied the bishop modestly. 'You see, I already knew that the surrounding hills gave back a powerful echo. When we raised our cry, the poor barbarians must have thought they were hopelessly outnumbered, so decided not to risk a contest. But that's all in the past.' He smiled sadly at Ambrosius – a smile of singular sweetness. 'Though I find the people still strong in the faith, much has changed in Britain since last I was here. Then the towns still had their decurions and bishops, who continued to run the public services, if imperfectly. Now all that is gone. Enlighten me my friend.'

'The old imperial system's completely broken down,' confirmed Ambrosius, handing his friend a brimming beaker. 'British beer; no more wine from Gaul, I'm afraid. More than once, I've appealed to Ravenna to re-occupy the diocese, but with the trouble in Gaul it seems there are no troops to spare. For the present, anyway. Everything here's reverted to a semi-tribal system of autonomous regions, with local warlords taking the place of hereditary chieftains.' He grinned wryly. 'Me, for instance. A warlord called Cunedda rules the North and Cambria, where his sons Keredig and Meiron have been apportioned subsidiary districts. Then there's Vortigern in Cantium. A fool, who's negotiating with two Saxon chiefs, Hengest and Horsa, for help against local enemies.' Ambrosius shrugged despairingly. 'It's like asking wolves to protect the flock.'

'But if your leaders were to combine against the common enemy?'

'Then we'd have no trouble driving off the Saxons,' declared Ambrosius with feeling. 'To say nothing of the Caledonian Picts or the Scots from Hibernia.' He sighed. 'But it'll never happen. Disunity has always been the Celts' Achilles' heel, from Vercingetorix and Boudicca onwards.' He paused, then added grimly, 'But in any case it may be too late. The thing we've all been dreading has begun to happen.'

'You mean the *adventus Saxonum*?'

The other nodded. 'The coming of the Saxons. As settlers, not raiders. Let me tell you what transpired at Anderida.'

The patrol from the Numerus Abulcorum, the unit of *limitanei* stationed at Anderida, grumbled under the unaccustomed weight of helmets and mail, issued from the stores on account of a recent increase in Saxon raids. All except Ludvig, a tough old *laetus*; a German ex-prisoner granted freedom and some land in exchange for military service under Rome. He had witnessed the departure of the legions under the usurper Constantine, and he was convinced that one day they would return. 'The eagles will come back, lads,' he would announce periodically, a remark which earned him much good-natured chaffing. 'Not this year, perhaps, but soon. They'll be back – just mark my words.'

Halting the straggling line of soldiers, the *biarchus* ordered the signaller to sound the recall, to bring back those on point duty before the patrol returned to the fort. The man raised a cowhorn to his lips, but before he could blow it the forward scout burst from a stand of pines ahead, frantically gesturing for silence.

'Saxons!' the man gasped as he reached the patrol. 'Three longboats approaching the shore about a mile ahead.'

Swiftly, the *biarchus* made his dispositions, first leading the patrol inland to avoid being spotted by the enemy, then approaching the landing-site under cover of a dense patch of bracken. Beyond the ferns, the ground fell steeply to a shingle beach which here threw out a long spit. In the lee of this natural breakwater, in the process of beaching, were the three Saxon craft, big clinker-built oared boats with a stepped mast to take a sail. The scene was curiously homely and unthreatening: women and children being helped on to the spit by their menfolk; saplings with netted root-balls, baskets of seed, bundled tools, all being offloaded with tender care; a puppy yapping with excitement.

'They look sort of . . . innocent,' whispered a young soldier.

'They do, don't they?' responded the *biarchus*. 'But they're not. Raids we can cope with – just. Settlers are something different. These people mean to take our land. Soon they'll be arriving by the boatload with every wind that blows from the east. So it's us or them.'

'You mean . . . we kill them all, even the women and children?' breathed the young soldier in horror.

'Just so, lad,' in a grim voice. 'Look, I don't like the business any more than you do. Just remember that cubs grow into wolves.'

With hand gestures, the *biarchus* spread his men in a semicircle to cut off escape, then gave the signal to charge.

The slaughter was swift, and total. Surrounded, taken by surprise, their backs to the sea, the Saxons stood no chance, and were cut down where they stood. The only survivor was the puppy, which the young soldier stuffed wriggling inside his tunic. The boats were stove in and sunk.

'Shouldn't we bury them?' suggested someone hesitantly. 'They may not have been Christians, but still . . .'

The *biarchus* shook his head. 'Leave them. Strewn along the beaches by the tides, their corpses may serve as a deterrent to the next arrivals.'

As the patrol neared Anderida, one keen-eyed soldier pointed to two specks in the sky heading north-west. He called out, laughing, 'Ludvig, you were right. Your eagles *have* come back.'

'We should begin with something strong and direct,' said Germanus, who was helping Ambrosius re-draft the letter to Aetius. He paused briefly then suggested, 'How does this sound? "To Aetius, consul for the third time, the groans of the Britons . . ."'

THIRTY-SEVEN

Not even Pallas could have built it faster or better
Inscription on the walls of Constantinople, commemorating their
rebuilding by the prefect Constantine in 447

'Good,' growled Arnegliscus to Aspar, as a *vexillatio* of heavy
horse, the Albigensian Cataphracts, thundered past. They were
the last unit of the Eastern Army to be inspected that day, on the
plain outside Marcianopolis, capital of the province of Moesia
Secunda and the largest city of Thrace. 'In fact, I have to say very
good,' he conceded stiffly. 'You've done an excellent job.
Congratulations.'

'Thank you, sir,' acknowledged Aspar, the Master of Soldiers'
second-in-command. He was grateful for the metamorphosis
Arnegliscus had undergone since the disaster of the Thracian
Chersonesus. The big German appeared to have learnt from
his mistakes at that battle; chastened, he had accepted the
unsparing criticism handed out by Aspar and by Areobindus,
his other leading general, and allowed them a free hand in
building a new army from the shattered remnant that had
survived the slaughter.

The defeat had forced the East Romans to sue for peace. In
the three years following the treaty drawn up between the Huns
and the veteran Eastern general Anatolius, Aspar and Areobindus
had achieved wonders in recruiting and training a new force to
resist the Huns, should they attack again. But in other respects
– quite apart from the harsh tribute exacted by the Huns under
the terms of the treaty – these had been terrible years. The winter
of the year of the Peace of Anatolius was the severest in living
memory, resulting in large-scale deaths of both livestock and
humans. There had followed dreadful floods which had washed
away whole villages, and in the capital there had been riots, plague,
and failing food supplies. In the east and south, the frontiers had
been threatened by Persians, Isaurians, Saracens, and Ethiopians.

Still, despite the onslaughts of nature, Huns, and hostile neigh-
bours, the East had survived. A new army had been raised, trained,
and equipped; thanks to Nomus, the Master of Offices, the Illyrian
section of the Danubius frontier had been quietly re-fortified and
re-garrisoned. And the sturdy peasantry and tradesmen (so
different from the semi-serfs of the West, ground down by rapacious tax-collectors), had shown commendable resilience and
toughness in face of a succession of catastrophes. Perhaps, Aspar
dared to hope, the worst was past and this year of the consuls
Aetius (for the third time) and Symmachus would mark a turning-
point in the fortunes of the East. But these hopes were to prove
vain.

Later that year, rumours began to filter across the Danubius hinting
at gathering storm-clouds in the north-west; Attila was reported
to be mustering his warriors for a second invasion of the East.
Then, on the twenty-sixth of January of the new year,* came the
greatest calamity of all: on a night of torrential rain, the citizens
of Constantinople were awakened by a violent earthquake.

Constantine, the Praetorian prefect, was working late in his
office in the palace on a knotty legal case when the tremors struck.
A loud rumbling, like a cascade of rocks, filled his ears and the
mosaic floor beneath him suddenly heaved upwards, flinging him
through the air to crash against a wall. In horrified disbelief, he
watched the pillars at the end of the room begin to twist and
bend like branches in a storm. Strong man though he was,
Constantine knew a moment of pure terror as he stumbled from
the building seconds before it collapsed behind him in an avalanche
of rubble. The moonlit scene in the sheeting rain was like a
description of the nether regions from Virgil's *Aeneid*: above him,
the mighty Hippodrome trembled but stood firm, but further
down the slope towards the Harbour of Julian on the Propontis,
buildings were swaying and toppling like children's toy brick
houses. Everywhere, the crash of falling masonry was punctuated
by the shrieks and moans of trapped victims. Fighting his instinct
to start organizing rescue teams, Constantine struck out west
towards the sea-walls, where the absence of large buildings should
make the going safer. In addition to key judicial and financial

* 447.

duties, Constantine was responsible for the maintenance of public works, the most important being the Walls of Theodosius, which guaranteed the capital's security.

The aftershocks and ominous rumbling stopped as suddenly as they had begun, the succeeding stillness and silence almost shocking by contrast. Hugging the sea-wall, which seemed to have sustained comparatively little damage, Constantine hurried past the harbours of Kontoskalion and Eleutherius, to reach the Theodosian Walls at the Golden Gate as dawn was breaking. The sun's early rays disclosed an appalling sight: tower after tower, together with the intervening stretches of rampart, reduced to jumbled heaps of brick and stone. Walking along the course of the bulwark, Constantine counted fifty-eight towers destroyed out of ninety-six – an open invitation to an invading enemy. And beyond the Danubius, the hordes of Attila were gathering . . .

It was a moment of supreme crisis, but Constantine rose to the occasion. Somehow, he had to find a solution to a seemingly impossible problem: how could he get the Walls rebuilt before the Huns were upon them? There weren't enough builders and masons in all Thrace, let alone Constantinople, to complete the work in time. Suddenly an idea came into his mind, one of those happy inspirations that can change the course of history. His first reaction was to reject it out of hand; it was crazy, it couldn't possibly work. But the more he thought about it, the more convinced he became that perhaps it just might. At any rate, there was nothing to lose by putting it to the test. Summoning the leaders of the opposing circus factions, the Blues and the Greens, he addressed them in the Hippodrome from the imperial box, the Kathisma: an unheard-of liberty, which carried the death penalty, but who was telling?

'Gentlemen, there are three things you should know,' he began. 'One, the Walls have collapsed for over half their length. Two, the Huns are about to attack. Three, the only people with sufficient organization and manpower to repair the Walls before the Huns get here, are yourselves. There's just one problem—'

'We don't like each other very much,' interjected one of his hearers. 'In fact, we hate each other's guts.' A roar of sardonic mirth greeted this sally.

'An understatement,' laughed Constantine, beginning to enjoy himself despite the dire circumstances. A tough, pragmatic individual, unflustered when it came to making rapid decisions which might have far-reaching consequences, he assessed the mood of his audience. These were hard, greedy, combative men, always spoiling for a fight, who lived for money and excitement. The most effective way to harness that raw energy, the prefect decided, was to pit the rival colours against each other as competing teams, each responsible for its own section of collapsed Wall. When he put the suggestion to them, it was greeted with delighted approval. Such a contest – on a mind-boggling scale, and with the added spice of a deadly race against time – provided just the sort of challenge they found irresistible.

'If we're agreed, here's the plan,' said Constantine. 'Many of you will have suffered damage or destruction of your homes, and loss or injury of family members, in the earthquake. Go home now and attend to your affairs. For those whose homes have been destroyed, temporary accommodation will be built. Injured relatives will have priority treatment at monasteries, and the field hospitals which will be set up without delay. Tomorrow, report outside the Walls with your faction's supporters. God bless you, and good luck.'

Work started the following day, on schedule. Sixteen thousand loyal supporters were divided up by the architects and master masons supervising the work, into gangs working in shifts, and field kitchens were set up to provide a constant flow of meals. To Constantine's relief and gratification, the Walls began to rise again with astonishing speed, the rival factions vying to outdo each other, while Anatolius bought time from the advancing Huns, by spinning out negotiations to repay arrears of tribute. In the incredible time of two months the ruined sections were rebuilt – not in any rough-and-ready improvised way, but as a massively solid, finished piece of work, with, in addition, a second lower line of walls and towers to its fore and, in front of that, a parapeted terrace, then a moat. As the last blocks were being mortared into place, the news arrived that the Huns, their numbers swollen by subject Ostrogoths and Gepids, were swarming forward, only days away. But Constantine was quietly confident that, behind his mighty barrier, the city was now safe. And so long as Constantinople stood, so would the Eastern Empire.

THIRTY-EIGHT

The enemy cavalry were not able to rout the Roman infantry;
standing shoulder to shoulder they formed with their shields
a rigid, unyielding barricade
Procopius, *History of the Wars*, c. 550

With mingled pride and sadness, Aspar watched his new army file out of Marcianopolis: pride because, starting from a base consisting of the demoralized survivors of the Thracian Chersonesus, he had built a formidable force, trained and equipped to the highest standards; sadness because, in engaging the hordes of Attila, many – perhaps most – would inevitably die. Ratiaria might be in Attila's hands, but the East's other workshops had worked night and day to provide his men with the finest weapons and armour that Roman industry and craftmanship could produce. No soldiers of his would face battle in cheap ridge helmets and stiff scale-armour cuirasses, as worn by Western troops. Instead, they would be protected by tough yet flexible coats of chain mail, and by helmets of the superior Attic type – unchanged since Alexander's day – complete with brow reinforcement and cheek-pieces, and with bowl and neck-guard forged from a single sheet of iron for maximum strength.

The army formed up in marching order on level ground outside the city: heavy cavalry such as the Arubian Catafractarii from the Black Sea province of Scythia; light cavalry like the Augustan Horse and First Theodosians; crack infantry units – the Fifth Macedonian Legion, the Second Thracian Cohort, the Third Diocletians, et cetera; specialist units – archers, slingers, catapult-men, doctors, armourers; the *bullistae* and *onagri*; the wagons loaded with arrows and javelins, armour, rations, and spares. Escorted by two famous palatine *vexillationes*, the Arcadians and Honorians, the three commanders, Arnegliscus, Aspar, and Areobindus, took their places at the head of the column. Arnegliscus raised his arm; all down the line the sonorous booming of the *bucinatores'* trumpets sounded, and the army began to move. Swinging along at the regulation pace of three Roman miles per hour, it headed westwards on the Nicopolis road: towards Attila, towards destiny.

'You've chosen well,' Arnegliscus told Aspar, as the two generals looked down on the imperial dispositions from the wooded slopes on the army's right.

'Thank you, sir,' acknowledged Aspar. 'Provided our men keep their nerve and hold the line, we should be able to block the Huns' advance – for a time, at least – and inflict heavy casualties. Realistically, that's about the most we can hope to achieve. We haven't the manpower for anything else.'

In the shadowy half-light of the first hour, the recently assembled units resembled black rectangular patches sewn on a grey cloak. The infantry were drawn up eight ranks deep, between high wooded ground guarding their right flank, and the River Utus* on their left. Heavy cavalry, mailed *clibanarii* and *catafractarii*, forming the wings, were stationed a little in front of the line, behind which were the archers, both horse and foot. Forming a protective screen several hundred yards in front of the main force were the light cavalry, mounted spearmen and *scutarii* with small round shields and javelins. Their job was not to try to stop the enemy but to slow its advance and cause maximum disruption, before falling back to reinforce the heavy horse. Positioned on the steep terrain on the right, wherever the ground was sufficiently level, catapults had been set up and the trees clear-felled in front of them so as not to impede the shot. Using the energy stored up in twisted hanks of sinew or hair, these formidable machines could discharge heavy bolts or round projectiles with terrific force, lethal up to several hundred yards. As an aid to aiming, painted stones marking various ranges had been sited in what would become neutral ground between the armies.

Scouts had reported that the Huns, bypassing the refortified section of the frontier in Moesia Prima, were approaching eastwards along the corridor of level land between the Danubius to the north, and the Haemus range** to the south. Here, in the neck of the corridor, in the province of Dacia Ripensis, Aspar, with the agreement of the other two generals, had chosen to

---

* The Vid, in Bulgaria.
** The Balkan Mountains, in Bulgaria.

confront the Huns. As Arnegliscus had implied, it was a strong position, allowing the imperial army to present a broad front to the enemy, thus utilising its manpower effectively, but with sufficient depth to provide stability. The river on the left flank, and the wooded bluffs on the right, ensured that the army could not be outflanked – always the greatest danger with the Huns. While favouring the Romans, the constricted nature of the site also prevented the Huns, who had overwhelming superiority in numbers, from deploying more than a fraction of their forces at one time.

Between the second and third hours, scouts galloped up from the west with the news that the Huns had broken camp and their van would soon be in sight. The *bucinatores* sounded their trumpets, and the army, which had been allowed to rest, was stood to arms. Two orderlies appeared before the army, carrying between them an improvised tribunal which they placed on the ground. Arnegliscus, the German master-commander, mounted the platform.

'Soldiers, we shall shortly be in battle with the Huns,' he began, speaking awkwardly, in clipped, guttural tones. 'For many of you, it will be your first battle, and you may well be afraid, because of what you have heard about the Huns as fighters. I tell you this: you need not fear the Huns. They are savages, barbarians. A Roman is worth two of them. The only reason they have been successful so far is that there are so many of them compared to us. Well, today their numbers will count for far less. As you can see from our position, they can only bring against us at one time the same numbers with which we will oppose them. Stand firm today, and we will show the world that Attila is not invincible.'

The little speech seemed to go down well, perhaps because, lacking the rhetorical flourishes which a Roman commander would have employed in addressing his troops, it came over as honest and sincere. The soldiers showed their appreciation by beating their shields loudly with their spears.

Soon after Arnegliscus had stepped down from the tribunal, dust-clouds on the western horizon signalled the approach of the Huns. The skirmishers, having done their work, came racing back ahead of the enemy to rejoin the Roman formations. Moments later, the Hun van swept down upon the Roman line. The front held firm; confronted by a hedge of blades, at the last second the enemy riders peeled away to left and right, taking casualties from the volley of darts and javelins that arced up from the Roman ranks.

After the shock and confusion of the initial encounter, both sides settled down to a grim contest of attrition. Time after time, Hun charges against the Roman line stalled, the horses balking in face of the wicked spear-points. Meanwhile, the Roman catapults, from their high ground to the right of the line, wreaked fearful damage on the Huns. The *ballistae* resembled giant crossbows, each arm being inserted into a column of sinews clamped in a frame. Cranked back with a lever-and-ratchet mechanism, when released by a trigger the bowstring discharged a heavy bolt along a groove. These projectiles, shooting downhill with tremendous force into the dense masses of Huns, sometimes skewered several bodies together, or turned horses into pain-maddened, uncontrollable liabilities. The other type of catapult, the aptly named *onager* or 'kicking ass', had an arm ending in a sling to hold a heavy ball. Also powered by twisted sinews, when wound down then released it was even more destructive, if less accurate, than the *ballista*; anyone struck by a lump of iron weighing twenty pounds, and travelling at enormous speed, if he was not killed outright was going to be put out of action – permanently.

The Romans' choice of terrain denied the Huns their favourite, and winning, tactic: outflanking then encircling their opponents. Being forced to fight on the Romans' terms on a narrow front put them at a considerable disadvantage; their strengths of speed, mobility, and firepower, were comparatively ineffective against a shield-wall maintained by armoured men, who could be attacked only from the front. And successive charges by the Roman heavy horse, invulnerable in mail, cut bloody swathes through their van, leaving heaps of dead and dying men and horses to impede others trying to attack the Roman front. Roman archers, too, shooting in safety from behind the rear rank, took a steady toll, as did the volleys of darts and javelins which the *pedites*, constantly supplied by runners bringing replenishments from the wagons, were able to maintain.

But the constant sleet of Hun arrows slowly began to thin the Roman ranks. Perhaps only one arrow in twenty found a mark, but so heavy and unremitting was the barrage that the casualty rate crept up inexorably. As gaps appeared, the file-closers pushed men up from behind to fill them, causing the Roman line to narrow dangerously from eight ranks, to six, to four . . . Sensing the situation was becoming critical, Arnegliscus removed his helmet, his long yellow hair allowing him to be instantly recognized, and rode along the Roman front exhorting the soldiers to stand firm. An obvious target, it was not long before his horse was killed beneath him; then he himself fell in the act of mounting a fresh steed, his brain transfixed by a Hun arrow.

Now in overall command, Aspar knew there could only be one conclusion to the battle. Had the sides been evenly matched, the day would have undoubtedly gone to the Romans. But with their huge preponderance in numbers the Huns could sustain enormous losses and still keep putting men into the field. Nevertheless, surveying the endless windrows of Hun dead that made the battlefield resemble a wheatfield after a hailstorm, Aspar felt a grim satisfaction. The Huns might win the battle, but it would be a Pyrrhic victory. It was clear that they had suffered losses on a scale which must leave them severely, perhaps permanently, weakened.

The fighting raged on until dusk. By then the Roman line had narrowed to a ribbon a mere two ranks deep – but still valiantly holding firm. As daylight began to bleed away, the Huns withdrew. Loading as many of the wounded as could be found on to the wagons, the Romans left the field and began to retreat eastwards, in good order. The formations they had maintained throughout the day were exactly delineated on the battlefield by the corpses of the slain, all facing the west. Whole *numeri* and legions had perished: the Third and Fourth Decimani, the Stobensian Horse, the Dafne Ballistiers, the Saracen Horse, the First and Second Isaurians, and many, many more. Though few had survived, their morale remained unbroken, for they had fought the Huns to a standstill, giving such an account of themselves that Attila must surely hesitate before again taking on a Roman army.

The following day, Attila inspected the field with a heavy heart. He had not taken part in the battle, for such was not his way; his was the mind that planned, not the hand that fought. The scale of the slaughter on the Hun side was immense – far, far worse than that suffered at Tolosa. It would take a generation to make good such losses. With a feeling akin to despair, Attila wondered, for the first time, if he could ever really beat the Romans, at least the Romans of the East. They were perhaps too populous, too organized, their cities too strong, for a barbarian people to defeat permanently. Especially now that they seemed, under strong leadership, to have discovered a new determination and fighting spirit. Or perhaps it was more a case of them having re-discovered the qualities that had made Rome great in the first place.

Had his life, despite all his fame and conquests, been a failure? In his dream of a Greater Scythia he had reached for the stars, but they had proved beyond his grasp. And now, perhaps, his invincibility as a warrior might begin to disappear, as the snows of the Caucasus melted in the spring. The Chinese had a saying: 'He who rides a tiger cannot dismount, lest it rend him.' Well, he was riding a tiger, the tiger of his people. He was old now and beginning to tire, but he had no choice except to continue to lead them in the course he had embarked them on, the course of slaughter and rapine. Even should that, in the end, bring about his and their destruction.

'What now, friend?' Areobindus asked Aspar, as the two generals, with what was left of the army, came in sight of the rebuilt walls of Constantinople.

'Now we ride out the storm,' replied the new Master of Soldiers, with a grim smile. He had no illusions about how terrible would be the vengeance that Attila would wreak on the Eastern Empire, for having the temerity to stand against him and inflict tremendous damage on his forces. The East would raise another army, as Rome had done after Cannae, but that would take time. Meanwhile, they must prepare to endure the whirlwind that the Scourge of God would surely unleash on them.

The battered but proud remnant of the great army that had marched out from Marcianopolis just weeks before, entered the capital by the Hadrianopolis Gate, to be cheered to the echo through the streets by the vast throng that had turned out to give them a heroes' welcome: news of their stand against Attila had preceded them. Shrewd and tough, the citizens of Constantinople knew the greatness of the debt they owed such men and their leaders. The Emperor might hide from the national crisis in his palace, and his chief minister Chrysaphius scheme only to enrich himself, but with men of the calibre of Aspar, Anatolius, and Constantine to steer the ship of state through the perilous waters that lay ahead, they were confident the empire would be saved.

That night, Aspar had a dream; a solemn funeral procession moved along the Mesé, which was lined by the mourning citizens of Constantinople, through the five great fora, past the Hippodrome and the great square of the Augusteum, to the Cathedral of the Holy Wisdom. The pallbearers placed the open coffin on the marble catafalque, which bore the inscription 'THEODOSIUS'.

He woke feeling disorientated. The vision had been so real, so vivid – it was more like a memory than a dream. He tried to put it out of his mind, but it kept recurring. Was it a portent? A warning? A sudden chill ran through him, as a third possibility presented itself. An admonition? Immediately, he closed his mind against the thought. He was no traitor; all his life he had served the Emperor loyally, and he would continue to do so. But a part of his mind – the Cassius part, he thought ironically – seemed to ask, 'But if the Emperor is unworthy, should not your loyalty be to the empire?' And so began a dialogue in his mind between 'Brutus' and 'Cassius', Cassius urging that the well-being of the state would be served by the removal of its present ruler, Brutus countering with the argument that the curse of the Roman Empire in the past had been ambitious generals wading through blood to seize the throne.

At length, after protracted mental debate, Aspar faced the stark truth. So long as Theodosius lived, the Eastern Empire would continue to pay tribute to the Huns – a disgraceful humiliation which no self-respecting state should endure, especially if that state was the heir to the greatest civilization the world had known, and the tribute extorted by a race of illiterate savages. And Theodosius was not yet fifty; he might live another twenty, even thirty, years. But if Aspar were to contrive the death of Theodosius and himself assume the purple, he would be condemned as yet another murdering usurper, an Arian and barbarian to boot, motivated by selfish ambition; the consequence might well be bloody civil war. No: the successor must be a man of stature, with a career of solid achievement to his credit, acceptable to Senate and Consistory, but a man who could never be accused of acting solely from ambition. A man also of spotless integrity, proven courage, and highest principle. Did such a paragon exist? Yes, Aspar knew just such a one. This very day he would approach him.

Cassius had prevailed over Brutus.

THIRTY-NINE

The river banks were covered with human bones, and the stench
of death was so great that no one could enter the city *
Priscus of Panium, *Byzantine History*, after 472

'"After the Battle of the Utus, in which, though victorious, he
sustained heavy losses, Attila appeared before the walls of
Constantinople. He did not linger; their massive strength obviously convinced him that it would be a waste of time to invest
the capital. Instead, the Scourge of God went on to vent his
heathen fury on the dioceses of Thracia and Macedonia, ravaging
without resistance and without mercy everything in his path from
the Hellespontus to the Pass of Thermopylae. The most strongly
defended cities like Heraclea and Hadrianopolis may have escaped,
but seventy others have been utterly destroyed: Marcianopolis,
Thessaloniki, Dyrrachium . . ."' Titus looked up from the letter,
just arrived by express courier from the Imperial Secretariat in
Constantinople, which he had been reading aloud to Aetius. They
were in the general's temporary headquarters, a suite in the archbishop's palace at Lugdunum** in the Gallic province of
Lugdunensis. 'I'll pass over the other sixty-seven, shall I, sir?'
    'And the rest,' sighed the general, nodding wearily. 'Just cut
to the end, and tell me what it is they want.'
    '"After our gallant army sacrificed itself at the Utus,"' continued
Titus, after briefly scanning the remainder of the missive, '"we
looked to the West for help, but sadly it was not forthcoming.
This despite the fact that our Invincible Augustus, the Most Sacred
Theodosius, the Calligrapher, has in the past given aid most gener-
ously, and on more than one occasion, to his Royal Cousin,
Valentinian, Augustus of the West. Our distinguished general, the

---

* Naissus (the present-day Niš), one of the cities destroyed by the Huns. Priscus
passed it en route to visit Attila in 449.
** Lyons.

291

Illustrious Anatolius, Count of the First Order, has had to make the best terms he can with Attila. These, however, are harsh indeed: the yearly tribute to be greatly increased, and a strip of territory south of the Danubius, from Singidunum to Novae,* to be ceded to the Huns – three hundred miles in length, and in breadth as much as a fifteen days' journey will encompass.

'"In hopes of mitigating these heavy conditions, a special embassy is to travel from Constantinople to Attila, who has agreed to receive it. This mission will be headed by a respected courtier, the Most Perfect Maximin, accompanied by one Priscus,** of Panium in Thracia, a scholar and historian of note. The observations of the latter, as to the mores of the Huns, may yield a useful insight as to how best to treat with these barbarians. It is greatly to be hoped that ambassadors from the West will join our embassy, as their presence could add weight to our pleas.

'"Esteemed Patrician, it is no secret that you have, or have had, ties of friendship with our present oppressor, the monarch of the Huns. This consideration might help to sway him in our favour. The citizens of the Eastern part of our One and Indivisible Empire beseech the Patrician of the West, in the event he cannot come himself, at least to send persons of substance to speak on his behalf. Such men should be familiar with both courts and camps, be of noble lineage and of consular rank. The Emperor Himself prays you will accede to this request; you would then leave the East a grateful memory of the name of Aetius. Farewell. Signed by the hand of Nomus, Master of Offices, the Most Perfect . . ." et cetera, et cetera. Sounds as if they're pretty desperate, sir.'

'I should at least have *tried* to help them!' cried Aetius, an expression of anguished guilt on his face. He looked appealingly at Titus. 'But how, in all conscience, could I? My army would have mutinied if I'd ordered it to the East, as Julian's legions did – and that was eighty years ago. Besides, Attila is, or was, my friend. It's hard to fight a man you've broken bread with. Anyway, all that's by the way. How could I have left Gaul, with the federates always ready to break out the moment my back's turned?'

---

* From Belgrade to Sistova, Bulgaria.
** Author of the fragmentary *Byzantine History*, which contains a vivid and detailed first-hand account of the embassy's visit to the court of Attila.

'No one, if he's fair, can blame you, sir,' said Titus gently, thinking how tired and lined the general's face had become, and how much his hair had greyed in recent months. 'You've got your hands more than full holding things together in the West.'

'I can't disagree with that,' concurred Aetius with gloomy emphasis. He began to pace the spacious chamber overlooking the confluence of the Rhodanus and the Arar,* which, since it had become his office, had been reduced to the usual state of chaos. 'With my field army shrinking steadily – like an icicle in the sun – these days I'm having to be more diplomat than soldier. Wielding the big stick's no longer the option it once was; I must now placate, where once I could compel. Never did I need Attila's Huns more. Keeping these touchy federates in line would try the patience of a saint. When King Chlodio died recently, the Franks couldn't decide which of his sons should succeed. So whom did they ask to arbitrate? Me. I chose the younger, Merovech, a decent lad who's showing promise as a ruler. But in spite of primogeniture not being a deciding factor with the Franks, the elder brother felt aggrieved and flounced off to Attila, whom he's asked to help put him on the throne.'

'And that could be serious?'

'It might. They've become formal allies, it would seem. That *could* give Attila a pretext for invading the West, I suppose. I just hope, for old times' sake, he'd never go that far. Half my time's spent ingratiating myself with the Frankish nobles, so as to persuade them that Merovech is the right choice.'

'And the other half?' ventured Titus with a smile, hoping to lighten the general's mood.

'What's this, a Socratic dialogue?' replied the other, with a wry grin. 'Don't humour me, my friend. You know the answer very well yourself. Ever since Theoderic and Gaiseric fell out over the latter's mutilation of the former's daughter, I've been working hard to build up a friendly relationship with Theoderic. We hope to be able to mount a joint Romano-Visigothic invasion of Africa, to punish Gaiseric and, with luck, get rid of him – which won't be easy, mind, as he's now Attila's ally. Still, he's played into my hands by making an enemy of Theoderic, who otherwise might be getting ideas again about expanding his territory eastwards

* The Rhône and the Saône.

into Provincia.' The general paused in his pacing to secure a banging shutter. He stood looking out of the window for a short while. 'The times we live in, Titus,' he mused. 'From here I can see, between the houses and the city walls, great empty spaces and derelict buildings. This city, once among the greatest in the West, has shrunk to half its size. Insecurity, declining trade . . . The aqueducts have stopped working, always the first sign that things are breaking down. Lead thieves; they strip the lining from the water channels. The city council's too strapped for cash to employ maintenance staff or an adequate force of *vigiles*.'

'To change the subject, sir, what, if anything, do we do about this appeal from Constantinople?'

'Not "we" my dear Titus: you. A trip to Eastern Europe as part of a diplomatic mission – it'll be a pleasant change for you.'

'Me!' exclaimed Titus, perturbed. 'Is that a good idea, sir? Remember what happened last time. And if Attila's only prepared to meet people of consular rank, that rather puts me out of the race, doesn't it?'

'It wasn't your fault that your mission to Attila failed. The timing was wrong, that's all. Litorius' blundering at Tolosa had just cost the lives of sixty thousand Huns, if you recall. As for your not having been a consul, well, while Caligula may have made his horse one, I can't do the same for you, I'm afraid. Not that it matters. Attila's stipulation isn't to be taken too literally. I doubt this Priscus fellow boasts a title to his name. Still, you'd better have one of some sort, I suppose. Let's see, top-ranking *agentes in rebus* became Most Distinguished under Gratian, but I'm pretty sure that went up to Notable early in the present reign. So, in order that you qualify, I now promote you to *princeps*, the highest rank in the courier service. Titus Valerius Rufinus, Vir Spectabilis: how does that sound?'

'I can live with it,' acknowledged Titus with a smile.

'I should think so! The things I do for you. Your title will need to be confirmed by the Consistory, but I'll make sure the application goes through marked "First Priority". Now, while officially your function on this mission will be to give backing to the Eastern envoys, I want you to try and arrange a private audience with Attila. His anger has had time to cool since Tolosa. There's just a chance that this time you may succeed in persuading him to become my ally again. I'll brief you later about what to say.

And while you're there, try to find out what happened to Constantius. He seems to have vanished off the face of the earth.'

'It's my guess he absconded with the gifts he was meant to take to Attila. I know you liked him, sir, but I felt there was something untrustworthy about him.'

'I suppose you may be right,' sighed Aetius. 'Pity. A talented young man, who could have gone far. Now, to decide who's going with you . . .'

FORTY

A luxurious meal served on silver plate had been made ready for us,
but Attila ate nothing but meat on a wooden trencher

Priscus of Panium, *Byzantine History*, after 472

Attila's palace, the Royal Village, Old Dacia (former Roman province) [Titus wrote in the *Liber Rufinorum*], 'in the consulships of Asturius and Protogenes, II Nones June.*

Soon after crossing the Danubius at Aquincum, the West Roman embassy (myself; Romulus, a senator, an affable nonentity included solely for the prestige his rank would confer on the mission; a modest retinue) was met by Hun guides sent by Attila. They conducted us eastwards for a further two hundred miles to Attila's camp, situated between the upper waters of the Tisa and the Carpathus Mountains. On the way, we stayed at Hun villages, where we were treated with impeccable politeness and hospitality, especially at one settlement owned by the widow of Bleda, Attila's brother. We were entertained with great kindness by the lady herself.

The Hun 'capital', which I visited nine years ago on my first, ill-fated, mission to Attila, is in reality nothing more than a vast, sprawling village of tents, lacking a single stone building, with one exception – a perfect copy of a Roman bath-house! It was designed apparently by a Greek taken prisoner in war. Anything more ludicrously inappropriate would be hard to imagine – like seeing a pearl stud in a pig's ear. The palace is on top of a hill within the village; it consists of a scatter of wooden buildings surrounded by a palisade. We were shown to our quarters, and invited to a banquet to be held that evening. To my surprise, the feast was arranged with considerable elegance: two lines of small

* 4 June 449.

tables, covered in linen, for the guests and their hosts down each side of a spacious hall, with the royal table, reserved for Attila and members of his family, on a raised platform in the middle. In contrast to the side-tables, which were spread with gold and silver platters and goblets (doubtless looted from the Eastern Empire in the recent campaigns), the royal board was furnished with wooden cups and dishes. In a calculated snub, we Romans were placed on the left-hand row, high-ranking Huns and subject German chiefs on the more honourable right. Unlike the non-Roman guests, who were tricked out in barbaric finery, Attila was clad in plain skin garments, lacking any ornament.

I found myself seated next to Priscus, the historian from the Eastern embassy, a garrulous, friendly little fellow who, when he thought no one was looking, would whip out his waxed tablets and stylus, and scratch down notes. He gave me a brief description of some of the characters facing us from the Huns' side of the hall. 'See those two opposite, the long-haired chap with the gold neck-torque, and the scholarly-looking type in the Roman dalmatic next to him? Edecon and Orestes,* the last two ambassadors Attila sent to Constantinople. They joined us on our journey from Constantinople. Edecon's some sort of chief among his own people, a German tribe called the Sciri who are now Attila's subjects and who provide his bodyguard. Orestes is Attila's secretary. Why on earth a Roman should choose to bury himself in this backwater, among a lot of unwashed savages, is beyond me. Of course, being a Pannonian and a resident in that province when it was ceded to the Huns, he may not have had a choice. And that oafish-looking fellow in the blue tunic, that's Bigilas, the interpreter. Watch what you say if you're called on to give a toast. He's a mischief-maker, who's quite likely to twist your words if he doesn't like your face.'

Contrary to my fears, the feast wasn't at all bad, though rather heavily dependent on goat's flesh and mutton. I was

---

* Orestes, as already noted, became the father of the last Roman emperor of the West, Romulus Augustus. Edecon was to be the father of Odoacer, who deposed Romulus to become the first barbarian king of Italy. An eerie coincidence.

relieved that the drink provided was not the local *kumiss*, a nauseating beverage made from fermented mare's milk, but Roman wine. This was undiluted, the Huns presumably being ignorant of the Roman practice of mixing water with the heavy imperial vintages. To my growing alarm and discomfort, with each course a cup-bearer presented a goblet of wine to Attila, who proceeded to toast the chief guests in turn. He barely touched the cup with his lips, but this privilege did not extend to those outwith the royal table; not to drain one's cup with each toast – or appear to do so – would clearly have been construed an insult. Consequently, despite unobtrusively contriving to spill a considerable amount of wine on the floor, I began to feel quite sick. Fortunately, the toasts were discontinued after the last course had been served, when we were treated by two bards to a tedious recitation of verses celebrating Attila's valour and victories.

This was followed by a grotesque performance by a pair of clowns, one Moorish, the other a Hun. Their buffoonish antics and 'comic' speeches in a garbled mixture of Latin, Goth, and Hunnish sent the opposite tables into paroxysms of laughter in which, for politeness' sake, we Romans had to pretend to join. Throughout this farce, Attila alone sat unmoved and gravely silent; except on the entrance of his youngest son, Irnac, when I was astonished to discover that the Scourge of God has a softer side. He hugged the little boy with a tender smile, pinched him gently on the cheek, and proceeded to dandle him affectionately on his knee. Soon afterwards, the royal party left the hall. Thankfully, I could now retire, and departed along with the other Romans, in my case, and I suspect in theirs, to nurse a throbbing head.

The following morning, Maximin was summoned for an interview with Attila. Titus' turn came in the afternoon. He was received in the same audience chamber as nine years previously, with Attila sitting on the same simple wooden throne. Now that he could see him close up, Titus was shocked by the change in Attila. Gone was the impression of coiled energy that had so impressed him. He seemed instead to be looking at a sick old lion, a lion whose teeth and claws could still rend, but whose great strength was beginning to run down.

'Well, Roman,' said Attila in his deep voice, 'I trust you bring me better news than last time, when you reported the loss of sixty thousand of my finest warriors. You may speak.'

'Your Majesty,' said Titus, bowing, 'my master Aetius, Patrician of the West, sends greetings to the King of the Huns, and wishes him good health and prosperity. He suggests that the time has come to mend bridges with the Romans – to cease making war against the subjects of Theodosius, and to become once more the friend and ally of the Romans of the West.'

'And why should the King of the Huns accede to either of these requests?' asked Attila mildly.

'From the East Romans, as I understand from Maximin, you already receive tribute, a shameful yoke for a proud Empire to submit to. But if these sums were to become fair recompense for protection for that empire from her enemies – the warlike Isaurians, the ambitious Persians, the savage Nubians – Scythia and East Rome could co-exist as friendly allies. The terror of Attila's name would of itself be sufficient to deter those peoples from attacking the Eastern Empire.'

'And the West?'

'It is my master's sincerest wish that the friendship that was once between you both might be resumed. For providing soldiers to watch the federates and ensure that they stay within the bounds of their assigned homelands, he is willing to grant you not only the titles of Patrician, and – together with himself – Master of Soldiers in all the Gauls, but also one-fifth of the revenues of the West. As peace and stability return, and taxes normalize, these revenues must increase. They would increase dramatically if you were to break off your alliance with Gaiseric, who is nothing better than a pirate, and if not assist, at least not hinder, the reconquest of Africa. He also sees a time when the empires of the Huns and the West Romans could become united – to the mutual benefit of both. And as a mark of his affection and respect, he sends this gift.' Titus unwrapped the present he had brought with him, a magnificent silver dish two feet across, showing scenes and objects in relief, wrought with the most exquisite Roman craftsmanship.

For a few seconds Attila stared in silence at the dish, then, taking it from Titus, he exclaimed hoarsely, 'See, here is the fight with the bear, at the moment when I pierced it with my lance. And here is Pegasus, the Arab steed I gifted to Carpilio, his son. The bison hunt. The Sacred Scimitar. Shooting the rapids of the Iron Gate. Truly, it is a noble gift,' he murmured, a hint of emotion in his voice, a yearning in his eyes, akin to the look Titus had noted when he greeted his child. But only for a moment. In a flash, Attila's features had composed themselves into their habitual expression of stern gravity.

'Your words are fair, Roman,' he declared judiciously, 'but I would remind you that in the past, where the West is concerned, I have given much but received little. You offer the same terms as did your predecessor, Constantius – allowing for his exaggerations. I was tempted to believe him, until it transpired that what he had told me was but a ruse in order to deceive me. Why then, should I believe you?'

'That I cannot say, Your Majesty,' responded Titus, with a sinking feeling that things were slipping away from him. His fears about Constantius had proved justified. To himself, he cursed the smooth-talking young aristocrat, and Aetius for having allowed himself to be taken in. 'Attila is famous as a judge of men,' he pressed on. 'I am happy that my honesty should stand upon his verdict. May I ask, Your Majesty, in what way Constantius played you false?'

'He is here. You may see him if you wish.'

His mind in a whirl, Titus could only nod. What could Attila possibly mean? Had Constantius turned traitor, to spy for Attila against the West?'

The King flung open the shutters of a window and invited Titus to look out. The Roman did so – and gasped in horror. In the middle of a grassy space stood a tall cross, on which was suspended a hideous thing that had once been a man – a skeleton, to which still adhered tattered scraps of skin and flesh. Things crawling in the empty eye sockets, lent to the skull a horrible semblance of life.

'I keep Constantius to serve as a warning to others who may be tempted to deceive me,' said Attila in sombre tones. 'How can I be sure, Roman, that you yourself do not harbour such intentions?'

Titus felt an icy knot of fear twist in his stomach. To end like that! He wetted lips which had suddenly gone dry. 'Your Majesty, I fear Constantius deceived us all,' he protested, keeping his voice steady with some difficulty. 'My master sent him to you in good faith – as he sent myself. Aetius' only fault lay with his judgement, not his heart. I myself distrusted Constantius, and tried to warn Aetius against him.'

'I am minded to believe you,' said Attila heavily, after a pause. 'You are, perhaps, that rare thing: an honest Roman. Though I have little reason to trust any of your race. To answer the question you asked earlier, Constantius was bribed to kill me – by the Eastern Emperor's chief minister, Chrysaphius.'

'But . . . you entertained Maximin, with kindness and generosity, Maximin, the emissary of that same Emperor!' exclaimed Titus, astonished and impressed. Theodosius could hardly have been unaware of Chrysaphius' plot, and so must have been involved, even if that meant merely looking the other way.

'We Huns may be barbarians,' remarked Attila dryly, 'but we respect the laws of hospitality.' He gave Titus a long and searching look. 'Go now, friend,' he said, in oddly gentle tones. 'Tell Aetius I thank him for his gift, and will reflect upon his words.'

After the Romans had departed, Maximin and Priscus for the East, Titus and his party for the West, Attila rode out alone into the steppe, to decide what should be his policy towards both empires. His instincts told him that further campaigns against the East would be unproductive. The Battle of the Utus had convinced him that, despite their huge superiority in numbers, the Huns could not expect to keep on winning against properly led and equipped Roman armies. Best, then, to settle for what he could get, while still in an apparent position of strength. The timid Theodosius would always favour a policy of appeasement; so let the Huns continue to accept tribute (which the wealthy East could certainly afford), but, as the Roman envoys suggested, not call it that. A face-saving formula could be devised by which the Huns would become the paid protectors of the East's frontiers. Actually, this would fit neatly with his present war against the Acatziri, a brave but primitive people to the east of his dominions. His campaigns there could be presented as a strategic move to guard the Eastern Empire's rear.

As for the West: could he after all have misjudged Aetius, have allowed Constantius to poison his mind against his one-time friend and ally? The Patrician's splendid present had moved him more than he had allowed Titus to see. Surely such a gift could come only from the heart? If Aetius was sincere about his proposal that they resume their alliance, should not Attila take up the offer? He was tempted, greatly tempted: wealth and titles, an honourable outlet for his warriors' fighting instincts, a possible union between two great empires. Perhaps he could dare once more to hope that his dream of a Greater Scythia might one day be fulfilled. Nothing need be decided at this juncture. In the meantime, he would stay his hand against the West, despite the clamourings of so-called 'friends' that he attack.

He was under pressure from Gaiseric; from the anti-Merovech faction among the Franks; and from Eudoxius, a one-time physician, now leader of the newly resurgent Bagaudae, who had sought refuge at the court of Attila. All these were urging him to invade, citing the present weakness of the West as providing a golden opportunity. They were parasites, he thought with contempt, jackals who followed the lion, hoping to snatch the leavings from his kill. He would resist their blandishments – at least until he had made up his mind regarding what his policy should be towards Aetius.

At that moment, the king's eye was caught by two birds, a plover, and a falcon in pursuit. The falcon soared above its quarry to prepare for its deadly stoop, but the plover had been at the game before and knew what to do. It dropped like a stone till only feet above the ground, then, keeping at that height, raced for the shelter of a distant copse. The falcon, easily pacing its prey, kept a parallel flight, yet dared not strike; it would have killed the plover, but the impetus of its stoop would have caused it to break its own neck. The two became specks in the distance; the lower speck reached the trees and disappeared, the upper soared above the tops and flew away, knowing it could do nothing against a bird in a wood. Attila laughed and turned his horse's head for home. The little drama he had witnessed could, he thought, serve as an exemplar of his own position.

In the spring of the following year,* – the consulships of Valentinian Augustus (his seventh) and of Avienus – Anatolius and

* 450.

Nomus crossed the Danubius to confer with Attila. The meeting was marked by a spirit of concord and goodwill on both sides, with Attila generously agreeing to abandon the strip of territory south of the Danubius, to drop demands for further return of fugitives and prisoners, and to draw a tactful veil over the plot to murder him. Tribute, rephrased as compensation for guarding the empire's frontiers, would continue to be paid, but reduced from that imposed by the terms of the previous treaty. For the general and the Master of Offices, the Third Peace of Anatolius was a diplomatic triumph, their years of patient and persistent effort crowned at last with success. For Attila, it meant a welcome, and honourable, reprieve from the necessity of waging constant war. Against this background, a resumption of his alliance with Aetius seemed increasingly attractive. Sunlit uplands of the spirit seemed to be beckoning the tired old warrior.

But these bright hopes were about to be dashed: by something tiny and insignificant, round, and of a blood-red colour.

FORTY-ONE

The Emperor Theodosius was thrown from his horse, injuring his spine
Theophanes, *Chronographia*, c. 800

Perhaps in compensation for his ineffectiveness as a ruler, Theodosius liked to ride large and spirited horses. It was as if he felt a need to demonstrate that here was a field, one not without an element of danger, in which he could display mastery. On the twenty-sixth day of the month named for Julius Caesar, in the year that the Third Peace of Anatolius was made, the Emperor, accompanied by a groom, was riding by the banks of the River Lycus, near the capital. After a spirited canter, as was his wont he dismounted and gave the reins to the groom, with instructions to walk the big bay stallion for a space and then return. Leaving his master resting by the waterside, the groom complied, but before rejoining the Emperor he made a small adjustment to the stallion's saddle.

On remounting, Theodosius found the horse suddenly uncontrollable. It began to buck and rear violently. His desperate efforts to calm it and retain his seat proved vain, and Theodosius was hurled from the saddle, to land with a crash on boulders by the river's edge. He tried to rise but his legs failed to respond. 'My back,' he whispered to the groom, 'I think it's broken.' Before going to summon help, the groom removed from beneath the stallion's saddle a tiny seed-capsule, scarlet, prickly, the fruit of a lowly shrub called 'burning bush'.

When he heard the news, Aspar at once sent word to Marcian, a senator and distinguished army veteran, then hastened to attend the bedside of the dying Emperor. Theodosius lingered for two days before expiring, unlamented, in the fiftieth year of his age and the forty-third of his reign. One month later, a retired officer, Marcian, a modest, upright man who had given Aspar nineteen years of loyal service, was invested with the imperial purple.

Renouncing the feeble policy of his predecessor, the first act of the new Emperor was to send, via his ambassador Apollonius, a polite but unequivocal message to Attila: the East would pay no further tribute to the Huns.

FORTY-TWO

*Sapor trampled upon the pact and laid hands on Armenia**
Ammianus Marcellinus, *The Histories*, c. 395

The wind blowing from Mount Ararat had a bitter edge. In the darkness, huddled beneath his cloak in a narrow gorge on the boundary between Roman and Persian Armenia, Julian shivered, and blew on cold-stiffened fingers. For at least the hundredth time since setting out from Antioch, he cursed the day he had accepted the lonely and dangerous commission on which he was now engaged. Of course, as a serving officer in the East Roman army, and from a family (connected to the distinguished soldier and historian Ammianus Marcellinus) with a long and distinguished military tradition to uphold, refusal had been virtually impossible. His mind drifted back twenty days to that fateful meeting with Aspar, East Rome's most powerful general, and the man behind the elevation to the purple of the present Emperor, Marcian.

It was with excitement mingled with trepidation that Julian presented himself at the commander's house in Antioch, the second city of the Eastern Empire. Antiochan born and bred (like his illustrious forebear Ammianus), Julian thought the city justly deserving of its titles 'Antioch the Beautiful' and 'the Jewel of the East'. Ushered by a *cursor* or messenger through the usual suite of halls to the building's colonnaded garden, he found himself in the presence of a soldier in plain undress uniform – undyed lined tunic with indigo roundels at shoulders and thighs, broad military belt, and round pillbox cap. Though the man bore no insignia of rank, something about his air of quiet authority told Julian he was in the presence of someone of consequence. Coming closer,

---

* The pact partitioned Armenia between Rome and Persia; Sapor (Shapur II) was a 'king of kings' of the Sassanid dynasty.

he recognized those delicate aquiline features in the dark-skinned face; they belonged to Aspar, great commander and hero of the Utus, under whom Julian had served in that selfsame battle.

'Welcome, young Julian,' said Aspar with a smile. 'I see you've recovered from that Hun arrow you stopped at the Utus. Nasty things, arrow wounds. Prone to infection unless they're treated straight away. Now, I expect you're wondering why you've been summoned from your unit at short notice. It concerns a spying mission in Armenia. I'm looking for someone young and fit, a good horseman with a proven military record. Oh, and preferably a bachelor. As a decorated tribune, *candidatus* of the top regiment of *scholae** in Constantinople, and an unmarried man to boot, I'd say you fitted those requirements pretty neatly.'

'I'm flattered, sir,' replied Julian, feeling his pulse quicken. 'But . . . surely there must be plenty of other officers as well as, or better qualified than, myself for whatever job you have in mind.'

'Don't sell yourself short, young man,' said Aspar briskly. 'I'm seldom wrong in my assessments. The qualities I've listed are not as common as you seem to think. At least not in the same person.'

'You said, sir, a bachelor would be preferred,' observed Julian, adding, with just a touch of asperity, 'I take it, then, the mission's dangerous.'

'There is some risk; I won't deny it,' said Aspar. 'But before you decide whether or not to accept the commission – and you have an entirely free choice in the matter – let me tell you what's involved.' Telling a slave to bring wine, he conducted Julian to a stone bench overlooking the valley of the Orontes, studded with vineyards and fruit trees, with the rugged spire of Mount Casius towering in the distance.

'What do you know about Armenia?' asked the general, pouring wine.

'Not a great deal sir,' confessed Julian. 'Isn't it a mountainous plateau between the Pontus Euxinus and the Mare Caspium, populated by tough individualists? I seem to remember it used to be an independent kingdom, until its partition into separate zones of influence between Rome and Persia, about sixty years ago.'

'A fair summary,' conceded Aspar, 'and correct as far as it goes.

---

* Imperial palace guards; see Notes p.437.

It's important also to bear in mind that the people have been Christian from at least the time of Constantine's conversion. The place has always been a cockpit between the great warring powers of East and West, even before the days of Darius and Alexander. Neutral zone or disputed territory? Take your pick. The present Great King of Persia, Yazdkart II, is, according to our contacts in the region, about to embark on an aggressive military venture. He apparently intends to invade eastern Armenia – the Persian zone – impose direct rule from Ctesiphon, and replace Christianity with Zoroastrianism, the official religion of Persia.'

'And the reason?'

'Oh, the usual thing – boosting his reputation by military conquest. Rome herself can give plenty of examples: Julius Caesar in Gaul, Claudius I in Britain, Trajan in Dacia, Septimius Severus in Caledonia; I could go on. If Yazdkart succeeds, that may well encourage him to try to extend his rule over West – Roman – Armenia. Which of course would constitute both a challenge and a military threat to the Eastern Empire. But he's made one big miscalculation which could prove to be his Achilles' heel.'

'And that is, sir?'

'Forcing the Armenians to accept the Zoroastrian religion. They're a proud, stubborn, independent lot, who'll resist tooth and nail any attempt to convert them from Christianity.'

'Especially if they get Roman help?' suggested Julian innocently. 'Unofficially, of course.'

'Quite,' confirmed Aspar with a smile. 'Unofficially. We mustn't be seen to be breaking the Treaty of Partition. Already, one Vardan Mamikanian is rallying the nobles in East Armenia to head a national resistance movement against the Great King. From our point of view, for Persia to get bogged down in a war of attrition, in difficult terrain, against a fanatical irregular army, would be highly desirable. Any ambitions Yazdkart may be harbouring to renew the age-old conflict between Rome and Persia, would then have to be shelved. Indefinitely. With Attila undecided as to which of the two Roman Empires to attack next, that can only be a good thing. There's just one problem.'

Julian looked dutifully expectant.

'The Tome of Leo.'

'The Tome of Leo?'

'It's all rather complicated,' said Aspar, refilling their goblets. 'I'll do my best to explain. Pope Leo in Rome has produced a treatise propounding the dual nature of Christ. Claiming, in fact, that He is both human and divine – a view the Western Empire apparently has no problem in accepting. Here in the East, it's quite a different matter. Most citizens believe, passionately, that Christ has only one, divine, nature, called monophysite.'

'Sir, I don't quite see—'

'Bear with me, young Julian,' interrupted Aspar with a smile. 'To prevent a damaging schism splitting religious opinion throughout the Roman world and further widening the growing rift between our two empires, plans are afoot to thrash out the merits of both points of view in a grand meeting of ecclesiastics, to be held most likely at Nicaea or Chalcedon. Probably the latter, as a mark of courtesy to Marcian, as it's just across the Bosporus from the capital. Its purpose will be to decide which is the correct position, monophysite or dual nature. The decision will have the force of dogma, to be accepted by Christians everywhere, on pain of excommunication. Unfortunately for the East – and in particular for the monophysite patriarch of Alexandria – the signs are that Leo's argument will prevail, as it has the support of our new Emperor. What on earth has all this to do with Armenia? you must be wondering. Well, the people are conservative, profoundly monophysite in their religious outlook. The chances of our forming a secret alliance with them might be put in jeopardy if the Eastern Empire were to abandon its present monophysite stance.' Aspar shrugged and spread his hands.

Julian stared at him in disbelief. 'It's absurd!' he exclaimed, stifling a disgraceful urge to laugh.

'Don't be heard saying that,' cautioned the general. 'Your family's pagan, isn't it?'

'Yes. We're among the few who still adhere to the old Gods. Naturally, we try not to draw attention to the fact.'

'Which means you can take an objective view,' murmured Aspar reflectively. 'As can I. Being an Arian, I'm able to view things from a perspective outwith the orthodox norm.' He shook his head. 'Things were so much less . . . extreme, even in Valentinian I's time. Whatever happened to good old Roman tolerance? But I digress. If a Romano-Armenian alliance is to be forged, it must happen *before* the conference takes place – for the reasons I've already stated. And that's where you come in.'

Which was why Julian was now waiting in this freezing gully a thousand miles from home. His mission: to make contact with Vardan Mamikanian, assure him of (clandestine) Roman support, discover all he could about supply routes, safe contacts, relative strengths and dispositions of Persian and Armenian forces, et cetera, then report back to Aspar as soon as possible. He had already arranged with a local headman, on the Persian side of the border, for a guide to take him to meet Mamikanian.

A shimmering greyness heralded dawn; then the jagged snow-clad crests of the surrounding peaks glowed pink. A rattle of loose stones sounded from below him in the gully; that would be the guide, Julian thought. A short time later, dimly visible in the growing light, a horseman appeared, a stocky, swarthy fellow with prominent features. 'You must be the Roman,' he grunted in passable Greek. 'I am to take you to Lord Vardan. Come.'

Unhobbling his mount, Julian followed the guide uphill on a stony path wide enough for only one horseman. They climbed steeply, through fields of primulas to the snowline, after which they had to dismount and lead their horses through drifts at times three or four feet deep. After several hours of exhausting struggle, they reached the summit plateau, where gravelly outcrops thrust here and there through the snow, stippled with bright dots of colour where tulips had taken root in crevices. All around them rolled a sea of snow-slashed mountains, with the twin peaks of Ararat pricking the far horizon. Descending slopes covered in tamarisk scrub and tulips, they reached the broad valley of the Araxes, with flocks of sheep and goats grazing on the short green sward. Turning east, they followed the Araxes downstream – easy riding after the mountain crossing.

At noon, they halted at a village, where they were given a meal by the headman in his house, an underground affair like all the dwellings in the place, roomy enough to house goats, sheep, cows, and poultry, as well as the humans. After dining well on lamb, veal, and barley bread, washed down with strong wine drunk through straws from a common bowl, they continued cautiously on their way, having been warned that Persian patrols had been sighted in the area. After some miles, they headed north up a stony side-valley leading towards Lake Sevan, a remote inland sea ringed about by inhospitable mountains among which, the guide told Julian, Vardan Mamikanian had his stronghold, which they could expect to reach in two days.

They had halted preparatory to making camp for the night, when the guide suddenly stiffened and pointed to the eastern wall of the valley, which glowed in the sun's last rays, in contrast to the shadowed western side. Julian looked; after a few seconds he saw, high up on the hillside, a tiny flash that came and went in a blink.

'Mica?' Julian suggested.

'Persians,' grunted the guide. 'Mount, Roman.'

Julian scrambled back into the saddle and spurred up the valley after the guide. Glancing back, he saw, moving down the hillside behind them, a cluster of dots from which issued winks and sparks of light. He looked over his shoulder from time to time, and was relieved to see that he and his companion were beginning to pull clear from their pursuers, who were encumbered with arms and armour. He had begun to relax when suddenly he heard a loud crack like a snapping branch, and his horse crashed to the ground,

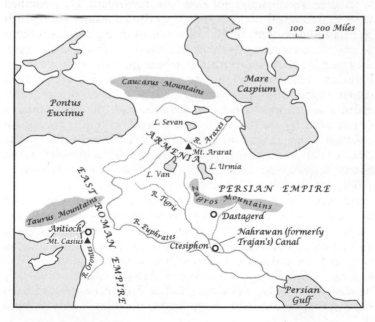

hurling him from the saddle. Winded and shaken, he got to his feet. He saw with horror his mount's dangling foreleg – clearly broken by catching between two of the boulders that littered the valley floor. The guide had pulled up and turned back, but Julian shouted to him to make good his escape. The guide bowed his head in acknowledgement of the inevitable, wheeled his horse and disappeared round a shoulder of hillside, leaving Julian alone, to face certain capture and interrogation.

In a reception hall in the palace of Dastagerd, the great fortified city and former capital of Persia, the Surena, the plenipotentiary of the Great King, waited for the day's first audience to begin. He was reading his favourite book, *The Book of the Laws of Countries*, a treatise written more than two centuries before by one Bardaisan, a Christian philosopher from the Roman client state of Osrhoene between the Euphrates and Mesopotamia. What a vision the man had, thought the Surena. It illumined, in a single brilliant image, the most important concept not only of Bardaisan's day but of the present too.

The vision, though grand, was so simple as to be blindingly obvious; yet it was strange how so few of the world's thinkers and leaders had ever realized or valued it. It was this: a narrow band of civilization encircling the world (or at least stretching as far as Ocean to the east and west) from Caledonia to Choson,* and comprising the empires of Rome and Persia, the Gupta Empire of northern India, the khanates of the steppes, and China. In central Asia the band, though perilously thin, remained vital and unbroken; witness the vibrant cities of the Silk Road such as Urumchi and Samarkand, and the mighty stone Buddhas of Bamian.** Within this ribbon had first appeared and then flourished all that was best in man's aspirations and achievements: agriculture and cities, writing – without which there could be no communication and storage of ideas – art and architecture, engineering, mathematics, music, astronomy, noble systems of philosophy and law, theories of democracy and natural justice, the great religions, et cetera, et cetera.

Yet, despite its supreme importance, the band was fragile, its

* Korea
** Alas, blown up by the reactionary Taliban government of Afghanistan, before its overthrow.

existence threatened by savage peoples to the north and south: the Germans in the swamps and forests of the west; nomadic hordes of Turcomens and Huns in the steppes; fierce Moors, Berbers, and Arabs in the southern deserts. Already, Bardaisan's golden chain was near to breaking in West Rome, where barbarians were threatening to destroy the very fabric of government and society. But instead of striving to understand, borrow from, and reinforce each other's cultures, so that civilization could be preserved and continue to develop, the great empires seemed determined to remain locked in senseless cycles of mutual destruction, or policies of barren isolation. Which was why the Surena remained resolutely opposed to anything which might threaten the precarious peace between East Rome and Persia – especially the mad Armenian adventure the king seemed determined to pursue.

All through the morning and well into the afternoon, the Surena interviewed a succession of informants bringing news from far-flung places: skippers who had voyaged to Taprobana and Paralia,* masters of caravans bringing silks from China or incense from Saba,** traders in ivory and gum from Axum and Nubia.† It was work he loved, and it helped him to spin a vast web of information of what was happening to the world outside Persia. Such knowledge was invaluable, providing him with the necessary insight to treat effectively with diplomats and envoys from other lands, and to proffer sound advice to the Great King regarding foreign relations. However, news was in short supply from one region, the Imperium Romanum. This was because the two empires of Rome together formed one vast single trading-area, with its own internal market and common currency, thus minimizing the need for external trade and contacts.

A servant had already lit the lamps in the audience chamber, and the Surena was preparing to leave, when a chamberlain appeared and, bowing low, said, 'Surena, a prisoner has just arrived under escort. Shall I have him brought to you?'

'No, no,' said the Surena testily. 'Tomorrow will be soon enough.'

---

* Ceylon/Sri Lanka and Malabar.
** the Yemen.
† Ethiopia and northern Sudan

'I venture to presume you may wish to see him now, Surena,' persisted the official. 'This one's a Roman.'

'Well, why didn't you say so? Of course I'll see him. Have him brought here immediately.'

Julian (who had divulged only his name and military rank) gasped as he was shown by the Surena into the palace's Great Hall. Roman trophies – arms and armour, more than three hundred standards and eagles – lined the walls in a glittering display.

'These we took from the battlefield of Carrhae, after the defeat of Crassus five hundred years ago,' said the Surena in excellent Greek, indicating the nearest array. 'And three hundred years later, these were from the army of Valerian when he surrendered to us at Edessa; and those we seized from your namesake's Julian's retreating legions a mere eighty-seven years ago, when some men still alive were in their infancy.' He paused, then asked, not unkindly, 'You wonder why I show you these things?'

Julian didn't think the reason was to humiliate him by reminding him of Rome's less than glorious record in her encounters with the Peacock Throne. His bonds had been removed and he had been treated with consideration by this courteous minister, clearly from the Persian caste of nobles whose code of courage, truth, and honour so resembled that of Rome – well, Rome of an earlier age, perhaps. 'Truly, sir, I cannot say,' he replied.

'It is intended as an object lesson in the futility of war between our two great nations,' went on the Surena. 'What have Rome and Persia, two civilized powers, to show for centuries of conflict? The deaths of untold thousands of their finest young men, the destruction of glorious cities, fertile provinces reduced to deserts, economies ruined by expensive wars – that is the true legacy. Neither side has profited one iota from the struggle, only suffered constant draining loss. Rome and Persia should be allies, not enemies; if that were to happen, each could enrich the other immeasurably.'

'I cannot disagree with anything you've said, sir,' said Julian carefully, impressed by the minister's obvious sincerity, but wondering when the hard questioning would begin. He did not have long to wait.

'Then what were you doing so far inside the borders of Persian Armenia?' demanded the Surena, in tones grown suddenly incisive.

Sensing that this man would see through any fabrication, Julian said nothing.

'Your silence speaks for itself,' said the other crisply. 'As I thought, you are a spy.' He shot Julian an appraising look. 'You will disclose to me all the deatails of your mission,' he went on in a quiet voice. 'Also everything you know about the state of Rome's two empires, the efficiency and readiness of her armies, her strengths and weaknesses, her leaders' ambitions and plans.'

'My knowledge of Rome's policies is extremely limited, and could be of little use to you,' said Julian dry-mouthed. 'Nevertheless, I would be betraying my trust if I were to divulge what little I know, or pass on any information regarding my presence in Armenia. For all I know, such information might be used against my country.'

'Noble words,' said the Surena, shaking his head. 'In the tradition of your Regulus, perhaps. But believe me, you will tell me; in the end you will tell me everything. Either voluntarily, or . . .' He paused, frowning. 'It would sadden me to have to hand over a brave young man like yourself to the torturers. They are very . . . efficient. The choice is yours. But to help you make up your mind, I think a second object lesson may be called for.'

Deep within the bowels of Dastagerd's grim state prison, a small procession – the Surena, Julian, three guards bearing torches, a gaoler, and, at the head, the castellan of the prison – clambered down dank staircases and tramped along corridors, eventually halting at the grille of one of the cells that lined the walls. The gaoler unlocked and opened the door, disclosing not the squalid hole Julian had expected but a fair-sized room illumined with oil lamps and furnished with rich rugs and couches, on one of which reclined a man clad in splendid if grimy silken robes. The prisoner stirred and sat up.

'He is a noble, so must be lodged according to his rank,' the Surena said. 'Even his fetters are of silver.'

'What was his crime?' asked Julian in astonishment.

'He converted from Zoroastrianism to Christianity – as have many Persians,' replied the minister. 'Regarding the lower castes of society – warriors, bureaucrats, the common people – the Great King is prepared to turn a blind eye should they become Christians. But for nobles and princes, who should set an example

315

to the rest of society, there can be no such latitude. To spurn the state religion, the Beh Den – the Good Faith – is for them a capital offence. So you see, in considering the Armenians worthy to embrace the faith of Zoroaster, the King is really paying them a compliment. This man's family, also Christian converts it has to be assumed, have fled into hiding. Naturally, as any man of honour in his position would, he has refused to tell us where.' The Surena's features creased momentarily in an expression of compassion. 'However, the Great King's wish is law and must be obeyed,' he said heavily, adding in an undertone, 'however distasteful those of us who have to implement its sentences may find it.'

The Surena held a brief conversation with the castellan, then turned again to Julian. 'It seems that after lengthy interrogation this prisoner remains obdurate. It is time, therefore, to try other methods.'

On a raised stone slab in the centre of the torture chamber, the naked body of the prisoner, face down and limbs extended, was held securely by straps around the wrists and ankles. Two menials in grubby loincloths hovered in the background. At a table was seated a scribe, ready to record any utterances by the victim. The Surena approached the prisoner and addressed him. The man remaining silent, the Surena nodded to the torturers to begin their work.

With a knife, one of the pair made a long incision in the back of the prisoner, who jerked against his bonds but made no sound. The bleeding wound was then forced apart and kept open by means of clamps. Removing a glowing crucible with tongs from a furnace in the corner, the second torturer poured a stream of white-hot metal into the wound. Agonized screams cut though the loud hissing of molten metal coming into contact with raw flesh; the prisoner convulsed on the slab, then fainted.

'They use copper which, having a higher melting-point than lead, inflicts a keener agony,' the Surena remarked to Julian, who was watching in horror. 'They will repeat the process, gradually extending it to more sensitive parts. Eventually the man will break – they always do. As will you,' he added grimly, 'if you choose to remain silent. Come, we have seen enough.'

They retraced their steps, Julian flanked by guards, to the prison's outer walls. 'Save yourself young man,' the Surena told Julian. 'You have witnessed what will happen if you refuse to talk. There can be no dishonour in co-operation. Afterwards, you will stay with me at my estate in the Karun valley, not as a prisoner but as an honoured guest, while this Armenian affair runs its course. We will hunt and hawk, and in the cool of evening listen to the music of the lyre and flute, and drink wine chilled by snow from the Sanganaki Mountains.' He stared intently into Julian's eyes. 'Say you agree.'

Mingled with terror, Julian felt an overwhelming urge to accept the Surena's offer. He opened his mouth intending to comply, but heard himself whisper, 'I cannot.'

The Surena raised his arms in a gesture of frustrated resignation. He nodded to the guards, who seized Julian by the arms. 'Then I can do nothing for you,' he said. 'You are a fool, Roman, but a brave one.' Turning on his heel, he walked swiftly towards the prison gates.

In the great menagerie of Beklal, near Ctesiphon, his capital city, Yazdkart II walked his horse, surrounded by vast herds of deer, zebra, and ostriches. Persia would be great once more, he mused as he rode among the grazing game. He, the Great King, would bring back the glorious days of Darius and Cyrus, Cambyses and the two Shapurs. Armenia would serve as a useful testing-ground. His forces would overrun the Persian protectorate and, should that renegade Vardan resist, he would be ruthlessly crushed. Christianity would be stamped out, and the people made to accept the one true faith. His victorious army would then press on into Western Armenia. Rome (East Rome, that is) would of course object. Well, let it. Yazdkart would welcome a challenge by the Romans. Perhaps the time had come for a final trial of strength between the two great rivals. His chief minister's report on how things stood in Rome's two empires, which was due for his attention this very day, should prove invaluable in helping him to shape his policy. It was in a sanguine and confident frame of mind that he cantered back to Ctesiphon.

Entering the Iwan-i Kisra, the royal palace in Ctesiphon, through the great central arch in the façade,* the Surena made his way to

---

* Still today the largest arch in any façade in the world. Prior to the invasion of Iraq in 2003, the ruinous façade was being reconstructed by the Iraqi Department of Antiquities.

the audience chamber, whither he had been summoned by the Great King.

He found Yazdkart enthroned, arrayed in the full panoply of a warrior-aristocrat, a drawn sword held upright between his knees. Before the royal throne and at a lower level stood three empty seats: for the Emperor of China, for the great Khaghan, the ruler of the nomads of central Asia, and for the Roman Emperor, against the time when these rulers came as vassals to the court of the King of Kings. In the face of this aggressive posturing, the Surena reluctantly decided that now was not perhaps the moment to press the King (as he had intended) to abandon his plans to invade Armenia. Bowing low before him, he said, 'Great King, as you requested, I have ready my report on Rome.'

Yazdkart frowned. 'We see no papers. Where are your notes, your memoranda?'

'Here, Sire,' replied the Surena, tapping his forehead. 'I need no parchment or papyrus. From earliest youth I have trained myself to dispense with such aids, by memorizing what I need to know from written or oral sources.'

'We are impressed; you may proceed.'

'Of the two Christian empires of the Romans,' the Surena began, 'the West need not detain us. It is weak, its coffers empty, half its territory ceded to fair-haired barbarians from beyond the Rhenus and Danubius. Only the genius of its great general, Aetius, has thus far safeguarded it from dissolution. Our only concern is with our neighbour, the Eastern Empire.'

'Whom we have cause to fear?' Yazdkart suggested hopefully.

'I think not, Sire. True, their new Emperor, Marcian, is taking a more resolute stance against Attila than his feeble predecessor, which may cause the Scourge of God, as the Romans call him, to switch his attentions to the West. Thus leaving the East free, in theory, to resume hostilities against us after a nine-year lapse.' The Surena paused, then added delicately, 'Hostilities which *we* began, Great King.'

'But they are strong enough to pose a threat?' persisted Yazdkart.

'Again, in theory, yes. East Rome is wealthy, densely populated, run well by gifted men, its armies being nurtured back to strength after their several maulings by Attila. But I believe its energies will now be directed solely to rebuilding their ravaged land; as ever, its priorities are economic not military. Armenia alone constitutes a potential flashpoint for war. But only if we demonstrate we have designs upon the Roman part of the protectorate. This, besides much else, I learnt from the confessions of a Roman spy who fell into our hands.'

'. . . the East, then, pacific yet strong,' mused the King, when the Surena had finished his report. As though tiring of the role of warrior-king, he sheathed his sword and propped it against the arm of his throne. 'Perhaps too strong for us to risk picking a quarrel with at this juncture?' His tone, though one of disappointment, held a tinge of relief.

'Exactly, Sire,' declared the Surena with feeling, the alarming spectre of a full-scale war beginning to recede. 'That, if I may say, Great King, is a commendably wise conclusion.'

In his office in the barracks of the palace guard at Constantinople, Aspar crossed Julian's name off his list of agents. Two months had passed since the tribune had left for Armenia, so it must be assumed that he was either a prisoner of the Persians, or else dead – most likely the latter.

Another fine young man sacrificed – for what? the general reflected with a heavy heart. Even if successful, Julian's mission would have been unlikely to affect the great scheme of things involving Rome and Persia to any significant extent. Whatever happened, the Great King was probably going to invade eastern Armenia; Roman aid to Vardan's freedom fighters would now probably not materialize; in any event, resistance would be crushed by the Persians and eastern Armenia become another satrapy. However, Yazdkart, who at bottom was a parchment tiger, would probably hold back from attacking Roman Armenia. So in the end little would change, and relations between Persia and Rome continue much as before. Meanwhile, there was the sad duty of a letter to Julian's parents to attend to. Having called for his secretary, Aspar began to dictate.

FORTY-THREE

Have I not given birth to God?
Protest of the Augusta Pulcheria to the Patriarch Nestorius,
against her exclusion from the Sanctuary of Hagia Sophia, *c.* 430

Returning Priscilla's wink from across the chapel floor, Honoria, exiled sister of Valentinian, the Western Emperor, felt the familiar excitement stir within her. The thought of their coming tryst helped to make endurable the tedium of the prayer session, led by Sister Annunciata, a Syrian ascetic to whom fasting, prayer, and mortification of the flesh were disciplines to be embraced eagerly, and whenever possible enforced on others. At last the interminable litany of invocations and responses came to an end, and the troop of chosen maidens, eyes modestly downcast, filed out of the building, which was richly decorated with mosaics, and tapestries they themselves had embroidered. They were preceded by Pulcheria, sister of the recently dead Theodosius and now consort of the new Emperor, Marcian, accompanied by her sisters Arcadia and Marina. The chapel formed part of the monastery into which Pulcheria had converted the Hebdomon, the second of Constantinople's three imperial palaces. It was located near the Golden Gate, and from it all males, barring eunuchs, were rigorously excluded. The eunuchs were all imported, mainly from Persia, castration being illegal within the Roman Empire.

Devout and iron-willed, Pulcheria commanded awe and admiration as 'the Orthodox One' among the populace. The semi-mystical veneration in which she was held owed much to her deliberate promotion of the cult of the Mother of God, *Theotokos* which, by analogy, transferred to the Augusta the virgin dignity of the unblemished Mary. Once, a bishop of Constantinople, Nestorius, had had the temerity to challenge her assumption of this role; he was silenced by an angry mob, then deposed.

Officially, the inmates of Pulcheria's convent had all been selected for their devoutness. Most were young women from good families, who had displayed a religious vocation. With some, this had proved to be a passing youthful enthusiasm; once accepted into the community, however, it was far from easy to be granted a discharge. A few had been taken in at the request of parents who found the upbringing of a difficult daughter beyond them, and who hoped that immersion in a strict devotional way of life would succeed, where they had failed. In these cases, a generous financial 'dowry' was an invariable condition of acceptance. The community therefore contained a small minority of desperate or rebellious members. It was to this category that Honoria, during her fourteen years' confinement in the palace, had always belonged.

The women entered a large colonnaded courtyard opening off the chapel. Here, for the next two hours, before partaking of a meagre midday *prandium* in common, they were free to meditate, peruse devotional texts, pray, or embroider hangings and altar-cloths. Conversation was frowned on, as constituting a frivolous distraction from more serious – that is, holy – matters.

'The eighth hour,' whispered Honoria, briefly brushing against Priscilla as they emerged into the courtyard. Neither woman witnessed the look of jealous hate on the face of Ariadne, Honoria's prior but now discarded lover, who, walking just behind them, had overheard the remark.

Pacing up and down as though deep in religious contemplation, Honoria reviewed her present circumstances with fury and frustration. Brought up in the Western capital, Ravenna, while still a child she had been raised by her mother Placidia to the title of Augusta, an appellation normally reserved for the consort of the Emperor. This conferred a status somewhere between high priestess and national figurehead, effectively debarring the holder from marriage. This had put Honoria beyond the reach of ambitious schemers, marriage to whom, it was felt, might form a danger to the state. Absolutely no thought had been given to her feelings, she fumed inwardly. Her mother and the government, for reasons of political convenience, had made her into a non-person. Honoria felt the injustice especially keenly as, with the onset of puberty, she began to develop strong sexual appetites – now denied any legitimate gratification.

Partly to spite her mother and the bloodless men of the Consistory who had condemned her to the life of a latter-day Vestal Virgin, partly to gratify her raging desires, at the age of sixteen Honoria began an affair with her chamberlain, Eugenius. The resulting pregnancy could have been hushed up and the world none the wiser; instead an outraged Placidia publicized the royal family's disgrace by exiling her daughter to Constantinople, after a period of severe confinement. Subjection to a life of strict religious observance would, it was believed, constitute both a salutary punishment and a corrective discipline. Chafing against the restrictions imposed by Pulcheria's monastic community (whose aspirations she totally rejected), and barred from finding an outlet for her passions through marriage, Honoria embarked on a series of clandestine Sapphic liaisons with some of the community's freer spirits. The latest was with Priscilla, who had recently displaced Ariadne in Honoria's affections. Ariadne, however, had not accepted her dismissal meekly, confronting Honoria in tearful rages in which she declared her undying love for the one-time Augusta, whom she accused of betrayal. To all of which, Honoria, infatuated with the comely Priscilla, responded with indifference, and in the end exasperated impatience.

At the eighth hour, a time assigned for private prayer, Priscilla slipped into Honoria's cell. 'It's all right – no one saw me,' she giggled shakily, her voice husky with excitement, and started tearing off her habit, an ankle-length tunic of coarse undyed linen. Within seconds the two women stood naked before each other, their eyes mirroring their mutual desire. Embracing, they locked mouths hungrily, then began to fondle each other's breasts with eager fingers, the nipples swelling erect and darkening. Leaning backwards on the bed, Honoria opened her thighs, gasped in ecstasy as Priscilla's lips found those other lips, and her flickering tongue caressed the swelling bud—

The door crashed open, revealing the skinny form of Sister Annunciata, flanked by two burly eunuchs. 'Caught – *in flagrante delicto!*' the nun shrieked in triumphant glee. Eyes glittering fanatically, she pointed at the cowering Priscilla, then turned to the eunuchs. 'Seize her!' she commanded.

Along with the other inmates assembled in the courtyard, Honoria was forced to watch while her lover, restrained by two eunuchs, was whipped by an enthusiastic Sister Annunciata till her back was bloody. To Ariadne, who had reported the assignation, the victim's screams were as music. Priscilla would be packed off in disgrace, back to her family. For Honoria, there was to be no such release.

Summoned before Pulcheria, she was told in icy tones that henceforth, following a spell of solitary confinement, she would be under constant surveillance, to prevent any recurrence of the disgraceful scene just witnessed.

'You should have shared Priscilla's punishment,' Pulcheria continued, 'but unfortunately, as the daughter of an Emperor, you cannot be chastised. Sexual congress with one's own gender is expressly forbidden in Scripture.' Her expression softened, and a note of concern entered her voice. 'Have you no thought for your own immortal soul, or for those of the women you have corrupted? The fires of Hell burn even more fiercely than the fires of lust.'

'I will pray for God's forgiveness, Your Serenity,' murmured Honoria in simulated contrition. She had long ago learnt the futility of fighting her rulers. As for punishment in the hereafter, she was troubled not one whit. She had been brought up in the Latin West, where the influence of paganism lingered more strongly than in the East, encouraging a more liberal and sceptical outlook. Here, religious fervour and obsession with the afterlife often dominated people's thoughts and behaviour.

'Within these walls, I am not "Your Serenity" but simply "Mother"' corrected the older woman mildly; since becoming Empress, she found that many in her little community were confused as to how to address her. 'Let us hope that God will hear you. Meanwhile, I shall confer with the holy Daniel* as to what penances are appropriate for you to undergo. His pillar is not yet so high that he cannot give advice to those who ask it. Now, let us pray to Christ together, that His light may show His erring child the way to true repentance and a purer life.'

Chafing against the restrictions – now even more severe – of a life she despised, tormented by desires she could no longer gratify,

---

* One of the astonishing 'pillar saints' who lived on top of columns, whose height tended to increase to avoid pestering by the pilgrims who flocked to such sites. The most famous was Symeon Stylites, who occupied the summit of a column near Antioch from 420 to 459.

Honoria grew more and more angry and desperate. Then, one day, a wild idea came to her, one which offered a chance of escape from her intolerable confinement, and a means of revenge on those who had imprisoned her. Before her resolution could waver, or common sense persuade her to desist, she penned a letter, little reckoning on the appalling consequences that would flow from its dispatch. The task completed, she gave it, together with a ring, to a faithful eunuch, charging him upon his life to deliver it in person, and to make sure that it was seen by no other eyes than those it was intended for.

PART III

THE CATALAUNIAN PLAINS
AD 451

FORTY-FOUR

*Honoria, the sister of Emperor Valentinian III, invited
Attila into the empire*

Anonymous, *Gallic Chronicle*, 452

Never had Attila felt so torn. The Council, convoked to decide
what should be done in this crisis, had assembled in an atmos-
phere of restless anger and uncertainty. Ever since the news that
the East was discontinuing tribute had landed among the Huns
like a fireball hurled from a catapult, hotheads had been clamouring for action. To be met with determined resistance was a
new, and disconcerting, experience for the Huns. From the time
they had burst upon the European scene seventy years previously,
no one had stood effectively against them. Until the Utus. Times
had changed in other ways, Attila thought as he looked round
the packed Council chamber. In his father's day, the Council,
which was open (in theory at any rate) to all adult males, had met
in the open and on horseback. Now it assembled in private, and
its membership was limited to senior members of prominent families, these having founded aristocratic dynasties, somewhat on the
Roman model.

The initial hubbub took rather longer to subside than usual,
Attila noted as he seated himself in the middle of the circular
chamber. Could it be that some of them, like pack animals challenging a leader grown old, felt that his powers were beginning
to wane? Best then, right at the start, to steer the meeting in the
direction he wanted it to go. He nodded towards Onegesius, he
of Roman bath-house fame, a man of moderate views and accom-
modating personality, as well as a personal friend. 'Speak, Ungas,'
he invited, using the Hun form of the name which the other, an
admirer of things Roman, had Latinized.

'Sire, as Marcian is refusing us tribute,' replied Onegesius in
reasonable tones, 'perhaps the time has come for the Huns to
change their ways. To rely on plunder as a way of life is surely

not a policy that can be sustained indefinitely. We were foolish not to realize that, sooner or later, the Romans would find the courage and the will to resist us. The Utus should have taught us that.'

An angry outburst, in which shouts of 'Coward!' and 'Traitor!' could be distinguished, followed his speech.

'Silence,' rumbled Attila. His basilisk gaze, moving round the chamber, instantly quelled the tumult. 'In Council any man may speak his mind freely, without fear. It should not be for Attila to remind you of this. Eudoxius, I heard your voice above the others. What is your complaint?'

The fugitive leader of the Bagaudae, a thin, intense man with burning eyes, declared, 'Since it is permissible to speak with frankness, Your Majesty, I shall not blunt my words. The shameful advice of Onegesius is not even to be thought of. You have a simple choice. Resume the campaign against the East, or – if the King of the Huns has no stomach for that course – attack the West. It has never been more vulnerable. Half the Frankish nation supports the claim of Merovech's brother, and would join you. The Huns have but to cross the Rhenus and Aremorica would rise. Gaiseric urges you to sound the war-horns, and would back you to the hilt. Unpaid, half-starved, the Roman army in Gaul grows weaker by the day. But if Attila prefers to stay at home and count his flocks . . .' Leaving the sentence hanging in the air, Eudoxius shrugged, and smiled offensively.

'Guard your tongue, Roman dog,' growled Attila. 'You are fortunate indeed to be a guest of the Huns and not the Vandals, or it would not long remain tenant of your mouth. Do not presume too far upon the laws of hospitality. There is another side to what you say. Half the Franks may support Merovech's brother, but the other half would certainly stay loyal to their King, who, by all accounts, rules his people justly and well. Gaiseric wants us to invade the West because he fears the Visigoths will join with the Romans to drive him from Africa. As for the Roman army in Gaul, I grant its circumstances may be straitened, but it can still win battles. Or have you forgotten Narbo and Vicus Helena?'

'Forgive me, Your Majesty,' retorted Eudoxius with false humility. 'You are right to remind me of those victories. One was achieved only with Hun help, the other was a glorious triumph against unarmed civilians. But no matter; the Romans indeed are doughty fighters. Attila shows wisdom in advising caution before engaging them.' Again the provocative smile.

'I will not stoop to answer that,' responded Attila with weary contempt, rueing the day he ever gave refuge to this agitator. 'You say we have but two alternatives. There is in fact a third choice.' And he went on to expound Aetius' offer made through his emissary Titus Valerius Rufinus: military service to keep the German federates in check; a share of the West's revenues; the possibility of future union with the West.

The response was not encouraging. Onegesius, with a few of the older and more experienced nobles, nodded and murmured in agreement. The remainder kept silent, apart from Eudoxius and a group of younger Huns clustered round him. They seemed to have formed a distinct faction, with the one-time doctor at their head. They shook their heads vigorously and muttered noisily in protest. Attila had an unfamiliar and disturbing feeling – that events, which he could no longer fully control, were moving ahead of him. He seemed to be witnessing the scene from the viewpoint of a detached observer. It was the first time since his clash with Bleda, before the Treaty of Margus, that his authority had been challenged. There was only one way to deal with the potential crisis: attack the ringleader and defeat him.

'Speak up, Eudoxius,' he challenged. 'We cannot hear you if you mumble like a toothless graybeard.' To his relief, a ripple of chuckles greeted this sally.

But Eudoxius could sting in return. 'Very well, Your Majesty,' he snapped, his face flushing with anger. 'Your fine suggestion amounts to this: the Huns to become the paid lackeys of a Roman general, one who by his folly cost the lives of sixty thousand Huns. We all know he was long your friend. It seems you place a higher value upon propping up that broken reed than on the welfare of your people. Otherwise, why has Attila withheld the contents of a certain letter from the Council?'

It was a shrewd and telling blow, Attila conceded silently, one he had not foreseen. He had assumed that only he was privy to Honoria's missive. How had Eudoxius found out about it, and how much did he know? The bearer, a Persian eunuch, had seemed trustworthy enough. Presumably, Eudoxius had noticed the man's arrival and had waylaid him on his departure. This was a supremely dangerous moment; unlike a Roman Emperor, a barbarian leader ruled ultimately by consent. Once perceived to be weak or unsuccessful, he was finished. Attila dared not call Eudoxius' bluff. Though it was unlikely that Honoria had confided in the bearer, Eudoxius might have forced him to reveal that the letter was from the disgraced sister of the Western Emperor, and that it came with a ring enclosed – a symbol which could have but one meaning. If Eudoxius' suggestion that important information was being kept from the Council, Attila's position would be severely compromised. There was only one way to draw the serpent's fangs before they could inflict a deadly bite: by forestalling him. But that would force Attila to follow the course he was least willing to adopt. However, there was now no help for it. The wily renegade had won.

'Ungrateful wretch, is this how you repay our hospitality?' he said icily, his words all the more menacing for being uttered softly. 'Suborning a king's messenger: in a Hun that would be treason. In a guest it is an inexcusable breach of trust which places you beyond the protection of immunity. Have you forgotten what happened to Constantius? Perhaps I should ask the Council to pronounce a fitting sentence.'

Eudoxius, realizing he had over-reached himself, and in so doing both forfeited his influence with the assembly and put his life in danger, turned ashen-faced. 'I . . . I beg your forgiveness, Sire,' he croaked, all his truculence deserting him. 'I but saw the messenger arrive. I know nothing of what it is he brought.'

'As well for you,' responded Attila sternly. 'On this occasion I will spare your worthless life. From now, keep silence. Break it, and I may not be merciful a second time.' Turning from the trembling Roman, he addressed the assembly, now become quiet and receptive. 'This poor apology for a man' – he nodded at Eudoxius – 'has presumed to anticipate the purpose of this meeting. Which was to inform you of the contents of the letter he dared to speak of. But before I told you of it, you first had to know all other options, that together we may choose the best path for our nation to follow. The letter is from the Augusta Honoria, wrongfully imprisoned these fourteen years in Constantinople by her jealous brother Valentinian, the puppet who disgraces the throne of Ravenna. In it, she entreats me to release her from a cruel bondage, offering in return her hand in marriage. And as a pledge of her affection and good faith, she included with her letter a ring.' Attila looked round the faces of his audience, now hanging on his every word. 'Should we decide to follow up the lady's offer,' he said with a judicious smile, 'I think we could reasonably insist on a substantial dowry – say, half the Western Empire. Shall we accept?'

The roar of acclamation that followed answered the King's question. He had survived, his leadership unscathed – indeed, strengthened. But at a bitter personal price.

That evening, sitting his horse by the banks of the Tisa, Attila withdrew from a bag suspended from his saddle-bow the silver dish that was the gift of Aetius. He retraced in his mind the scenes depicted on it, each representing a stage in a long and eventful friendship. Now circumstances had decreed that it was impossible for him to keep it. Instead, it would become a worthy votive offering to Murduk, the great God of War. 'Goodbye, Aetius, old friend,' he murmured in sorrow. 'This is the hardest day of Attila's life, for from this moment we two are enemies.' He flung the dish high in the air above the water. It spun in a glittering arc, then plunged with a splash into the river. For a moment, he glimpsed its fading sheen beneath the surface, then it vanished from his sight.

Riding homewards, Attila said a final farewell also to his dream of building a Greater Scythia. Nothing now remained for him except to lead his people in a bleak and bloody cycle of warfare, plunder, and destruction. He who rides a tiger . . . Of a sudden, the third part of Wu Tze's prophecy echoed in his brain: 'The wounded eagle turns on the ass, which leaves it to attack the first eagle.' The wounded eagle: the eagle of East Rome, whose empire he had ravaged. The ass: the wild ass of the plains – in other words, the Huns. The first eagle: the symbol of imperial Rome, the Empire of the West. It all fitted together. The East had mauled the Huns at the Utus, and were now refusing tribute; the Huns had then decided to switch their attack to the Western Empire. What was the last part of the seer's prophecy? Resolutely, Attila closed his mind against recall. Perhaps his actions were indeed already written in the scroll of Fate. But he would continue to act as though he alone controlled his destiny.

When Attila's intentions (and consequently the tenor of Honoria's fatal letter) became public knowledge, the guilty princess was sent away, an object of horror, from Constantinople to Italia. Her life was spared, but she was married off in indecent haste to an obscure nobody, who was happy to receive a generous fee in return for going through the forms of marriage as her nominal husband. Then, safely insured against the marriage claims of her would-be deliverer, Honoria was consigned to perpetual imprisonment.

FORTY-FIVE

Attila's terrible horde: warlike Rugians, savage Gepids, Scyri, Huns,
Thuringians . . . poured across your plains, O Belgica
Sidonius Apollinaris, *The Panegyric of Avitus*, 458

Gripping the shaft of his late father's *angon*, a wickedly barbed
javelin with a long iron head, Cleph crouched behind an oak on
the edge of the clearing, which was bisected by the path along
which Gisulf should soon come riding. The silence of the great
Thuringian Forest, which covered much of his tribe's, the
Thuringi's territory, was broken only by the patter of raindrops
on the ground, still carpeted in early spring from the autumn's
fall of leaves.

With a cold, controlled fury, Cleph thought of his father's
death last summer at the hands of Gisulf, an arrogant young lout
of the local chieftain's *comitatus*. Cleph's father, a *kerl* or peasant
farmer, had remonstrated with Gisulf when the latter had carelessly ridden through his field of standing wheat. Gisulf's response
was to club the older man aside with his spear-butt. The heavy
iron cap-spike had connected with his temple, delivering an un-
intentionally fatal blow. Later, confronting Cleph, Gisulf had
tossed a Roman *solidus* at the lad's feet.

'*Wergeld*, in payment for your father's life,' the warrior had
declared loftily. 'A lot more than his man-worth, considering he
was only a *kerl*.'

'I refuse it,' replied Cleph, spitting on the gold coin, 'as is my
right.'

Clearly dismissing as an empty threat the implied claim to
exact blood-vengeance, Gisulf shrugged and rode on laughing,
leaving the *solidus* glinting in the mud.

But Cleph had been content to bide his time. Over many
weeks he had noted Gisulf's habitual movements, while at the
same time allowing the warrior to become lulled into a false
sense of security. Of late, Gisulf had taken to keeping a tryst on

each Wotan's-day with a wealthy widow in a nearby hamlet. Cleph knew the route his enemy would take, having trailed him on several occasions, and now from his hiding-place listened for the sound of Gisulf's approach.

At last it came, muffled by the damp earth of the track: the thud of hooves. Then into the clearing cantered Gisulf, a heavy-set young man mounted on a rawboned destrier. Hefting the *angon*, Cleph drew back his throwing-arm, waiting for the moment when the other would have just passed level, exposing his broad back as a perfect target.

Suddenly Cleph heard a faint, muffled booming – the moot-horn! This was the prearranged call to arms for all owing allegiance to Etzel,* whether Huns or subject Germans, a summons which, issuing from the dread King of the Huns, would brook not the slightest of delays. Instantly lowering the *angon*, Cleph turned and made off through the trees at his best pace, in the direction of the horn-blast. His vengeance would keep, he told himself. Gisulf was living on borrowed time, which would elapse as soon as campaigning with Etzel should be over.

From the Mare Suevicum to the Danubius, from the Rhenish lands to the Imaus Mons,** wherever the war-horns sounded, men ceased whatever task they were engaged in, and hastened to their local muster. A fisherman casting his nets off the mouth of the Viadua river† abandoned them and rowed for shore; a shepherd in the Carpates foot-hills left his flocks; a farmer ploughing in a forest clearing in Boiaria‡ unyoked his oxen and hurried from his field; a fowler in the marshes of the River Vistula laid down his snares unset; a hunter in the Caucasus, about to loose an arrow at an ibex, let down his draw . . . Such was the effect of Attila's huge authority. Obedience, instant, total, was the one inalienable condition he demanded from his subjects, the least infraction of which was punishable by crucifixion or impalement. But his rule could be generous as well as stern: devoted or courageous service often rewarded with a costly gift such as a mail shirt, a jewelled cup, a golden dish.

* The Germans' name for Attila.
** The Urals.
† The Oder.
‡ The Carpathians; Bavaria.

From every quarter of Attila's vast realm, rivers of armed men began flowing towards the upper Danubius: Gepid horsemen from the Carpathus foothills, dark-skinned Alans, blue-eyed Sciri and Thuringians, mounted Ostrogoths, above all countless Huns from the limitless steppelands above the Mare Caspium, the Pontus Euxinus, and the lower Danubius. All these, and many other, lesser tribes, who acknowledged Attila as overlord, merged at last into one enormous horde as they converged on the assembly place, the northern shore of Pannonia's Lake Neusiedler.

When the last contingents had arrived, the great host, headed by Attila himself, clad in a simple coat of skins and carrying no weapon, began to move north-west towards the Belgic provinces of Gaul.

FORTY-SIX

Very many cities have been destroyed: Aluatica, Metis . . .[*]
Hydatius, *Chronicles*, sixth century

Even in March of that fateful year, the consulships of Marcian Augustus and Adelphius, and the one thousand, two hundred and fifth from the founding of Rome,[**] ice-floes still dotted the Rhenus at its junction with the Nicer.[†] On a hill-top overlooking the confluence, Bauto, an Alamann shepherd, drew his cloak more closely around him and scanned his flock with anxious eyes. After such a bitter winter, he would have to be especially vigilant with newborn lambs these next few weeks: the foxes' hunger would make them bold. Just then his keen eyes picked up something strange, what appeared to be a bank of mist obscuring the foothills of the Wotanwald, whose peaks defined the eastern horizon. Odd, he thought. The day was cold and cloudless; even distant objects stood out sharply. Not a day for mist, that was sure. What was that sound, like a far-off murmuring? Must be the wind. But the murmur grew in volume to a steady reverberation like a roll of drums or rumble of thunder. It seemed to be coming from the mist, which was rapidly getting nearer. In fact it was not mist at all, he realized, but a line of billowing dust-clouds among which sparked and glinted a myriad points of light. It was an army. But an army such as no man had seen before, for surely it could not be numbered in mere thousands, but only in scores, perhaps hundreds of thousands. Bauto watched in awed fascination as the vast host poured through the mountain-passes and rolled in a spreading tide towards the Rhenus. Forgetting his sheep, he turned and began to run downhill with loping strides, to warn the villagers of Mannheim.

[*] Tongres, Metz.
[**] 451.
[†] The Neckar.

'Attila has no quarrel with the Romans, only with the Visigoths,' declared Valentinian to Aetius. They were in the reception chamber of the palace of Ravenna's imperial apartments. The Emperor waved a roll of parchment. 'He guarantees it in this letter, which expressly states that he wishes to be my friend. *My* friend,' he went on in spiteful triumph. 'He makes no mention of you, Patrician.'

'This is folly, sir,' rejoined Aetius wearily; he was unable to bring himself to address Valentinian, whom he despised, as 'Your Serenity'. 'Are you so blind that you can't see what his game is? Divide and rule, or in his case conquer. He's trying to set the Visigoths against the Romans and vice versa, also you against myself. In your case, he's obviously succeeding. I imagine Theoderic in Tolosa has also received a letter such as you have there, assuring him that Attila's only quarrel is with the Romans.' He pressed on bluntly, 'I notice you've omitted what the letter goes on to say: that Attila insists on his marriage to Honoria taking place, together with a dowry of half the Western Empire – terms which the government has naturally refused. Also that he replace myself as Master of Soldiers in Gaul.'

Valentinian stared at Aetius in astonished fury. 'How do you know this?' he shouted. 'The letter is privy to myself.'

'I have my sources; the Consistory does not consist entirely of servile fools,' retorted Aetius. 'There are some whose priority is to serve Rome, rather than seek advancement by flattering yourself.'

'Who are these traitors?' shrieked the Emperor, trembling with rage. 'I demand their names. I will have them banished – no, executed.'

'You don't really expect me to tell you?' responded Aetius with amused contempt. 'Some of us have principles, even if you do not.' Since Placidia's death less than four months previously, Valentinian's obsessive fears had increased alarmingly. Whatever her faults and limitations – and they were many – the Empress Mother had been a restraining influence on her son's worst tendencies. With Placidia gone, the character of the young Emperor had degenerated markedly. Free to indulge his baser urges, he had begun to resemble, in his acts of wanton cruelty and unhealthy obsession with sorcery, two of his most infamous predecessors, Caligula and Heliogabalus. More serious, in Aetius' view, was the

rise of a pro-Valentinian faction among the courtiers and councillors of Ravenna. With the Western Empire facing its greatest
ever crisis, the need for the Roman government to show a united
front against Attila could hardly have been greater.

'But all this is wasting time, sir,' went on the general impa-
tiently. 'Even as we speak, the Belgic provinces are being
overrun. Aluatica and Metis have fallen and their populations
have been massacred. Attila, with a vast horde of Huns reinforced by subject Germans – Rugians, Heruls, Thuringians,
and especially the Ostrogoths and Gepids – the whole host estimated to number anything up to half a million, has crossed the
Sequana and laid siege to Aureliani.* He has had to delay his
advance by waiting until spring, for grass to provide fodder for
his horses, granting us a vital respite. But we cannot afford to
wait any longer. Unless we intercept him now, Attila will take
the whole of Gaul.'

'You have a plan, I suppose,' sneered Valentinian.

'On its own, the Roman army in Gaul is simply not strong
enough to stop Attila,' pointed out the general. 'I have to persuade
Theoderic to join us with his Visigoths. Together, we would have
a chance.'

'I told you, Attila's intention is to destroy the Visigoths,'
snapped the Emperor, 'the tribe that represents the biggest threat
to Rome. To seek to prevent him from achieving that is sheer
perversity.'

'You haven't taken in a thing I've said,' said Aetius in frustration. 'Well, with or without your co-operation, I intend to march
for Gaul. I'll take what forces are readily available. That includes
your palatine troops, sir.'

'Permission refused, General,' said the Emperor, smiling
maliciously. 'Try to insist, and I will personally order them to
disobey you.'

Aetius decided to let it go. It would be unfair to the *scholae*, the
Emperor's personal bodyguard, to subject them to a test of loyalty.
He would make do with whatever units of the Army of Italy, which
consisted almost entirely of auxiliary regiments, he could get
together at short notice. Bowing ironically in farewell, he
murmured, '*Mit der Dummheit, kämpfen die Götter selbst vergeblich.*'

* Orléans.

'I heard that,' said Valentinian sharply. 'You will tell me what it means.'

Aetius shrugged. 'If you insist, sir,' he replied, his expression blandly innocent. 'It's a saying attributed to Alaric, the illustrious father of our mutual friend Theoderic, when the Roman Senate foolishly rejected his generous peace terms after he'd invested Rome. That refusal resulted in Alaric losing patience, and his Goths taking and sacking the City. Its meaning is: "Against stupidity, even the Gods struggle in vain."' And, instead of backing out of the royal presence as protocol demanded, Aetius turned on his heel and strode from the chamber, his mood marginally improved.

'Well, that's that,' said Aetius in calm resignation, as the door closed behind Theoderic's ambassador. He and Titus were once more the sole occupants of the general's office in his headquarters in the archbishop's palace at Lugdunum. 'We did our best, but it wasn't enough. With Theoderic committed to defending only the Visigoth homeland in Aquitania, and refusing to join us in a combined operation against Attila, the outcome's not hard to predict.'

'You mean, we're going to be defeated, sir?'

'Almost certainly. Without the Visigoths, we haven't a chance. Attila will engage us separately and crush each of us in turn.'

'And what will happen then?' Titus felt the first stirrings of dread, as the sombre reality of the position began to dawn on him.

Aetius shrugged, his expression bleak. 'Put starkly, it'll be the end of Western civilization. The Huns will destroy everything in their path, and massacre those they can't sell as slaves. Then, when there is no more plunder to be had, they will withdraw, leaving total devastation in their wake. Attila himself may cherish higher goals, but even he can't prevail against the will of his nation. I know these people, Titus. They can never adapt to civilization. They'll loot what they can from it – gold and slaves – then destroy the rest.'

'Won't the East help us?'

'Hardly. We failed them in their hour of need, remember? Attila would never have crossed the Rhenus if he'd felt there was any risk of the East attacking his rear.' Aetius looked at his senior courier earnestly. 'If you haven't already done so, I'd advise you to prepare your will,' he said gently, a hint of affectionate concern in his voice. 'I had hoped that Attila would hold back from invading the West,' he mused. 'After all, you did say the signs were hopeful when you returned from seeing him. What made him change his mind, I wonder?'

'Well, for all his power he's hardly a free agent, sir,' replied Titus thoughtfully. 'I learnt quite a lot about the factors influencing his policy, during the visit. Especially from Maximin and Priscus, the ambassadors from the Eastern Empire, which had been at the receiving end of Hun aggression for eight years. I really think he wanted to accept your offer of what amounted to . . . well, virtual partnership in running the Western Empire. He was certainly affected by your gift. Just for a moment he let his guard slip; I could tell he was moved, also how much your friendship had meant to him. But the pressures on him to invade the West were enormous. King Gaiseric, the Bagaudae of Aremorica, the anti-Merovech faction among the Franks – they were all pushing him in that direction. Add to that the new tough stance that the East, with its huge resources and now committed leadership, is taking against the Huns, who were badly mauled at the Battle of the Utus. And finally, the business of Honoria's letter, which provided him with a perfect pretext . . .' Titus smiled ruefully, letting the unfinished sentence hang in the air. 'Perhaps he hasn't any option.'

'Neatly put, Titus Valerius,' conceded the general. 'That probably sums up his position.' He sighed in frustration. 'If only Theoderic could have seen the bigger picture.'

'He did once, didn't he?' recalled Titus. 'You remember sir, after the shambles of Tolosa, when the Visigoths were thirsting to avenge themselves on us. Who was it persuaded them to make peace with you, rather than engage in a bloody battle in which both sides would have been the losers? It was Avitus, wasn't it?'

'You're right, it was,' said Aetius slowly, a thoughtful expression forming on his face. 'That might be the answer. Well done, Titus – I should have thought of it myself. If anyone can talk Theoderic round, it has to be Avitus. Let's see, he's finished his term as Praetorian prefect of Gaul, so presumably he's now back on his estate in Arvernum. How far's that? A hundred miles? The great military road from Lugdunum to Divona* virtually passes his villa. The imperial Post's still functioning – just. With relays of fast horses you can be there tomorrow.' He clapped his agent on the shoulder, and grinned. 'Well, don't just stand there. On your way, my friend.'

* Cahors.

FORTY-SEVEN

Hail Avitus, saviour of the world
Sidonius Apollinaris, *The Panegyric of Avitus*, 458

Imposing in his senatorial toga – an archaic survival from the days of the Republic – Avitus faced the assembly of Visigoth chiefs ranked behind their aged king in the great basilica of Tolosa. They were clean-shaven, clad in dalmatics or Roman-style tunics – indistinguishable from Romans in fact, save by their tall stature and blond colouring. Theoderic alone, with his long moustaches, and white hair falling to his shoulders, retained the fashion of his ancestors.

'Your Majesty, nobles of the mighty nation of the Visigoths,' Avitus began, in a mild and friendly voice, 'I thank you for your welcome, and applaud your courage in deciding to resist – alone – the Scourge of God. Indulge me, while I touch upon your past. These Huns Attila leads are the same cruel savages who drove your forebears from their homes, condemned your nation, like the Israelites, to wander forty years. But where the seed of Abraham had only the desert in which to pitch their tents, the fair expanse of the Roman Empire was the scene of your exile. I will readily admit that many times during your long sojourn your people have been wronged by Rome, as – let us be frank – Rome has been wronged by you. But there has been much of friendship also. It was the Romans gave you refuge from the Huns, and your warriors have filled our legions, proving among the staunchest of Rome's defenders. Stilicho, Rome's great commander, many times spared Alaric when he could have destroyed him. Athaulf, brother of that mighty leader the father of your present king, married Galla Placidia, mother of Rome's present Emperor. And you were finally granted your homeland – Aquitania, the fairest of Gaul's provinces – by the Emperor Constantius, Valentinian's father, who married Placidia after Athaulf's death. Many are the mutual ties that bind the Romans

342

and the Visigoths. Search your hearts, and, if you are honest, which I know you are, you will acknowledge that what I say is but the truth.'

Avitus paused. There was a general murmur of agreement, and nodding of heads. So far, the senator thought, he had his audience's sympathy. But that would change in an instant to hostility, if he misjudged things. He must proceed with circumspection.

'Yet our two peoples, who should be friends, are enemies. That is indeed a pity, never more than now.' He allowed his voice to rise. 'You think you can prevail against the Huns, that because, eleven years ago outside this very city you slaughtered sixty thousand of them, you can again defeat them. I tell you, that is folly and delusion. Attila comes against you with ten times that number; do you really think you can prevail against such odds? You will, of course, fight valiantly – as you always do. But you will be destroyed. And it will have been a useless sacrifice. Your widows and orphaned children will be slaughtered or enslaved, your churches desecrated and your habitations razed. The Visigoth nation will vanish from the earth as if it had never been. Is this what you want to happen? For believe me it will happen, if you hold to your present course.' He paused again, gauging the mood of his hearers. A tense silence gripped the assembly.

'Let the Romans and the Visigoths put their differences behind them, and join together against our common enemy,' he continued, once more lowering his voice. 'Then, when the other federates – the Franks who are loyal to Merovech, the Alans and Burgundians – see the example we have set by our alliance, they will be encouraged to join us. Only if all Gaul combines to resist him can we defeat Attila.' He raised his voice again, to finish almost on a shout. 'Divided we can only fail; united we shall win. Visigoths, avenge your ancestors!'

The senator waited anxiously for his hearers' reaction. For a few seconds, not a sound was heard throughout the great building. Then Theoderic turned towards his following. 'Avitus speaks wisely,' he declared. 'Let us join the Romans.' His words were greeted with shouts of assent, which gradually blended in a mighty crescendo of approval.

As he breathed a huge sigh of relief, Avitus realized that he was shaking and soaked with sweat.

FORTY-EIGHT

I myself shall throw the first javelin, and the wretch who fails
to follow my example is condemned to die

Jordanes, *Gothic History*, 551

'Nothing, my lord,' the messenger told Anianus, Bishop of Aureliani, an ecclesiastic noted for his zealous piety. 'Not a sign of any relieving force, I'm afraid.'

'If they don't come soon, it'll be too late!' cried the bishop, too distracted by worry to conceal the desperation in his voice. 'Listen to that.' In the distance, a regular thump-*crash* could be heard, as the Huns' great battering-rams, designed and built by captive Romans, thudded against the city walls, dislodging cascades of shattered masonry with every blow. 'But we must have faith,' he muttered, more to himself than to the other, 'faith that the Holy Shepherd will not abandon His flock to the Scythian wolves. Return to the ramparts, friend, one last time, while I renew my supplications to our Father.'

With a feeling that it was a hopeless exercise, the messenger hurried from the forum, which was crowded with anxious citizens, back to his post on the battlements, and bent his gaze towards the south. As he expected (and feared), the horizon remained empty of anything that moved. No – wait. There was something, surely: at the very limit of his vision, a tiny pale spot which seemed to grow as he watched. A dust-cloud! Pulse racing, he pelted back to the forum, barged his way through the densely packed throng and gasped out his news to Anianus.

'It is the aid of God!' exclaimed the bishop. Immediately his cry was taken up by the townsfolk, who, headed by their spiritual leader, poured on to the walkways behind the walls' crenellations. The dust-cloud, now clearly visible, was suddenly blown aside by a gust of wind, revealing serried ranks of armoured Romans marching beneath their standards, together with a multitude of fair-haired giants armed with spears and shields.

'Aetius and Theoderic,' declared Anianus, his voice trembling with emotion. 'Fall on your knees, good people,' and give thanks to God for our deliverance. Let this fourteenth day of June be ever noted in the calendar, in commemoration of His favour extended to our city of Aureliani.'

'Look, they're going!' shouted a soldier, pointing to the scattered suburbs beyond the walls. Like a fast-ebbing tide, the Huns were pulling out, leaving their siege-engines behind. Before the van of the relieving force had reached the city gates, the Huns were no more than a dust-cloud in their turn, rolling swiftly east towards the Sequana.

'They've crossed the Sequana, sir,' announced the scout, pulling up his lathered mount before Aetius.

'And?'

'They're pressing on to the north-east, sir – even faster than before, I'd say.'

Dismissing the man, Aetius allowed himself to hope. Attila had seen the huge size of the force marching against him at Aureliani, not only Romans and Visigoths, but also Franks, Burgundians, Alans, and Aremoricans. Being always as prudent as he was bold, the Hun king had decided to withdraw. Could it be that Attila, daunted by the sheer scale of the alliance his invasion had provoked, had decided to return home?

'What do you think, Titus?' he asked his aide, tried and tested in the course of many campaigns. 'Will he push on to the Rhenus?'

Looking at his commander's haggard face, etched with lines of strain from holding the Western Empire together, while wearing himself out winning over the federates in Gaul while also countering the hostile machinations of Valentinian, Titus felt a stab of pity. In the same position, Titus would doubtless find himself clutching at any straw. But for Aetius that would be a dangerous luxury. The general was exhausted, utterly drained by coping with demands which would have broken lesser men. Small wonder, then, if he had allowed his judgement to be clouded by a temporary weakness. Suddenly, Titus knew where his duty lay. He must ensure that his master's mind remained clear and objective, even if it meant destroying any false hopes he might long to cling to.

'I don't think so, sir,' replied Titus gently. 'That would be unlike Attila. Invading the West is the biggest commitment he's ever made. He can't afford to back down; to do so would be to shatter his prestige and thus forfeit his grip on his empire.'

'But you saw what happened at Aureliani,' objected Aetius, in a tone bordering on querulous. 'That was two days ago, and he's still retreating.'

'It is not a retreat but a tactical withdrawal, sir. If he'd stayed, he would have been squeezed between our forces and the walls of a hostile city – a worse position would be hard to imagine. If he'd offered battle then, he would have risked defeat in the very heart of Gaul, with no avenue of retreat. Believe me, sir, he'll stop and face us as soon as he finds ground favourable to himself.'

Aetius shook his head and passed a hand over his face. 'You're right, of course,' he acknowledged with a weary smile. 'What have I been thinking of?' He clapped the other on the shoulder. 'Thank you, Titus Valerius – a true Victor to my Julian.* "Ground favourable to himself" – that means an extensive, level area, where he can deploy his horse-archers to the best advantage.' The general's brow furrowed in thought for a few moments. 'There's only one place in this region that fits that description: the Locus Mauriacus – or the Catalaunian Plains, as it's usually called – huge plains to the south of Durocatalaunum** – that's a small town about fifty miles north-east of here.'

And so it proved. On the night of 19 June, Attila's headlong retreat slowed; his rearguard was overtaken by the allies' van, which led to a bloody clash between the Franks and Gepids. While the confused skirmishing was raging in the moonlight, Aetius, leaving his generals Aegidius and Majorian† to contain the situation, rode off to reconnoitre the terrain. A risk, but one he felt he had to take. Although he intended making a wide flanking detour to avoid the Hun positions, the chance of encountering outlying hostile pickets couldn't be discounted.

Dawn disclosed a vast and, at first glance, absolutely level plain stretching away on every side to the limit of his vision. Underfoot, the ground was firm and dry, a circumstance causing the Huns

---

* One of Julian's generals in that Emperor's Persian campaign, Victor risked censure by wisely advising against a rash attack on the city of Ctesiphon.
** Chalons-sur-Marne.
† He was West Roman Emperor from 457 until 461, when he was deposed and put to death.

to betray their presence by a great pall of dust rising several miles to the south. Aetius' heart sank. The Locus Mauriacus was perfect for the manoeuvring of Attila's cavalry, which would give him a clear advantage over the Roman-led coalition with its comparatively weak horse. Reports put Attila's force at half a million – surely an over-estimate. But even allowing for exaggeration they could scarcely number less than a hundred thousand. Against which Aetius could field twenty thousand Romans, twenty thousand Visigoths, and perhaps a similar number for all the other allies put together. A maximum of sixty thousand, at best a little more than half the numbers Attila had at his command.

With a sick feeling of despair, Aetius acknowledged a grim fact: unless he could devise a way to neutralize the odds against him, he faced certain defeat. Then, at that stark moment, he noticed something which lifted his spirits from despondency and sent them soaring. His observing of it Bishop Anianus would undoubtedly have ascribed to Divine Providence, Aetius thought irreverently. With a wry chuckle, he wheeled his horse and spurred for the Roman lines.

In a private chamber in the imperial palace of Ravenna, Valentinian, white-faced and shaking, scanned the latest dispatches from Gaul. 'He gave us his word, Heraclius,' he cried in a trembling voice to the plump eunuch standing nearby. 'In his letter to us, Attila swore that his only quarrel was with Rome's enemy, the Visigoths. But now we learn that all the federates in Gaul, the Ripuarian Franks excepted, have combined against him. What can this mean?'

'It means, Serenity,' said Heraclius, the emperor's favourite, and chief adviser, 'that Attila has played you false. Deceit is his stock-in-trade, and playing one enemy off against another. I fear his plans of conquest are not limited to Aquitania, but extend no doubt to all of Gaul, perhaps also Italia, and even Hispania.'

'Why were we not warned?' wailed Valentinian. 'We are surrounded by fools and cowards – Aetius especially. He should have foreseen Attila's intentions and taken steps to counter them. Can he still stop the Huns, do you suppose?'

'We cannot count on it, Serenity,' replied the eunuch imperturbably. 'In that respect, the record of Rome's Eastern armies is hardly an auspicious precedent.'

'Then we must prepare to leave!' exclaimed the emperor. 'Go at once to Classis, Heraclius. Charter a galley, the fastest you can find, to transport immediately to Constantinople ourself, the Augusta and her daughters, I suppose, and key members of the Council, and as many court servants and imperial guardsmen as can be accommodated.'

'And also one whose chief concern is Your Serenity's abiding welfare?' Heraclius suggested smoothly.

'Yourself, you mean? Yes, yes, but hurry. Others may well have read the auguries.'

'It shall be done, Serenity. The vessel will be ready within the hour. But before I go, perhaps I may caution against immediate embarkation.'

'Why, pray?' snapped Valentinian

'Just that supposing Aetius were to prevail against Attila, Serenity, then return to Italy to find the throne vacated . . .' Heraclius shrugged, and spread his hands suggestively.

'We take your point,' said Valentinian worriedly, after a pause. 'Aetius has long striven to undermine us and usurp our power. You think he might be tempted in our absence to usurp the throne itself?'

'The history of Rome, Serenity, is sadly strewn with examples of ambitious generals seizing the purple – the usurper Iohannes in your infancy, to name but one.'

'Very well,' conceded the Emperor reluctantly. 'Charter the ship, but we shall not sail immediately. If Attila wins, I daresay we'll get advance warning before he has time to cross the Alpes.'

'A wise decision, Your Serenity.'

The allied camp near Durocatalaunum [Titus wrote in the *Liber Rufinorum*], Province of Lugdunensis Senonia, Diocese of the Gauls. The year of the consuls Marcian Augustus and Adelphius, XII Kalends Jul.* First light.

We reached Aureliani just in time. The Huns were already in the suburbs when the Romans and their allies arrived on the scene. Rather than let his army be trapped around the walls of the city, Attila, ever the cautious tactician, abandoned the siege and pulled back across the Sequana. This

* 20 June 451.

was a major gain for Aetius, and a setback for Attila: the capture of Aureliani would have given the Huns a strong base from which to launch an offensive against the Visigoths' homeland, Aquitania.

My admiration for Aetius knows no bounds. On receiving the news that the Visigoths had decided after all to join us, he immediately set about negotiating with the other federates in Gaul, which involved prodigious journeyings and feats of persuasion. The upshot: a huge force, united in fear and hatred of the Huns, has been assembled in an amazingly short time. To the Roman army and their powerful ally the Visigoths have been added large contingents of Alans, Franks, Burgundians, and even Aremoricans (perhaps, late in the day, the last-mentioned realized that rule by Rome is preferable to 'liberation' by Attila). How strange, and heartening, to witness Roman soldiers collaborating in the most friendly way with their erstwhile enemies. Our only weak link is Sangiban, King of the Alans, who treacherously tried to betray Aureliani to Attila and switch his allegience to the Huns. Fortunately, the conspiracy was detected and annulled, and Sangiban has now rejoined the fold. But he and his people will need watching.

The federates seem well enough equipped, especially the Franks and Visigoths. All have round shields, and either a spear or several javelins apiece, as well as arms such as knives or throwing-axes. Most still scorn body-armour, but many now have helmets. The wealthier own swords and horses. Whatever our German allies lack in discipline, they more than make up for in courage and resolve. Our own Roman troops are steadier and better trained, although their armour and weapons generally could be in better shape – some are patched up and kept in service long after they should have been scrapped. The trouble is that many of our weapons *fabricae*, like those at Augusta Treverorum or Lauriacum* which lie within federate or abandoned territory, are no longer in production, while the ones in Gaul that are – as at Durocortorum and Argentorate Stratisburgum** until

* Trier and Lorch.
** Reims and Strasbourg.

their recent sacking by Attila, that is – operate on a much-reduced scale because of cut-backs in central funding. Much of our gear now has to come from *fabricae* in northern Italia, at Cremona, Verona, et cetera. Unaccountably, a few months ago supplies for a time stopped coming from this source. (Aetius suspected the jealousy of Valentinian at work.) However, when Aetius had three managers charged with peculation, resulting in their dismissal and imprisonment, supplies miraculously resumed.

The scale of Attila's devastation in northern Gaul is truly appalling – far worse than the reports had led us to believe. Most places of any size between the Rhenus and the Sequana have gone up in flames, and indiscriminate massacres have routinely followed the capture of a city. One hears blood-curdling stories of the atrocities committed by his Thuringians: accounts of victims tied between horses and torn apart, or staked down and crushed beneath wagon wheels are chillingly convincing. They have had one positive effect, though: to give an iron edge to the allies' determination that Attila must be defeated.

Calling in his wings from around Nemetocum and Vesontio* as he retreated from Aureliani, and closely followed by our coalition's forces, Attila has chosen to make a stand south of the town of Durocatalaunum, where the terrain favours his cavalry. The area is one enormous plain, flat and dreary beyond imagining, its monotony unrelieved except by stands of poplars and winding tributaries of the Matrona river** on which the town stands. We have pitched our tents within sight of Attila's entrenchments,† after some heavy skirmishing in the night, when our van caught up with some of Attila's German allies. Everyone expects there will be a great and bloody battle today. Morale is high, though I would say the mood is one of grim resolve rather than excited optimism. Apart from last night, when he went off to scout the lie of the land, Aetius has been everywhere,

* Arras and Besançon.
** The Marne.
† Still clearly visible in 1851, according to Sir Edward Creasy, in his splendid *The Fifteen Decisive Battles of the World*.

chatting with the soldiers round their camp fires, briefing leaders, visiting the sick, checking supplies, et cetera. The man's energy is inexhaustible. Just the sight of his famous battered cuirass and (carefully dis-arrayed) scarf is enough to put new heart into everyone.

Though officially I shall not be fighting, my position as a courier should ensure that I see more of the conflict than most soldiers. I have already made my will and dispatched it to my head steward at the Villa Fortunata with instructions that, should I fall, all my property is to pass to my son, Marcus, now a fine young man studying law at Rome. To him also I bequeath the *Liber Rufinorum*, our family's archive, whose compilation I trust he will continue. I have prayed to my God, the Risen Christ, and am at peace. Holding the Chi–Rho amulet given to me all those years ago in the cathedral at Ravenna, I feel that the souls of my dear wife Clothilde and my father Gaius look down on me from Heaven, lending me strength and encouragement against the coming fray.

I close now in haste; Aetius has returned from his scouting expedition and has summoned me.

When he reached the Roman lines after surveying the Catalaunian Plains, Aetius handed his blown horse to a groom and sent a messenger to fetch Titus. Looking round, he could see that Aegidius and Majorian had done a good job of pitching camp, following the night encounter with Attila's rearguard. Approvingly, he noted the neat rows of the legionaries' leather tents, with patrolling sentries and even a rough-and-ready ditch and stockade – Trajan would have been proud! Even the federates' lines, stretching away into the far distance, seemed reasonably well ordered – for German dispositions, anyway. Titus appeared, and Aetius sent him to order the *bucinatores* to sound Arise, and to request the allied leaders to assemble in the command tent.

Surveying the motley array of German warriors and Roman officers who filed in, Aetius chuckled to himself. What would Hadrian or Constantine have thought, if they could have seen a Roman general solemnly preparing to discuss tactics with fur-clad barbarians?

'Good morning gentlemen,' he said cheerfully. 'I trust you slept well. My apologies if my summons has caused you to delay your breakfasts, but I can assure you there will be plenty of time for that. The Huns are not yet astir, and my guess is that Attila is in no hurry to join battle. Clearly, he got a rude shock when we turned up in strength at Aureliani. He'll probably play safe and postpone the fighting till late in the day, so that he can fall back under cover of darkness, should that prove necessary. I propose to exploit that. I've discovered that there's high ground behind the Hun position, on their right. If we can occupy the hill while they're unprepared, that'll give us an enormous advantage. Torismund' – he smiled at a fair-haired giant standing beside his father, King Theoderic – 'does the task appeal to you?'

'Definitely, sir,' said the young man eagerly.

'Excellent. Best be on your way, then. God speed and good luck.

'Your Majesty,' said Aetius, turning to Theoderic when Torismund had left to collect his assault force, 'it is only fitting that the honour of commanding the right wing should fall to yourself.' The venerable King inclined his head in assent. 'Then I, together with the Romans and our other allies, apart from the Alans, will take the left.

'Now, Sangiban,' he continued, in tones suggesting he was addressing an old and trusted colleague, 'I have reserved the most important post especially for you; the centre. This is where Attila is most likely to concentrate his main attack, using his best troops, the Huns. Who better than the King of the Alans to match against the King of the Huns?' Ribald laughter from the Germans and Romans greeted this observation: everyone knew that Sangiban had tried to desert to Attila. The King, whose dark complexion hinted at his Asiatic origins, could only nod unhappily. 'But don't worry,' went on Aetius reassuringly. 'You'll have friends on either side, to keep an eye on you.' More laughter at the thinly veiled threat that, should Sangiban try to repeat his treachery, it would be instantly spotted and punished by those flanking him.

'Right, I think that's everything,' concluded the general. 'When the fighting starts, it'll be a straightforward pounding-match, with no opportunity for elaborate tactics, and victory going to the side that doesn't break. The lines will be so extended that there'll be no question of the Huns trying their favourite encircling trick. I suggest you let your men eat and sleep their fill for the time being: they'll fight the better for it. My scouts will keep me informed of what the Huns are doing; I'll send word when it's time for us to take up battle positions. Enjoy your breakfasts, gentlemen.'

Surveying the great wall of wagons behind which his forces were deploying, Attila felt unaccountably depressed. This despite the fact that, both tactically and strategically, he had done nothing which could be faulted, and was now in a very strong position. Given the circumstances, his decision to withdraw from Aureliani had been wise, as had his disengagement from Aetius' Frankish vanguard in the night. The plains where he was encamped were ideal for the deployment of his Hun and Ostrogoth cavalry. His forces greatly outnumbered those of the Romans and their allies. So why was he so low in spirits?

Part of it was sheer weariness. If he defeated Aetius today – and all the signs were that he would – what then? The subjugation of the entire Western Empire, to be followed, perhaps, by an epic contest between himself and Gaiseric for domination of the barbarian world? There would never be an end to it, he thought despairingly. Together with his people, he was locked into a perpetual campaign of bloody conquest, in which war became its own self-fulfilling justification, and forward momentum the only choice. The Hun warriors themselves, he had noted, seemed to share his despondency, probably because of the withdrawal from Aureliani. Lacking the patience and perspective of the Romans, who could rally no matter how many times they were defeated, to his unsophisticated fellow tribesmen retreat and failure must seem like the same coin. Perhaps if they were to receive news of a favourable divination, that would help to restore their morale.

Summoning his shamans, Attila asked them what the immediate future held. After slaughtering two sheep and examining their bones and entrails, the augurs remained ominously silent. Pressed, they confided that the omens predicted Attila's defeat, whereupon he dismissed them with instructions to keep silent regarding the prophecy. Unconcerned on a personal level, for he was not in general superstitious, Attila decided that the next best thing to an auspicious augury would be to encourage his troops with a rousing speech. His army was so enormous that only those within a limited distance could hope to hear him, but the gist would be relayed back to the others, and the mere sight of their leader addressing them should have the desired effect.

When the vast multitude was assembled, Attila mounted a rostrum erected on a wagon-bed. 'Faithful Huns, loyal Ostrogoths, intrepid Rugians, bold Sciri and Thuringians, stout Gepids and Herulians, fellow warriors all, today we shall win a great and glorious victory surpassing all our previous feats of arms, against the Romans and their misguided friends. Of those, the Visigoths alone are worthy of our steel. As for the Romans themselves, they pose no threat; weak and timid, they dare not fight like men, but cower in close ranks for comfort, like lobsters in their iron shells. Fight bravely, and your gods will protect you. I myself will throw the first javelin, and the wretch who fails to follow my example is condemned to die. But such a one does not, I think, exist among you. Tell me that I am right.'

A chorus of affirmation grew and swelled, blending at last into a thunderous acclamation by the entire army. When it had died away, he dismissed the host, whose components returned to their stations. His troops' confidence and fighting spirit were now, Attila judged, fully restored, and his own black mood had lightened somewhat.

As he prepared to return to his tent to snatch a little much-needed rest before the battle, a scout came galloping up. 'Serious news, Sire,' he gasped. 'The Visigoths are about to occupy a hill overlooking our right flank.'

Attila's mind reeled. What hill? Earlier reports had assured him that the terrain was totally flat and featureless. But these plains were so vast that a lone eminence could easily have been overlooked, especially in the half-light of dawn. He should have surveyed the ground himself, of course; he would have missed nothing of tactical significance. This was what happened when a leader lost his concentration, Attila thought grimly. Within moments he was in the saddle, issuing orders to secure the hill before the Visigoths could take it – even as the feeling grew within him that it was probably too late.

FORTY-NINE

A conflict terrible, hard-fought, bloody, and monstrous
Jordanes, *Gothic History*, 551

Screened by a stand of willows on the banks of the Matrona, Titus watched Torismund's Visigoths, crouching low, approach the hill on foot, then begin its ascent. They got halfway to the summit before being challenged. Issuing from the Hun camp, a large body of horsemen galloped to the base of the hill, then, dismounting, swarmed up its face on a parallel course to the Germans. But Torismund's men gained the top well ahead of their pursuers. Turning, the Visigoths charged down upon the Huns with such impetus that the latter were broken and scattered before they could make a stand. Wave after wave of Huns tried to dislodge the Visigoths, only to fall back each time with heavy losses; eventually, further attacks were abandoned. Titus thought Attila must have decided that trying to storm what was virtually an impregnable position was too expensive. Hugging the shelter of the riverside trees, Titus returned to camp to report to Aetius.

'First round to us,' observed the general. 'Let's hope our luck lasts.' He shot a keen look at his courier. 'You realize that, potentially, Attila's got one huge advantage over me.'

'I can't think what, sir.'

'Your belief in me is touching, Titus. However, there's no gainsaying that among his followers Attila's word is absolute, giving him a control over his forces which I can only envy. The Romans apart, I don't have a real command at all. The federates are here of their own free will, because it's at last penetrated their thick German skulls that they've a lot more to lose by not fighting Attila than by combining against him. They could turn round now and march off, and there wouldn't be a thing I could do about it.'

'But that's not going to happen, surely?'

'Let's hope not. I don't trust that Sangiban an inch, but I think we've managed to contain him. The rest should stay in line – provided nothing happens to upset them.'

The day, just one short of the longest of the year, wore on: a bright, cloudless day, with just enough breeze to prevent it becoming oppressively hot. The sixth hour passed and the sun began its descent from the meridian; still there was no movement from behind the wagons the Huns had drawn up in front of their entrenchments. Then, at the eighth hour, scouts came galloping up to Aetius' command tent with the news that Attila was at last beginning to form his order of battle. As Aetius had predicted, the Huns took the centre. On their right were the Rugians, Heruls, Thuringians, Gepids, and those Franks and Burgundians who had not joined the Romans. This right wing was commanded by Ardaric, King of the Gepids. On the left were the Ostrogoths, under the three brothers who jointly ruled the tribe, Walamir, Theodemir, and Widimir.

While the Huns and their subjects were moving into position, Titus galloped to the federate leaders with orders from the general to take up their posts. Soon, the Catalaunian Plains resembled an ant-hill into which a child has thrust a stick – men swarming everywhere, the armoured ranks of marching Romans contrasting with the loose formations of the federates. The air was filled with the harsh braying of the Goth war-horns, and the sonorous booming of Roman trumpets.

'What now, sir?' asked Titus, reporting back to Aetius.

'We wait, Titus, we wait,' replied the general calmly. 'There's nothing more that I personally can do. As I've said, I don't control the federates. Everything now depends on whether they stick to the agreed plan. There's one good omen: my scouts tell me that Attila himself has taken the field at the head of his Huns.'

'And that's *good*?'

'Certainly. It shows he's worried. The one thing Attila never does is take active charge in a battle; he leaves that to his captains. He's obviously concerned that this time, unless he leads his warriors himself, they may face defeat.' A look of sadness settled on the general's face. 'I never thought to see it happen, Titus,' he said quietly. 'Myself and Attila, my oldest and closest friend, taking up arms against each other. A bit like Cain and Abel.' Then his face cleared, and he said briskly, 'I want you to join Torismund on his hill. From up there, you'll have an excellent prospect of the battlefield. If you see anything major developing – a break-through by our side or theirs, for example – report back to me.'

From the summit of the hill, crowded with flaxen-haired warriors, most of them extended on the grass resting or asleep, Titus looked out over the plains. He was awed by the vast extent of the dispositions, which stretched away before him to left and right almost to the limit of his vision: six enormous ragged blocks of men and horses. On his left, the Ostrogoths, faced by their kinsmen on the opposing side, the Visigoths; in the centre, Attila's Huns opposite Sangiban and his Alans; away to the right, Attila's other subject tribes, looking across a mile or so of ground at Aetius' Romans and the remainder of the federate allies.

For perhaps half an hour, the two great hosts stood motion-less as if in silent contemplation of each other, then a mournful blare of horns sounded from Attila's centre and the Hun cavalry rolled forward, like a swiftly spreading stain. The usual manoeu-vres followed – successive waves of horsemen advancing, wheeling and retreating, shooting volleys of arrows which looked to Titus like sudden shadows flitting over the ground.

Anxiously, Sangiban, in the third rank of the Alans, watched the Hun van, led by Attila himself, hurtle towards his front. The ground began to shake as the drumming of half a million hoofs grew to a sustained roar. Now he could see the enemy clearly: squat, powerfully built men with flat Oriental faces, controlling their huge mounts with knees alone as they fitted arrows to the strings of their bows. These were the deadly, recurved, composite weapons that, in conjunction with their horsemanship, had made the Huns the most feared warriors in the world. Sangiban knew that (in theory), so long as infantry kept formation protected by their shields, cavalry would not press home a charge against an array of spear-points. The reason was that, while men can be driven on to self-destructive acts, horses cannot. But would his men hold their line? They knew they shared their King's disgrace, and were demoralized and fearful. It would not take much to make them break.

Suddenly, with a loud hissing like a nest of angry serpents, the air went dark with arrows. Most thumped into shields or clanged off helmets, but enough found their mark to create gaps in the line – a momentarily lowered shield was all it took for a shaft to pierce a throat or eye.

When only feet from the Alan line, the Huns wheeled away to right and left, the leading riders weaving back through the open formations to make room for those behind, thus enabling a constant succession of charges to be maintained. The terrifying sight of wave upon wave of fierce horsemen bearing down on them, the pitiless sleet of arrows, and the screams of wounded men, began to take their toll. To Sangiban's horror, his worst fears were confirmed as, despite their officers' frantic efforts, the Alan front began to disintegrate. In twos and threes, then groups, the men turned and tried to fight their way back through the ranks to escape that terrible archery.

Slowly at first, then with accelerating speed, the Alan line buckled and fell back. Panic began to sweep through the ranks, then suddenly the whole Alan formation broke in disorder, became a fleeing mob. Penned like sheep between the Ostrogoths on one flank and the Romans on the other, the struggling fugitives could find no refuge from the unremitting arrow-storm. The retreat became a rout, the rout a massacre, as the Huns swept the shattered remnant of Sangiban's troops from the field.

Meanwhile, on the right flank of the allied army, the Visigoths were also under attack from cavalry, that of their Ostrogoth cousins. Brave, with high morale, led by a heroic and respected veteran, unlike the Alans the Visigoths maintained their shield-wall intact against repeated charges. The method was simple but effective, provided every warrior kept his nerve – no easy task when confronted by a mass of charging horsemen. Locking his shield with those of his companions on either side, each man planted his right foot forward and fixed his spear-butt firmly in the ground, holding his weapon inclined between his shield and that of the man on his right. Again and again, the Ostrogoth cavalry swept up to the wooden barrier and hurled their javelins, hoping to break the Visigoth line, only to wheel round as their mounts balked in face of the deadly frieze of spear-points.

'Well done, my heroes!' shouted the aged Theoderic, his long white locks streaming behind him as he rode along the ranks to encourage his men. 'Only hold fast, then they can never break us.'

But his courage in exposing himself proved fatal. Arcing through the air, a heavy Ostrogoth *angon* struck him in the chest and, mortally wounded, he fell from his horse.

Instead of discouraging the Visigoths, however, his death had the opposite effect. Burning for vengeance, they surged forward, no longer a defensive shield-wall, but a charging mass fronted by a bristling hedge of blades. So ferocious and determined was their attack that the Ostrogoths were forced to give ground, retreating stubbornly pace by pace, fighting all the way. Both sides, being Germans, mostly scorned the use of armour or lacked the wealth to own it, which resulted in frightful wounds and a high casualty rate. A spear-thrust in the torso was almost sure to pierce a vital organ, while a blow from a sword could inflict spectacular damage. Pattern-welded, edged with razor-sharp steel, these fearsome weapons – almost exclusively the preserve of nobles – could slice off heads and limbs with ease, and in the right hands cleave a man from skull to crotch.

On the left flank, the Romans waited, silent, motionless: cavalry, consisting of light scouting squadrons, heavier Stablesian *vexilla-tiones*, and one or two formidably armoured units like the 'Equites Cataphractarii Ambianenses'; infantry, comprising a few of the old legions still proudly bearing their eagles, now outnumbered by the newer units with their dragon standards – the Celtae et Petulantes, Cornuti et Brachiati, and many others, the red crests of their helmets a vivid contrast to the sombre grey of their mail. Beyond the Romans, the remainder of the German allies stood in loose formation, mainly unarmoured infantry with spears and shields. Their chiefs were mostly mounted, many wearing *Spangenhelm*s and body armour, and armed with swords.

A message-carrier came posting up to Aetius, who was seated on his horse a little way in front of his troops, flanked by his two chief generals, Aegidius and Majorian.

'Sir, it's the Alans!' gasped the messenger. 'They're falling back – Attila's got them on the run!'

'Splendid,' said Aetius, smiling enigmatically.

'They're falling *back*, sir.'

'Thank you, Tribune,' replied Aetius crisply, 'I heard you the first time. Off you go now and find out what's happening on the right wing. Dismissed.'

'Well, gentlemen, Attila's taken the bait it would seem,' Aetius remarked with satisfaction to his two generals. 'Now to see how well young Torismund can play his part.'

Some time later the galloper returned with news of heavy fighting on the right: the Visigoths were apparently beginning to gain the upper hand.

'Tell the trumpeters to sound the advance,' Aetius ordered him. Then, turning to his generals, 'To your posts, gentlemen.' He shook each by the hand, then added quietly, 'May God be with us. Jupiter or Christ? Perhaps it does not matter what we call Him, for surely He has heard our prayers and will grant us victory this day.'

As the last deep notes of the *bucinae* died away, the whole left wing began to move – infantry in the centre, cavalry on the flanks. Both Roman and German foot advanced in attack formations, *cunei*, which, despite the name, consisted of broad-fronted columns rather than triangular wedges. Carapaced in armour, legs swinging as one at the regulation marching pace, the Roman columns resembled monstrous metal centipedes. The enemy – Attila's German subjects other than the Ostrogoths – surged forward to meet the Roman-led wing, chanting their war-cry and banging spear-butts on shields. As the gap between the two forces narrowed, the Roman *campidoctores* began to call out their ritual training admonitions: '*Silentium*; *mandata captate*; *non vos turbatis*; *ordinem servate* – Silence; obey orders; don't worry; keep your positions.'

On the command '*Jacite*', a storm of javelins and lead-weighted darts arced up from the Roman ranks, who then immediately locked shields fore and above, in the ancient but tried and tested *testudo* formation, to form an impenetrable 'tortoise-shell' against which the enemy missiles thudded harmlessly – in contrast to the Roman volley, which took a heavy toll. Then the two sides slammed together with an earth-shaking crash. For a while, the battle swung to and fro, with neither side gaining the advantage. Then slowly, inexorably, the allied forces, stiffened by the steady and disciplined Roman contingents, began to push Ardaric and his Gepids back.

From Torismund's hill, Titus was able to observe the progress of the battle from the start. In the centre, under relentless pressure from the Huns, he saw Sangiban's front begin to waver and buckle, and a great concave salient form in the Alan line as Attila's onslaught started to take effect.

The Ostrogoths were now in action against the Visigoths, while to his right the two wings of the opposing armies were as yet unengaged. Gripped by a dreadful fascination, Titus watched as the battle slowly began to evolve its own patterns and rhythms. In the centre, the Hun advance pressed relentlessly forward, while to the left, after some ferocious fighting, the Ostrogoths were beginning to fall back. Now, on Titus' right, the Romans and their allies were moving, meeting head-on Attila's subject Germans under Ardaric. For a time, the outcome of the battle swayed in the balance. Then the two wings of Attila's force, its weakest sections, began to crumble. With shocking suddenness, they broke, first the left wing then the right, and streamed back in headlong flight, looking like a scatter of moving dots, pursued by the dark clumps of their victorious foes. Around Titus on the hill, the Visigoths formed up at Torismund's command, and charged downhill to attack Attila's retreating forces from the rear.

With his wings disintegrating, Attila's centre – now isolated by its forward momentum against the retreating Alans – was dangerously exposed on both flanks. Suddenly, Titus saw the genius of Aetius' plan: calculating on the Alans' expendability, he had ensured that the Huns' initial success became their downfall. Leaving Torismund and his men to deal with Attila's broken wings, the other Visigoths and the Romans, together with the other federates, abandoned the pursuit to smash into the Hun centre from either side. So mighty was the impact that Titus could hear, faint with distance, the clash of shields meeting and the ring of steel on steel. Then, guiltily aware that he had allowed events to overtake him, he began to scramble down the slope to where he had left his horse tethered.

Badly mauled, the Huns managed to make it back to their entrenchments where, from behind the wagon-wall, their archery kept their foes at bay, until the coming of darkness caused the allies to withdraw.

Although far from destroyed as a fighting force, Attila's army had sustained enormous losses, and he knew that he had been soundly beaten – his first defeat. Curiously, the thought did not trouble him – the reverse, in fact. He realized, with a stab of wry astonishment, that his chief feeling was one of relief. No more struggle, no more never-ending demands on his ability as a leader to conquer more and yet more lands, and reward his people with a constant bounty of pastures, gold, and plunder. Life as King of the Huns had become a burden he was ready to lay down. Tomorrow the Romans and their German allies would close in for the kill, like hunters with a bayed lion. But he would cheat them of their greatest prize, himself. For Attila, there would be no captive chains, no exposure to jeering mobs as he was dragged behind a Roman chariot to face a shameful death. No; he would die magnificently, and in a manner befitting a king, so that generations down the ages would recount with awe and admiration how Attila had perished.

He gave orders for a great funeral pyre, consisting of the saddles of his cavalry and his own finest trophies, to be erected within the wagon-walls, and issued instructions to his most trusted captains to set fire to it when the final assault came – as it surely must on the morrow. Then, seated atop the monstrous pyramid, he prepared to wait out the night, his last on earth.

The moon rose, illuminating a stark and dreadful scene. Between the two fields of myriad flickering lights that marked the rival camps, and extending on either hand for as far as he could see, the dead lay strewn in heaps and windrows where they had fallen, for the fighting had ended too late for burial to be possible. Attila cast his mind back over his long and eventful life. He would not dwell with regret on his unfulfilled ambitions for his people; the time for that was past. Instead, he would savour those defining moments when the blood ran high and keen, with the senses at their sharpest – when he faced the challenges that marked great turning-points in his life.

He recalled how, as a boy of ten, he had fought a lynx which had attacked the flock he had been guarding. Braving the great cat's snarling spitting rush, riding the pain as its claws raked his arms and chest, until he managed to draw his knife and plunge it into the creature's neck. Then his first raid: riding as a youth at his father's side against a Sarmatian war-band, his thrilled surprise at seeing warriors fall to the arrows he shot in quick succession from the powerful recurved bow of laminated wood and sinew that was his father's gift. He remembered Margus, where he had stamped his authority on the Huns, and forced the Romans to a shameful treaty. Incidents in his long friendship with Aetius (now, such were the strange workings of fate, his deadly foe) paraded in his memory – the great hunt where Carpilio, the Roman's son, had faced the bear; the shooting of the rapids of the Iron Gate . . .

Attila jerked awake, chilled and stiff. The moon had set. The shimmering greyness of the false dawn came and went, leaving the night blacker than before. Then a rosy flush appeared in the east and a tide of light spilt over the horizon, gradually suffusing the wide expanse of the Catalaunian Plains. The time had come, Attila told himself with a kind of defiant exultation. He would embrace death joyfully, with no regrets.

An hour passed.

When the camp beneath him was fully astir, and the full light of Midsummer's Day exposed a silent battlefield, empty save for corpses, Attila knew that the Romans would not come. He was being allowed to escape. A wave of weary disillusionment engulfed the tired old warrior. The struggle would resume, and once more he must take up the burden of leading his people, a burden grown so heavy as to be well-nigh unendurable.

As Attila began his retreat towards the Rhenus, he heard again the final words of Wu Tze's prophecy: 'The eagle is joined by the boar, and together they put the ass to flight.' The eagle was Rome; the boar was the favourite emblem of German warriors; the wild ass of the plains represented the Huns. The meaning was clear: Rome and Germany would join together to defeat the Huns. All along, the seer's prediction had proved correct, Attila reflected, with gloomy wonder. In the end, it seemed, no man was master of his fate.

Titus exclaimed in disbelief, 'You let him go, sir! Why?'

Aetius looked up from scanning a tally. All over the battlefield moved little knots of men, burial parties, and assessors compiling lists of the fallen. They were all Romans, the Visigoths and other allies having left the Catalaunian Plains for their homelands. In the case of Torismund, elected king on the battlefield after his father's death, he had taken Aetius' advice to return without delay to Tolosa, to prevent his brothers challenging his succession.

'It was the wisest course,' said Aetius. He gestured at the buzzards wheeling overhead. 'Would you wish their feast prolonged? This has been Rome's bloodiest victory. Another day's fighting would have all but wiped out the remaining legions, cohorts, and *auxilia** of my army. Attila is a wounded tiger – best let him escape, to lick those wounds. He may still be dangerous, but he can never again be the menace he was before. Besides, we need him.' He smiled at his courier enigmatically.

'*Need* him?'

'Indeed. Without the fear of Attila to make the federates stay friends with Rome for their own safety, they'd start carving out more territory for themselves. Unless I get fresh Roman troops, which there isn't the money to raise, I'd never be able to stop them. Which is why I persuaded Torismund to head for home as soon as possible – just in case he was tempted to start getting above himself.'

'A shabby way to treat our staunchest ally,' said Titus, unable to conceal his disgust at the general's cynicism. 'Without the Visigoths we'd probably have lost.'

'Not "probably" but certainly,' conceded Aetius. 'To spare my Roman troops who, being virtually irreplaceable, are too valuable to be squandered, I had to ensure that the Visigoths bore the brunt of the toughest fighting. Pitting barbarians against barbarians – that's been a policy of all our generals regarding federate troops, in order to cut down on Roman casualties. I salute the Visigoths; they performed magnificently.'

'But might that not have dangerous repercussions? They're bound to feel exploited.'

'Which is why I want them as far away as possible,' observed Aetius, like a lecturer expounding an elementary point of logic. 'At this moment, despite their losses, they're elated by victory. Resentment will come later – against myself, against Rome. But that's a price I'm prepared to pay for victory against Attila.'

'I see,' said Titus, both impressed and shocked by this revelation of the general's calculating craftiness. He paused, then added gently, 'But there was another reason, apart from keeping the federates on side, why you spared Attila, wasn't there?'

Aetius shrugged, then gave a wistful smile. 'True,' he admitted; 'the most important reason. He was my friend.'

---

* 'Cohort' was a sub-division of the old legion. 'Auxilium' (a 'regiment') was the name for one of the new formations replacing the legion.

PART IV

ROME
AD 451-5

FIFTY

And God breathed life into the dead and lifeless hand and she stretched out to take the tome

Theophylact, *Chronicles*, seventh century

'Chalcedon!' screamed Valentinian, leaning forward in his throne to point an accusing sceptre at the sturdy old man in pontiff's robes who stood before him. 'A boatload of bishops to the Bosporus! Did you hear that, Heraclius?' The emperor turned to the plump eunuch, his chief adviser, standing beside the throne. 'He means to ruin us.' To the pope he continued, 'Do you have the least idea how much this expedition will cost in fares, in board and lodging, in expenses? And for what? A vast quantity of hot air expended in theological hair-splitting.'

Pope Leo controlled his temper. 'With respect, Your Serenity, to determine the true nature of Christ can hardly be dismissed as hair-splitting,' he countered, with some difficulty keeping his tone reasonable. Had he been dealing with Valentinian's predecessors, Honorius, the Emperor's pious and gentle uncle, or his grandfather, the great Theodosius, who had knelt in humble supplication before Ambrose, Bishop of Milan, this conversation would have been very different. With disapproval, Leo noted the colossal statues of pagan gods and emperors that lined the walls of the great audience chamber of Domitian's palace in Rome – which city the Emperor increasingly favoured for his residence over Ravenna. It was said that Valentinian was a Christian in name only, that in secret he practised the black arts of sorcery and divination. But of course it was wise to keep knowledge of such rumours to oneself.

'The matter is closed,' snapped Valentinian. 'The state cannot afford it. Tell him, Heraclius.'

'I think, Your Serenity, the Treasury might *just* be able to find the funds,' said the eunuch smoothly. 'The defeat of Attila last month liberated monies which otherwise would have been earmarked for the war. Besides, the state's contribution to the expenses of the trip need not be very great. The Church's income from legacies and donations is considerable, and would help substantially to cover costs. And it would enhance your imperial prestige, Serenity, if for once Rome could be seen to be dictating terms to Constantinople.'

'It would hardly be dictating,' Leo protested; then he rumbled into silence as Heraclius shot him a warning glance. A tough and experienced negotiator, Leo knew enough about the ways of the world to understand the game Heraclius was playing. Vain, profligate and vicious, heading a corrupt and inefficient government, Valentinian was widely unpopular. To block a key papal delegation would cause enormous offence, not only to the bishops but to their flocks throughout the Western Empire. It would be disastrous for the Emperor's already tarnished image. Bishops were powerful men, with strong influence on public opinion and increasingly involved in civic administration, as the decurions, overburdened by responsibilities, sought escape by flight, or by enrolling in the army or the civil administration. Heraclius was astute enough, Leo realized, to know that any crisis affecting Valentinian might affect his own position, possibly resulting in his being made a scapegoat.

'I would of course be at pains, Your Serenity, to ensure my delegates made clear to the assembled Council that they came only with your consent,' Leo said tactfully. 'And with your blessing too, I trust.'

'Oh very well then, go – go!' cried the Emperor peevishly. 'Empty our coffers, impoverish your sees – what do these things matter so long as Christ is served?' He waved his sceptre dramatically in a gesture of dismissal, covering his eyes with his other hand. 'See to the arrangements, Heraclius, and speed them on their way.'

'What's happening to the Roman world, old friend?' Marcian asked Aspar, as the old Emperor and his Master of Soldiers strolled in the gardens of Constantinople's main imperial palace. 'People seem more concerned over what constitutes the exact Divinity of Christ than over repelling Huns or Germans. When I was a child, the first Theodosius was on the throne and the empire was still one. Theodosius may have been obsessed with enforcing Catholic orthodoxy, but his priority was always the security of the state. He died leaving the frontiers intact and strongly defended. God, how things have changed!' He stared moodily downhill at the old Wall of Septimius Severus, which here formed part of the sea defences. 'The West crumbling, the East preoccupied with theological minutiae – the legacy of Greek philosophy, I suppose. The people pay more heed to Daniel on his pillar than they do to any edict of mine. Meanwhile, the empire continues to drift apart, like a cracked ice-floe. To help stop the rot, I suppose I had to convene this wretched Council, but believe me it went against the grain. There are weightier matters claiming my attention – rebuilding the country after Attila's ravages, for a start.'

'As to the Council, you had no choice, sir,' assured Aspar. (The long association between the two men had led to the dropping of the honorific 'Your Serenity'.) 'We simple soldiers may not like it, but this new world has to embrace religious obsessions – sorry, attitudes.'

'Already, I've lost the thread of my reasons for convoking the assembly,' groaned Marcian. He clapped Aspar on the shoulder. 'Remind me, please, old friend. It was your idea in the first place.'

'You may recall, sir, the case of one Eutyches who championed the monophysite doctrine that Christ has only one, wholly divine, nature. For this he was charged three years ago with heresy, and condemned by a small council at the instigation of Flavian, the Patriarch of Constantinople. Flavian received the backing of Pope Leo in the West, whose view – that Christ's nature is both human and divine – of course directly contradicts monophysitism. A year later, however, the case came up for reconsideration at the Council of Ephesus. Dioscorus, the ultra-monophysite Patriarch of Alexandria was in the chair, and the council was packed with his episcopal supporters – staunchly monophysite Egyptians and fellow believers from Palestine.'

'And the result was a foregone conclusion, I suppose?'

'It could hardly be anything else, sir. The council's verdict was to vindicate Eutyches, condemn Flavian, and set aside Pope Leo's judgement as expressed in a written treatise, *The Tome of Leo.*'

Marcian frowned. 'Forgive me, but I seem to be missing something. Exactly why is all this so important?'

Aspar laughed. 'I confess my own head's beginning to spin a bit. Essentially, it's a political rather than a religious issue, and the nub is Constantinople, the imperial capital – your city. For Dioscorus of Alexandria to have humiliated Flavian of Constantinople is both a snub to the pope and a challenge to your authority.'

'Thank you,' said the Emperor. 'It's all coming clear now. Dioscorus must be taught a lesson and, very publicly, put in his place. Right? Everyone, in both empires, must be left in no doubt that, in matters of doctrine just as much as government, Constantinople, the seat of the Emperor and of his patriarch, has the final say. And the best way of ensuring that is to reopen the Eutyches case. By pitting Leo against Dioscorus, figuratively speaking, in public debate, and making sure that Leo wins, we shall establish our supremacy in the most telling manner possible. That's the position more or less, isn't it?'

'Admirably summarized, sir. Flavian himself would be impressed.'

'Then let's drink to success.' Signalling a slave to bring wine, the Emperor pointed to where, two miles distant on the opposite Asian shore, the neat little city of Chalcedon gleamed white in the warm October sun. 'Looks peaceful, doesn't it?' he murmured. 'But in a few days, now that the papal delegates have docked, it'll be war to the death over there – metaphorically speaking – with no quarter given or taken. Mind you, with Rome, Constantinople, and the Eastern Emperor arrayed against them, I don't see how the monophysites can win. Ah, here's the wine.' The slave filled goblets and handed them to the two men. Before raising his cup, Aspar dribbled a little wine on the ground.

'Aspar?' queried Marcian, with a puzzled frown.

'A libation, sir. Just in case the old gods are watching. After all, we may as well enlist all the support we can.'

Black and hideous, the skull-like head of the mummified Saint Euphemia, martyred in the Great Persecution under Diocletian, grinned up at the two boys, junior singers of the church named for the saint, who gazed into the open coffin with a mixture of disgust and fascination.

'Ugh!' Simon, the younger, shuddered. 'I don't think I want to go on with this, George. Let's go home.'

'Afraid she'll be waiting to grab you one dark night?' mocked his companion, waving his arms and uttering low moans. 'All right, all right,' he went on hastily, seeing real fear register in his friend's face. 'Sorry. Come on, Simon, don't back out now. It'll be fun – just think of their faces when I pull that thread.'

'All right,' conceded Simon hesitantly. 'But no more fooling.'

'Choirboy's honour,' promised George solemnly. 'You remember how to tie that slip-knot round her finger?' Simon nodded, holding up a knife and a spool of black cobbler's packthread. George went to the back of the church, climbed down the stairs leading to the crypt, and positioned himself below a small ventilation grille piercing the floor of the nave above. Presently, the end of a thread descended through the the grille. Taking hold of it, George called, 'Ready?'

'Ready,' came back Simon's voice from above.

George tugged, but the thread barely moved. He rejoined his friend, who said, 'It's catching on the edge of the coffin.'

George felt the lip of the casket's head end. 'Wood's rough,' he said. 'Soon fix that.' Taking one of the lighted candles from the altar, he dribbled wax on to the offending area. Having checked that the thread ran smoothly over the waxed surface, he returned to his post, and at the signal tugged again. This time, he was able to pull in several feet of thread, and after a tiny resistance drew in the rest.

'Perfect,' said Simon, sticking up a thumb as George returned to the nave. He pointed to the saint's right arm, which now rested across the withered chest instead of along the mummy's side.* Pronouncing the rehearsal an unqualified success, they replaced the arm in its original position, then hurried giggling from the church.

Preceded by candle-bearers, chanting singers, censer-swingers, and acolytes, and headed by the Emperor and Empress, the commission and delegates making up the Fourth Ecumenical Council filed in solemn procession into the church of St Euphemia in Chalcedon. Members representing the monarchical bishopric of Rome and the patriarchate of Constantinople took their seats in the nave to the right of the altar, those of the patriarchates of Alexandria and Jerusalem to the left. Between the two groups, on raised benches behind the altar, were seated the commission or

---

* Re the retention of pliability in some mummies' limbs, see Notes p.439.

guiding panel of ten ministers and twenty-seven senators. Before the altar, like some mute and grisly president, in her open coffin lay the shrivelled corpse of St Euphemia. On her chest reposed a copy of *The Tome of Leo*.

In a brief address, Emperor Marcian welcomed the assembly and asked God to help steer them to a right decision; then he and Empress Pulcheria departed. The head of the panel then opened proceedings by summarizing the opposing positions of the Roman and Alexandrian parties, after which he invited the Roman lobby to comment.

A grizzled Gallic bishop was the first to speak. 'Since Christ was born of woman, though begotten of the Holy Ghost,' he began, speaking in a strong southern Gaulish accent, 'it surely follows that His nature is both human and divine. Yet is He very God of very God, being of one substance with the Father.'

'Amen to that,' quavered an aged delegate from Thracia. 'Nestorius, whom I knew when he was but a presbyter in Antioch, was right, you know. Christ Himself was not born, but only the man Jesus. Hence Mary cannot rightly be called the mother of God. Jesus was but a man; however, a man, er, clothed, as it were, by the Godhead, as with a garment.'

'Sit down, you fool,' hissed the delegate next to the Thracian. 'Nestorianism was declared heresy at the Third Ecumenical Council.' Standing, he addressed the panel. 'I beg the Commission to excuse my reverend friend from Philippopolis. Clearly, his years have caused him to forget the Twelve Anathemas drawn up by Theophilus of Alexandria against Nestorius, and ratified by Pope Celestine.'

'Yet those very Twelve Anathemas, formulated by my predecessor, were the basis of Eutyches' doctrine that Christ has but one nature: divine!' shouted an emaciated scarecrow with blazing eyes, from the opposite benches: Dioscorus. 'The same Eutyches whose monophysite beliefs you now seek to condemn.'

'Silence!' thundered the convener. 'I will not tolerate such unseemly interruptions. The Patriarch of Alexandria will have his chance to speak in due course and at the proper time. As for the delegate from Philippopolis,' he went on, glaring sternly at the offending cleric, 'we will overlook his lapse on this occasion. But he would do well to bear in mind that Nestorius, whom he esteems so much, is languishing in exile in Egypt's Great Oasis.

'Now, to clarify the issues we are here assembled to discuss, I propose to ask my learned colleague on the panel, Zenobius of Mopsuestia, to expound the doctrines of *an-homoios* – that is, the Son as different from the Father – and *homoios*, which defines the Son as similar in essence with the Father; also *homo-usios*, which declares the Godhead to be of the *same* essence as the Father . . .'

Early in the morning of the Council's final day, as soon as the sacristan had opened the doors of St Euphemia's church to check that all was in order, George and Simon slipped inside and hid. When the sacristan had gone, they attached the thread to prepare their 'surprise', after which George descended to the crypt while Simon concealed himself behind a pillar. He had a clear view of the church's interior, and was within easy reach of the staircase to the vault, so he could warn George when the moment arrived.

'. . . and in conclusion,' said the convener, 'having heard and carefully weighed the arguments put forward by the disputing parties, and taken into consideration the preponderating view, I shall announce the findings of the Commission, which are as follows.' He glanced around the assembled delegates: those supporting Leo looked eager and excited, the ones favouring Dioscorus sullen and subdued.

'That Christ is both human and divine as stated in the sacred *Tome of Leo*, being of the same nature with the Father according to His divinity, and of the same nature with us according to His humanity, a union of the two natures having taken place, wherefore we confess one Christ, one Son, one Lord.

'Accordingly, the doctrine that Christ has one nature only, that of God, is hereby declared to be anathema, and we decree that anyone subscribing to this doctrine be deemed a heretic.

'In consequence whereof, the verdict of the Council of Ephesus, vindicating the Monophysite teaching of Eutyches is hereby declared null and void.

'And moreover we decree that Dioscorus and those bishops of Egypt who supported him at Ephesus be now condemned, but that the rest, by reason that we think them more led astray than that they consented with a ready mind, be pardoned, provided they submit.

'And now, with gracious thanks to Their Serenities Marcian

and Valentinian, joint Augusti of our One and Indivisible Empire, to Leo, Monarchical Bishop of Rome, and to Flavian, Patriarch of Constantinople, in the name of the Father, the Son, and the Holy Ghost, I declare this Council closed.'

As the convener finished speaking, a susurration, like leaves in the wind, arose from the assembly, mingled with gasps and cries of astonishment. All over the church, delegates rose to their feet, pointing to the body of the saint in its coffin. Incredibly, but indisputably, a stick-like arm was rising in the air; it reached the vertical, then flopped on to the mummy's chest, its talons clutching at *The Tome of Leo* . . .

'A miracle?' said Marcian, angrily pacing the atrium of the villa in 'the Oak', Chalcedon's most exclusive suburb. He had been assigned the sumptuous residence during the sitting of the Council, for ease in monitoring its progress. 'This is the last thing we need, Aspar. Now the findings of the Council are going to have all the credibility of a fairground trick. The credulous fools. A corpse's hand rising to clasp the *Tome*? I've never heard such nonsense in my life!'

'I'm as puzzled as you are, sir,' responded the general. 'But they all swear they saw it – those who weren't dozing at the back, that is. I don't think we can just dismiss it, sir. Both John of Antioch and our own Flavian have confirmed they saw it happen, and a more hard-headed pair of pragmatists would be difficult to find.'

'Then it must be a trick,' fumed Marcian. 'We've all heard of phials of saints' "blood" which liquefy on certain days, or statues of the Virgin which supposedly weep real tears on Good Friday. It's got to be something on those lines, or . . . Perhaps the warmer temperature in the nave, compared to that in the crypt whence the body was removed, made arm muscles contract. For God's sake Aspar, don't look at me like that – I know it sounds far-fetched. But a miracle? No, that I can't accept.'

'Why don't we examine the lady for ourselves,' suggested the general soothingly.

'Good idea. Lead the way.'

'No signs of interference, sir,' pronounced Aspar, rising to his feet beside the coffin.

'I have to agree,' said Marcian reluctantly, dusting down his knees. 'This bending isn't good for my arthritis, you know,' he grumbled; then abruptly, pointing down at the coffin's head. 'Hallo, what's this?'

'Just a blob of candle-grease,' said Aspar, stooping to examine it.

Ignoring the stiffness in his knees, Marcian bent down to have a closer look. 'There's a mark here,' he observed suspiciously. 'Look,' and he indicated a faint groove on the surface of the wax. 'Something funny here, Aspar.'

'You know, sir,' said the general innocently, 'I wonder if it might not be a mistake to be *too* thorough in attempting to disprove that a miracle occurred. After all, it's bound to be seen as a manifestation of divine approval for the Council's findings. Judiciously presented, the "miracle of Saint Euphemia" needn't do us any harm.' He paused, then added reflectively, 'Any harm at all.'

'Aspar, I can't believe I heard you say that,' said Marcian indignantly. 'Not for a moment would I countenance such—' He stopped, shook his head, then burst out laughing. 'Well, perhaps you're right. Sleeping dogs, eh? You old reprobate, there are times when I despair of you.'

FIFTY-ONE

The sudden bursting of an artery flooded his lungs
with a torrent of blood

Jordanes, *Gothic History*, 551

Fear gripped Attila as he awoke. He could not move. Every muscle was immobile, as though his whole body were clamped by bands of iron. He willed his flesh to respond; slowly, slowly, beginning with his hands and feet, the power of movement returned until he was able, painfully and stiffly, to rise from his couch. The condition, brought on by over-taxed muscles reacting after a long and punishing lifetime in the saddle, had begun some years ago and had gradually worsened, until now he dreaded retiring each night in case the morning found him alive but paralysed. He could imagine no greater horror. It would be like being buried alive. No, worse; because then the agony would swiftly pass, whereas this would be a living death.

Calling for his horse, he rode out from his palace far into the steppe, not drawing rein until he reached the foothills of the Carpathus, his refuge when he wished to be alone to commune with himself. In a mood of quiet desperation, he reviewed the happenings of recent months, and the likely shape of events to come. After the defeat by Aetius, he would have desired nothing better than to make peace with the Romans and spend the remainder of his days consolidating his great empire, and perhaps trying to salvage something of his abandoned plans for a Greater Scythia. But that path was closed to him for ever. Fate had decreed that, however much he might wish it otherwise, he must always lead his people in never-ending wars of conquest. So, tired and dispirited, he had last year invaded Italia. Aetius' federate allies refused to serve outwith Gaul; with a limited number of Roman troops he could only harass, not seriously impede, the Hunnish horde. Worldly arms proving ineffective, the Romans had resorted to spiritual weapons; the fierce old pope (aptly named Leo, Attila thought), had met him at Lacus Benacus,* urging him to withdraw forthwith, or risk incurring divine punishment. Rather than God's wrath, however, it was the destruction of Aquileia, the sacking of Mediolanum and Ticinum,** and the partial payment of Honoria's dowry, commuted to gold, that had encouraged Attila to return home, without loss of face. But that was not enough. Even now, the Council was pressing for a fresh assault on Italia, should the Senate not deliver up Honoria herself.

He was, he thought with weary resignation, like the sharks that swim in Ocean, the mighty sea encompassing the earth: doomed to keep moving or sink into the vast depths and die, crushed by the unimaginable weight of water above. What had it all been for? he wondered. He was the oldest man he knew, yet his long life had accomplished nothing of lasting value. He had fame; the name of Attila would echo down the ages. But it was a fame based on the butchering of tens of thousands, of countless cities razed and lands laid waste. Was that a fame worth striving for? His was a barren legacy. Those closest to him he had lost: his brother Bleda, whose life he had been forced to take; Aetius, his one true friend, now become his deadliest foe. The vast empire he had forged, by leadership and ruthless will alone – could that survive his death? Or would his sons quarrel over their inheritance and, weakened and divided, fail to stop the subject nations breaking free and tearing it apart? Ellac and Dengish, his ablest sons, were brave and resolute, but in truth probably lacked the force of character to unite their siblings and hold the huge fabric together.

Sadly, he turned his horse's head for home. He had little inclination to return, but today was his wedding-feast, the bride, the latest of many, a young girl named Ildico. She had been chosen by the Council, Attila suspected, to prove to the Huns that their King, though old, was still virile and potent. He felt a flash of resentment that it had come to this: paraded like a stud bull at a market, to gratify the expectations of his subjects who, in their ignorance, needed the myth of an all-powerful monarch to sustain them. Perhaps, he thought wryly, he was coming to resemble King Log in the fable by that Greek slave.

* Lake Garda.
** Pavia.

Arriving back at his capital late in the afternoon, Attila was greeted by a great throng of women. Forming long files, and holding aloft white veils of thin linen so as to cover the spaces between the columns, they preceded Attila to his wooden palace, while choirs of young girls marching beneath the linen canopies chanted hymns and songs. Outside the principal gate, surrounded by attendants and with the wedding guests ranged behind, waited his new bride. A slave presented Attila with a goblet of wine, raised on a small silver table to a height convenient for the King as he sat his horse. Attila touched the goblet with his lips, bowed briefly to his wife-to-be, a frightened-looking youngster scarcely visible beneath layers of bridal finery, and dismounted.

A shaman performed a brief marriage ceremony, then the couple, followed by the bride's retinue and the guests, proceeded through the gateway and into the great hall, bright with wall-hangings and Oriental carpets, and lined with tables for the wedding guests. As at the reception for the Roman envoys five years before, the royal table, raised on a dais above the level of the rest, was laid with wooden cups and platters, in contrast to the gold and silver vessels on the other tables.

Punctuated by performances of minstrels, clowns, and jugglers, course followed course in monotonous plenty; each was a variation on mainly three ingredients, mutton, goat's flesh, and millet. Toasts, in fermented mare's milk, millet beer, and Roman wine – to Attila, to his bride, to each member of the bride's family, to the prominent nobles among the guests – were proposed and returned in an interminable succession. Although, as was his wont, he ate and drank sparingly, the sheer number of toasts and courses began to tell on even Attila's iron constitution. But, he being host and bridegroom, courtesy compelled him to sample every serving and each health drunk; nor could he decently retire before the conclusion of the feast. At last, as the first rays of dawn began to filter through the shutters of the hall, the final course was cleared away and, ill and exhausted, Attila was able to retire with his bride to the bedchamber.

With enormous thankfulness, the king lay down on the bed, indicating to Ildico that, instead of joining him, she should rest on a nearby couch. He felt a pang of compassion for the poor trembling child, waiting to be ravished by a man old enough to be her grandfather. She need have no fear. Let her choose some handsome young page to be her bedmate, and, to keep the Council and the people happy, any offspring be passed off as Attila's. A smile played briefly round the grim old warrior's lips as sleep claimed him.

Attila awoke, conscious of a terrible lancing pain beneath his breastbone. He tried to call out, but only a feeble croak issued from his throat. When he tried to rise, his stiffened muscles refused to obey his will. The pain increased, becoming un-endurable. Suddenly, something seemed to tear inside his chest and his gullet filled with warm liquid; he tried to breathe, found himself choking . . .

Later that day, concerned about his master's non-appearance, Balamir, Attila's loyal and devoted groom, broke into the royal bedchamber and found the King dead, lying in a great pool of blood. Ildico was crouched beside him, her head hidden by a veil. It was clear that an artery had burst, drowning Attila in his own blood.

The funeral was of a scale to reflect the King's mighty exploits. His body was solemnly exposed beneath a silken canopy; the nomads shaved their hair and gashed their faces, while chosen squadrons wheeled round the corpse, chanting a funeral song. The corpse was enclosed within three coffins: of gold, of silver, and of iron, then placed within the dry bed of the River Tisa, which had been diverted from its course by captive Romans. The waters were then restored to their natural channel and the pris-oners executed, that the spot should remain secret for ever.

As news of the King's death spread throughout the Roman world, it was everywhere greeted by a vast collective sigh of relief – nowhere more than in the East, on which Attila had vowed to wreak terrible revenge, for its defiance in withholding tribute.

FIFTY-TWO

*The ring came to rest on particular letters appropriate
to the questions put*
Ammianus Marcellinus, *The Histories*, c. 395

Anonymous in *cuculli* or hooded cloaks, the two figures – one stocky and muscular, the other tall and athletic – plunged ever deeper by torchlight into the squalid warren that was Rome's Fourth District, the Subura. Walled in by towering *insulae*, tall, badly built blocks which were forever catching fire or falling down, the narrow streets were clogged with filth and rubbish, infrequently removed by gangs of private refuse-collectors. Gone were the old public services that until fairly recently had maintained high levels of security and hygiene throughout the city's fourteen districts. Law and order, fighting fires, cleansing, and public health – all were now contracted out by the City Prefect to private concerns for whom profit was the priority, with corner-cutting and shoddy standards ever more widespread.

His hugely developed shoulders and forearms deterrents to any would-be mugger, the first of the pair threaded the maze of alleys with a sureness born of long familiarity, halting at last at the base of a huge tower which dwarfed all the buildings around it. This was the famous Insula of Felicula, the tallest structure in Rome, and as much a visitor attraction for Rome as the Pyramids were for Egypt.

'Legs and lungs in good shape, Serenity?' chuckled the man, his informal manner bordering on insolence. 'You'll be sorry if they're not – we're in for a climb of sixteen storeys.'

'You've been paid to do a job, Statarius, not talk,' snapped his companion, throwing back his hood to reveal the face of the Emperor. 'Just lead the way.'

'Whatever you say, Serenity,' responded the other, unabashed. 'Just trying to be friendly.'

Damn the fellow's presumption, thought Valentinian as he

followed the man up the steep stairwell. These swollen-headed charioteers, the darlings of the mob, considered themselves as good as anyone, even their Emperor. Still, lack of respect was a small price to pay for the assignation he was about to keep. If you wanted a nefarious deal arranged, a charioteer was always your best choice. This one, Statarius, 'Slowcoach' (the ironic nickname bestowed on account of his being the fastest driver in Rome), had been recommended for his network of shady contacts.

And nothing could be shadier than this present business. But Valentinian had been driven to it. All his life he had had to suffer the humiliation of being ruled by his mother and then Aetius. At least Placidia had always had his interests at heart, her prestige as the Augusta ensuring that he was accorded the deference his position as emperor demanded. But Placidia was dead, and the Patrician now treated him with open contempt, as though it were Aetius – a mere general – who ruled the West. Why, ambassadors and potentates addressed their missives directly to him, bypassing the court in Ravenna – as though the Emperor were a cipher who could be ignored, irrelevant to the conduct of affairs. It was insufferable. Worse, it surely meant that Valentinian stood in personal danger. With Placidia gone, what was there to prevent Aetius from taking that final step and seizing the purple for himself? If the empire's turbulent history proved anything, it was this: a dethroned emperor was never suffered to live. Hence this mission: to try to discover what fate the future held in store, for himself and for his Master of Soldiers. Maybe the Patrician's star was on the wane, the Emperor thought hopefully. Attila's death had removed the West's most pressing peril; and therefore perhaps the need for Aetius, as well.

Up, up, up, till at last they reached the sixteenth floor. Valentinian was pleased to note that his breathing was less laboured than his guide's. He was proud of his body, and careful to maintain it in peak condition by regular sessions in gymnasia. Statarius knocked at one of the doors on the landing. It was opened by a white-haired man, stooped and ancient but redeemed from any hint of decrepitude by a pair of glittering black eyes, which seemed to Valentinian to strip away his outward show of haughty indifference and lay bare the secrets of his soul.

'Niall MacCoull, Serenity,' announced Statarius, 'a Scot from Ireland. For some of these Celts, the veil separating this world from the next is very thin, enabling them to make contact with the world beyond the Styx – or should that be the Jordan?'

Telling Statarius to wait outside, Valentinian followed the old man into a dusty chamber, empty save for some flickering oil lamps, a truckle bed, a chest, and a curious apparatus standing in the middle of the floor.

'Right, let us begin,' declared the Emperor. He intended to appear masterful, but confronted by those penetrating eyes he felt unsure, inadequate, his words sounding in his ears like the shrill demand of a petulant schoolboy.

'In a little, sir,' replied the seer, politely but without subservience. 'First, I must attune myself with the Beyond, in the hope that some spirit may answer whatever questions you wish to put.' Closing his eyes, he commenced to mutter, in an unfamiliar tongue, a prayer or incantation.

Feeling uncharacteristically subdued and, now that the moment of truth had arrived, distinctly apprehensive, Valentinian moved to the room's one window, unshuttered this warm July night, and looked out over Rome. From a height of two hundred feet, illumined by the moon, a great western section of the sleeping city lay spread beneath him: the fora of four emperors, a forest of silvered pillars; the looming bulk of the Capitol; and beyond, bounded by a great loop of the Tiber, the shining levels of the Field of Mars studded with theatres, circuses, and baths, all transmuted by the moonlight into strange abstract shapes like demonstration models from a mathematician's study.

'It is time,' said the seer, opening his eyes. 'Come.'

Valentinian approached the apparatus in the centre of the chamber. It consisted of a circular metal plate engraved round the rim with the letters of the alphabet, and surmounted by a tripod from whose apex a ring was suspended by a thread. Setting the ring swinging in a circular motion, the diviner said, 'The auspices are favourable. Ask what you will.'

Valentinian licked lips which were suddenly dry; sweat sprang out on his palms. He opened his mouth to ask the question he had prepared but no sound issued from his throat. At the third attempt, the words came tumbling out in a rush: 'Who will die first, Aetius or myself?'

Disbelievingly, he watched as the ring interrupted its oscillation to make a tiny but palpable jerk as it came opposite the letter

'F', before continuing its circuit: 'L', 'A', and 'V'; the name could only be 'Flavius', thought Valentinian in horror, the first of his own names! Then he recalled that Aetius' *praenomen* was also Flavius. He would have to wait for the next name to become manifest, before—'Enough!' he cried hoarsely, overcome with sudden nameless fears. With a sweep of his arm he hurled the tripod to the floor, then he rushed in terror from the room.

Statarius would have to go, thought Valentinian, following the charioteer along the way back to the palace. Divination, sorcery, call it what you will – any attempt to foretell the future, or to influence the outcome of events by contacting the spirit world, was a capital offence. In the case of an emperor being involved, that could hardly apply; but, despite being in a sense above the law, emperors were still expected not to break it. As Ambrose had put it, 'The Emperor enacts laws which he is the first to keep.' Valentinian knew that emperors who continued to act unacceptably or tyrannically, or who openly flouted the will of the Senate, never died in their beds: Nero, Caligula, Commodus, Heliogabalus, Gallienus . . . The list was lengthy; and sobering. If news got out that Valentinian had been dabbling in the Black Arts, the loss of imperial prestige would be enormous. It might well lead to his being overtaken by the very fate he feared, but had just shrunk from discovering.

   Could Statarius be trusted to remain silent? Probably not. Charioteers were notoriously boastful and arrogant. To rely on the discretion of a man from that class would be to make himself a hostage to fortune – a risk he could not afford. An 'accident' would have to be arranged. Nothing obvious; Statarius was extremely popular, and suspicion of foul play would rouse the dangerous fury of the mob, the pampered underclass who, thanks to the state-funded dole, saw no necessity to work and lived only for the Circus and the Games. Valentinian recalled that in his grandfather Theodosius' time the imprisoning of a popular charioteer had had consequences that rocked the throne. Care and discretion must be his watchwords.

The stall gates of Rome's Circus Maximus flew open, and the four chariots representing the rival factions of the Blues, Greens, Whites, and Reds burst forth. Each driver strove to reach the inside track round the *spina*, the long barricade running down the centre of the Circus, which the chariots must circle seven times. The roar issuing from three hundred thousand throats was deafening, the loudest shouts coming from supporters of the Blues, the colour of Statarius. The vehicles thundered along the right-hand lane, swept round the *spina*'s far end, and hurtled down the opposing track. As they completed the second turn, *erectores* removed a dolphin and an egg from their respective crossbars at either end of the *spina*, signifying that the first lap had been run.

As the race continued, Statarius employed his favourite tactic of hanging back until an opportunity should present itself to cut in from behind, cross the path of the other chariots, and reach the inside track – an extremely dangerous manoeuvre, calling for the utmost skill and coolness. In the emperor's box, Valentinian began to gnaw his lip with worry. Four dolphins down and Statarius was still in the race. That fool of a *sparsor* in charge of cleaning the Blues' chariot, who had been bribed to saw partly through the shaft, must have botched the job.

The Emperor's anxious thoughts were distracted by a collective gasp from the crowd. Taking advantage of a momentary gap between the two chariots in front of him, Statarius urged his four horses to top speed, shot between the vehicles, and drew level with the leader. Then he laid his whip on the shoulder of his rear left-hand, horse. The best of the team, this was a *centenarius*, a horse which had won a hundred races. Swift and sure-footed, the *centenarius*, not yoked to the shaft but held only in traces, responded to the touch of the whip by surging forward, and swung in front of the other chariot. The two yoked centre horses, selected for their pulling power, maintained the momentum while the offside animal, running in traces like the *centenarius*, jerked the equipage round, co-ordinating the manoeuvre.

Suddenly, there was a loud crack as the shaft, subjected to tremendous stress, snapped where it had been weakened. Horses, driver, and chariot went down in a tangle of flailing limbs and splintering wood, which somersaulted twice before slamming against the *spina*. While attendants rushed out to clear up the *naufragium*, the 'shipwreck', Valentinian sent the editor of the Races, who was beside him in the imperial box, to find out how Statarius had fared. 'Dead, Serenity,' announced the man on his return. 'Killed outright – a broken neck.'

'Thank God,' breathed Valentinian, feeling himself go limp with relief.

'Serenity?' said the other in shocked amazement.

'I'm glad he did not suffer.'

The man's face cleared. 'I see, Serenity. Rome is indeed fortunate to have an Emperor who cares for the least of his subjects – even a mere slave and charioteer.'

FIFTY-THREE

You have acted like a man who cuts off his right hand with his left

An imperial adviser's reply to Valentinian III, on being
asked to approve the murder of Aetius, 454

Never have I seen Aetius so confident and positive [wrote
Titus in his journal, at the Palace of Commodus in Rome]
as in the days before he left for Rome to meet Valentinian.
This was to promote the plans – already well advanced –
for the marriage of his son Gaudentius with the Emperor's
daughter Eudocia, thus uniting the house of Aetius with the
royal line of Theodosius.

He was, despite everything, saddened, I suspect, to hear
of the untimely death last year of Attila, his greatest friend
turned bitterest foe. If so, he does not show it. Nor does
he openly express concern regarding a serious consequence
of Attila's removal from the stage of history. For, while
solving an immediate problem, the King's death has created
another, possibly even a greater. It was the terror Attila
inspired that enabled Aetius to unite the federates and
Romans in common cause. That threat has now passed. But
with an overstretched Roman army (its numbers much
reduced in consequence of the Battle of the Catalaunian
Plains) to deal with the federates should they again cause
trouble, can even a leader as inspired as Aetius maintain
control? Only time will tell.

Meanwhile, I made ready to journey from Aetius' base
at Lugdunum to Rome, ahead of the Patrician and his
retinue, to prepare lodgings and give notice to the palace
of his coming.

'Here's your pass to use the *cursus velox*,' Aetius told Titus, handing
him a scroll. 'Head down the Rhodanus to Arelate, then along
the coast via the Julia Augusta to its junction with the Via Aurelia

in Italy. After that follow the Aurelia to Rome – with relays of fast horses you should do it in a week. Make an appointment to see the Master of Offices and warn him of my coming; as the Emperor's in Rome, the court and Consistory will have moved there from Ravenna. Also get him to arrange an interview with the Praetorian prefect, who'll clear it with you to secure the use of Commodus' Palace for myself and my entourage.'

'Valentinian won't like it, sir,' observed Titus dubiously. 'Aren't the imperial palaces his personal property?'

Aetius shrugged. 'He may not like it, but that's immaterial. He knows he can't refuse a request from the Master of Soldiers. Anyway, Prefect Boethius is a friend of mine. He'll smooth things over if Valentinian proves difficult.' He glanced at a water-clock on a stand. 'Barely past the second hour.' He grinned and clapped Titus on the shoulder. 'With hard riding, you'll be in Arelate by sunset.'

In a chamber in the central, private, block of the Domus Augustana, Domitian's immense brick-faced concrete palace on Rome's Palatine Hill, Valentinian was ensconced with his *amicus principis*, his favourite, the eunuch Heraclius.

'Commandeering our Palace of Commodus,' fumed the emperor. 'The man's presumption knows no bounds! And, to add insult to injury, he dispenses with a formal request but sends instead a lackey, this agent Titus, to inform us he intends to requisition our property. Perhaps he thinks himself above his sovereign?'

'I would hesitate to say that he does not, Serenity,' replied Heraclius. 'I would advise you have a care for the safety of your person. Today the Palace of Commodus, tomorrow . . . the Palace of Domitian?' Smiling and plump, he spread his hands. 'Is Heraclius being too fanciful? I do not wish to cause Your Serenity undue alarm, but it would be wise, perhaps, not to dismiss such considerations lightly. Remember what happened to Gratian, and to the second emperor to bear your name – done away with by ambitious generals. It is no secret that Aetius intends to press the suit of his son Gaudentius for the hand of your daughter, the Princess Eudocia. One cannot but wonder: why is this of such importance to him? Should the union come to pass, and a male child be born . . .' He left the sentence hanging in the air.

'Don't fence with me, Heraclius,' snapped Valentinian. 'What is it you're suggesting?'

'Why, nothing, Serenity,' the eunuch replied smoothly. 'Merely observing that, as such a child would be of royal blood, Aetius might be tempted.'

'Tempted!' exclaimed Valentinian, turning pale. 'Tempted to usurp our throne in the name of his son or grandson? Is that what you're saying?'

'I'm saying Your Serenity should be careful,' said Heraclius in his soft, whispering voice. 'Just in case. Aetius, as we know, is no respecter of persons. He destroyed Boniface, he humiliated your mother, he rides roughshod over your decrees. Who knows what such a man might venture, to advance himself? I advise you, when you meet him, not to be alone or unarmed.'

'Thank you, Heraclius,' said the emperor. 'You are a loyal friend. If only all our ministers were as concerned for our welfare. You may leave us now. We shall ponder what you have said.'

The eunuch bowed and backed out of the chamber, a spiteful smile playing round his lips. Like his master, he had felt the lash of Aetius' scorn in the past. Perhaps the score could now be evened.

Handing his sword-belt to the duty *centenarius*, Aetius dimissed his bodyguard, a company of tough young Germans, hand-picked for their fighting skills, and all of proven loyalty and courage. Unarmed and alone, he advanced towards the gates of Domitian's Palace. As they swung open, he reflected that his agent Titus and others had cautioned him against seeing Valentinian without taking precautions for his own security. The Emperor was in an angry, suspicious, and unstable mood, they had said, and he had not concealed his resentment of the Patrician's presence in Rome. But Aetius had brushed the warnings aside. What could Valentinian possibly do to harm him? Shout? Threaten? If the Emperor attempted to arrest him, his bodyguard, as soon as they got wind, would make short work of Valentinian's – who were scorned as toy soldiers, for all their splendid uniforms.

Aetius strode to the entrance of the left-hand, official, block of the three that constituted the palace, whence he was conducted by a *silentiary*, one of the aristocrats who served as palace ushers, through the triclinium and peristyle into the audience chamber. This was a vast hall, ablaze with vari-coloured marble and lined with enormous statues. At the far end was Valentinian, enthroned. To Aetius' surprise, he was flanked by numerous courtiers and eunuchs, among the latter, the well-fleshed form of Heraclius.

For a moment, Aetius felt a twinge of unease; he had expected to meet the Emperor alone. Then his concern changed to contempt. Clearly, Valentinian felt intimidated and, to give himself moral support, had felt the need to surround himself with lick-spittle lackeys guaranteed to reinforce his every statement. For the moment, however, Aetius told himself, he must mask his true feelings. In a matter as delicate and important as a royal marriage, diplomacy above all was called for. He advanced with measured steps towards the throne, then, halting three paces before it, bowed his head.

'You have come, I suppose, to press your son's claim to our daughter's hand,' declared Valentinian in a loud voice, leaning forward in his throne.

'Hardly a claim, Serenity,' replied Aetius mildly; for once, in the knowledge that tact would help his cause, addressing the Emperor by his honorific title. 'The Princess Eudocia herself, I understand, desires the marriage as much as does Gaudentius.'

'Or as much as you do,' accused Valentinian. 'Are you sure the marriage reflects not more your own ambitions than our children's happiness?'

'What ambitions, Your Serenity?' asked Aetius, puzzled. 'Naturally, I would feel immensely proud if my family were to be joined with the illustrious House of Theodosius. But apart from the vicarious prestige I would gain thereby, I can see no advantage accruing to myself.'

'You lie!' shouted the Emperor. 'For you, the marriage would be but a first step to seizing the purple – if not for yourself, for your son, or your grandson should there be one. You would use the name of Theodosius to cloak your usurpation with legitimacy.'

'With respect, Serenity, that is nonsense,' protested Aetius. 'It is the empire, not myself, that would benefit from such a union. You yourself, to the sincere regret of all your subjects, have as yet no male heir. Should that, unfortunately, remain so, and should the union of my son with your daughter be blessed with male issue, the dynasty of Theodosius, which has lasted these seventy years, would be secure. That would mean stability, Serenity – a priceless boon. The soldiers welcome continuity because it guarantees security of pay and donatives. Thus the threat of usurpers plunging the empire into chaos – which has been the curse of Rome – must be very greatly lessened. Would I, who have dedicated my whole life to the preservation of the West, risk putting the state in jeopardy by making a bid for the throne?'

'You would!' shrieked Valentinian, spittle flying from his lips. 'Traitor, your smooth words do not deceive me. All along, you have robbed my mother and myself of the power that was rightly ours. But the final accolade, the purple and the diadem – those you shall never have.'

Drawing a sword concealed beneath his robes, Valentinian rushed at Aetius and plunged the blade into his breast. Immediately the whole swarm of imperial attendants, drawing hidden weapons, followed suit, hacking and thrusting like men possessed, in their eagerness to emulate their master. Moments later, blood gushing from a hundred wounds, Aetius fell dead at Valentinian's feet.

I have just heard the dreadful news that Aetius has been murdered [Titus wrote in the *Liber Rufinorum*]. I feel the loss almost as keenly as I did those of Gaius and Clothilde. He represented all the best of Rome – courage, honour, perseverance; to serve him has been the greatest privilege I could have sought. As for the vicious coward who struck him down, I can find no words strong enough to express my loathing and contempt.

Reports are coming in of a bloodbath at the palace: Aetius' friends summoned secretly then dispatched, Boethius the Praetorian prefect among them. Proclamations are being made throughout the city that Valentinian was provoked and killed Aetius in self-defence. No one believes them; Aetius' bodyguard swear that he was unarmed when he entered the palace, and, in their present mood of grief and fury, will not hold back from saying so. Rome is in uproar, and it would not surprise me to hear that the mob had stormed the Domus Augustana.

The consequences of the murder for the West will probably be catastrophic. Is there anyone who can take Aetius' place? The death-blow that Valentinian dealt him may prove to be the death-blow for the empire. I cannot write more at this time; my mind is too distracted by sorrow and confusion.

FIFTY-FOUR

His attendants also surrendered, considering it a disgrace to survive
their King* or not to die for him if the occasion required it
Ammianus Marcellinus, *The Histories, c.* 395

As Hercules slew the vile monster Cacus for his treachery
[Titus wrote in his journal], so Vadomar has avenged the
slaying of his master Aetius, by dispatching, in the thirty-
first year of his reign and the thirty-seventh of his worthless life, Valentinian, the third of that name, Emperor of
the Romans of the West. Some (though few, I think) will
call it murder; to me, it is no more than just retribution for
a heinous crime. Perhaps you've heard that the killing was
carried out by two Huns who had served Aetius, Optila and
Thraustila? Mere progaganda – a fabrication designed to
shield the palace guards from blame. Judge for yourselves.
I give you Vadomar's own story, just as he gave it to me.

I was born, I think (we Germans not being so nice in such
matters as you Romans), in the year when Gaiseric took
the Vandals into Africa, which makes me, at this time of
telling, twenty-five or twenty-six. My father was a farmer
and when need arose a warrior, in the country of Gundomad,
a lesser chief – or *regulus*, as you would say – of the
Alamanni. Unlike the Burgundians or even the Saxons, the
Alamanni, as the name tells you, are not one people but a
loose gathering of Hermunduri, Suebes and others, settled
in the old *agri decumanes* between the upper Rhenus and
the Danubius. Gundomar, whose stronghold of the Runder
Berg looks down upon the Nicer, is not a warlike lord, his
housecarles mainly time-served veterans who once fought

in the armies of Rome. To stay at home, then, held little hope of plunder or renown for bold young men. Being myself of a restless temper, and thinking a life of toil behind the plough little better than bondage, in my eighteenth year I joined the war-band of one Hermann, who led us across the Rhenus into the province of Maxima Sequanorum in eastern Gaul. This he was able to do unhindered. Half of Rome's great armies had been killed in the wars against the Goths, the losses being made up by stripping the empire's marches of their troops, leaving them unwarded.

Sadly, Hermann showed little of the cunning of his great namesake who, in the reign of your Emperor Augustus, destroyed Varus' legions in the Teutoburgerwald. From our camp in an abandoned villa, we raided the neighbouring countryside. To little gain. The land was empty, the Romans long ago having left their farms and villas for the safety of the towns. Instead of searching for unwasted parts of the province, or pressing on into mid-Gaul, Hermann, lured by the thought of easy booty, chose to lay siege to Argentaria.* It was a witless thing to do; Germans, as everyone knows, lack the skill or patience to take a place guarded by walls. He seemed to think the townsfolk would either soon give in or pay us gold to leave them be. When, after three weeks, neither of these things had happened, our war-band started to break up. Sullen and hungry, many of Hermann's followers drifted back across the Rhenus, he lacking the force to stop them. Unwilling to return home with nothing to show for ourselves, however, I and a boon comrade – a simple fellow, but loyal to a fault and who would gladly share his last crust with you – thought to seek our luck in the service of Rome. This has long been a worthy calling with our people. And so Vadomar and Gibvult began to seek out the whereabouts of the Army of Gaul. Which, after a weary trek across the Vosegus Gebirge then up the dales of the Mosella and Mosa, we found patrolling the marches of the Frankish Settlement in Second Belgica.

The Norns, who weave the web of men's lives, must that day have looked on us with favour. We were being taken

---

* Horburg in Alsace.

towards their camp by the sentries who spotted us when, as we entered a glade, there burst from the far side a huge boar, followed by a man on horseback with a levelled hunting-spear, a high Roman officer by his silvered armour. Seeing our party blocking his way, the boar turns at bay and charges his foe. Affrighted, the officer's steed rears and throws his rider. But before the boar's tushes can rend the helpless man, I hurl my spear – at handling which I am skilled through long usage. It strikes in the neck, making the brute stagger and fall. Before it can rise, Gibvult and I, racing to the spot, swiftly dispatch it.

The Roman officer, getting shakily to his feet, clasped our hands in turn. 'A close call,' he said with a wry grin. (Though he spoke in Latin, both Gibvult and myself had enough knowledge of that tongue from talking with the veterans at home, to understand him well enough.) 'But for you two, I would now be dead or badly wounded. I'm sorely in your debt. If there's any way within my power to repay that obligation . . . ?' He smiled and spread his hands.

When we told him our wish was to join the legions, he declared, 'Rome welcomes volunteers, especially brave young Germans. In these hard times few follow the Eagles from choice. But carrying a spear in the ranks? A poor reward for such a service as you've done today.' Borrowing tablets from the *biarchus* in charge of the sentries, he scratched a message on the wax and returned them to the man, saying, 'See that the general gets this.' He turned to us. 'A recommendation to the commander-in-chief that you be allowed to join his bodyguard.' Remounting nimbly, he waved and cantered off.

The *biarchus* whistled and shook his head solemnly. 'Well, you're in luck all right,' he said enviously. 'Know who that was? Only Count Majorian, that's who. Second-in-command to General Aetius, the man who runs the empire.'

And so we joined the Eagles. But before we could join Aetius' bodyguard of *bucellarii* – mostly Franks and Alamanni drawn from the *auxilia palatina* and *vexillationes palatinae*, the best units in the army – we had to undergo a time of training.

394

Some Germans (but only those who have never fought the Romans) think that, because at present Rome seems weak, her soldiers must be cowardly or badly trained. Having served in Rome's Army of Gaul, I can say with truth that this is not so. Along with other recruits, we were taught, both on foot and mounted, to use spear, sword, javelin, and lead-weighted darts, practising on wooden dummies, later against fellow soldiers using blunted weapons. We were drilled without pity till some recruits dropped on the parade-ground. That never happened to Gibvult or myself, thanks to our having practised hard with weapons from boyhood, like all Germans. Above all, we learnt discipline: to keep steady in formation, and to obey orders – that comes hard to Germans, which is why, in almost all our battles with the Romans, we have been the losers. You see, Titus Valerius, we Germans, unlike you Romans, have never trembled before a schoolmaster's rod. That is, I think, the reason why we are bolder in battle than you, but why your discipline is better. Anyway, having passed our training tests – with eagles held high, as they say – Gibvult and I joined the general's bodyguard. Splendid was the war-gear they gave us as full-fledged *bucellarii*: shirt of mail, helmet of the Greek or Attic type, which is stronger than the ridge-helmets worn by ordinary troops, *spatha* of fine Hispanic steel, tough oval shield made from layers of laminated wood, a lance, a spear.

As for Aetius, whom I accompanied on his last campaigns in Gaul and by whose side I fought on the Plains of Catalauni, this I can truly say: he was the best man I ever knew. Bold, frank, open-handed, never asking of another what he would not do himself, he was a leader such as Germans love to serve. Gladly would I have laid down my life for him when he met the Emperor in Rome. But that was not to be, for he entered the palace alone.

Truly is this Rome a mighty *Stadt*. Riding down the Flaminian Way, we (that is, Aetius with his bodyguard and a small train of officers and attendants) came to the city from the north, with the Tiber flowing to our right. Standing in the middle of a dreary plain, Rome is guarded by a high brick wall full twenty miles round,* made by order of Emperor Aurelian against inroads by my own tribe, the Alamanni. Passing beneath the portcullis of the Flaminian Gate, a great arch through the battlemented curtain with strong towers clad in white marble on either side, we kept on down the same road (now a street) past the huge drum of Augustus' tomb with two tall columns from Egypt standing before it, then through the Arch of Marcus Aurelius and under the mighty aqueduct called Aqua Virgo. (Understand, this being my first visit to the city, I did not then know the names of these buildings or anything about them, but found out later.)

And so, passing beneath the Mount of the Capitol crowned with stately buildings, we entered the famous Forum Romanum, surrounded by more temples, basilicas, and statues than I could number. Our path then led along the Sacred Way beneath the Palatine Hill, and through the Arch of Titus to the Colosseum, the biggest thing made by man that I have yet seen. How, I asked myself, to find words to tell of such a marvel? Then beside me, lost in wonder, Gibvult breathed, 'It's a cheese – a great cheese!' I cuffed him playfully and made to mock him for an ignorant barbarian, when it struck me of a sudden he was right. A monstrous cheese is truly what the Colosseum looks like – well, from a distance, anyway. But such a cheese as might have graced the board of Odin.

From the Amphitheatre of the Flavians it was but two hundred paces to where we were to stay, the Palace of Commodus, Aetius having sent ahead to make sure the place was ready against our arrival. (You, Titus, were the messenger on that occasion I believe.) What Valentinian thought of this 'borrowing' of imperial property (which was like to add to the tally of his grievances against the Patrician), I can only guess.

For Gibvult and myself, who thus far had known only the rough life of the backwoods village or the camp, it was strange indeed to eat in marble halls and sleep on beds of down. Aetius, who was a hard taskmaster when need arose,

---

* In large measure impressively intact today.

but an easy one when things were quiet, while making preparation for his meeting with the Emperor (of whose purpose we of course knew nothing) gave his bodyguard leave to see the sights of Rome, taking turns to do duty at the palace. I could fill a book (if I could write) telling of the wonders of the city. But that would weary you, Titus, my friend, so I shall speak only of those things that struck me most: the Colosseum (which I have already touched on); the Baths of Caracalla and of Diocletian, the size of towns in Gaul; the Circus Maximus near half a mile in length; the Forum of Trajan flanked by a wondrous mall with covered markets, shops, and galleries; the Pantheon's stupendous dome; the Basilica of St Peter below Mount Vaticanus outside the Walls, the empire's greatest church they say; the Insula of Felicula, a gigantic tower block out-topping Trajan's column and accounted one of the wonders of the Roman world; above all, the mighty aqueducts snaking through the city like Orms* above the rooftops.

Such works, it almost seemed to me, mere men could not have wrought, but only Gods or giants. They made me wonder: how was it that the people who had made such marvels could let their city, which even Hannibal had not dared assault, be taken by the Goths? (Though, saving a few great villas on the Caelian which – too badly damaged to be restored to their former state – have been patched up and made to serve as hospices, there's little sign today of the Great Sack, which many Romans still recall.) The pagans say that Rome's luck went out with the closing of the temples, which made the Gods withdraw their favour. However that may be, one thing is sure: the folk of Rome today show little of the hardy spirit of their forebears, who conquered Carthage, then the world.

Each day you can see crowds of poor (and shamefully the not so poor) gathering on steps throughout the city to await a dole of bread, pork (in season), and oil. This any free head of family can claim by showing a little slip called a *tessera*. Fed by the state, these pampered leeches show little wish to work, but spend their days in the baths (to which a trifling

---

* In Teutonic mythology, Orms or Worms were giant serpents.

coin gains entry), where they mingle freely with the great and wealthy. Or, if Games are being held in the Circus or arena at the Emperor's expense (or of the quaestors, praetors, senators, and consuls), they live for nothing but betting on the outcome. Huge sums are spent on these shows, one given by Petronius Maximus (about whom more hereafter) costing, I've been told, four thousand pounds of gold.

But do not the patricians set the plebs (for such in olden times were called the higher and lower ranks of citizen now termed *honestiores* and *humiliores*) a good example of behaviour? Rather, the opposite is true. The nobles think only of pleasure and display, flaunting their wealth in rich apparel and carriages of gold or silver, which they drive at furious speed around the city, careless of harming passers-by.

Touching on which, Gibvult and I caused pride to have a fall. We were strolling in one of the narrow streets of the district called Subura, when towards us, whirling along at breakneck speed came one of these equipages driven by a youth in billowing silken robes. Scattering before this would-be Diocles,* folk leapt for safety into alley-mouths and doorways. A glance between my friend and me decided us to teach this arrogant puppy a lesson.

Scorning to jump aside, we stood our ground – though on my part, I confess, with a thumping heart. The horse, though a noble animal, is not (save for endurance) a brave one. Confronted, his nature is to flee, as Gibvult and I had learnt when practising cavalry tactics against ranked infantry. Sure enough, the matched pair drawing the conveyance reared up before us, pawing the air and pitching the driver from his seat; his fall was broken by his landing in a pile of ordure. Grabbing the horses' bridles, we pulled their heads down and calmed them. Then, laughing, we walked past the prostrate youth, who was dashing filth from his face and screaming threats. Little we cared; Rome's *vigiles*, the urban cohorts, had been disbanded and replaced by *vicomagistri*, nightwatchmen. Anyway, who would dare arrest two bold young Germans in the service of the Master of Soldiers?

---

* A famous charioteer, the first to win a thousand races.

Came the day of Aetius' meeting with the Emperor. We of his bodyguard escorted him to the Palace of Domitian, an awesome block of brick-faced concrete on the Palatine. Leaving us at the gates, Aetius removed the baldric holding his sword (no weapons being permitted in the presence of the Emperor) and gave it to our *centenarius*.

'Stand easy, lads,' he said. 'I'll be at least two hours; so you can be free until the fifth. You two' – he pretended to glare at Gibvult and myself, and shook his head in mock reproof – 'try and stay out of trouble till then. Oh yes,' he continued with a grin, 'I heard about your little escapade in the Subura.' Then, addressing the whole company, 'Fifth hour, remember. Dismiss.' And with a casual wave, he strode off through the palace gates, which the imperial guards, recognizing him, had already opened.

It was the last time I ever saw him.

As, about an hour later, Gibvult and I were wandering among the stalls of the Forum Boarium, I became aware of a distant murmur from the Palatine Hill above us. The murmur grew and spread, became a swelling roar: the sound of many voices raised in query and concern. Suddenly the crowds around us were caught up in the clamour; a chill struck my heart as I began to pick out phrases: 'He's dead . . . Who's dead? . . . They say it's the Patrician . . . murdered by the Emperor himself . . . I heard it was Boethius, the Prefect . . . No, it was Aetius I tell you – slain by Valentinian's own hand . . .'

I stood in frozen disbelief while the rumours dinned in my ears and the world seemed to swim around me. Then Gibvult and I were running towards the source of the noise, barging through the shouting throng. We found an angry mob gathering outside Domitian's Palace. Behind the locked gates a triple row of white-faced guards stood with levelled spears. A group of Aetius' bodyguard were dragging a beam from a nearby building-site, clearly meaning to use it as a ram to force the gates.

'Drop it!' Crackling with authority, the voice of our *centenarius* cut through the uproar, and he positioned himself in front of the gates. 'You want to break through these? You'll have to start with me. In an hour I'll be taking a roll-call back at our quarters. Anyone not on it –' his eyes, charged with flinty menace, surveyed the bodyguard – 'will be on a charge. Spread the word. Get moving – *now.*'

No one missed the roll-call. Afterwards, the *centenarius*, struggling to master strong emotions, addressed us confidentially. 'The rumours are true, lads: the Patrician's dead. And yes, before you ask, it was indeed the Emperor who killed him. And no, there's nothing you or anyone can do about it, because the Emperor's above the law.'

Angry shouts broke out: 'He shouldn't get away with it . . . Aetius was worth ten of him . . . Bad emperors have been dealt with before – think of Attalus and Iohannes.'

The *centenarius* let the fury and resentment burn themselves out, then raised his hand for silence. 'I feel the same about this as you do, lads,' he said. 'Removing the dog-tag on its thong from around his neck, he held it up. 'You were all given one of these when you joined the army. And you also had to swear an oath, to be – well, come on; let's hear it.'

'Loyal to the Emperor,' came the mumbled response.

'Good. Remember it.' After a pause, he went on musingly, 'Of course, if anything – God forbid – *were* to happen to Valentinian, I suppose you'd just have to swear loyalty to whoever took the purple.' He winked, then added, 'You didn't hear that last bit, by the way. Dismiss.'

During the weeks and months that followed, a tense calm seemed to grip the city. While continuing to occupy our quarters in Commodus' Palace, we heard that, beside Aetius, Boethius, the Praetorian Prefect, had been murdered; also the Patrician's closest friends and associates. Recalling the dark days of Sulla, proscription lists of 'traitors' were posted, and at the same time public announcements (which nobody believed) proclaimed the Emperor's deliverance from a dastardly plot to overthrow him, and praised his courage in turning the tables on a would-be assassin. As to why the Emperor had really murdered the unarmed Patrician we could only guess, but jealousy and spite were thought to play a large part. As common soldiers, we of the bodyguard were safe enough, we thought – so long as we kept our heads down, as our *centenarius* never tired of reminding us.

With Placidia and now Aetius dead, who was running the empire? Now that Valentinian was spending more time in Rome than in Ravenna, would the whole machinery of government be transferred? Who would be the new Master of Soldiers? (Avitus was heavily tipped.) And, whoever it turned out to be, would he still require our services, or would he choose his own escort? No one seemed to know the answers to these questions. Yet the wheels of the administration kept turning – creakily, it must be said, but they turned. Our pay was often in arrears but we always got it eventually. I believe that this was due, in part at least, to the persistence of one of Aetius' *agentes in rebus*, in reminding the paymaster of our existence. (Now who, Titus, could that agent have been, I wonder?)

Perhaps the strangest thing of all at this strange time was the regaining of some of its ancient power by the Senate. The Senate, that toothless tiger, whose only function these four hundred years had been to legitimize who came to power! But with Valentinian (now the most hated man in the empire) cowering in his palace, someone had to make decisions, and that someone could only be, collectively, the Senate. Chief spokesman of this august assembly was one Petronius Maximus, about whom, because he was about to play such a large part in my life, I shall now tell you something.

Petronius Maximus: wealthy senator, twice consul, thrice Praetorian prefect of Italy, member of the ancient and famous Anician family, cultured man of letters, liberal patron, generous host, popular with all – could this cornucopia of distinctions be held by just one man? The answer, if that man happened to be Petronius Maximus, was that it could.

My first meeting with him came about in this way. The bodyguard was having its midday *prandium* of bread and cold meat, when a *biarchus* appeared and summoned Gibvult and myself. We followed him out of the palace to where a Nubian slave was waiting. 'You're to go with this fellow,' said the *biarchus*. 'Seems some senator wants to see you; don't ask me why.'

Mystified and not a little curious, we followed the slave through narrow streets, up the slopes of the Caelian, beneath the arches of the Claudian Aqueduct, and through the old Servian Wall into the Fifth District, one of the most salubrious in the City. Soon after, we entered a private square adorned with statues, which fronted an imposing mansion. We were led through a number of halls opening one into another, in the fifth of which, the *tablinum*, we halted. It was a spacious room, with pigeon-holes and open cupboards filled with scrolls and codices. Scant furniture, but what there was was beautifully crafted in metal or rare woods. Wall-niches held one or two fine bronzes.

In the midst of this austere elegance, a middle-aged man in a plain but expensive dalmatic was seated writing at a table. He waved us to a bench and kept on writing for a little longer, then, consulting a water-clock beside him, laid down his stylus and looked up. A strong Roman face beneath a full head of well-groomed silver hair. 'Four hours for study, four for writing, four for friends and relaxation, four for business,' he said with a smile. 'These make up my day, aside from sleep. Each must get its due – no more, no less. I am Petronius Maximus. You've heard of me perchance?'

If anyone had not, he must be either deaf or witless. Everyone, even we uncouth Germans, knew of the great senator. 'Who in Rome has not, Your Gloriousness?' I replied, using the correct if absurd-sounding form of address.

'Fronto, bring wine for our guests,' he told the slave, then, turning to ourselves, 'You must be wondering why I sent for you.' He eyed us appraisingly. 'I require a certain task to be carried out, for which I require two suitable young men. They must be brave, know how to handle themselves, and above all be trustworthy. I made enquiries of your *centenarius*; he recommended you two above all others in your unit. Also, it came to my ears that you clipped the wings of a certain young blood – my nephew, actually – driving at reckless speed through the Subura. I applaud; the young puppy needed taking down a peg. More importantly, it tells me you're the sort of men I'm looking for. It takes courage to halt a galloping pair. Forgive me if I ask a personal question: what is your present rate of pay?'

'Thirty *solidi* per annum,' I replied, intrigued. 'Plus rations, uniform, and fodder for our mounts.'

'Would you be interested in trebling that?'

Gibvult and I exchanged the briefest of glances. 'We'd be interested,' we said in chorus. 'Provisionally,' I added. Where was the catch? I wondered. For that sort of money, there had to be one.

At that moment, Fronto returned bearing a tray on which were a silver flagon and two glass drinking-vessels decorated with hunting scenes in relief. Placing the tray on a table, Fronto filled the glasses, handed one to me, and was in the act of passing the other to Gibvult, when it slipped from his hand to smash on the mosaic floor. He began to tremble, and his skin turned from black to dusky grey.

'Oh, Fronto,' murmured Maximus, shaking his head, the angry glitter in his eyes belying the mildness of his tone. 'My Rhenish beakers – irreplaceable.'

The mess was quickly cleared up and Gibvult supplied with a fresh tumblerful, but the trivial incident had taught me several things about our host. I realized as I sipped my wine – vinegary stuff from the Vatican vineries – that he thought Gibvult and myself unsophisticated barbarians who would neither notice that they were being fobbed off with an inferior vintage, nor expect it to be diluted with water in the Roman fashion. The reactions of Maximus and his slave to the breaking of the beaker showed that Fronto could expect to be severely punished. Maximus clearly had an arrogant, mean, and cruel streak, which gave the lie to his reputation for benevolent urbanity.

'What would this task involve, Your Gloriousness?' I enquired.

'For a start, a transfer from your present unit to the *scholae*, the imperial bodyguard. An enviable advancement, most would think.'

'What, serve Valentinian?' I exclaimed in outrage. I stood up, as did Gibvult, his face suddenly gone red. 'I'm afraid, Senator, you've chosen the wrong men.'

To my amazement, Maximus beamed delightedly. 'Splendid,' he declared. 'Just the reaction I hoped for; you've proved beyond doubt your loyalty to your murdered master, Aetius. Please hear me out. I will explain.'

Whatever strings Maximus pulled to secure entry for Gibvult and myself to the *scholae* (mainly sprigs of noble families), we were not to know; for a man of his influence it would not be difficult, I think. Suffice to say that a week from our meeting with the great man, we were reporting for duty with the *scholae* at Domitian's Palace. We were issued with splendid parade armour: muscled cuirass and crested helmet, fashioned by the *barbaricarii*, smiths who normally made armour only for officers. Our duties were light: mainly standing outside the main entrance to the palace looking impressive, or escorting the emperor on the rare occasions when he left it. At first, some of our new comrades tried to make mock of us, resenting us as low-born upstarts, I suppose. However, in a fight arranged on waste ground in the Fourteenth District, Transtiberina, Gibvult and I demolished their two champions. After that, we were accepted.

As for the task for which we had been chosen, our only instructions at this time were that we note the Emperor's behaviour towards his wife, the Augusta Eudoxia, a kind and gentle lady, daughter of Theodosius, the late Eastern Emperor. Maximus had assured us that the purpose of our posting to the *scholae* was not to serve the Emperor but to help see justice done for the memory of Aetius; details would be disclosed to us later. On no account were we to communicate with the senator; he would make contact and give further instructions in due course. Although Maximus, accompanied by his beautiful wife, was a frequent guest at the palace, neither by word nor look did he ever acknowledge our presence.

Then, early in the year following that of Aetius' murder, the summons came. Gibvult and I were off duty in our barracks when a slave arrived from Maximus, requesting that we accompany him to his master's villa.

'Your duties at the palace are congenial, I trust?' asked the senator, when we were ensconced once more in his *tablinum*.

'I've no complaints, Your Gloriousness,' I said. 'They're hardly taxing, after all.'

'*Ja, sehr gut,*' confirmed Gibvult, whose command of

Latin was rather less than mine, causing him to lapse at times into German.

'And the Empress?'

'He neglects her, although clearly she loves him; why, I can't imagine. I've hardly once heard him address a civil word to her.'

'He treat her shameful – worse than a *Hund*,' declared Gibvult hotly. 'In Germany, such a man would be *Ausgestossene*, outcast. And she such a kind lady, always with smile or *Trinkgeld* for us *Soldaten*.'

'I see,' mused Maximus. 'Your opinion, then, would be that the marriage is a sham – at least on the Emperor's side; that Valentinian no longer has any interest in his wife?'

'That is correct,' I said. I sensed that, bizarrely, the senator was pleased by this intelligence.

'So presumably he looks elsewhere to gratify his desires?'

'I've no means of knowing,' I said. Where was all this leading? 'The *scholae* are never with the Emperor on any occasion that could be termed intimate. You'd have to ask the palace eunuchs – especially Heraclius, who has the emperor's ear. But I'd be surprised if you weren't right, Your Gloriousness. After all, Valentinian's fit, healthy, and still young.'

Maximus rose and began to pace the room, then halted and stood with furrowed brow, lost in thought. Eventually, 'You have proved yourselves both discreet and reliable,' he said in a low voice, almost as if he were speaking to himself. He turned to face us. 'The time has come to take you into my confidence. I'm sure you need no reminding that anything I say must go no further than these walls.'

Gibvult and I assured him that our lips were sealed.

'Then I must tell you this: the Emperor has begun to cast lustful eyes on my wife. She is the soul of honour and fidelity, and would never willingly betray the marriage bed. But that would not deter Valentinian, for whom to desire something is but the prelude to possessing it. He has no honour and would not scruple to force himself upon my wife, if he could find the opportunity. Despite my high position, how could I prevent him? After all, he is the Emperor.'

Gibvult and I exchanged concerned glances. To be party to this knowledge was horribly dangerous.

Maximus must have noticed, for he continued, 'Why am I telling you all this? I will keep nothing from you. Should Valentinian succeed in ravishing my wife, I would be compelled to uphold the honour of my *gens*, the Anicii.'

'By disposing of the Emperor?' I suggested bluntly.

Maximus gave a wry half-smile, then shrugged. 'As a Roman, and Anician to boot, I would have no choice.'

'And we would do the "disposing",' I observed sourly, as realization dawned. Maximus was planning nothing less then seizing the purple for himself – a move which might well succeed, given Valentinian's huge unpopularity. Avenging his wife's honour would give Maximus a convincing motive for killing Valentinian, as well as being guaranteed to enlist public sympathy. I could see it all clearly. The information we had given the senator, slight though it was, had convinced him that the time was ripe to use his wife as bait for Valentinian's lust. Gibvult and myself, chosen because of our proven loyalty to Aetius and, I suppose, our boldness, were simply to be convenient tools to implement the deed. Well, no matter. If falling in with the senator's plans, however base, would enable us to avenge our beloved leader, we could ask for no greater privilege. I looked at Gibvult, and we both nodded.

I turned to Maximus. 'Whenever you are ready,' I declared heavily.

'Excellent; we understand each other, then,' he returned briskly. 'Instructions will be given you in due course. Meanwhile, you will carry on as normal with your duties at the palace.' He shot us a calculating glance. 'Never fear – you'll both be well rewarded.'

Something snapped inside me. 'You Romans think that everything must have its price!' I heard myself shout. 'Can't you realize that some things are done for honour's sake alone? Come, Gibvult.' And turning on our heels we marched from the *tablinum*.

Soon after that second meeting with Maximus, Rome was rocked by a scandal, the details of which the senator did nothing to conceal; in fact, short of putting up posters, he did everything he could to publicize them. What happened was this. In a gaming session with the Emperor, Maximus lost heavily – more than he could afford to settle on the spot. Valentinian insisted that the senator surrender his signet ring as a pledge that he would repay the debt. Following the incident, Valentinian had a message sent to Maximus' wife purporting to come from her husband (together with the ring as proof of identity). She should come at once to the palace to attend the Empress Eudoxia on some urgent business. Unsuspecting, Maximus' wife complied. On arrival at the palace, she was taken to a remote bedchamber where she was raped by Valentinian. Predictably, when word got out (as Maximus made sure it would), the Emperor's stock plumbed even lower depths.

Despite the scandal, in a gesture of defiance in the face of public opinion, the Emperor announced that he intended shortly to open, in person, a display of military Games to be held in the Campus Martius – a great plain in the west of Rome, between the Tiber and the city's hills. The day before the event, I was approached by one of Maximus' slaves, who handed me a note. It contained five words: 'When he drops the *mappa*.'

My pulses quickening, I sought out Gibvult. 'Tomorrow the Emperor will start the Games by dropping a white cloth,' I told him. 'That's when we strike.'

He took the news calmly. 'Better make sure we're picked for duty, then,' he grunted, without looking up from the task he was engaged in – buffing up his cuirass with a paste of fine sand and vinegar. 'And check our swords are keen.'

Because of the extra spit-and-polish involved, attendance at ceremonial occasions was not exactly welcomed by members of the *scholae*; so it was easy enough to ensure our names were on the duty roster.

It was a cool, bright, mid-March morning when the procession set out from the Palatine, the Imperial couple accompanied by the guard and followed by a train of courtiers and attendants. Along the Sacred Way we passed through the Forum Romanum, where we were joined by the Senate (headed by Maximus), resplendent in their archaic togas, then below the Capitol, and on up the Flaminian Way.

Turning left off the great street at the Arch of Diocletian, we headed into the Campus Martius past the Pantheon and the Stadium of Domitian, to a roped-off open area where the contestants were assembled. The first event was to be a display of mounted archery by units of the *vexillationes palatinae*, the cream of the cavalry. The participants began lining up a hundred paces from a row of targets, which they would gallop towards, then shoot at as they passed.

Accompanied by Heraclius, and flanked by select members of the *scholae* (which I had made sure included Gibvult and myself), Valentinian mounted the steps of the podium. He took the white cloth that Heraclius handed him, and raised it aloft. I have to admit that, vile degenerate though he may have been, he was certainly imposing. With the purple robe and glittering diadem setting off his tall, athletic figure, he looked every inch a Roman emperor.

'Let's take Heraclius as well,' Gibvult whispered. I nodded, my heart beginning to thump violently. Everyone knew that Heraclius had poisoned Valentinian's mind against the Patrician. But for the eunuch, Aetius would still be living.

The *mappa* dropped.

Time seemed to freeze as we drew our swords and closed on Valentinian. He turned towards us, hand still uplifted, eyes widening in shock as the glittering blades moved towards his breast. I was vaguely aware of the riders surging forward from the starting-line, the crowd rising, mouths opening to shout encouragement. The illusion of time slowing lasted a mere heartbeat; I felt my sword jar briefly against bone, then it slid deep into Valentinian's chest. I wrenched it free, blood spurting from the wound, saw Gibvult withdraw his own reddened blade. With a choking, gurgling cry, Valentinian staggered and collapsed. Stepping over the dying Emperor, we cut down Heraclius before he had grasped what was happening. At our feet, the two figures twitched briefly, then were still.

Slowly, the hubbub of the crowd died away as news of the killing spread. Then the vast silence was broken by a stentorian voice, that of Maximus: 'People of Rome, you are free. The tyrant Valentinian is dead.'*

A mighty shout (clearly pre-arranged) issued from the assembled ranks of senators: 'Romans, behold your new Augustus, Petronius Maximus.'

A brief pause, then from the packed multitude arose a swelling roar, 'Maximus Augustus! Maximus Augustus! Maximus Augustus!'

With the permission of the new Emperor (whose purpose anyway we had served), we left the *scholae* and, having had our fill of Rome and Romans, prepared to return to our homes in Germania. But before departing, we received a message that one Titus Valerius Rufinus, who had been an officer on Aetius' staff, desired to see us. It could do no harm, we thought. We decided I should speak for both of us, and the meeting was arranged.

The rest you know, Titus Valerius, my friend.

My tale is done [wrote Titus in the *Liber Rufinorum*], as will soon be Rome's, if Romulus' vision should prove true. The twelve vultures he saw represented, according to the augur Vettius, the twelve centuries assigned to the lifetime of his city. Fable that may be, yet I cannot think the Empire of the West will long outlive the man whose genius alone for so long nourished hope for its survival. Maximus is no Aurelian to subdue the barbarians and restore the state. Already, in Gaul the Franks and Visigoths begin to push beyond their boundaries, and our army there is starved of men and resources to contain them. Hispania is ravaged by Bagaudae and the Sueves, Africa in Vandal hands, Britain lost beyond recovery. Only Italia, Provincia, and central Gaul remain inviolate. But for how long? Our armies dwindle by the day; the Treasury is empty; we look to the East for aid – which does not come.

* On 16 March 455, by an eerie coincidence almost exactly five centuries to the year and the day from the murder of Julius Caesar, on the Ides (15th) of March 44 BC.

Let my son Marcus, if that should be his wish, take up this history where I leave off. But it is to Constantinople, not Ravenna, that he must turn his eyes. West Rome may fall, but East Rome will live on. *Vale*.

AFTERWORD

The murder of Valentinian III ended the Theodosian dynasty which, for all its defects, did provide a measure of stability to the crumbling Roman state. Deprived of the inspired leadership of 'the great safety of the Western Empire', as a Byzantine chronicler has described Aetius, that empire entered its terminal decline. Valentinian's successor, Petronius Maximus, lasted barely three months before being lynched by an angry mob, as he prepared to flee Rome ahead of a Vandal assault on the city.* He was briefly followed by Avitus, who had served Aetius so well in Gaul but who, falling foul of the Senate (enjoying a temporary, astonishing revival of its power) was sentenced to death by that assembly. Next, German warlords proceeded to set up a succession of puppet emperors (of whom Majorian, another former colleague of Aetius, alone showed any promise), the last of whom, Romulus Augustus (sic!) was deposed in 476, bringing to an end the Roman Empire in the West.

Gaiseric, who contributed more to the destruction of the West than any other individual, outlasted that empire by a single year. Like the Huns', the Vandals' legacy was entirely negative, their name linked for ever with cruelty and destruction. Two generations after Gaiseric's death, they were routed by the East Roman army of Justinian and, like the Huns, wiped from the slate of history. (After Attila's death, the Hun Empire rapidly disintegrated, leaving no mark on posterity except a memory of massacre and devastation with which the name of Attila, 'the Scourge of God' will ever be associated.)

Was the work of Aetius, then, all for nothing? By no means. Although he probably appeared too late on the scene to rescue the Western Empire, not only did he save Europe from Asiatic domination, but his career helped to make possible the future harmonious co-existence between Germans and Romans within

---

* This resulted in a second (and much more destructive than that of 410) Sack of Rome.

the limits of the former empire. The Catalaunian Plains was the Western Empire's greatest (although final) triumph. The victory was due to a new development of seminal importance: Romans and Germans *combining* to repel a common enemy. This contrasts with previous Roman policy towards federate 'guests': reluctant toleration and containment as with the Visigoths and Franks or, in the case of the Burgundians, military suppression. Henceforth, the political dynamic lay with the constructive interaction between the two peoples, a process which survived the dissolution of the empire itself.

The conversion of the Frankish king Clovis to Catholicism in 498 – an example followed eventually by other German monarchs – removed the last major barrier to co-operation between Germans and Romans. (Hitherto, the Franks, like other German tribes, had been Arian Christians, heretics in Roman eyes.) Aetius laid the foundation on which Theoderic (no connection with the Visigothic kings of that name) was able to build his successful Romano-German synthesis in Ostrogothic Italy. This, despite renewed conflict between the two peoples in the course of Justinian's re-occupation of the West, was to prove a lasting achievement. From it developed European medieval civilization, embodied politically in the empire of Charlemagne and the Holy Roman Empire, whose heir is, arguably, the European Union.

The two thousand years of the Christian era have been significantly occupied by Rome. The Western Empire lasted almost a quarter of that period, the Eastern nearly three-quarters, surviving (admittedly in increasingly attenuated form) until 1453 – less than two generations before the birth of Henry VIII, which, in the long perspective of history, is the day before yesterday. Rome's influence on architecture, law, languages, ideas, the arts, religion, government, etcetera, etcetera, has been immeasurable – and lasting. To take just one example: for nearly two centuries British India was ruled by classically educated young men, who took as their model for government that of Imperial Rome; on the whole, whatever one thinks of the morality of imperialism, they made a pretty good fist of running the subcontinent. Rome's legacy has, in the main, been a noble one, whose preservation and transfer owes not a little to Aetius – 'the last of the Romans', as Procopius described him.

AUTHOR'S NOTE

Regarding the history of the Roman Empire in the fifth century, we know pretty well *what* happened, but not always why or how it happened. This requires the writer of historical fiction to flesh out the skeleton of available fact with speculation as to the motivation and personality traits of real persons. For example, we don't know if Attila planned to build a 'Greater Scythia', as I have suggested. But it is at least arguable that he might have done. Great military leaders have tended to harbour ambitions beyond the mere acquisition of plunder and territory – Alexander and Napoleon, for instance.

Such creative guesswork aside, I have, except in a few instances, kept to the known historical facts as closely as possible. (The story of Attila and Aetius is so extraordinary and dramatic in itself that it needs little in the way of embellishment.) The exceptions are as follows. The Burgundians have been relocated to Savoy a few years before this actually happened. My character Constantius is a conflation of two real persons of that name. Even Gibbon admits that the two Constantii 'from the similar events of their lives might have been easily confounded'; so I don't feel too guilty about uniting them. I have made him the key figure in Chrysaphius' plot to have Attila murdered, rather than Edecon or Bigilas (Vigilias), the two agents most closely involved in the conspiracy. Ambrosius' meeting with Germanus is conjectural, but certainly within the bounds of possibility when the difficulty in precisely dating events in Britain for this period, is borne in mind. According to some scholars (Winbolt, Musset, *et al.*), Ambrosius was active in the early to mid-fifth century; others (e.g., Cleary) place him late in that century. Like Aetius, Ambrosius Aurelianus (sometimes given as Aurelius Ambrosius), who is thought to have come from a consular family, has earned the epithet 'the last of the Romans'. The estimated date of Germanus' second visit to Britain (440–44) virtually coincides with that for the third appeal for help to Aetius (445), permitting, I think, a

413

fictional conjunction. Irnac I have presented as a child rather than the young man whom Priscus saw. And Daniel, Constantinople's 'pillar-saint', I have placed on his column ten years before he first sat on it. In addition, I have made a few minor changes to topography: part of the necropolis of Tarquinii (the Etruscans' southern capital) has been translated a hundred miles north – but still within Etruria – to the valley of the Garfagnana; in Gaius' transit of the Black Forest I have telescoped one or two features (for instance, bringing the Triberg Falls a few miles further south), and have relocated the Himmelreich from the western to the eastern end of the Höllenthal. The above changes were made in the interests of dramatic emphasis or rounded storytelling, and on that count are hopefully excusable.

As for sources, Gibbon's *Decline and Fall of the Roman Empire* (still the most vivid and readable general account), E. A. Thompson's *A History of Attila and the Huns*, and *The Later Roman Empire* by my old lecturer, A. H. M. Jones, were essential background reading. Of the many books kindly lent to me by my co-publisher Hugh Andrew, the following were especially valuable: *Fifth-Century Gaul: A Crisis of Identity*, a series of papers edited by John Drinkwater and Hugh Elton; *The Early Germans* by Malcolm Todd; Peter Brown's *The World of Late Antiquity*; *The Germanic Invasions* by Lucien Musset; and – a real treasure – *The Rome that Did Not Fall* by Stephen Williams and Gerard Friell. Some primary sources that I found extremely useful were: *Notitia Dignitatum*, a list of senior army and civil posts with units, for both halves of the empire, compiled *c*. 400; *The Histories* of Ammianus Marcellinus, which gives a marvellous picture of the late Roman world in the period just before that of my story; Ptolemy's *Geographia*; and excerpts from the *Byzantine History* of Priscus of Panium, which includes an eye-witness account of the Eastern embassy's visit to Attila's court.

R. L.

APPENDIX I

DID ATTILA REALLY DESERVE HIS SOUBRIQUET 'THE SCOURGE OF GOD'?

The received understanding of Attila's soubriquet *Flagellum Dei*, the Scourge of God, is of a ruthless barbarian leader heading a horde of bloodthirsty savages on a rampage through the Roman Empire. There is an undeniable element of truth in that image. To contemporaries, however, the epithet had a somewhat different meaning. Attila was seen as just retribution sent by God to chastise the Christian Romans for some (unspecified) collective fault or omission. Catastrophes, whether caused by man or nature, then tended to be regarded as the consequence of divine disapproval. Which perhaps lends a fresh perspective to the interpretation of Attila's nickname. Had Attila been Christian instead of heathen, would he still have been seen as the Scourge of God? It's a moot point. The Vandal monarch Gaiseric, who *was* Christian, and whose tally of destruction and atrocities was not so very inferior to Attila's, was never known by anything other than his own name.

Judged by the standards of the ancient world, Attila may not have been quite the monster he appears to us. 'Greatness' in that world tended to be equated with scale of conquest, large numbers of enemy killed or enslaved being a bonus – vide Alexander 'the Great', Pompey 'the Great', *et al*. One condition of a Roman general's being awarded a triumph was that enemy dead should number not less than five thousand. (Julius Caesar boasted of having slaughtered a million Gauls.) By this yardstick, Attila would certainly qualify as a legitimate contender for the palm of greatness! 'Attila the Great' – it sounds preposterous, but only perhaps because he left no legacy. Had the vast empire he built up endured, and not disintegrated immediately following his death, his reputation might today be very different. History, after all, is written by the winners.

On a personal level, Attila compares favourably with many supposedly 'civilized' Greeks and Romans. His legendary simplicity of dress and lifestyle (skin garments, wooden cup and platter) was in refreshing contrast to the ostentatious pomp and luxury of the imperial courts of Constantinople and Ravenna. Although his punishments could be cruel (crucifixion and impalement were favourite forms), he could – as befits magnanimous monarchs who are above acts of petty revenge – display mercy and forgiveness. For example, when Bigilas/Vigilius, the chief agent in the bungled conspiracy to assassinate Attila, was brought before him, the King disdained to punish the man as being so insignificant as to constitute no threat. This surely displays a certain nobility of character, which contrasts with the jealous vindictiveness of Valentinian III, who slew his chief general, Aetius, with his own hand, or the rancorous spite shown by the Empress Eudoxia in hounding the saintly John Chrysostom to his death.

Attila's onslaught on first the Eastern then the Western Roman Empire, has created an indelible image of a power-hungry megalomaniac. The truth is that he had little choice. By inheriting the Hun throne, he became shackled to a juggernaut. The only way to hold the Hun nation together, and maintain personal power by rewarding his followers, was to wage war – incessant, *successful* war. Failure to maintain that momentum would have resulted in his swift replacement (and almost certain liquidation). So, by a (very) generous re-interpretation of history, Attila could be portrayed more as a man of his time and the prisoner of circumstances, than as the Scourge of God.

APPENDIX II

WHY DID THE EASTERN EMPIRE SURVIVE WHILE THE WESTERN DID NOT?

The West finally succumbed in 476, but the East survived for many more centuries. Why? A hundred years before the West's collapse, Rome was still a mighty power with an immense army which, though stretched, was dealing capably with enemies on many fronts. These extended from the Rhine to the Euphrates, as Ammianus Marcellinus, an army officer turned historian, shows us in his *Histories*, that magnificent picture of the late Roman world, at a time when it was the *West* that was seen as the stronger of the two halves of the empire. In his vivid pages, the only hint of coming disaster lies in his account of the Battle of Adrianople (Hadrianopolis) and its immediate aftermath: a conflict (involving the destruction of East Rome's army and the death of her emperor) whose effects, initially at least, seemed confined to the East. However, events in the next few decades were brutally to expose the true reality of the empire's situation: the West had serious deep-seated weaknesses, not fully apparent till after the death of Theodosius I in 395, while the East was in fact far stronger and more stable than it seemed in 378, the year of Adrianople. These differences become clear if we compare the two halves of the empire in three areas.

First, the frontiers. The West, with its extremely long frontier – the whole of the Rhine and upper Danube – was far more exposed to barbarian inroads than the East, which only had the lower Danube to worry about. (Persia, on its eastern border – potentially a far greater threat than any barbarian federation – was a civilized power which on the whole kept its treaties.) Unlike the East, whose poorer Balkan provinces could serve as a buffer zone to absorb barbarian attacks, leaving the richer eastern and southern provinces inviolate behind an impregnable Constantinople, the whole Western Empire, bar Africa, could easily be penetrated by barbarians once they had crossed the boundaries. Also, the East became adept at passing on invaders to the West, once they had tired of plundering the Balkans. (Vide Alaric and the Visigoths.)

Second, the economy. The East was far wealthier and more productive than the West, which still had great tracts of forest and undrained bottom land. Moreover, wealth in the East (with its generally fair tax system, and well-to-do land-owning peasantry) was much more evenly distributed than in the West. Here, an immensely rich senatorial aristocracy lived lives of luxury in contrast to the great mass of the population, who existed dangerously close to subsistence level. Yet it was the poor – mostly agricultural labourers or smallholders – who had to shoulder an unfairly high proportion of the tax burden, in addition to paying rent to the great landowners from whom they leased their plots. Much territory in the West was lost to German invaders who, though most eventually settled down as federates, paid no tax. A shrinking tax base, difficulty in recruiting, and massive losses incurred in barbarian wars, made the task of putting a strong Roman army into the field increasingly difficult for the Western government. Signs of the growing disparity between the two halves of the empire were: in the West, disaffection and decline in patriotism, with many driven by poverty into flight to the estate of a powerful lord (relief from the tax-collectors traded for serfdom), outlawry, or open rebellion as in the 'Peasants' Revolt' of the Bagaudae; in the East, a much more homogeneous, prosperous, and stable population.

Third, the government. In the West, Rome's curse of usurpation by ambitious generals or politicians lingered on: Firmus, Magnus Maximus, Eugenius, Gildo, Constantine III, Constans, Attalus, Jovinus, John (Iohannes) Petronius Maximus. Compare this with the situation in the East, where in the whole of the same period, 364–476, there were only *two* attempts at usurpation – by Procopius at the very beginning and Basilius at the very end – both of which were easily put down. In the East the civil service was staffed by efficient middle-class professionals, much less prone to graft than their Western counterparts. In the West, the sale of offices (*suffragium*) was endemic, tending to create a corrupt bureaucracy more concerned with lining its pockets than with serving the state. And the curial class, once the backbone of Western administration, had been demoralized and decimated by an ever-increasing workload imposed on it from Ravenna. In the East, all power was concentrated in Constantinople (like the status of Paris in France until very recently), with the civil service mandarinate, Senate (a service aristocracy, as opposed to the Western club of 'grands seigneurs'), army, patriarchate, Emperor, and Consistory, combining to form a smooth-working administrative whole. Being forced to work in close proximity to each other, and thus able to establish a system of mutual checks and balances, none of the above entities could become dis-proportionately powerful. Instead, accountability, and co-operation between all state departments, received strong reinforcement. In the West, where the machinery of government was weaker and more fragmented, this did not happen.

Given the above differences, it is not difficult to see why the West – afflicted by administrative, economic, and social breakdown, and militarily too weak to stem barbarian encroachment – collapsed in 476, while the more prosperous and stable East was able to survive for another thousand years.

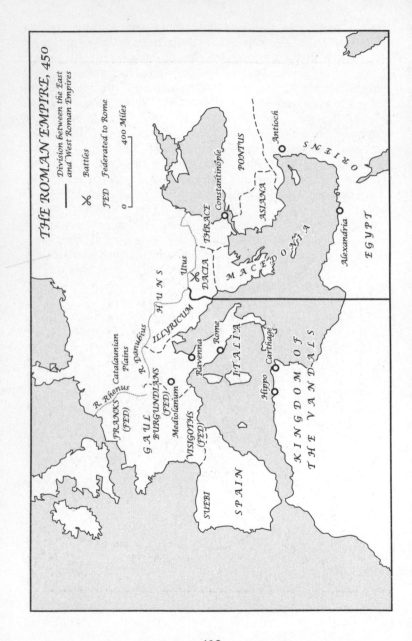

THE ROMAN EMPIRE, 450

— Division between the East and West Roman Empires

✗ Battles

FED Federated to Rome

0   400 Miles

FRANKS (FED)

R. Rhenus

Catalaunian Plains

GAUL

BURGUNDIANS (FED)

Mediolanum

VISIGOTHS (FED)

SUEBI

SPAIN

R. Danubius

ILLYRICUM

HUNS

Utus

DACIA

THRACE

Ravenna

Rome

ITALIA

Hippo

Carthage

KINGDOM OF THE VANDALS

Constantinople

PONTUS

ASIANA

MACEDONIA

ORIENS

Antioch

Alexandria

EGYPT

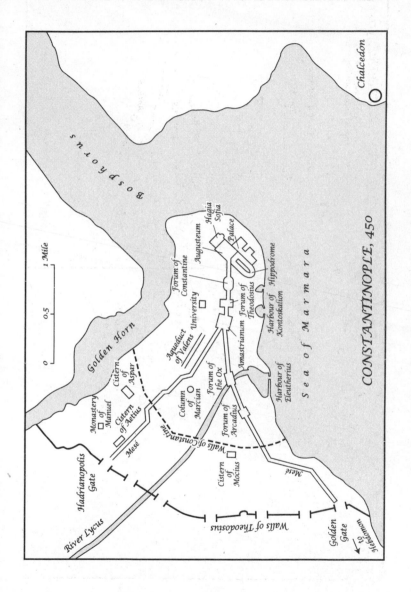

CONSTANTINOPLE, 450

Chalcedon

Bosphorus

Golden Horn

0   0.5   1 Mile

Sea of Marmara

Monastery of Manuel
Cistern of Aspar
Cistern of Aetius
Aqueduct of Valens
University
Column of Marcian
Forum of Constantine
Forum of Theodosius
Amastrianum
Augusteum
Hagia Sofia
Palace
Hippodrome
Harbour of Kontoskalion
Harbour of Eleutherius
Forum of the Ox
Forum of Arcadius
Walls of Constantine
Cistern of Mocius
Mesé
Mesé
Hadrianopolis Gate
River Lycus
Walls of Theodosius
Golden Gate
to Hebdomon

421

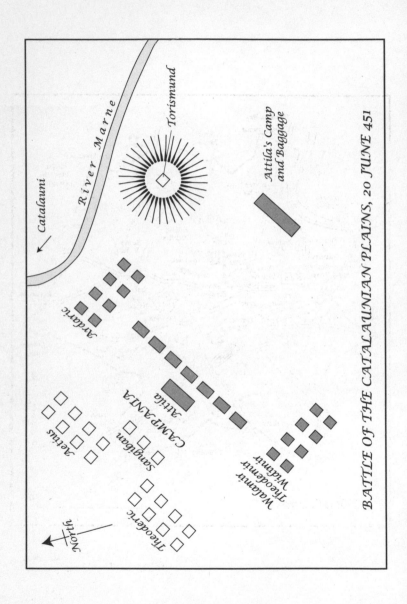

BATTLE OF THE CATALAUNIAN PLAINS, 20 JUNE 451

Catalauni

River Marne

Torismund

Attila's Camp
and Baggage

Ardaric

Attila

CAMPANIA

Walamir
Theodemir
Widimir

Aetius

Sangiban

Theoderic

North

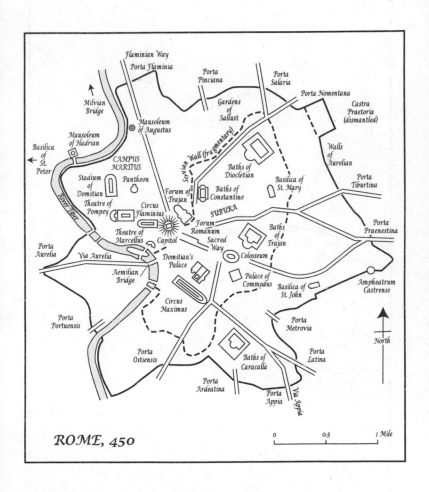

ROME, 450

Flaminian Way
Porta Flaminia
Porta Pinciana
Porta Salaria
Porta Nomentana
Milvian Bridge
Gardens of Sallust
Castra Praetoria (dismantled)
Mausoleum of Augustus
Mausoleum of Hadrian
Basilica of St. Peter
Serviàn Wall (fragmentary)
CAMPUS MARTIUS
Baths of Diocletian
Walls of Aurelian
Stadium of Domitian
Pantheon
Baths of Constantine
Basilica of St. Mary
Porta Tiburtina
River Tiber
Theatre of Pompey
Forum of Trajan
SUBURA
Circus Flaminius
Porta Praenestina
Theatre of Marcellus
Forum Romànum
Baths of Trajan
Porta Aurelia
Capitol
Sacred Way
Colosseum
Via Aurelia
Domitian's Palace
Aemilian Bridge
Palace of Commodus
Ampheatrum Castrense
Basilica of St. John
Porta Portuensis
Circus Maximus
North
Porta Metrovia
Porta Ostiensis
Porta Latina
Baths of Caracalla
Porta Ardeatina
Porta Appia
Via Appia

0   0.5   1 Mile

423

NOTES

Chapter 1

11 'The year of the consuls Asclepiodotus and Marinianus, IV Ides Oct.' The Romans dated important events 'from the founding of the city – *ab urbe condita*' or AUC (753 BC), but for most dating purposes the names of the consuls for any given year were used, one from Rome, the other from Constantinople. Dating from the birth of Christ was introduced by one Dionysius Exiguus, only in 527. Dates within any given month were calculated by counting the number of days occurring *before* the next of the three fixed days dividing the Roman month: Kalends, the first day of the month, the Nones on the 5th or 7th, and the Ides on the 13th or 15th. (In March, May, July, and October, the Nones fell on the 7th and the Ides on the 15th, in the remaining months on the 5th and 13th respectively.) Thus, the Ides of January happening on the 13th of that month, the next day would be termed by a Roman not the 14th, but the 19th *before the Kalends of February*, reckoning inclusively, i.e., taking in both the 14th of January and the 1st of February; and so on to the last day of the month which was termed *pridie Kalendas*.

Chapter 2

19 'ridge helmets'. These had replaced the classic 'Attic' helmet (familiar to all from every Hollywood Roman epic ever made) in about 300, except in the Eastern, more Hellenic half of the Empire where (from representational evidence) Attic-style helmets continued to be worn until at least the time of Justinian (527–65). For convenience, and speed of construction, the bowl was made in two sections, joined by a central strip or 'ridge'. The vastly increased army under Diocletian must have called for 'assembly-line' techniques in the state arms factories (*fabricae*) in order to meet production targets.

Notes

Chapter 3

23 'Jordanes, *Gothic History*'. The *Gothic History* was a summary of a much fuller work (unfortunately lost), *De rebus Geticis*, by a Roman, Magnus Aurelius Cassiodorus, 468–c. 568 (*sic*). Cassiodorus – historian, statesman, and adviser to Theoderic, the Ostrogothic king of Italy – whose very long life encompassed both the fall of the Western Empire in 476 and its partial recovery by Justinian – may in his youth have consulted veterans of the Catalaunian Plains. If so, he would have incorporated the knowledge gained into his great work. In 551 he commissioned Jordanes, a Romanized Goth, to make a summary version of his work: *Gothic History*.

Chapter 4

30 'Augustine, the saintly Bishop of Hippo'. The influence of Augustine (354–430) on Western thought has been profound, especially regarding Catholic belief, from late Roman times to the present. His doctrine of predestination (with its corollary of 'the Elect') has helped to shape the mindset of many, from Calvin and Wittgenstein to the 'acid murderer' Haig. It was mined, to brilliant effect, by James Hogg in his seminal novel *The Confessions of a Justified Sinner*.

32 '*ludus latrunculorum*'. A board game not dissimilar to chess, in which one piece was taken by being trapped by two enemy pieces. The player who captured most opposing pieces won.

34 'the chain of forts established by Diocletian'. Their well-preserved remains can still be seen today.

35 'seen service at the Milvian Bridge'. The Milvian Bridge outside Rome was the scene of Constantine's victory over his rival Maxentius in 312, and of his vision which brought about his conversion to Christianity. The bridge is still in use.

36 'drawers'. It used to be thought that Roman soldiers – like men in Highland regiments, did not wear underpants. However, the recently discovered 'Vindolanda tablets' at Hadrian's Wall, contain evidence that they sometimes did.

38 'a Blemmye, judging by his tribal markings'. The Blemmyes' homeland was Nubia, to the south of Egypt. They were a part-Semitic, part-African people.

44 'The *cursus velox*'. The *Cursus Publicus*, or Imperial Post, covering some 54,000 miles of road, was an amazing feat of organization

and efficiency. While its primary function was the delivery of government and military dispatches, it also catered for the transport of imperial freight and the conveyance of official personnel. If the news was urgent, it could reach its destination very rapidly, by means of a special dispensation within the system – the *cursus velox* or express post. Changing horses every 8–12 miles, a good rider could cover 240 miles in one day. The system reached its peak in the fourth century, but began to break down in the fifth with the disruption caused by barbarian invasions.

44 'it was all built underground'. The well-preserved remains of this villa, known today as 'Maison d'Amphitrite', can still be seen – as can those of several more of these remarkable underground buildings.

46 'who might almost have stepped down from the Arch of Constantine'. As an artistic convention, representations of soldiers on the Arch are mostly shown wearing classical armour and helmets (obsolete by this time in the West, though retained in the East for many more years). Some of the panels on the Arch were filched from Trajanic monuments.

Chapter 5

54 'He had failed'. It is recorded that Augustine spoke for over two and a half hours at Carthage, against the Feast of the Kalends – in vain. The Feast continued in the West as long as urban life survived; when the Arabs conquered Roman Africa in the seventh century, they found the Kalends still celebrated.

Chapter 8

66 'scale armour or chain mail'. Most book illustrations (and, unfortunately, films and TV programmes) depicting Roman soldiers of any period from 200 BC to AD 400, show them wearing ubiquitous 'hoop armour', *lorica segmentata*, along with (naturally) classical helmets and curved rectangular shields. This efficient type of body-armour was in use by the early first century (specimens have recently been discovered at Kalkriese, the probable site of Varus' military disaster in 9 AD) and is last seen (in a carving) c. AD 230 in the time of Alexander Severus – a good run, but of only perhaps 250 years as opposed to 600. It was superseded by scale armour (*lorica squamata*), chain mail (*lorica hamata*), and lamellar armour (small vertical iron plates) –

possibly because of its weight, and the fact that its complex construction made it relatively slow and expensive to produce.

Chapter 10

74 'the German's bid for power'. Germans were never acceptable as Roman emperors and could only rule indirectly through puppets of their choice. This despite the fact that Spaniards, Africans, Illyrians, and an Arab had all at various times donned the purple – without anyone objecting on ethnic or cultural grounds.

74 'the great Anician family of Rome'. The Anicii were, like the Symmachi, one of those great Roman families whose influence was felt in the corridors of power at the highest level. They were connected by blood to, among others, Eparchius Avitus (Emperor, 455–6), and in marriage to Emperor Theodosius I, to Petronius Maximus (Emperor, 455), to Eudocia, widow of Valentinian III, and perhaps to the Spanish usurper Magnus Maximus.

75 'Gaius Valerius acquired an unofficial *agnomen*'. The Romans were sometimes referred to as 'the people with three names'. From an early period they adopted the Sabine practice of using a *praenomen* or personal name (chosen from an extremely limited stock – Titus, Quintus, Marcus, etc., usually abbreviated to T., Q., M., etc.) – followed by a *gentile* or tribal name ending in 'ius', such as Julius, Claudius, or Tullius. This, in the case of patricians, was followed by a family name or *cognomen*, often originally deriving from a personal peculiarity: Caesar (having a full head of hair), Cicero, Naso, etc. Occasionally, as a mark of distinction, a second *cognomen* or honorific *agnomen* such as 'Africanus' or 'Germanicus' was added. By the fifth century, the system had loosened up a little, to the extent of widening the choice of personal names, and occasionally the affecting of more than one family name. In general, however, naming practice remained remarkably conservative and consistent throughout the whole Roman period. Incidentally the style 'Julius Caesar', referring to Caius Julius Caesar, is a modern adoption and wouldn't have been used by the Romans themselves. They would have called him Caius (interchangeable with Gaius), or Caesar, or Caius Julius, or Caius Caesar; never by a combination of the *gentile* and family names.

76 'the Altar of Victory removed from the Senate'. This was bitterly opposed by Symmachus, city prefect of Rome, consul, orator,

man of letters, and distinguished member of one of the great influential Roman families, the Symmachi.

76 'the pursuit of *otium*'. Leisured scholarship was the preserve of the senatorial aristocracy and country gentlemen in Rome and the Latin provinces, as well as in the Eastern Empire. This created a remarkably uniform, if sterile, classical culture which survived in the Western Empire right up to the end in 476, and even beyond.

77 'Many of their leaders copy Roman dress and manners'. Sidonius Apollinaris, who visited the Visigoth court of Theoderic II, draws a flattering pen-portrait of the monarch, and describes Gallo-Roman aristocrats being sumptuously entertained by Visigoth courtiers displaying the courteous manners and wit of Roman gentlemen.

Chapter 11

81 'like a latter-day Cincinnatus'. In Rome's early days, the ex-consul Cincinnatus was summoned from the plough to lead Rome against the Aequians; that tribe defeated, he returned to ploughing his farm.

Chapter 13

91 'Ariminum's five-spanned bridge . . . triumphal arch'. The bridge is still in use today, and the arch spans a main road into Rimini.

Chapter 14

101 '*Ad Kalendas Graecas*'. The Roman Kalends was the usual day for paying rents, accounts, etc. But as the Greeks used a different mode of reckoning, a postponement of payment 'to the Greek Kalends' simply meant a refusal to pay altogether. Popularized by Emperor Augustus, the expression became a synonym for 'never'.

Chapter 15

107 'his son-in-law Sebastian'. 'the virtuous and faithful Sebastian' (Gibbon) was subsequently hounded implacably by the agents of Aetius, 'from one kingdom to another, till he perished miserably in the service of the Vandals', a Catholic martyr of Arian persecution.

109 'he will be outlawed'. After the Battle of the Fifth Milestone,

Aetius and the remnants of his force managed to retreat to Gaul. Defeated, disgraced, declared a rebel by Placidia, he then withdrew to a fortified estate inherited from his father, where he attempted to hold out. However, besieged by imperial troops and nearly falling victim to a murder attempt by Sebastian, Aetius soon realized that his position was untenable. Accompanied by a few loyal followers, he slipped away in secret and escaped to Pannonia, to be granted sanctuary by his faithful friends the Huns.

Chapter 17

119 'the sword had been gifted to him by a herdsman'. The full story is recounted by Priscus of Panium in his *Byzantine History*, which contains a graphic account of his visit to the court of Attila.

123 'both an Aristotle and an Arrian to Attila's Alexander'. Aristotle was tutor to the young Alexander, Arrian (second century AD) his biographer.

124 'even copied by the imperial cavalry of China'. This seems to have occurred *c.* 300 BC. Gradually tunic and trousers spread among the Chinese population, displacing traditional flowing robes and tight shoes to become the Chinese national dress. Today, this ubiquitous costume is giving ground to Western clothing, itself a throwback to Persian dress, introduced into Britain by Charles II: a long, open-fronted jacket worn over waistcoat and breeches – the embryonic three-piece suit.

125 'if Ptolemy is correct'. The foremost of classical geographers, Ptolemy flourished in the mid-second century AD. His *Geographia*, a standard work of reference up to the Great Discoveries of the fifteenth century, shows on its great world map lines of latitude and longitude (calculated from Ferro in the Canaries), Europe and the Near East reasonably accurately, and – distorted though recognizable – the main features of Asia and Africa as they were known in his day.

127 'a drink called *chai*'. Tea is thought to have been introduced to China from India before 500. 'Brick tea', steamed and compressed tea dust, is only one-sixth the bulk of loose tea, making it an ideal article of trade.

127 'rhinoceros and elephant'. That is, woolly rhinoceros and mammoth. John Ledyard in his 1787–8 journal, *A Journey through*

Russia and Siberia, noted seeing large quantities of such bones in the vicinity of Irkutsk. Significant amounts of commercial ivory have been recovered from mammoth tusks.

128 'still permitted to discuss all matters freely'. But not for much longer. Within a few generations they were to be closed by order of Justinian, one symbol of the winding up of classical culture.

Chapter 18

138 'between Scylla and Charybdis'. In Homeric legend, these were two sea-monsters who dwelt on either side of a narrow strait, constituting a deadly peril to passing seafarers. In modern parlance, 'between Scylla and Charybdis' would translate as 'between a rock and a hard place'.

Chapter 22

165 'one of those German legends'. The Burgundian campaign, of which this was the prelude, was in fact to become the subject of one such saga, the *Nibelungenlied*, which conflates several separate events, and even features Attila.

Chapter 23

169 'an Aurelian to wipe out the Alamanni sweeping into Italia'. Aurelian, huge in character as well as physique, was instrumental, along with his predecessor Claudius II and his successor Diocletian, in rehabilitating (in a bleak and totalitarian fashion) the Roman Empire after its near-eclipse in the third century. Rome is still (mostly) surrounded by the defensive walls he built against incursions by the Alamanni.

Chapter 25

194 'a race of uncivilized allies'. At the time Sidonius was writing, the Visigoths were attacking Arvernum (Clermont-Ferrand in Auvergne) of which Sidonius, son-in-law of Avitus, had become bishop.

196 'the milestone marking the centre of Gaul'. It has since been moved a few miles to the town of Bruère-Allichamps, south of Bourges, to mark the supposed geographical centre of France.

197 'Revessium'. Also known as Ruessio or Ruessium, it was the capital of the Vellavi tribe, allies of Vercingetorix against Julius Caesar.

197 'the fierce and volatile Arverni'. Under their famous leader

Vercingetorix, they inflicted on Julius Caesar his single reverse at Gergovia in 52 BC.

197 'Avitacum, the estate of Senator Avitus'. Sidonius Apollinaris, son-in-law of Avitus, has left us a description of the place. There are views of the hills and across Lac d'Aydat, heated baths, outhouses, women's quarters, and a summerhouse. Sidonius talks of drinking snow-cooled wine while watching fishermen on the lake; and he describes the rural sounds of frogs, chickens, swans, geese, wild birds, cattle, cowbells, and shepherd's pipes. A scene straight out of Virgil's *Georgics* – ironically, painted as the Western Empire tottered towards its final collapse.

Chapter 26

202 'the recently enacted Law of Citations'. This was compiled under Valentinian III in 426, in an attempt to clarify the rather ramshackle mass of sometimes conflicting Roman legislation; a further improvement, the Theodosian Code (compiled in the Eastern Empire) followed in 438. The stately fabric of Roman law which we know today and which forms the basis of Scots law and the legal systems of other nations, is the great *Digest* of Justinian, a selective condensation of Roman laws from Hadrian to 533, the year of the *Digest*'s publication.

202 'Papinian was to have the casting vote'. Aemilius Papinianus was the most celebrated Roman jurist before the time of Justinian. He was put to death by Caracalla in 212 AD.

203 'But this could happen only once'. Penance would obviously incur prior admission of the sins to be expunged. But that was very different from the present practice of Confession followed by Absolution, on a regular basis. This only became formalized in the fourth Lateran Council of 1215, and received final confirmation in the Council of Trent, 1545–63.

Chapter 28

214 'another Zama'. Zama was the decisive battle in North Africa, in which Scipio the Younger inflicted a crushing defeat on Hannibal in 201 BC. The long and bitter struggle against Carthage brought out the best in the Roman character, creating a patriotic resolve akin to the 'Dunkirk spirit', or the sentiments expressed in Robert Burns' poem, 'Bruce's Address at Bannockburn'.

219 'sowing dragon's teeth'. A reference to an incident recounted in the Greek legend of the Golden Fleece, where warriors sprang up from land sown with dragon's teeth.

220 'Orestes, his young Roman secretary'. A brave and talented man who, after the death of Attila rose to become Master of Soldiers in Italia, Orestes was the father of the last Western Roman Emperor, Romulus Augustus – those names a chilling echo of Rome's founder, and of her first Emperor.

Chapter 29

223 'Sirmium, the mighty Illyrian city'. Mitrovica, in Kosovo, along with Belgrade, is by a macabre coincidence once more associated with a policy of genocide and 'ethnic cleansing'. For Huns read Serbs. Illyria, comprising the East's Balkan provinces, should not be confused with Illyricum, the West's most easterly diocese.

226 'the city was . . . systematically demolished'. The capture and destruction of great cities like Sirmium, hitherto thought impregnable, especially to barbarians, must have dealt the Romans a terrible psychological blow, creating panic and hopelessness.

227 'the circus faction of the Greens'. The Greens and the Blues were the opposing supporters of the rival chariot-racing teams in Constantinople, distinguished by those colours. They could wield enormous influence, as in the 'Nika' riots of 532, which almost toppled the emperor Justinian. Shades of Celtic *v.* Rangers! The Blues tended to identify with the emperor and the Establishment.

Chapter 30

237 'in extending their conquests so far westward'. Recent discoveries have confirmed the vast distance the Huns migrated from their original homeland, which was probably to the north of Korea. In north-west Hungary, the last area to fall to them, a Hunnic hoard has been found, containing small gold horses, identical to others discovered in a huge arc extending across eastern Europe, and Asia as far as eastern Siberia.

239 'a grotesquely inflated nose'. Europe's only antelope, the saiga formerly existed in enormous herds across the steppelands of Asia and eastern Europe. Almost wiped out in the severe winter of 1829, it is making a comeback and is now protected. Its salient

feature, a hugely enlarged nose, contains structures to warm the air and filter dust from it.

241 'a mighty aqueduct'. Built by Emperor Valens in 375, much of it is still standing, having been in use until the late nineteenth century. A classic Roman structure, it dramatically spans a valley in a double series of superimposed arches.

242 'four mighty horses in bronze'. They were looted by the Venetians after their capture of the city in 1204, and are now to be seen adorning St Mark's Cathedral in Venice.

Chapter 31

245 'King Chlodio'. Chlodio was the great-grandfather of Clovis (Chlodovec), whose reign was of seminal importance for two reasons: (i) under Clovis, the Franks became the dominant power in Gaul, henceforth to be known as Francia – France; (ii) Clovis' marriage to a Catholic princess led to his, and his people's, conversion from Arianism, which helped to unite Gallo-Romans and Germans in his kingdom.

246 'a mighty *comitatus*'. The warrior society of the early Germans shows remarkable parallels to that of the Highland clans or Border reivers in Scotland, where a successful war-leader would attract a retinue of armed followers who adopted his surname. (The word 'surname' was coined in the Borders.)

Chapter 32

256 'Eratosthenes . . . was said to be able . . . to measure its circumference'. His method was brilliantly simple. By comparison of the sun's relative position at two separate points on the earth's surface (north–south), the angle subtended by the measured distance between these points was calculated. 360 degrees was then divided by this angle and the result multiplied by the distance. This gave a measurement astonishingly close to the modern estimate of 24,000 miles. Pure geometry – pure genius.

Chapter 36

272 'To Aegidius, consul for the third time'. Perhaps from the similarity of the names, Gildas is confusing Aegidius with Aetius, to whom the appeal was actually sent. Aegidius at the time was serving under Aetius in Gaul, as was Majorian, the future

emperor. Aegidius was destined to become 'Master of Soldiers throughout the Gauls'.

277 'as the patrol neared Anderida'. Pevensey – Anderida to the Romans – held out until 491. The entry for that year in *The Anglo-Saxon Chronicle* says: 'In this year Aelle and Cissa besieged Andredesceaster and slew all the inhabitants; there was not even one Briton left alive.'

Chapter 37

281 'Constantine rose to the occasion'. As did the emperor – in the only way he knew how. Theodosius led a penitential procession of ten thousand, barefoot, with hymns, icons and relics, to the Hebdomon palace for a great service of supplication.

282 'a massively solid, finished piece of work'. And still standing: a tribute to Roman engineering genius – and the terror inspired by Attila. They held firm against all attacks for another thousand years, until finally falling to the Turks in 1453. A contemporary inscription on the Walls commemorates Constantine: '*Constantinus ovans haec moenia firma locavit* [Triumphantly, Constantine raised these stout ramparts].' An ambitious reconstruction scheme has recently restored part of the Walls to their original glory.

Chapter 38

287 'Attila must surely hesitate before again taking on a Roman army'. The Battle of the Utus was in fact the last occasion when the Huns defeated a Roman army.

Chapter 39

292 'a strip of territory south of the Danubius . . . to be ceded to the Huns'. Probably Attila's aim was not to occupy this strip but to create a 'cleared zone' to facilitate any future re-invasion of Roman territory.

Chapter 40

301 'Constantius was bribed to kill me'. For full details of the conspiracy masterminded by Chrysaphius, see Gibbon, *The Decline and Fall of the Roman Empire*, Chapter 34.

Chapter 42

307 'regiment of *Scholae*'. Based in Constantinople, the imperial

bodyguard consisted of seven élite cavalry regiments known as *scholae*. A select group of forty chosen from their number and known as *candidati*, formed the Emperor's personal retinue. Individuals from the *scholae* often served as imperial agents, carrying out missions in the provinces.

307 'a mountainous plateau between the Pontus Euxinus and the Mare Caspium'. Armenia was the interface for the Roman world's equivalent of 'the Great Game'. For Afghanistan, read Armenia; for Britain, Rome; for Russia, Persia. After being occupied by other powers for nearly two millennia, from Rome and Persia to Turkey and the Soviet Union, Armenia has at last regained its autonomy.

308 'Take your pick'. In the fifth century, it was dawning on the Roman world, especially Constantinople, that theirs was but one state among many: a perception which contrasted with the fourth-century view that Rome comprised the entire civilized world. The weakening of West Rome and its growing divergence from its Eastern partner, the re-emergence of Persia as a formidable power under the Sassanids, the sudden rise of Attila's vast empire: all contributed to the shattering of this comfortable illusion. The new reality is illustrated by the diplomatic missions, in the mid-fifth century, of Olympiodorus of Thebes (in Egypt) to Rome, to Nubia, to the Dnieper – accompanied by a parrot speaking pure Attic Greek.

309 '*before* the conference takes place'. As the Council of Chalcedon, it duly did take place the following year, 451, when the Persian invasion of Armenia also occurred.

315 'In the tradition of your Regulus'. Regulus was a Roman consul who, despite knowing the likely consequences to himself, conveyed to the Carthaginians (during the First Punic War) the Senate's rejection of their offers of peace. According to legend, he was then executed after being hideously tortured.

317 'Perhaps the time had come for a final trial of strength'. That time did come, though not for many years. The 'final solution' of the centuries-old conflict between Rome and Persia was to be as cataclysmic as it was unexpected. Early in the seventh century, a ferocious Persian general, Shahrvaraz, overran the southern provinces of the East Roman Empire; but in a series of brilliant campaigns the territory was all recovered by the heroic Emperor Heraclius. Then, without warning, fanatical

Arab armies inspired by the teachings of Muhammad, swarmed out of the south in the 630s, and in a few short years had swallowed up Persia and reduced the East Roman Empire to an Anatolian rump.* Roman Christianity in Africa, Egypt, Palestine, and Syria was permanently replaced by Islam.

Chapter 49

359 'On the left flank, the Romans waited'. This was the last great field battle fought by the Roman army in the West. (The Roman troops of Majorian, by the time he became emperor, and – after the collapse of the Western Empire in 476 – those of Syagrius, were virtually private armies.) But even after the end of empire, vestiges of Rome's army lingered on. In 482 a Danubian unit sent to Italy for its final pay instalment; and Procopius writes of soldiers in Frankish service clinging nostalgically to their old legionary structure, complete with standards and traditional Roman uniform. This in the 550s, a century after the Catalaunian Plains. Even in Britain, abandoned by the legions *c*. 407, units of the *limitanei* struggled on, until the last of them was wiped out by the Saxon invaders in 491.

Chapter 50

370 'we shall establish our supremacy in the most telling manner possible'. It has been said that the Council of Chalcedon (October 451), 'the accursed Council' to the monophysites, split the East Roman Empire irreparably, ultimately facilitating the Muslim conquest of Egypt, Palestine, and Syria in the seventh century. This is a fallacy. The imperial administration, coupled with the heroic struggle against Attila (and later that of Heraclius against an aggressive Persia), forged a strong, unified, and patriotic state, in which the Emperor, from Marcian onwards, came to be seen as the 'little father' of his people, and a conscientious arbiter in theological disputes. Although the findings of the Council undoubtedly created strains within the empire, they were never serious enough to harm its fabric.

371 'the saint's right arm . . . now rested across the withered chest'. Some places seem to have the property not only of arresting the

* The Balkans had already been virtually lost to the Avars, a warrior people from the Steppes.

process of decay in a corpse, but of preserving the flexibility of muscles and ligaments. A notable example of this is to be found in St Michan's Church, Dublin, where the corpses of (reputed) crusaders have been preserved, their limbs still perfectly pliable, by the moisture-absorbing magnesium limestone of the vault.

Chapter 51

379 'news of the King's death'. Following Attila's demise in 453, his German subjects successfully rebelled, and his empire, without Attila's huge personality to hold it together, rapidly disintegrated, leaving no mark on posterity except a memory of slaughter and destruction on an epic scale.

Chapter 52

382 'Valentinian approached the apparatus'. For a description of a séance using the type of apparatus described in this chapter, see Ammianus Marcellinus, *The Histories*, Book Two. It bears an uncanny resemblance to a modern séance using a ouija board, or alternatively a circular table with letters of the alphabet round the edge, and a wineglass or tumbler in the centre.

383 'the imprisoning of a popular charioteer'. This was carried out by the army commander at Thessalonica, who was then lynched by the mob. As punishment, Theodosius I had seven thousand citizens massacred. In consequence, Ambrose, Archbishop of Milan, refused to admit the Emperor to Mass until he had done penance. A spectacular demonstration of the growing power of the Church, and a harbinger of the medieval doctrine of 'the Two Swords'. Theodosius kneeling before Ambrose: the image has an eerie parallel to that of Emperor Henry IV of Germany at Canossa, barefoot in the snow before Pope Gregory VII.

Chapter 54

397 'a few great villas on the Caelian . . . made to serve as hospices'. One such was the House of the Valerii, which remained derelict and unsaleable for some years after the sack of Rome.

409 'the twelve centuries assigned to the lifetime of his city'. 753 BC is the date generally accepted for the founding of Rome. The twelfth century would then elapse in AD 447. The Western Empire actually fell in 476. Allowing for some latitude in dating

such a distant event as the founding of the city, the prophecy is uncannily accurate.

Afterword

411 'not only did he save Europe from Asiatic domination'. The consequences of a Hunnish conquest would have been potentially both devastating and permanent. Gibbon cites instances where whole tracts of Central Asia were reduced in a few years to uninhabitable deserts by invading nomads, whose destruction of forests, irrigation, and infrastructure had effects which lasted for centuries if not permanently.

412 'From it developed European medieval civilization'. The building-blocks of medieval Christendom were already in process of formation by the time of the late empire. Feudalism: protection in return for service – was concomitant with a breakdown of security, with powerful landlords recruiting bands of armed retainers, or *bucellarii*, and peasant labour from *coloni* fleeing barbarians or rapacious Roman tax officials. The Germans' sense of honour, love of fighting, and respect for women, provided the germ from which the medieval Code of Chivalry would one day develop. And the Church Militant, with its doctrine of the Two Swords, was beginning to flex its muscles under Theodosius the Great – himself forced to kneel in supplication before Ambrose, and do penance for his sins. Shades of England's Henry II after Becket's murder.